Also by Sebastian Faulks

Paris
Echo

Paris
Echo

A NOVEL

Sebastian Faulks

Henry Holt and Company   New York

Henry Holt and Company
Publishers since 1866
175 Fifth Avenue
New York, New York 10010
www.henryholt.com

Henry Holt ® and 🏛 ® are registered trademarks of Macmillan Publishing
Group, LLC.

Library of Congress Cataloging-in-Publication Data

Names: Faulks, Sebastian, author.
Title: Paris echo : a novel / Sebastian Faulks.
Description: New York : Henry Holt and Company, [2018]
Identifiers: LCCN 2018013873 | ISBN 9781250305657 (hardcover)
Subjects: LCSH: Americans—France—Paris—Fiction. | Women historians—
    Fiction. | Immigrants—Fiction.
Classification: LCC PR6056.A89 P37 2018 | DDC 823/.914—dc23
LC record available at https://lccn.loc.gov/2018013873

Our books may be purchased in bulk for promotional, educational, or business
use. Please contact your local bookseller or the Macmillan Corporate and
Premium Sales Department at (800) 221-7945, extension 5442, or by e-mail at
MacmillanSpecialMarkets@macmillan.com.

First Edition 2018

Designed by Meryl Sussman Levavi

Printed in the United States of America

1   3   5   7   9   10   8   6   4   2

For Hector, *mon ami*

Qu'est l'histoire? Un écho du passé dans l'avenir.
Un reflet de l'avenir sur le passé.
What is history? An echo of the past in the future.
A shadow of the future on the past.

VICTOR HUGO, *L'Homme Qui Rit*

The Métro furnishes the best opportunity for the foreigner
to imagine that he has understood the essence of Paris.

FRANZ KAFKA, *Diaries*

Fourmillante cité, cité pleine de rêves,
Où le spectre en plein jour raccroche le passant!
Teeming city, your streets filled with dreams,
Where daylight ghosts confront the passer-by!

CHARLES BAUDELAIRE,
from "Les Sept Vieillards," *Les Fleurs du Mal*

Paris
Echo

Maison Blanche

I WAS TAKING A PEE IN THE BATHROOM WHEN I CAUGHT SIGHT OF MYSELF in the mirror. My face looked so beautiful that I turned to look more closely, spraying the tiles round the toilet in my hurry. I shook my *zib* and put it back inside my boxers so I could study my face. It was like someone had drawn a faint shadow beneath the cheekbones, then put a touch of mascara on my lashes. The eyes had a depth I'd never seen before. I put my head to one side and smiled, then furrowed my brow as though I was being serious, but the eyes stayed the same—twinkling with a kind of humor and experience. This was the face of someone old beyond my years.

How could it be I'd never noticed before just how beautiful I was? Not regular handsome maybe like an old-time film star and not indie blank like a modern one. More a mix of soul and sexiness. With noble bones.

I flipped the glass to magnifying and back to normal. I held a hand mirror up to turn the reflection on itself, so it sat right-way-on. I backed against the wall, then went fisheye close. It made no difference. True, I'd smoked a little *kif*, but only a little, which was all I liked, and I'd had a Coke to keep my sugar level up (a tip from a boy in my year). I felt happy to think this person was me. No harm could come to someone who looked like that. The ways of peace and righteousness were ours. Not to mention soft-skinned girls and travel to distant places.

We stared into one another's eyes for a few more minutes.

Then he spoke.

He said, "You got to get out, man. You gotta get out."

I felt myself nodding in agreement.

Because I'd known this anyway, for quite a while. There was nothing shocking in what he said, it was more of a relief.

"Go now."

"I will. Any day now."

 ● ● ●

We lived just outside the medina, the old town, in a whitewashed house. There was another family on the ground floor, but an outside staircase led to our front door. We had the top two floors and a roof terrace with a view towards the sea. My stepmother used to hang the washing up there, which pissed my father off. "How can I bring people home when they have to sit next to a row of wet shirts?" I had nothing against my stepmother except that she was not my mother. That, and the fact that she always repeated herself. Once she'd locked on to a piece of news or a point of view, she couldn't let it go. "All our problems are caused by the Arabs of the Gulf, especially the Saudis," she told us one January. In September she was still saying this like something she'd just stumbled on.

In the middle of the terrace was a *taifor,* a kind of low table. It had a woven cloth, orange and red, and small shiny discs that reflected the sun. On it was a box of cigarettes and colored glasses for tea. My father asked men he hoped would invest in his business to come up and admire the view while he unlocked his supply of whiskey. He offered it round with a leer that made me feel sick. There were tons of places in town you could buy liquor. Some of them had only boxes of tissues or cat food in the window, but everyone knew you couldn't run a specialist tissue shop. You only had to go a few paces in, past the Kleenex, and there were rows of Johnnie Walker and Glenmorangie above the lager and Moroccan wine.

Then my father told me to go and do some studying. Down in my room at the back of the house, I opened my books. I was studying economics, though "studying" may be too strong a word. True, I'd done well at school when I was young, but it was only because I was good at languages. I'd learned French from my mother, who was half French herself. Her father was from a French settler family in Algeria—one of those they called *pieds noirs,* or black feet, because the original ones (a hundred years before) had had shiny leather shoes. Normally the generations of settlers married others of their own, French people, but my grandfather took a liking to an Algerian woman in Oran (Algerian Granny) and they were married, though in what religion I don't know. They moved to Morocco and then to Paris, where my mother, Hanan, was born one day in the early fifties. I don't know why they had such itchy feet. Maybe they saw trouble coming in Algeria. I guess the Arab name was a gesture from my French grandfather to his Algerian wife now they were stuck in Paris. *Hanan,* any dictionary will tell you, means "mercy" or "clemency," so maybe he was trying to be nice.

It was in Paris that Hanan, my mother, was brought up and where perhaps she should have stayed. But in her early thirties she went to Morocco on a visit to some cousins and it was there she had the misfortune to meet and marry Malik Zafar, a would-be businessman, who, in 1986, became my father.

My mother died when I was ten. Or maybe I was nine. I wasn't aware at the time how ill she was and went off to school one day telling her I hoped her "cold" would be better by the evening. She did look thin and had trouble speaking. I was later told she had had cancer of the esophagus, though I hardly knew what either word meant. Her legacy was my ability to speak French.

For a time, I went to the American School of Tangier, where the lessons were all in English and the girls wore Western clothes. There were daily doses of classical Arabic, as well, but it got too expensive for the son of a flaky businessman. I was sent instead to a school in the Ville Nouvelle, where I got distracted, stopped reading and only just scraped into college at the end of it.

And at college there were more girls. There was also a woman who taught politics, Miss Aziz. She had hair so black it had a purple glow in the light that came through the lecture-room windows. It was thick, with a slight wave, chopped off just above the shoulder. Like other women, she wore trousers most of the time, but once she wore a black skirt to the knee with a white shirt and three rows of big red beads. Towards the end of class, I noticed that a thin strip of white lace had slipped below the hem of the skirt and settled on the black nylon that covered her legs.

We were all majoring in economics. It was a dull subject, but my father made me do it. Miss Aziz's politics class was a compulsory module in the course and it had a bit of history in it too. One day she told us about the wars of the last century and how the Europeans came to North Africa. She talked about the colonizers as though she wasn't sure they were quite human. They were cultured all right, the way she told it, but they were addicted to killing in a way that no number of symphonies could make up for.

All this was new to me. I didn't know exactly when the Europeans had first come to my country or what they wanted from us. But they'd left a lot behind in the names of boulevards, squares and churches. Listening to Miss Aziz describe the Spanish and the French as creatures of a slightly different species, I wondered if this was how they'd seen us, too, when they first arrived in North Africa—primitive bandits on a coastal strip above an endless desert. Bandits with religion.

Miss Aziz, at first glance, seemed to do the right things. She was patient with the questions of the class, and when Dr. Ahmed, the head of department, put his head round the door and asked her for a word she placed her book facedown on the desk and hurried after him. But what was different about her was that she seemed to carry a world in her head that was not the world we knew. She never returned an essay late and she was polite to Hamid, the toothless janitor who swept the courtyard while the rest of us just laughed at his fat ass when he wasn't sitting on it. And I can't imagine Miss A. ever raised her voice in the staff room. So why did she give off this sense of rebellion?

Laila, my girlfriend, noticed the same thing. She used to call Miss Aziz "the Messenger." It was the name of an American television show in which an average family had adopted a boy who turned out to be an alien. It was a comedy aimed at children, but it was a cult at our college. The kids in the family were always begging to be taken away to his home planet, but the Messenger, who was like an ordinary boy except for two extra fingers (and some telekinetic powers), was too grateful to the mom and dad for rescuing him to take the children away, even on a day trip. For all I know, it was a hidden message, sponsored by some religious group—however shit your life is, you've got to keep believing; don't run away.

While my father poured his whiskey down the throats of his guests (they never invested, they just drank), I sat on my bed and opened a course book. I was bored. Who cares about history, even if Miss Aziz is teaching it? What's the point of remembering stuff that happened before you were born? We weren't "remembering" it anyway. We hadn't been there—neither had our teachers, nor anyone else in the world—so we couldn't "remember" it. What we were doing was "imagining" it. . . . And what was the point of that?

If I wasn't distracted by thoughts of escape, it was by thoughts of Laila. In my room, pretending to study income distribution, I used to send her text messages on the fancy phone she'd given me when her father bought her a new one. Sometimes she sent me back a picture of herself, playing with her dog or drinking Fanta on the veranda of her house.

I hadn't slept with Laila. I was nineteen, and I hadn't slept with anyone. When she first arrived at college, I'm not sure the other guys noticed how pretty she was. At that time, she had very short dark hair, almost like a boy's, and they all drooled over pictures of blond girls with hair to the shoulders. But I spotted the weight under her white shirt when she leaned across a table, even though everything was properly buttoned up. Girl students were allowed to wear pretty much what they wanted. Laila's clothes were modest, but somehow you could tell they were good quality. Maybe she got them sent from abroad or bought them online. After a week or so settling in, she became more confident. She was always laughing. For a while I was afraid she was laughing at me, but then I decided she was just carefree. She didn't like computer games as much as I did, but she was crazy about *The Messenger*. That was the moment we clicked. "I love it, I love it, don't you?" she said when the subject came up. "I love the way he's always sneaking up on people. And when he's amazed by something in our world he doesn't understand, he just says—"

"'Frozen fireballs . . . Count me in!'" we both said at once.

I invited her to come to my house and watch *The Messenger* one evening when my parents were out. She had no shame about watching a kids' program. We sat through five or six episodes on the trot. She mentioned some other shows I'd never heard of, so I guessed at her house she'd got more TV channels. Some of these programs weren't even shown in the United States, I think, they were just made for export to a youth audience.

Every evening I went up on the roof to smoke a cigarette and looked out towards the sea, in the direction of Europe. If you looked the other way, south over the city, the trees and hills soon became semi-desert. It was all brown, with scars of mining and digging, the last attempt to get something out of the sand, with tipper trucks and lorries parked up and conveyor belts of dirt.

But what happened if you looked north? What went on up there across the sea? Spain, France, where the invaders had come from . . . Way beyond that, Germany. The people in Europe all had new cars and watches. And green woods and forests. The labels on the clothes had been put on by who they claimed to be, not knocked off in China like ours. The girls were blond and wore short dresses, showing their legs. The bars weren't hidden in expensive hotels or in underground dives where you might get beaten up by an old alcoholic. The liquor places were on every corner, and women drank there too, ordering wine and cocktails.

Smoking my cigarette, I pictured this, through the low clouds and the gray sea on which I could see a far-off container ship.

I knew I had to go, but it was hard to get the courage up. My father would explode if I said I was quitting college. He really thought four years studying was going to make a difference—that with a degree I'd somehow have life on a string. I knew the only way to escape from all this was to leave the country. All that was holding me back was Laila and the feeble hope of sleeping with her.

Laila lived in a big house about a mile out of town. Inside her own grounds she wore Western skirts and dresses as well as the usual jeans. They weren't very short, but they were elegant and you could see the honey-colored skin of her legs. There was a housekeeper, Farida, a woman with sleepy eyes. She wasn't old, she was middle-aged, maybe thirty-five. She was tame like a cow. She brought in tea, she swept the floors, pushed back the stray bits of hair that came loose from her clip. She adored Laila, who was the only person who could make Farida lift up her heavy eyelids into a smile. The rest of us she drifted between, putting down cups, picking up ashtrays. Or else you'd see her carrying armfuls of washing down the corridor to a distant laundry. Sometimes lying on my bed at home I imagined that Farida asked Laila to her room at the back of the house and asked her to undress her and help her shower at the end of her long day's work. There was a lot of kneeling down and straps and buttons to undo and many underclothes before Farida was ready for the shower, by which time Laila seemed to be naked as well, which was only fair.

The trouble with having fantasies was that I was never sure I was alone. In my bedroom wall was a *moucharabieh*, a carved wooden screen that gave onto the landing, where anyone could see through the gaps. In the small towns the shopkeepers spied through the shutters and the screens and only opened up when there were enough people in the street. You never knew if you were being watched. All my life was like that.

Laila had a younger brother called Billy and a cute little sister called Najat and they'd sometimes barge in when we were watching *The Messenger* or playing cards, but they didn't hang around. In the last year at the boys' school, the year before college, I'd given a kicking to a kid who'd been making life difficult for Billy, so he was kind of grateful, plus he could take a hint. I also gave him a Radiohead T-shirt of mine. Actually he was a bit of a dude and was growing up so fast I'd thought he'd soon outrank me.

Was I in love with Laila because she'd given me some encouragement and was therefore my best bet? I don't know. But it pained me to see her and to go home without having done it with her. It really hurt. If I'd been offered the chance to sleep with all twelve girls in our lecture group one after the other or just Laila, just her . . . No contest, even if the twelve included Wasia and Kashira, who by any normal standards were both smoking hot.

I didn't discuss Laila with other boys, though we did talk about sex in general when we were hanging out. If Laila's name came up, I changed the subject. But on my own I thought a lot about how great it would be just to feel my *zib* sliding up inside her. Just that simple thing. I thought it might feel really quite hot, almost burning on the skin. By then of course, thinking about it, I had a huge boner.

My stepmother did nothing. Like all the women I knew, she lived mostly indoors and went out in the afternoon to the houses of her sisters or her friends. We weren't rich because my father's schemes never came to anything, but we weren't as poor as some families in the medina. We had a cleaner, for instance—a very large unsmiling woman who came in once a week. She only charged a few coins. And my stepmother did the cooking. I think she was interested in that. The other thing she liked was birds. She had two cages with small songbirds in them. "They remind me of my childhood in the Rif Mountains," she said. She also left the door open onto the roof terrace so others could fly into the house, which was built round a light well with a glass roof. The golden-beaked sparrows always found their way upstairs and out again.

• • •

A couple of days after the guy in the mirror told me to get going, I looked at some flights on the Internet, but they were expensive. Maybe I could get one of the ferries to Europe that were advertised all over town.

You gotta get out . . . Well, all right then. I'd be better off not torturing myself by seeing Laila every day. I'd done so little work I was likely going to fail my exams at the end of the year. Even if I didn't, even if I completed the course, it still wouldn't get me a job worth having. I'd have a degree in economics and business studies with a Miss Aziz Special in politics (including five hours' free history). No one was going to hire me for that. "Go to the building site, you jerk," that's what they'd say. "Go and join the line with the skilled masons and plumbers." So I *was* going to leave. I was going . . . Somewhere. Some*real*where. Some*fucking-proper*where. Paris probably.

I knew almost nothing about Paris, but it was in Europe, they were Christian, they had bars, girls, old buildings, cinemas . . . So before the courage could leave me, I leapt off the bed and went upstairs. As I came near the door of the living room, a strange thing happened. I began to be outside myself, watching. I could see myself as a third person, my T-shirt and jeans, two spots on the chin, skinny arms and messed-up hair.

I saw myself going to tell my father.

There was me, Tariq, going into the living room. My father was sitting on a sofa where he was looking through his glasses at some papers.

"What do you want?" he said. "Can't you see I'm busy?"

"Sorry. What are you doing?" said Tariq.

"Accounts. They never end. Why aren't you doing some work? I'm sure you've got reading to do."

"No, I'm up to date with my reading," said Tariq, pushing back the hair from his forehead.

"Dinner's in an hour. You can tell me what you want then. And your stepmother. You know how much she worries."

"I'm leaving. I'm going to live somewhere else."

"God give me strength. You want to give up your studies?"

"Yeah, but that's not the reason."

"So what is the reason?"

"I want to live in a different place, a better place."

My father laughed and put down his papers—so without them he'd be free to laugh harder. "Where? Fez? Algiers? I know you always wanted to go there. Think you're a man for the big city?"

"No. That would just be . . . bigger."

"Where then? Malaysia?" He was really gasping now. "Australia? Why not? Go and be a sheep farmer."

"Paris, I think."

"What on earth for? You don't know anyone there."

"No, but I'd like to see where my mother grew up. Find out some more about her. And I can speak the language."

"Think they'd understand your accent? Anyway, they hate us, the French. They always have."

Tariq rubbed his chin. "I don't think they'd hate me. I think I'd fit in. There's a lot of us there."

"Oh yes, sure. Living in filthy tower blocks in the *banlieue*."

"I don't mind where I end up."

"And how are you going to live?"

"Like a peasant." Tariq seemed to think for a moment. "Like a hero."

My father dabbed the corner of his eyes with a handkerchief. "And what are you going to use for money?"

"I don't need money," Tariq said. "I'll live off my wits."

"*Your* wits!"

"I hope so. You know I can speak English like a native."

"Yes, like a native of America. All that TV."

"And French. My mother—"

"You truly are a ridiculous child," said my father, his shoulders no longer heaving. "Go and do some work."

He picked up his papers and put his glasses on again. Tariq backed slowly towards the door. It looked like he was hoping my father would stop him. With his hand on the doorknob, he hesitated.

"Well?" My father looked up from his papers. "What are you waiting for?"

Back in my room I heaved out a backpack and stuffed some clothes in it. I took my passport and all the money I'd saved up. It didn't come to much, though it included some euros I'd got from a Spanish tourist for showing him round. Then I went into the bathroom and took a long hard look at my reflection. The lighting wasn't so good as the time before and my face looked a bit greasy.

Oh fuck it, I thought. Let's go.

After walking for about fifteen minutes, I got a lift with a lorry. There were crates of *limonada* and Sprite rattling behind us. The driver gave me a cigarette. We drove past Laila's house and from high up in the cab I could see over the wall onto the lawns. There was a covered electric lamp glowing on the veranda. I wanted her to come out of the house, but I also couldn't bear the thought of seeing her. I felt for a moment as though someone had grabbed my lungs and was squeezing me to death. Fuck, was this what a heart attack feels like?

I shut my eyes and let the road take me away.

• • •

Maybe I shouldn't say how I got into Europe. A long airless night in the back of a lorry in a cargo hold—not something I want to go into or remember. And for sure Marseille wasn't how I'd pictured it. I suppose a freight terminal's not the best place to enter a country.

There are good and bad things about being nineteen. One of the good things is you can sleep pretty much anywhere—on a beach, in a field, or in my case between two pallets on the metal floor of a curtain-sided truck. I wasn't even stiff as I fiddled with the fastenings of the canvas, waiting till we were some way out of the terminal. When the driver stopped at what I thought must be a traffic light, I hopped off.

France at last. Except I could have been in any industrial area. Warehouses, roundabouts, lorries, everything in concrete or metal, the most human thing the words on the signs—Saint-Martin de Crau, Martigues. Even this ass-end of the country looked rich to me. All that expensive fuel turning into smoke as the drivers worked the gears, revving up to get the wheels turning under the big loads. To say nothing of the cargo itself, the loot that was weighing down the giant red tractor-trailers of Norbert Dentressangle. I walked towards what I thought might be a service area, but turned out to be a weighbridge.

It was an hour before I got myself into a café attached to a filling station where I ate a cheese sandwich from a cellophane wrapper. I didn't have enough euros for a train to Paris, so I thought I'd better try hitchhiking. I knew that Lyon was in the right direction and Bordeaux wasn't. But I guessed most of the lorries would be headed for Paris anyway, so it was just a question of getting one to stop.

The toilets were pretty bad. The stench . . . It was as though there'd been an outbreak of dysentery. And the mess on the floor. Is it like that in their own homes—with torn paper on the tiles with piss and water squelching underfoot? But I needed to wash somehow, so I did my best while trying not to gag.

Back in the cafeteria, I noticed a girl on her own. She had brown oily hair and looked like she hadn't slept for days. She was maybe four or five years older than me and she didn't immediately look away when I caught her eye, so I ordered a coffee and took it to the next table.

"Where are you going?" I asked in French, trying not to sound African.

"North," she said.

"Have you got a car?"

She shook her head. "One of these lorry drivers'll offer me a lift."

"Is that safe?"

"It's fine. Tonight he'll ask me to suck his cock. I'll say no."

"Right . . . Shall I travel with you? It'd be safer . . . I mean, I can make sure nothing bad happens."

She managed a smile, but she looked so exhausted. "All right. But if you slow me down, you'll have to leave me on my own."

"Sure. My name's Tariq."

"Sandrine. I'm going to the bathroom."

On her way back she stopped to buy a Chupa Chups and said something to a gray-haired man sitting on a stool, stirring his coffee with a plastic stick. When he'd finished, he nodded towards us and we followed him out to his lorry. It was a medium-size green Iveco with room for three up front and a bunk behind. The driver had a ribbed zip-up sweater with a shirt and tie underneath.

Sandrine winked at me as he maneuvered us out onto the slip road. I didn't know what the wink meant. This guy was a soft touch? He was a Christian fanatic? Europe was strange.

One thing was for sure, the French radio was no good. A man and a woman were talking over each other at a thousand miles an hour. But even that was better than the music. French pop! I didn't like to say anything in case Sandrine was a fan too.

The driver turned out be called Maurice and he wasn't much of a talker. I thought that was maybe why he'd picked us up, for some company, but he seemed happy with his own thoughts and le shit pop music.

It must have been an hour before he said something. *"La vallée du Rhône."* The Rhône Valley. He said it with a big wave of his hand, like he owned it or he'd been born there. Perhaps in his previous life he'd been a schoolmaster.

I asked him where he came from.

"Le Pas-de-Calais." You'd think it was Hollywood he sounded so proud—and if you came from anywhere else you weren't being serious.

He was headed home after a two-week trip. I asked if it was hard to be away from his family for such a long time and he told me he wasn't married. There was a pause. I said I was aiming for Paris, but he only grunted. Sandrine had been asleep for a good twenty minutes, her head nodding against the back of the cab, her mouth slightly open. I wanted to check her out properly, but if you stare at people when they're asleep it sometimes wakes them up. I felt it was a bit unfair as well—she didn't look that great with her mouth open.

At some point I must have nodded off too. The jabbering of the man and woman on the radio wove in and out of a dream. Then my stepmother merged into the *speakerine* to tell me off about running away from home. Several times she told me how wrong it was.

"*Lyon*," said Maurice, waking me up. "*On s'approche de Lyon, le ventre de la France.*" The belly of France. I sleepily asked him why and he told me it was known for its cooking. Snails in garlic, fried liver with sage, apple and cherry tarts with cream . . . Maurice's little speech seemed to exhaust him. "Too many Algerians in Lyon, that's the trouble," he said and slumped back into silence as the lorry ground to a halt in the traffic of the ring road. "Always have been."

It was getting dark and my stomach was rumbling as I pictured the kind of restaurant Maurice had described. Sandrine said she needed to go to the toilet, but he told her to wait. Eventually we came to a service area about an hour north of Lyon and left the autoroute.

We pulled over in an area reserved for lorries and Maurice said he was going to a truckers' café. He told us we could get food at the petrol station. Could that really be it?

Sandrine and I looked at each other in disbelief. Then she led me over to the place where Maurice had gone and we looked through the steamed windows. Inside it men were eating pâté with long loaves of bread and plates of sausages with mashed potatoes and ketchup. It sure wasn't the menu Maurice had talked about, but it looked pretty good and there were bottles of red wine with no label at intervals on the tables among the fat *camionneurs*.

"*Salaud*," said Sandrine. Bastard. In the garage shop, while Sandrine was in the toilet, I bought another sandwich in a wrapping. It was meant to be cheese, but it was nearly all crumby white bread. A thin rain was falling when we crossed the parking outside and Sandrine pressed something into my hand. It was a chocolate bar.

"Have it. I took a whole lot while the guy was changing the paper roll on the till."

"Where are we going to sleep?"

"In the back of the lorry. If he lets us. Do you like sausages?"

"I'm not sure. Are they pork?"

"Not really *pork*. They're just odds and ends. Come here and keep watch." She led me round to the back entrance of the drivers' canteen.

I was left standing in the rain for at least fifteen minutes before she came back with a plate in her hand.

"Have some. Use your hands, boy."

I took a sausage and pushed it through the mashed potato.

"Put some ketchup on it. Do you like it?"

"Yes. How did you get it?"

"Waited for the right moment."

"No one saw you?"

"No. They don't care anyway. Most of the people in the kitchen are kids. Some of them probably illegal."

The sausage had a peppery taste. "Are you illegal?"

She laughed. "No. I'm French."

Sandrine took the plate to a bin, then marched into the café where Maurice was finishing his dinner. She certainly had balls, this girl. Through the steamed-up window I could see the drivers laughing and pointing while Sandrine stood with her hands on her hips. Eventually Maurice stood up and came out into the drizzle. He walked over to his lorry, took a blanket from the bunk behind the driver's cabin then unlocked the back and told us to get in. There was room to lie down on a wooden pallet between the tied cargo.

"Don't fuck in my lorry. I'll hear you if you do," said Maurice, throwing in the blanket and closing the doors behind him.

We lay down and made ourselves comfortable. There was a bit less space than I'd thought and Sandrine's hip was touching mine. She wasn't my sort, Sandrine, with her lank hair and gray skin, but it was dark now and when she turned over I felt one of her breasts for a moment on my elbow and I immediately got a hard-on.

"Is it okay?" I said. "Will you have to . . . You know. Do anything with Maurice?"

"Nothing. No. I'm not his type."

"What do you mean?"

"I'm too old for him. He's a pedo."

"How do you know?"

"The shirt and tie. That's why I chose him. The worst are the married ones. They want you to do disgusting things."

In the middle of the night I woke myself up coughing. Sandrine was sitting up, smoking a cigarette.

"Is that safe?" I said. "We don't know what's in the cargo."

She ground it out on the metal floor of the truck. "I couldn't sleep," she said.

"Where are you going?" I said.

"Don't know. Paris at first. Then maybe England."

"Why do you want to go there?"

I sensed she was smiling in the darkness. "I want to see the rain and the fog and the queen on horseback in her crown."

"Really?"

"Not really. I know some people there. I think I'll be safer in London."

"English people?"

"Yes."

"What are they like?"

"English people?"

"Yes." I'd never met one. Except an old pervert who lived in the casbah.

"I'll let you know. I really want a smoke," said Sandrine.

"You just had one."

"I mean weed. Have you got any?"

"No. I didn't want to be stopped."

"I can't sleep without it. Unless I have sex."

"Do you want me to—"

"How old are you?"

"Twenty-three," I said.

"I don't believe you." She put her hand on my trousers. "Oh. Sorry, boy. I thought you might have . . ."

I thought about Miss Aziz's skirt and Laila's *qooq* and Farida's breasts and all the usual things, but for once it was no use. My *zib* was like a dormouse.

Eventually we both fell asleep and in the morning I found I'd come in my underpants, something that often happens if I'm not at home but in a strange bed, or in this case lorry.

Maurice opened the doors and the gray light came pouring in. I squinted out and saw he had a smirk on his teacher's face.

"I'm going to get breakfast," he said. "We leave in twenty minutes."

By noon we could see the outskirts of Paris and half an hour later Maurice dropped us at a junction as he headed round the Périphérique until he could pick up the road for Calais, the Hollywood of the North.

I watched the green Iveco indicate then merge. Sandrine and I walked for a long time towards the middle of the city. It was a relief to get away from that music on the radio.

"What are you going to do in Paris?" said Sandrine eventually.

We were still on a dual carriageway with modern blocks on either side, but at last there was a Métro station, Maison Blanche.

"I don't know," I said. "Maybe find out about my mother."

It was hard to talk against the roar of traffic.

Gare du Nord

I LOWERED MY CASES FROM THE TRAIN ONTO THE PLATFORM AT THE Gare du Nord. "I'm sorry . . . *Pardon,*" I said to the people behind me, as I flipped the pack onto my back and set off to drag my luggage up the length of the Eurostar. The casters roared on the concrete.

There was no ticket collector at the gate, but as I headed for the taxis I was met by a man who, like many others circling, looked North African. *"Où allez-vous, Madame?* Where you go? You want taxi?"

"Yes, I do. Isn't there a line?"

"Where you go?"

"La Butte-aux-Cailles." It sounded odd when spoken aloud; in English, it was "Quail Hill."

"Eighty euros."

"What?" Did I look especially gullible or was it just that I was female?

"See here." The man produced a book of tables that looked official, like logarithms. "Is good price. Look." He jabbed a column. *"C'est bon."*

By now we were outside the station, where the taxi line doubled back beneath a glass-roofed awning.

"Non, merci," I said. *"J'attendrai un vrai taxi."* I'll get a real cab.

There was some muttering among the men, but they didn't linger, seeing other confused travelers coming their way.

"Salope," said one.

"And fuck you too," I said, at the back of the line but shielded from the hustlers by a later arrival. I felt like smacking a cigarette from its pack and had almost got as far as opening my bag before I remembered that after years of struggle I'd quit six months before. It was raining lightly on the roof of the shelter.

The next North African was a licensed driver, who loaded my bags into the trunk of his Renault and waved away my apologies for how heavy they were. I sat back and sighed. *Allez.*

He swept me down boulevards of obscure character—Magenta, Beaumarchais, L'Hôpital, with travel agencies, peeling plane trees, refrigerator showrooms, offices, more travel agencies . . . What was there so urgent to escape? And could the journey really be this far? I'd always thought of Paris as compact within its various gates or *portes.* At last we came to somewhere I'd heard of, the Place d'Italie, after which the sat-nav took us down streets that seemed unfamiliar.

I saw a name, the rue de l'Espérance, and thought it was an omen. "Dear Mom and Dad, I am living off Good Hope Street in Quail Hill." It sounded like a tony address in Boston; perhaps I'd be invited to a dinner given by the Lowells so I could meet the Cabots from next door.

There was something strange about the narrow street where I was dropped off. The buildings were not on the usual Haussmann design of grand but repeatable efficiency; there were low stuccoed houses with iron railings in front. The street itself had the bare trees and flat light of an Utrillo painting; and, as in the Montmartre townscapes of Utrillo, there was no one there.

The key was with the manageress at the *laverie-pressing* on the corner. A few minutes later, I'd hauled my bags to the door and let myself in. The apartment was on the first floor and it didn't take long to get the feel of it. The living room or *salon* at the front had a small balcony; a hallway opened on a bedroom to the left with an internal bathroom. At the end of the hall was a tiny kitchen and a second bedroom, large enough only for a single bed and a nightstand. The original parquet was intact throughout the apartment under thin rugs; the main rooms were bigger than they'd looked in the e-mail attachment, but the furniture was cheaper and more worn. It was no problem; some flowers and a couple of woolen throws would fix it.

After moving around the lamps and chairs, I had the *salon* set up as a place where I could work. The dining table was big enough to hold

books, a laptop, city maps and papers. I wasn't planning any dinner parties, so I could push it up against the wall. In the kitchen I found some
UHT milk, but there was nothing else in the refrigerator. On a shelf in
a cupboard were some half-used packets of pasta, folded over and held
by elastic bands, and some ginseng-powder capsules.

In the hall, by the Wi-Fi router, there was a child's exercise book with
details of local services. The nearest supermarket was three blocks
away, which would do for coffee, bread and milk for the morning; the
notes recommended several better shops, but they could wait. And as
for dinner . . . It was still only a little after six, but I was hungry—and
what was the point of Paris if you couldn't just wander into the street
and find somewhere? I grabbed a book to read and, as I was getting
ready to leave, remembered my parents and my brother, Warren, who
was currently visiting with them. I managed to send an e-mail on my
baffling new phone, the loan of which had been my department's
farewell gift. The Wi-Fi seemed erratic, but it lasted long enough for
me to hear the whoosh as the message left. "Arrived. All good. More
later. H. x"

As I was putting the phone away, it pinged. Surely my parents
couldn't have answered so quickly? No; but the connection had lasted
long enough to download three e-mails. Two were junk and the third
one read:

"Hi, Hannah, hope this finds you. I heard from Nathalie at UCL that
you were bound for Paris, maybe even here by now. I'm still laboring
over the Romantics (though Sylvie and I parted company some time
back) and would love to meet up one day if your work allows. Best
wishes, Julian F. x"

Julian Finch was an Englishman I'd met during my first visit to Paris,
when I attended some of the lectures in a literature course he taught.
His specialties were French Romanticism and New Wave cinema (his
course on Truffaut and *Les Quatre Cents Coups* was his big draw with
the students). It would be interesting to see how he was getting along
without the large Passy apartment that had belonged, I was pretty
certain, to Sylvie.

"Of course," I replied. "Just arrived. Maybe one day next week. H."

Before I could gather my things, Julian had e-mailed back, asking
for my cell number. A minute later, my phone rang.

"I don't suppose by any remote chance you're free tonight?"

I looked again at my watch. "Well, I guess I could be." What was the point in pretending?

"I live off the rue du Faubourg Saint-Denis. Bit of a comedown from the rue des Marronniers, I know. If you go to the Métro Strasbourg–Saint-Denis and start walking, there's a bar on the right about five minutes up called the Mauri Sept. Could you make it by eight?"

"I don't see why not. The Morissette? Like Alanis?"

"What?"

"Never mind. See you there."

The reason I'd first come across Julian ten years earlier—the reason I'd been in Paris at all—was that I'd applied for a junior-year program there. I was a history major and most people going on the course were language students, but there were two places reserved for nonlinguists; the idea was that as well as some compulsory classes there would be time to research your own project. My knowledge of France at the time was limited to a half semester's work on the Algerian War of 1954–62—in which the Algerians had defeated their French colonial masters in a conflict of insane savagery—and an essay on Léon Blum's socialist Popular Front in 1936. I doubted that my high-school French would be good enough and was excited when my application was accepted.

I went on a crash course in spoken French in Boston in the summer and waved goodbye to my parents in September with a breezy *au revoir*. From Paris I sent long letters home that my mother and father, so they said, were delighted to receive. But did it ever worry them that I seemed to have time to write at such length? Shouldn't I have been going to parties and exhibitions, or picnics on the Seine? Maybe my parents didn't think like that; neither of them, for all their European roots, had ever left the United States.

The truth is that, however much I may have been struck by Paris and its beauty, by its sidewalk cafés and its trees and bridges, by its cathedral floating on the stream and all the other charms to which no sane person could fail to respond a little, I was lonely. The language students stuck together and I found them childish. I sometimes visited a boy from England who had a room in an old woman's flat off the Avenue de la Grande Armée, but it was not enough to take away the sense of isolation. And as for making friends with any Parisians, the language seemed too great an obstacle. It was one thing being able to make myself understood in my faulty French, quite another to follow a Parisian conversation in a noisy bar.

Everything changed one evening at the American Library. Julian Finch had alerted us all to the existence of this excellent refuge, well stocked and all but free to students, and he himself was that night chairing an event, which, having nothing better to do, I'd decided to go along to. There I met a man who put an end to my sense of isolation, but at a cost that ten years later I was still paying. For a few months, my letters home became euphoric. And then they stopped.

When I finally returned home that July, I'd lost almost twenty pounds in weight and my parents were shocked by the sight of me. Reluctantly, I agreed to a course of weekly visits to Dr. Pavin, a psychotherapist, though she seemed to think my problem had its roots in childhood. No sympathy from my mother or arm around the shoulder from my father could persuade me to confide in them—though at the beginning of my senior year, back in college, I did sit up one night talking with my roommate and best friend, Jasmine Mendel. Even with Jasmine, I was unable to describe the extent of my unhappiness. There was nothing in my own experience or in my knowledge of the lives of others with which to compare it, so I thought it best to lock it all away and try to think of other things. My mother told me I seemed "cold," and I found it impossible to convince her that when you've found yourself so far out of your depth you cling to certainties, things you know you can deal with. And you keep clinging for as long as it takes.

During all that time in Paris—the lonely part and the ecstatic later days—Julian had been a background presence. To some, not me, he was more than that. He was not what you'd call handsome and he had this sort of British reserve, but I think many of the female students were a little in love with him. It happens. He was both professional and happily married, or so we thought, to a Frenchwoman called Sylvie, who made the occasional appearance at functions or readings, looking friendly in a bored sort of way, smoking and checking her phone for messages. The male students also liked him because as well as movies he sometimes talked about soccer (which he called "football") and he didn't condescend to them.

In the course of the year, Julian quite often had lunch with a group of students at a café on the Boulevard Raspail. He always ordered a pitcher of Côtes du Rhône for us all to share, though I didn't drink wine in the middle of the day; and almost every time, I remembered, he got a beer, a *demi pression,* then the eggs mayonnaise with anchovy. The only time we'd ever met *à deux* was when we had dinner after seeing a student play near the Bourse and I embarrassed myself by confusing *onglet,* a cut of steak I'd never heard of, with the identically pronounced *anglais.* He teased me about being so serious; he called me "Mrs. Jellyby," after a character in Dickens who was obsessed by helping the African poor, and once wondered out loud if I was a born-again Christian.

His sense of humor wasn't the same as mine, but I could see he meant no harm and I liked the way he dealt with his students. Perhaps I also sensed something strained or unhappy in him then—a sense that the large apartment in the Sixteenth, the glamorous wife and the offer of publication of his book were not as satisfying to him as others presumed. But probably I'm imagining that, because at the age of twenty-one, I'm afraid, I was too preoccupied by my own feelings to wonder about people older and more secure than I was.

Dinner with Julian, I decided as I took a bath and washed my hair, would help ease me back into Parisian life. I chose a black wool dress that showed I'd made an effort. I wore it with boots, a leather flying jacket and a silvery costume necklace. For a moment I worried that it all looked a bit much, like a rock star attempting a comeback, but the outfit made me feel safe.

I was early at the station, so I walked up and down the noisy main road to kill some time. At the junction with the Boulevard de Strasbourg, middle-aged Chinese women with shopping bags and parkas were leaning against the rail in pairs, catching the eye of solitary men. It was a strange version of domesticity: "Come home and pay me for sex, but not till you've helped unpack the shopping."

Going up the rue du Faubourg Saint-Denis, I found it hard not to smile at how different it was from the smooth stone expanses of the Sixteenth, where Julian's married home had been. On the rolled-down metal blinds of the shop fronts were the solid blocks of graffiti that had shocked me when I'd first seen them as a child on the New York subway. This was an old street that seemed to have lost itself without finding a new identity; its life was only in the people outside the bars, smoking cigarettes. I passed several such places, heard music, but couldn't find a bar called the Morissette. I had by now been walking for ten minutes so it was clear I'd gone past it. Retracing my steps, I came eventually to the red awning of Le Mauri 7.

The Morissette, the Mauri Sept . . . Of course. Typical of my problems with French. Inside, everyone seemed to be twenty-three years old and most were playing table football. Julian was sitting near the door. When he had returned with drinks, I apologized for being late and explained my confusion over the name of the bar.

"Alanis Morissette was a big thing back in '96, the year I was last here," I said. "We all listened to that record *Jagged Little Pill* a hundred times."

"I had you down as more of a Joni Mitchell type," said Julian, clinking his beer glass against mine.

"I liked her too. They know how to pour their hearts out, those Canadian girls. So you live nearby these days?"

"Yes. In a small street just up there. It's what in London they call a mews. It's where they used to keep horses. I live above a brasserie. I originally had my eye on a place in the Passage du Désir, just up the road, but the gates into it were closed when I came and I never got to see it."

"So your way into the passage of desire was barred?"

"Story of my life."

I didn't mind providing the feed. I knew Julian had always thought of me as a humorless social campaigner, and I liked it that he had me slightly wrong; it gave me some extra protection.

"And what exactly is your project in Paris this time?" he said.

I felt myself pushing my hand back through my hair as I exhaled. "It's a long story."

"There's a short version?"

"Yes. I'm here to research the experience of women in Paris under the German Occupation, 1940 to '44. It'll be a chapter in a book my head of department, Professor Putnam, is putting together."

"It's a fascinating period. But someone told me you'd given up university after your doctorate? I thought that was a shame."

"I did for a time. I went to work in Africa for two years on an

AIDS-education program. When I got home I was a little lost. My old friend Jasmine Mendel suggested I apply for a position as a postdoc. The department had some money for once."

I felt the short version of my life had gone on long enough. "And what about you?" I said. "Are you still in the nineteenth century?"

"Yes. I'm halfway through a biography of Alfred de Musset for an English publisher. You know who I mean?"

"A Romantic, wasn't he?"

"Yes. Famously George Sand's lover. He wrote plays, a memoir and a lot of poetry. Not a front-rank poet, I suppose, but an interesting one."

"He wasn't the guy with a pet lobster on a lead?"

"No. That was Gérard de Nerval."

"And there are publishers in London who'll take a book on a not-front-rank nineteenth-century French poet?"

"Luckily there's *one*. I'm putting quite a lot of stress on the autoscopy angle."

"The what?"

"Autoscopy. It's when you have the sense of being outside yourself and seeing yourself as another person. Auto, self, scope, vision. De Musset had it a lot."

"As a poetic device or a nervous symptom?"

"That's the question. Both, I think. But it's not the doppelgänger thing; it's more interesting. Sometimes he found himself walking towards himself in the Tuileries."

"That sounds good."

"Yes. He made it very sad. In his best poem, 'La Nuit de Décembre,' he describes this person who's dogged him all his life, in different cities, at different ages."

"And who is it?"

"I'm not going to tell you. You'll have to read the poem for yourself."

I stood up to go to the bar. "You were always good at tantalizing your pupils. At tricking us into reading more."

"I never really had a gift for teaching, I'm afraid," said Julian. "I always looked on it as a nuisance that took time away from my own work."

Returning with the drinks, I said, "I was sorry to hear about Sylvie. What happened?"

"God, you're quick off the mark. Not even waiting till dinner."

"I didn't know there was a set time for personal questions."

"Between the main course and the cheese, I think," said Julian.

"You used to like me being frank. Or 'American,' as you called it."

"I like your honesty. The way you admitted to being free tonight."

"A Frenchwoman wouldn't do that?"

"No. I'm sorry if I seemed pushy. I've become rather impulsive, living on my own. But I knew you'd be—"

"Hungry?" I said, putting down my beer glass.

Two hours later, when I was walking home from Tolbiac station, a little flushed by wine, I saw a figure slumped on a step at the end of my street. It didn't look like a regular doorway sleeper, a *clochard*; in any case, the Butte-aux-Cailles was not really hobo country and this was not a bearded man but a young woman, in dirty but once-good clothes.

"Are you okay?"

There was no reply.

"What's your name?"

"I came out to get some food. I got lost."

She looked feverish.

"Where do you live?"

"The Olympiades."

"I don't know that. Do you have a phone?"

"No."

"You'd better come with me. We'll get you back there tomorrow."

"All right."

"What's your name?" I asked again.

"Sandrine," the young woman said, allowing herself to be helped to her feet.

Back at the apartment, I put a duvet and blankets on the bed in the little storeroom and moved my suitcase out of it; then I heated some vegetable soup from a carton. I saw no reason to distrust this feverish kid.

Stalingrad (by night)

I HADN'T COME TO PARIS ON A MISSION, IT WAS JUST TO ESCAPE FROM MY father and stepmother and the torture of *not* sleeping with Laila. Can you run away from a negative? You bet. Had I really "run away" in any case? No one had tried to stop me going.

Plenty of people had headed up from Morocco to France looking for work, though my father said the French had recently become less welcoming. He didn't put it as nicely as that. What he said was: "They always hated us. Once they'd murdered and tortured and killed and taken everything they wanted from us in our country, they just let us hang, the bastards. Then a few bombers from the *banlieue* gave them an excuse to hate us more." That was how he put it.

He went on a bit about jihad and brainwashed virgins, but I'd stopped listening by then. I didn't care about colonial wars that had happened before I was born. I only knew that my mother had been born and brought up in Paris, had lived the best part of her life there. Her name was hardly ever mentioned at home and there were no pictures of her on shelves or tables in our house. It was as though my father resented her for dying. Once when I was going through his desk drawers looking for cigarettes, I did come across an envelope with some old photographs in it. One of them showed him as a young man standing with a woman in a floral dress who had large eyes and black hair. I looked, but could see nothing of myself in her. It *might* have been my mother, though there was no sign of affection or attachment between the two of them, they weren't holding hands or anything, so it could have been a secretary at his office or someone he'd met at the beach. I think he tried to be a ladies' man in his younger days, when that sort of thing was easier to pull off, before a lot of women wrapped themselves in black. They got that idea, by the way, from watching the news on cable TV, which showed their sisters in places like Iran and Yemen. It was like a fashion thing. At the same time, they were seeing U.S. television for the first time and started wearing lots of makeup. And so: the hijab-mascara combination . . . Frozen fireballs, count me out.

When Maurice had left us, Sandrine and I kept walking into Paris.

"What are you going to do?" she said.

"I suppose I'll get a job."

"Just like that?"

"Maybe I can teach Arabic."

"No one wants to learn Arabic. They want *less* Arabic."

"All right, English then. But the first thing I've got to do is eat," I said.

Half an hour later we were inside the city itself, on a wide street, cold, with a dreary park to one side. Sitting in the doorway of a building was a homeless girl, huddled with all her belongings and a look of misery on her face, like she was posing for a picture called *Despair.* She was probably East European, not bad-looking if you'd put her through a hot car wash and bought her new clothes. Her hand was stuck out in a half-hearted way, but what you noticed was how the look of maximum sorrow never let up, not for a second. Sandrine bent down and put a coin in her McDonald's cup and said something I didn't hear. She stayed leaning over, talking to the beggar girl while I looked up and down the street.

"There's a place we can go not far from here," Sandrine said, standing up.

We got walking again. PONSCARME, said the sign on a bus stop. It didn't look like Paris at all. The buildings were new, they looked like children's playthings with funny shapes and bright colors, but it seemed poor as well. And it was so cold compared to home. We kept walking on down these blank streets past the odd Chinese and Vietnamese place with paper lanterns in the window, but we couldn't afford them.

It's hard to say exactly what I'd expected. I hadn't *studied* Paris, I'd just seen a few films over the years and got an impression from the Internet of somewhere very old-fashioned. Not old-fashioned like the medina at home, which had been the same forever—but a place where the buildings all looked similar, with huge black roofs but lived in by ordinary people in heated flats where they kept small dogs and the stairwell was filled with the smells of different dinners. What movie had I got that from? But, it wasn't like that at all, not the bit we were in anyway. It was so twentieth-century and concrete and hard and opened up to the sky with no alleys or big wooden doorways. "Unforgiving" might be a word for it.

Sandrine took my arm and pushed me down a side street. We came to the back of what looked like a school. We went inside a bright room with a canteen along one wall and a couple of old men sitting at a table. We put our backpacks on the floor and went over to the counter, where a dozy African woman handed us some aluminum containers with food inside and a plastic spoon and fork.

"Do we have to pay?" I said.

The woman said nothing, just shook her head slowly. Then she gave us an apple and a piece of bread. We took it over to an empty table.

"What is this?" I said. There was meat of some kind, wrinkled and gray in a sauce with pieces of onion. It smelled bad.

"Tripe, I think," said Sandrine.

"Is that pork?"

"God knows. Cow, maybe."

"What is this place?"

"The girl in the doorway told me about it. It could be a religious thing, or Red Cross maybe."

"I can't eat this."

"Just have the bread. We can buy some coffee and chocolate. I've got a few euros left. She told me about the soup kitchen at Stalingrad, too. We can try there."

"What else did she tell you?"

"She thinks maybe we can find somewhere to stay in one of those tower blocks. She was there herself but she got kicked out."

"Everyone round here seems to be Chinese."

"Is that a problem for you?"

"I suppose not."

But it was. I'd never met Chinese people before and to me they all looked odd. Their heads had no sharp features, they were flat like a cartoon face when someone's whacked it with a pan.

"Do you want to find somewhere to sleep for free?" said Sandrine.

"Sure. But I thought you were going to England?"

"I think I'll wait a few days. I don't feel well."

It was true she looked even grayer than before as we set off for the Métro. We went down the steps and Sandrine stood in front of the wall map for a long time working out our route.

"When we get to the barrier," she said, "just jump it."

I put down my backpack and vaulted over. She passed over my bag and hers, then did the same, though it wasn't so easy for her and I had to give her a hand.

The train took us fast for three stops, then we had to change lines. I'd never been on an underground railway before and I noticed that each stop was different. At Opéra the wide station had tracks in both directions, so the people waiting could look across at one another. At Château-Landon our single track was squeezed into one little tube and the station had red seats. It wasn't a bit like home—the daily bus to college out of the medina, down the boulevard into the shabby Ville Nouvelle. It was exciting.

There was no one sitting opposite me, so I could stare at my own reflection in the window. The lighting made me look tired, with dark smudges under the eyes, but in other ways quite handsome. We held each other's gaze and neither of us blinked.

At the small stops there were a few film posters on the curved walls, but the big stations had pictures of food, of burgers, or of "all the tastes of Italy," of kids leaping, hands above their head, made healthy by drinking special yogurt—or of clothes, with giant women with no skirts showing their legs close-up in colored nylon tights and open coats with bright shop logos. There was a warm, tarry smell.

About this time I noticed that Sandrine was laughing at me. "Your eyes," she said. She made a goggling expression with her tongue hanging out and I pretended not to care. I thought the Métro was cool.

At Stalingrad, we went down some steps not up, because the tracks were outdoors and elevated, held up on iron supports, like a viaduct. They looked like something I'd seen in a cop film set in Chicago. Boy, was it a cold and run-down place. On the Boulevard de la Villette we went past a giant food market called Goa. In each of its bulging windows was the name of a distant place—China, Japan, the Antilles, Africa, the Indian Ocean and God knows where else. France was meant to be famous for its cooking but this place sold food from anywhere *but* France. The bits of wall between the windows were covered in graffiti.

The soup kitchen under the raised tracks was full of Africans, maybe from Liberia or Senegal, places farther south than where I lived, people with dark-black skin—men with white eyes and things to sell wrapped in bright bits of cloth. Under the ironwork, while the trains rattled over us, they traded cell-phone covers and drugs while they waited for the soup. They spoke French in loud nasal voices, sounding angry or urgent. Some of them looked at me suspiciously—as though I wasn't hungry enough or black enough—but no one stopped me from claiming my cup from the woman at the table. It was better than the stuff in the canteen down by the Place d'Italie. It was hot and it had some lentils and carrots and tasted okay with the bread. The cup was made of styrofoam like we had at home in cheap coffee places, but it wasn't very big or full.

One of the *not*-so-good things about being nineteen is that you're hungry all the time, and one cup of soup with a piece of their funny bread, not round and flat like ours but torn from a long tube or baguette, was nothing like enough. I managed to get hold of a banana, a black one, before Sandrine dragged me off.

We walked for a long time again, but I couldn't say where. I had the impression it was an area not many people chose to be. Sandrine had begun to cough and she looked really ill. We stopped in a doorway and she sat down, leaning against the wall. It was starting to get dark already.

"I need a rest," she said.

"Where are we going to sleep?" As I asked the question it did hit me for a second that I really should have thought of this before. I hadn't planned even the simplest things. I'd just wanted to leave. And I'd been *told* to leave.

"There's a guy I know. It's a bit further on. He's called Yves. I've used his place before."

"What does it cost?"

"Nothing."

"Are you going to have to suck his cock?"

"No. You are."

"I don't think I can do that."

"I'm teasing you, boy. He used to be a junkie. He likes helping people."

"What sort of drugs?"

"Heroin. Crack."

"Oh no. That's bad."

"I thought everyone took drugs where you come from."

"Only *kif.* Or *majoun,* where you mix the *kif* with dates and nuts and stuff." (I hated *majoun* actually, you never knew if you'd had enough until it was too late, but I didn't say so.)

I was thinking I'd better get a job pretty quick. Hanging out with all those Chinese was not my idea of fun. And then the Africans. When was I going to meet a French girl? I thought about Laila and how nice it would have been if only she'd been there, especially with her father's credit card.

When Sandrine had had her rest, we started walking again and I must have got a few paces ahead because I was on my own when a woman stopped me. She'd been standing in a doorway of a building next to a canal and she was carrying two shopping bags. Her French was pretty bad, but I could just about understand. She was asking if I wanted to go back to her flat, which was nearby.

This seemed like a good break. Sandrine was struggling and I really didn't want to sleep on the floor of some opium den, even if we ever got to find it.

"Thanks," I said. "How far?"

"Fifty euros."

The French word for "how far" is *combien,* which is also the word for "how much," so I explained the mistake and said, still in French, "No. I mean, is your place a hundred meters, two hundred meters from here?"

As I was talking to her, I saw that she was wearing a lot of makeup. Her reply was spoken so fast and with such a strong accent that I couldn't make it out. By this time Sandrine had caught up with me. She looked ready to drop.

"This woman's offered me somewhere to sleep," I said. "Her flat's nearby."

Then to the woman I said, "Can my friend come too?" In reply she poured out some torrent of stuff, of which I could make out only filthy words. Sandrine took my elbow and said, "Come on. It's not far to Yves's place now."

At the end of the street, I said, "She seemed nice at first, but then—"

"How old are you, boy?"

"Twenty-three. I told you."

"No. Really."

"All right. Twenty."

"Honestly?"

"Almost."

"You just met your first Parisian hooker."

"But she had a shopping bag and a wedding ring."

"And she wasn't standing under a lamppost singing Edith Piaf."

I didn't know who Edith Piaf was, but after a bit I said, "You can stop laughing at me now."

Yves's place was on the top floor of a building like the Goa food market, really dirty with metal-framed windows, and there weren't any beds. At least he was there when we rang the bell from the icy street and he remembered Sandrine and he let us in. Yves was a big man with a beard and overalls. He looked like an American car mechanic—in fact he looked a lot like a character in *The Messenger* called Buster Bee. He gave us each a piece of baguette with a tiny round cheese in a red wax coat.

There were four or five other people sitting round, but there was just one couch so two of them were on the floor. Sandrine had a thin sleeping bag attached to her pack, so she rolled it out and lay down and fell asleep pretty much straightaway. Her face was flushed.

Sitting with my back to the wall, I had a cigarette and listened to the others.

"I had this room in Clichy-sous-Bois in one of the big towers. It was cool but this fucking *métis* chucked me out 'cause his brother and his kids were arriving in the back of a fruit lorry. So then I'm on the street and the *schmitts* picked me up for no fucking reason at all . . ."

Everything was someone else's fault. They all had so much anger and they used bad words about other races, even the African did. I didn't know exactly what all the slang meant, like *métis* means half-caste and that may be okay, and *schmitt* I guessed was a cop, but some of the other words for Arabs and Africans and Jews—*bougnoules, youtres*—didn't sound nice. I managed to escape to the bathroom where I cleaned my teeth, came back in and lay down close to Sandrine on the floor and hoped they'd all shut up soon. I didn't have a sleeping roll or anything, but I put on a spare sweater and made a pillow with two clean T-shirts.

The thing was, I wanted to get as much of Sandrine's body heat as I could without catching her filthy virus. I stuck my ass against her and kept my head turned the other way.

Through the night, Yves came and went, talking in a normal voice, as though no one had told him it was bedtime. Some of the others went droning on with their hard-luck tales and a new woman arrived in the middle of the night. I must have slept at some time or another because I know I had strange dreams. One thing I knew for certain—I wasn't going to spend another night in this place.

The next morning we took the Métro back down to the Place d'Italie, near where we'd had (or *not* had in my case) the tripe for lunch the day before. The idea was to find the beggar girl and see if she could get us into a room in one of the towers nearby.

I felt I'd somehow fallen out of normal life. We didn't know the name of the girl, so we asked other street people if they knew where she was. Suddenly this was my world—not Miss Aziz or Laila and her garden, but this: Let's find a down-and-out and ask if he knows when a home-less person whose name you don't know might be back on her step. It was still only about eight in the morning, a time I'd normally be asleep, but we'd already had hours awake and had crossed the city. This other world I'd tumbled into hardly seemed to sleep.

Eventually, we did get some names, and by late morning we were walking over an esplanade where the buildings had wavy red roofs in some cartoon oriental style. Les Olympiades, it was called, because all round were big towers named—God knows why—after cities that had hosted a summer or winter Olympic Games. Athens, Cortina, Tokyo, Sapporo . . . It was like a sci-fi thing where a planner had been given too much money. The shopping center was called the Pagoda. What the hell did pagodas have to do with Olympic Games or the Thirteenth arrondissement? Frozen fireballs . . .

Floor 21 of Sarajevo was where we ended up. It was Chinese. Every-thing was Chinese in the whole tower. There was a small room with a single bed with no bedclothes and we could share the bathroom with eight other people. The owner was a Chinese woman of about fifty, whose name was something like "Baco." She was hard-faced, flat-faced, but she gave us till the end of the week to pay and I told Sandrine I could earn money somehow. Sandrine really just needed to go to bed and sleep off this thing that was attacking her. There was no chance of her getting anywhere near England for the time being.

We made her comfortable with her sleeping bag and I lent her my sweater, which meant I had just my T-shirt under a sports top with a hood. It was acrylic, though, which is quite warm, so I thought I'd be okay out on the street. We put together the euros we had and I went off to get cheap food. I asked Baco where to go.

"*Ton frère*," she said.

Was this a curse? Like saying "fuck your sister?"

"*Mon frère?*" I said politely. "*Je n'ai pas de frère.*" I haven't got a brother.

"*Non, non! Ton frère, ton frère!*" she shouted.

Eventually, after a lot of screaming and looking for bits of paper and pen, we got there. There was a big supermarket called Tang Frères. It wasn't really old Baco's fault. Ton, Thon, Temps, Tang—it's all the same to them.

It was immense. I mean, we have a covered market in the medina which is big, with maybe forty stalls, but this was five times that. Every spice, every noodle, every type of cabbage from any country east of India was there. There was half a mile of ready-cooked stuff, but it cost too much. Ground pork was the big thing at the meat counter, but though I'm not religious it's just not something I could eat, so I got some chicken pieces, very cheap, piles of noodles for almost nothing, a bag of five-spice and some greens and a container of hot soup. I also got a two-liter Sprite and lugged it all back to Sarajevo.

I had a go at cooking it, but Baco pushed me to one side and took over. I took in some soup to Sandrine to keep her going. It smelled a bit fishy, but she said it was fine. Baco did a pretty good job on the chicken and threw in a few bits of onion and garlic from a plastic bag above the door. The noodles expanded to fill a huge pan. I offered her some of it in return for the cooking, and afterwards I felt full for the first time since I'd left home. Almost too full, in fact. It occurred to me that since arriving in France I hadn't had a dump.

It wasn't great, that little apartment in the Chinese tower. I slept on the floor because Sandrine needed the bed. She lent me the spare clothes from her bag to pad the linoleum tiles a bit, but it was hard on the hip bones. Through the night the others came and went, banging doors, flushing toilets, talking in loud voices.

On the third morning, I went out and walked up and down the cold open streets. God, I was missing Laila. And Farida. And Miss Aziz. I was even missing my parents and the room where I was always over-looked. I was wondering whether this whole venture had been such a good idea.

I went into some restaurants with paper lanterns and asked if they needed help. Anything. Washing up. Sweeping floors. They just frowned at me, then gabbled oriental stuff I didn't understand. I could tell they didn't want me because I didn't have a flat face like them.

On one of those windy boulevards, near Tang Frères, I ran across our original doorstep girl, the one who looked like the painting of Despair. She'd got a dog and wasn't looking quite so miserable. I told her Sandrine still seemed in a bad way and I was desperate for some work. "I don't think the Chinese like me," I said.

"No. They're racists. Why don't you look in the *banlieue*? It's full of people like you."

"How do I get to the *banlieue*? Does it have a Métro station?"

"It's the big blocks outside the city. Go up Line Thirteen. Saint-Denis, all round there. Are you a Muslim?"

"Yes. Are you?"

She smiled. "I don't believe in God."

"Neither do I. But I'm still a Muslim."

"Go on, crazy boy. Line Thirteen."

She was laughing and I asked her why. Thirteen, she told me, was the line of despair—from Châtillon-Montrouge in the south to the souks of Saint-Denis beyond the northern city limits. The trains had no drivers, but the platforms had doors to stop you throwing yourself on the track.

Well, thanks for the tip, Doorstep Girl. There were other things about the Métro I was learning fast, like don't change lines at mainline sta-tions, especially Montparnasse, unless you want an extra fifteen-minute walk.

When I got there, Saint-Denis looked like it was home to people they didn't want inside the city walls. Arabs and Africans mostly. It wasn't like the casbah at home where everyone looks the same, comes from the same tribe. Some people here had black skin, some had brown. What they had in common was they all looked cold. They all looked wretched. They didn't come from the good places of Africa or the Middle East, anywhere you'd actually want to visit, but from the bits that had been put on the map by famine and beheadings.

I spent the night in some sort of artists' studios in a modern block with a yellow door. A guy of about my age told me I could sleep there free if I got in before it was dark and hid. This worked fine, but it was cold in there and it didn't open up again till nearly ten the next morning. There was a toilet on the floor below, so I could take a pee, but I hadn't brought a toothbrush and still hadn't had a dump.

It took me two days, going into almost every shop or builder's yard, until I finally got lucky at a fast-chicken place called Paname Fried Poulet. The owner was an Algerian with a pockmarked face and they churned out fried nuggets in striped buckets to eat in their front room or—if you had any sense—to take away. I could be a kitchen help for eight euros an hour. He didn't ask to see any ID. It was cash, the Métro was free so long as I could leap the barrier, so I told him yes, I'd start the next day. I just needed to go home and tell my girlfriend (I thought this sounded good, like I was settled or responsible). The Algerian, who said his name was Hasim, gave me an odd look, but said okay.

Strasbourg–Saint-Denis

I N THE MORNING, SANDRINE SEEMED BETTER. I FIXED HER UP WITH coffee, bread and jam; as an afterthought, I also left out some cheese and a banana. The night before, after she'd taken a long soak in the tub, we'd sat up talking for an hour or more; she told me she was trying to escape a violent husband and had plans to stay in England. I loaned her some clean clothes, including a sweater my mother had given me at Christmas—which I'd packed only for fear that she'd be offended to come across it still in my closet at home.

"I'll be back later," I said. "If you're feeling all right, we'll get you back to your apartment. There's a key here if you need to go out before then. Read any of the books you like the look of. There's a television, though I don't know how it works."

"Thank you. You speak good French."

"I can speak it okay. My problem's understanding it."

Soon I'd forgotten about Sandrine. I took the Métro to École Militaire and cut through the rue Saint-Dominique to walk up the windy Avenue Rapp. Most people thought the Seventh arrondissement was dull, a lesser version of the Sixteenth across the river. But there were some fantastic art nouveau designs high up on the avenue's big apartment buildings; there were backstreets with cheap hotels and small delis if you knew where to look. In a narrow clothes-mending shop a woman sat at a treadle in the window, staring out, as she might have done in the days of Victor Hugo. And for me there was the added attraction of the American Library in rue du Général Camou, where, bewildered and alone, I'd first found refuge among the accents of Boston and the Midwest.

Almost nothing had changed there. I took out a six-month subscription and had my photograph taken at the issue desk. The stacks were warm and full; they covered every discipline, but I always thought their specialty was the Franco-American story, the long unrequited passion of one nation for another. Here you could find all the early pilgrims, drunk on sex and *fine à l'eau,* the lovers of the racetrack at Enghien, the Train Bleu, the zinc bars and the clubs of Pigalle. Then came the wartime reminiscences of doctors and diplomats and soldiers, men like Ambassador Bullitt and Sumner Jackson of the American Hospital in Neuilly, who'd helped save Paris from the Nazis. In the ten years since my last visit, there seemed to be a new generation of young men in horn-rims who had come to lay their tributes at the feet of the indifferent mistress.

The chairs in the reading room were still hard, and the ban on food and drink was still in force; the only change over the years was the patter of laptop keyboards. I photocopied "La Nuit de Décembre" from the *Collected Poems of Alfred de Musset* and sat down to look at it. I expected it to be fey and feeble, something with which I might dare to tease Julian when we next met; but at first glance it seemed to have a mournful music. Coming to the American Library when my real material lay elsewhere had been a frivolous thing to do, but I'd wanted to reconnect with my past before I pushed out into the unknown.

Although my student room in those distant days had been north of the river, near rue de Charonne, ten minutes' walk from Bastille, I'd spent my afternoons on the Left Bank, like many dreamy students, straining for the ghosts of Hemingway and Sylvia Beach. But I couldn't afford the Closerie des Lilas and all I found near the Boulevard Saint-Michel were souvenir shops and doner kebabs; the terraces of the Saint-Germain cafés were full of foreigners drinking expensive coffee. I saved up for two weeks to go to the brasserie where the existentialists had met their publishers, but it gave me food poisoning with a forty-eight-hour fever.

My only regular human contact was with my landlady, a foulmouthed Lyonnaise, from whom I picked up an accent that was almost French—a rare thing for an American, people told me. Comprehension was a different matter, and I struggled to understand the rapid talk, which seemed to have too few vowel sounds. With reading, there was no problem: The spelled-out words offered all the variations you'd expect. But in speech . . . How could they get through life, I wondered, making the same sound for *teint* and *thym* when the words had only one letter in common? "Context," said our language tutor. But in conversation with Parisians I began to speak less fluently than I could; I allowed my accent less Lyon and more Boston in the hope they'd slow down and give me a chance of distinguishing between *ont, ans, am, ent, ant, en, on, emps, ang* and all the other ways of making the same sound.

After a few weeks, my loneliness became self-perpetuating and I began to make excuses. I did talk, it was true, to the teacher when it was my turn during evening language classes, but my attempts afterwards to lure the other students out to a café met with excuses of work and home. In silent libraries and in the seclusion of my rented room, I could fill the hours with study and research. There was no online world then in which to find virtual companionship; there were only books, which I was being a good student by reading, while the girl eager to make friends could be shut away.

On that first important evening at the American Library, I noticed a man sitting in the next row, reading a book while we waited for the event to begin. He looked up for a moment and glanced round the room over the top of his glasses, perhaps to rest his eyes. I met his gaze and half-smiled, as if I knew him or had once been introduced. His eyes swept past me, then returned to his book, leaving me to wonder why I'd given this twitch of recognition.

The librarian introduced Julian Finch, who gave a résumé of the life of the main guest, an American travel writer, a fleshy woman in her fifties who looked unwilling to be there. Julian did his best to prompt some anecdotes or some reflections on what "travel writing" really meant, but the writer was both conceited and unresponsive, and I had time to look again at the man whose eye had caught mine. He had untidy chestnut hair and a darker-brown beard with some gray in it; he wore a fawn corduroy jacket and a pale-blue shirt. He looked scruffy yet clean. I guessed he was in his early forties, twice my age at the time. In my mind, I had him down as a publisher—of poetry, perhaps. He lived with a difficult French wife and two small children somewhere in a place with a view of the river. Near Bastille. Even rue de Charonne maybe.

Holding a glass of wine afterwards, I found myself next to him. It was easy enough to start talking. "Have you read . . ." "Do you know . . ." I lost him for a moment in the crowd but lingered in the cold doorway as the library staff began to close the building.

"Hannah, come and join us all at dinner," said Julian, including me in a group of eight people going to a restaurant.

No one questioned my right to be at the table. I was at least on nodding terms with two of the librarians—American women in their thirties, friends with one another. The conversation was conducted in English; with its flow of wine and sense of camaraderie (which came, I guess, from relief that the event, while hardly a success, was at least over and done with), it was the kind of noisy evening I'd envisaged being part of every night in Paris. The man whose eye I had caught was Russian and his name was Alexander (or perhaps "Aleksandr," I thought, leaning across to hear what he was saying). He was a playwright, though it seemed he also had something to do with the Russian embassy or its cultural department.

As we were all standing up to leave, I asked (with a daring fired by loneliness and a half liter of red wine) if he had a card so I could be in touch about "some research" I was doing. He had no card but wrote a phone number on a piece of paper I tore from my notebook. A few days later, I began a month of afternoon visits to his apartment off Boulevard Barbès. He was separated from his wife in St. Petersburg and had come to Paris to "shake up the pieces of my mind," as he put it. He was restless and critical and always seemed amused by what he saw when we went together to a café or a cinema. He was able to take everything in his stride: There was no mishap or rudeness, no piece of good luck, that he couldn't make part of his commentary on the world. It was two weeks before we kissed and another week before we slept together, which was when, in retrospect, I was immediately out of my depth. It hadn't felt like that at the time, though; it had seemed then to be exactly right— *tout à fait comme il faut,* as though it had been preordained.

My previous experiences with men hadn't amounted to much. In my freshman year, mostly to please Jasmine, my ever-encouraging roommate, I'd gone out with a couple of boys in the year ahead. I enjoyed sex up to a point but found it difficult to see why or how this led to anything like a "relationship," when the boys' interests were so different from mine. The following year I took up with Max, a young man I met at a charity fundraiser. We spent months together in bars and clubs and in the back bedroom of the apartment he shared with two other students. Our discussions sometimes lasted most of the night and I felt myself grow close to him; I couldn't keep my eyes from smiling and feet from running towards him when we met after any sort of break. But Max seemed to back away from my attempts to give expression to this tenderness, and I began to think his deeper feeling was for other men. Or maybe that was an excuse. Maybe I just wasn't pretty or alluring enough.

In a way, it was a relief. I could tell Jasmine that I'd tried. I hadn't been priggish or anything like that; I'd "slept around," a bit; I'd had my heart broken, half broken anyway, by the last boy, Max. But this dating, pairing thing was a relic of some prehistoric necessity (food, warmth, money) colored by novelists anxious for a story; and as for sex, well, it was fine, more than fine sometimes, but it was just a moment, really, while the great world of the past—of injustice, of vanished, valuable lives—lay all undiscovered out there.

• • •

At four in the afternoon, reconnected with my twenty-one-year-old self, aching a little, bleeding a little, I left the American Library. On the way home, I stopped at the Carrefour and bought some food for dinner; then, in the hope that Sandrine would be up to joining me, I put in a bottle of wine as well.

When I let myself into the apartment, I heard voices from the sitting room, where I found Sandrine on the couch. Opposite, in an armchair, smoking a cigarette, was a young man with curly hair.

Sandrine stood up. "This is Tariq. I found my way back to the Olympiades and left him a note. I hope you don't mind."

"No, that's fine," I said. "Have some tea."

"Thank you. Tariq and I were sharing a room. On the twenty-first floor of Sarajevo. We met at . . . well, we met at a cargo terminal."

I filled the kettle and laid out some cups on the kitchen counter. It was one thing looking after a young woman in distress—and I was intrigued by Sandrine—but this uncouth boy smoking in the apartment didn't figure anywhere in the matrix of my obligations.

Over green tea, I found out that he'd run away from his home with no fixed idea of where he was going. His mother had been half French, the daughter of a French colonial settler and an Algerian woman; as a result, he not only spoke good French but viewed Paris as some sort of lost motherland (not that he put it like that: I had the impression that his first aim in the city was to find a girlfriend). He seemed shallow and self-obsessed, narcissistic almost, though there was some comedy in the way he described his work in a fast-food shop in Saint-Denis.

I was on the point of getting up and making it clear that he should be on his way, but he anticipated me.

"Would it be all right if I slept on the floor of Sandrine's room? Just for tonight? It's so cold back in Sarajevo."

"You'd better ask Sandrine."

"Maybe one night, if that's okay," said Sandrine. She looked me in the eye, woman to woman. "He's no trouble."

"All right. One night. But he can't smoke."

"Thank you," said Sandrine. "Tomorrow we'll go back to the Olympiades."

"Oh God," said Tariq. "Baco and the shared toilet."

• • •

That evening, I looked at the photocopy of "La Nuit de Décembre" and for my own amusement began to write a translation. The language was mostly simple. It told a story of how, at each period of his life—schoolboy, lover, libertine and so on—the poet was visited by a figure in black who resembled him as a brother: *"qui me resemblait comme un frère."* To begin with, it was charming, especially in the schoolboy scene, when the figure read the poet's own book, resting his forehead on his hand, "thoughtful, with a sweet smile." Later it was more menacing; so, for instance, when the poet was kneeling by the deathbed of his father, the dark figure came and sat beside him, his eyes red with weeping and *"son glaive dans sa poitrine."*

I tried to go online to find a translation of *glaive*. I wondered if it was some religious symbol that was in the chest, or *poitrine*, of the apparition. The Wi-Fi refused to give me a single saucer of connection, but I was intrigued enough to go to the storeroom and ask for Sandrine's help.

I knocked softly and heard a grunt and a rustling from inside. Tariq, in his boxer shorts and T-shirt, opened the door halfway.

"I'm sorry. Is Sandrine asleep?"

"Yes."

"It doesn't matter." I paused. "I don't imagine you can help. Do you happen to know what the word *glaive* means in French?"

"*Glaive?* I think it's a sword. There was an old folk song my mother used to sing to me when I was a child that had the word in it. I'm not sure, but . . ."

"That makes sense. Thank you."

He seemed to be in a hurry to close the door, so I left him and went back to the living room, where I continued the translation. There was plenty more of the poem to go before the identity of the strange Vision would be revealed.

I went down the hall to the kitchen and closed the curtain, then listened at the door of the storeroom. There was no sound. I locked the front door and went to my own room. In bed, I read for a few minutes, then turned out the light.

It was not anxiety about having two strangers in the flat that kept me awake. It was the memory of Aleksandr and of what he had revealed to me. I didn't like to be reminded that there was a more full-blooded, truthful version of myself that I'd decided to kill off in the interests of a manageable life. I turned on the pillow and made myself think of work, of the research that lay ahead, of the lives of women in Paris under the Germans. Theirs was true hardship. My own problems were nothing that sleep couldn't ease or wash away.

Tolbiac

LAILA HAD NEVER SLEPT WITH A BOY, SHE TOLD ME. THAT WAS NORMAL for most girls at home, but it weighed with her. It was a big thing, this little thing—lying on her back, which presumably she did every day, and simply parting her legs. How hard was that? It seemed such a small gesture, but I did understand that it was somehow more than that for girls of her age. It was not so much the religious thing, it was emotional. That's what she told me.

Her family were different from the rest of us. Her father was a businessman who was meant to know important people like sheikhs and presidents. Laila never said so, but that was the rumor. He wasn't a big deal to meet. He was quite short and spoke softly. He had thick gray hair and a mustache and expensive glasses that made him look clever. There was always luggage of his in the hallway, a briefcase and a couple of leather bags with airline tags, CAI, MAD, CDG. But he'd moved his family around with him and Laila had lived in Beirut and other places that were less strict than we were. He'd picked up some Western customs and he was rich enough to do what he liked when he was back home. They went to the mosque occasionally but that was about it. One of the things he'd done was have a tennis court built in their garden. There was a public tennis club in town, but your own private court was completely unheard of.

In the old streets of the medina and the casbah you can never tell what's going to be behind a door. A gate might open onto just a room, or it might give onto a courtyard with a fountain. Laila's house, a mile along the coast, was like that but more surprising. Behind the white wall with its studded door was a garden the size of a small park with trees that had been there for a hundred years. The first time Laila asked me in there it was like going to a foreign country. For a start, there was the dog, Sasha. Most of the dogs in town had been poisoned or shot over the years. There were some police Alsatians, a mutt who guarded the synagogue and the very occasional stray, but nobody *owned* a dog, any more than anyone owned the cats that slept in the covered market. Sasha, who was large and hairy, was allowed to climb on the sofas and the beds. He nuzzled into Laila's neck and she kissed him on the head until he jumped down suddenly, his balls swinging in front of her face, and chased a squirrel.

Ah, Laila. I'd spent a lot of time thinking about her on the twenty-first floor of Sarajevo. When I'd got back to Olympiades after my first day at Paname Fried Poulet, Sandrine wasn't there. I asked Baco, but she didn't care. At least without Sandrine I got to sleep on the bed, though it was hard to drop off with the others doing their door-banging and arguing. I wasn't hungry because I'd eaten some of the less weird-looking chicken pieces at work which I'd stuck in a piece of baguette and I was bloated from the days I hadn't visited the can. I did wonder a bit where Sandrine had got to.

The next day I was on the early shift and when I got back about four after work, I found Baco to give her some money for the room.

She put it in a purse and said, "Your girlfriend leave a note."

As she handed me a piece of paper, she said, "What the matter, young man? You look . . ." She made a face.

"It's my belly." I pointed. "Here."

She cackled. "You no go toilet? You eat baguette. I see in your room. That way no one go! Come with me."

She handed me a plate of greasy-looking noodles with bean sprouts and fried onions. Perhaps it was her way of saying thank you for the rent.

"Eat this." She splashed on some chili sauce. It tasted better than it looked.

I read Sandrine's note. "T, I have found a better bed. Come round if you like. There is food and the <u>heating works</u>. S."

She gave an address nearby, in rue Michal, and I set off. Soon after Sandrine let me in to the warm apartment, I began to feel a mighty stirring, and half an hour later I emerged from the internal bathroom.

"What have you got against this woman?" said Sandrine. "You haven't even met her."

"Nothing," I said, hearing a key in the lock. "But she's American, right?"

"So?"

"So she's going to take one look at me and think I've come to blow up the Eiffel Tower."

"Maybe she's not like that."

There was no time to say more, as the landlady herself came into the room. Hannah was early middle-aged—Miss Aziz country, that no-man's-land where they're getting on but not quite your parents' generation. I had the impression she was not that keen on men, or not this one anyway. I guessed she was a teacher of some kind. But the apartment had radiators in each room that gave out heat, unlike old Baco's which were colder than the wall they were screwed into.

Sandrine got Hannah to agree to let me stay the night, though she didn't look that happy about it. I just hoped she wouldn't go to the bathroom for a bit.

In the middle of the night I climbed into bed with Sandrine. I thought she couldn't still be infectious.

"What are you doing?"

"I'm getting in."

"No, you're not."

"I'm sick of sleeping on the floor. And I've been at work. I've paid the rent at Sarajevo. For both of us."

"Big deal. I'm not going back to that tip anyway. Turn over, I don't want your wretched little cock sticking into me."

"Couldn't you just . . ."

"No, get off. Why don't you get one of the Chinese whores to do it for you? There's plenty round the Olympiades."

In the end she did allow me to stay, half-hanging off the side, but it was better than lying on the floor at Baco's.

When I arrived next morning at Paname at eight, there was no sign of pockmarked Hasim, so I walked around for a bit to keep warm.

One of the things I liked about Paris is the way they tell you the name of the street on every corner. At home, there's the odd sign put up by the French in the Ville Nouvelle, but not at every junction. In the medina, people *know* where things are, they don't need signs. Yet in Paris, even in Saint-Denis (which in places was a bit like the medina), you're told where you are every few steps.

Rue Bacon was a street name I couldn't help noticing on my early-morning stroll. Had some spiteful Christian mayor stuck it in there to annoy the Muslims? Like Shellfish Synagogue or Pork Chop Mosque? It was a quiet little street, in fact, ten minutes off the hubbub of the main market. There was a tree with pink blossoms and a notice about a lost cat that went on for ages. "Don't let this impostor into your house . . . He is not lost! He is an opportunist and a thief." I suppose it was meant to be funny, but in the photocopied picture the cat looked like he meant business.

Hasim had opened up by the time I got back. I explained that I'd been there on time and he nodded in acceptance. The thing about Hasim was that he looked beaten. I suppose he was religious and submitted to kismet or the will of Allah or some such thing. He told me he was proud of his little restaurant (you wouldn't call it a "restaurant," it was a kitchen with a wipe-down counter and a few chairs in the room out front, but I didn't tell him that) and that "Paname" was a traditional nickname for Paris. It referred to Panama, the country where the canal and the hats come from, but he didn't know why it also applied to Paris. Frozen fire-balls.

"And what about "Fried," I asked him, where had that come from?

"Everyone knows what 'fried' means," he said. "Think of KFC."

I suppose Paname Fried Poulet with its striped cardboard buckets was as close as Hasim could get to the Kentucky brand without being run out of town by Colonel Sanders. The word *poulet* was also a bit doubtful. I wouldn't say that what we fried in that deep basket was definitely *not* chicken, but I wouldn't swear that the odd bit wasn't from some other vertebrate.

In charge of cooking was a man called Jamal, also Algerian, I guessed. Where Hasim looked so worn down by life, Jamal had a bit of spark in him. He was about forty-five, I think, and he wore an apron and rubber clogs to make himself look like a chef. He had a belly and a double chin with gray stubble on it. He had been brought up near Lille, he said, though he was evasive about it, and his first language was French. Occasionally, when he wanted me not to understand, he spoke some sort of Algerian dialect with Hasim.

My basic work was cleaning the floor with a mop and wiping the surfaces with a pungent cloth. Hasim lived in fear of a hygiene inspection and he'd rather the food taste of Javel than risk losing his license. About nine in the morning two sacks of frozen bird bits were dumped at the back door. Soon afterwards came crates of sliced-up frozen potato from a wholesaler even farther out of town. I think they came from Romania or Bulgaria, maybe driven in the back of an Iveco by a perv like Maurice.

The "cooking" first involved thawing out the meat in a low oven. My job was to go through the frozen sack, chuck out the odd foot and beak then arrange the rest on a flat mesh with a sort of trough below to catch the drips as the meat thawed and began to ooze. Jamal meanwhile prepared three bowls of different coatings. He had his own words for the stuff in the kitchen. On the board behind the counter out front, the choices were "American," "Italian" and "Oriental." To Jamal they were "Farmyard," "Mafia" and "Nuclear." He had a heavy hand with the cayenne, though there was one regular who asked for "Oriental Super," which Jamal called "Anthrax." The potato bits he cooked from frozen in a basket dipped in bubbling fat, most of which was collected from the trough. There was a sump beneath the fryer that I offered to open so we could drain it off and put new oil in. Jamal told me it was the age of the oil that gave the food its special taste and that Hasim would fire me if I touched the sump. Oil was expensive.

I didn't want to go straight back to Tolbiac after work that day. I wasn't sure if I'd be allowed to spend another night at the American's and I thought I'd stand a better chance if I arrived late, looking cold. Also, I quite fancied smoking a little *kif,* so I made for Stalingrad on the Métro, thinking one of the Africans beneath the tracks might deal me in. I had a few euros left in my pocket.

At Place de Clichy, I jumped off and went across town on the raised outdoor section over Barbès-Rochechouart by the Tati department store, an area that also looked promising, I thought, if Stalingrad let me down.

God, I loved the Métro. The speed of it, the weird names of the stations. Barbès-Rochechouart! I mean, what was *that*? And the views across the city . . .

For some reason there was less activity than when I'd first been to the soup kitchen, with Sandrine. There was still a table, but no vat of hot broth, just a few bananas and some bits of baguette, which I now knew to avoid. There were only a dozen or so people lurking there. I asked a young guy if he knew where I could find some mild *kif*, but he didn't seem to understand. I showed him a ten-euro note, and he scuttled off. A burly man in a leather jacket came towards me. I find these big West African faces hard to read. Like in Hollywood films sometimes you don't know if the black guy is the loyal cop who'll take a bullet for the boss or Mr. Nasty who's about to blow your fucking head off.

As he began to speak I found that I was outside myself, watching, as I'd been that night at home when Tariq had gone into the sitting room to tell my father he was leaving. This Tariq looked a little scared as he listened to Mr. Big African. He nodded his head like a kid being told off by the teacher. If he'd been a dog he'd have rolled on his back. The African was telling him that the whole place was about to be closed down. The police didn't like it. There was going to be a raid any day and if he had any sense Tariq would stop waving his money around and get the hell out of it.

I was back inside myself by the time I felt the last of his hot breath on my face. I thought of offering to buy a pink phone cover with a cat's face, just to make the visit worthwhile (maybe I could give it to my new landlady). Instead, I went for a walk to try to calm down. I went up Boulevard de la Chapelle, then turned up rue de Tanger—Tangier Street— because the name reminded me of home. It was a shit road of modern buildings that someone had presumably stuck in to replace old ones. There was a better bit by a roundabout with rue du Maroc (Morocco), another alley of soulless junk, before I came back onto a big avenue.

I was shaken by the African under the tracks, I admit, and I wasn't concentrating on where I was going or on my surroundings (I never do, much). I did notice a green shop that dealt in *dératisation* and *désinsectisation,* two words new to me—though the huge pictures of rats and cockroaches in the window, along with the traps and bags of poison, made it clear what it was for. Maybe I should make a note of the number to pass on to Hasim—perhaps they'd come and de-rat and de-roach, then give him a certificate.

Soon I was back at Stalingrad station and it was now late enough to start heading back to Sandrine's new flat and take my chances with the American. I was in a funny state of mind, I must admit, having seen myself beneath the tracks, then having those reminders in the street names of the place I'd left behind.

It was cold, out there on Avenue de Flandre. Suddenly, I was starting to cry—which was something unheard of for me. I fought it back, swallowing and coughing, ashamed of myself. But this city just wasn't the Paris of cafés and girls I'd seen on television and on the Internet. And I was so lonely.

Then, as I was climbing the steps to the platforms, I saw a young woman coming down the other way. She met my eye, and held it for a moment. She had a coat that was unbuttoned, beneath which she wore a short woolen dress with leather boots to the knee and gray woolen tights. Her hair was half-covering her face as she leaned forward. The dress slipped a little up each thigh in turn as she took the steps down. I caught a glimpse of dark lipstick. A leather bag on a long strap was slung diagonally across her front. In the moment her eyes met mine I knew she was the other half of me, and I could never rest, or truly live, until I had her. I knew she knew it too.

As she went past me, she tossed her ticket down on the steps, and I noticed she had folded it several times into the shape of a "V." Then she was gone.

* * *

Although it was dark and there were at least eighteen stations on the way, it was still quite early when I reached the Place d'Italie. I'd taken the pink line that goes north–south from La Courneuve–8 Mai 1945 to Mairie d'Ivry. Even for a Métro fan like me, these station names sometimes seemed a bit much. What was so great about a single day, 8 May 1945, that it had a station named after it?

It was too soon to arrive at Sandrine's new place looking cold and homeless. On the other hand, I couldn't face going back to the twenty-first freezing floor of Sarajevo. So I thought I'd take Sandrine's advice and go and find a Chinese hooker.

The problem was, I'd never done this before, nothing like this existed at home, apart from the big hotels on the bay where the Gulf Arabs and the Russians went and fucked themselves blind on whiskey and cocaine. I wasn't sure if I was looking for a red light or a lady with a poodle or what. And would she laugh at me for being young, and would she have syphilis or AIDS and would my *zib* rise to the occasion? After half an hour of going up and down the streets near the Olympiades, I was so cold I had to take a chance on a shop called Beijing Beauté Massage. It didn't say it was a brothel, but it looked a bit like it. It had paper flowers in the window and a price list of different treatments, one of which, the half-hour Swedish, I could just afford. At least it would be warm in there.

The metal-framed door let out a ring when I pushed it open. There was no one at the reception desk, but after a moment a Chinese woman in an overall came out with a bucket and a mop and asked me what I wanted.

"A massage, please."

She went behind the desk. "Which one?"

I pointed at the list. "That one. Half an hour."

"Thirty euros." She held out her hand and I paid up.

She pushed the mop and bucket to one side with her foot and said, "Come."

She led me through a door at the back, down two steps and into a dark room with a mattress on the floor.

"You lie here, I come back."

So the cleaner was the masseuse?

I said, "Do I take my clothes off?"

"Yes. Then lie down."

"All of them?"

"Yes."

She sounded a little angry. I'd never had a massage, but in movies there's a table with a hole for your face and hot towels and windy music. I lay down on the mattress. At least the sheet was clean, though with no clothes on I was still cold.

After a couple of minutes the cleaner came back. She lit two candles and I saw she was now wearing a short dress with bare legs. She wasn't bad-looking in a way, but she still seemed a bit annoyed, as though she'd rather be mopping.

She took a cell phone out of the pocket of her dress and checked some messages, then knelt down beside the mattress. I shut my eyes and waited. I felt something cold on my back. Oil. Then she began to rub it in with circular movements of her hands. After a bit she went down to the back of my legs.

"How old are you?" she said.

"Twenty-three."

She didn't say anything, just kept running her hands up and down my legs. She put on more oil and gave my butt a good going over and one of her fingers trailed over my *tizi*. No one had ever touched it before and it gave me a bit of a shock.

"You no like?"

"No, I like."

Then her hand worked further through, between my legs, and touched my balls, which also made me jump a bit, though I wouldn't say it was unpleasant. My *zib* having a life of its own, I had a huge boner by now anyway. There followed a bit more shoulder-rubbing and working down my arms, which was quite boring.

After about ten minutes, she said, "You turn over now."

About time, I thought, as I rolled onto my back, my *zib* nodding in agreement. I wasn't expecting any compliments, but I thought she might say something. Instead, it was back to the oil and working along my shins. As she came towards the top of my thighs, I was beginning to strain at the leash, but then her phone went off and she stopped to answer it. She rubbed a thigh with one hand in a half-hearted way while she gabbled Chinese into the phone. Eventually the other guy got off the line and she turned back and, showing some sort of consideration for the first time, brushed her fingertips against my bursting *zib*.

"You like?"

You bet. "Yes."

"You want more?"

"Yes."

"Is thirty euros more."

"What? I've already paid."

"Is extra."

"I haven't got thirty euros more."

"How much you have?"

My jeans were hanging from a hook on the door, so I stood up and went over. I felt a bit of a fool, what with the boner. I fished around in my pockets. "Fourteen . . . No, wait. With the coins, eighteen. I can bring the twelve later."

She let out a snort as I lay down again, but after a bit of chest and thigh work, she touched the *zib* again and it snapped to attention. To move things along, I began to think of Laila helping to undress Farida while Miss Aziz looked on. Just as I was getting to the good bit, when Miss Aziz began to undo her own skirt, there came the sound of a baby crying. The Chinese woman pulled her hand away and stood up quickly.

"Wait. I come back."

After lying there for about ten minutes, listening to the baby howl, I put on my clothes and let myself out into the freezing street.

• • •

That evening Hannah, the American, cooked some dinner in the apartment and invited me to eat with her and Sandrine. It was something called "meatloaf" which she said her mom used to make. I was worried it would have pork in it, but she promised it was "ground beef with oats, some tomatoes and a couple of secret spices." It was better than it sounds.

Afterwards, I lit a cigarette and, to make conversation, told them a bit about my day. I didn't mention the massage because I felt ashamed. I had wanted an epic experience with Laila, not an expensive fail with a working mother.

"Do you mind not smoking in the apartment?" said Hannah.

"Sorry. Anyway, what's your job? Are you a teacher?"

"No, I'm a postdoctoral researcher. I'm here researching a chapter for a book. About Paris under the German Occupation."

"The Germans occupied Paris?"

She passed her hand over her mouth. "Yes."

"Why? When?"

"From 1940 to 1944. Did you not know that?"

"History's not my subject."

My face was hot and I needed to get back into the game. "I noticed today there's a station on the Métro called La Courneuve–8 Mai 1945," I said. "Do you know what happened then? If you're a historian?"

This seemed a good gambit to me, so I was surprised when both women laughed, Sandrine making noises like a donkey.

"It's VE Day," said Hannah. "The end of the Second World War."

"Did you really not know that either?" said Sandrine.

"Obviously not," I said, but it came out a bit defensive, so I tried to sound blasé. "These Métro stations, eh? What names! Barbès-Rochechouart. What a mouthful! Or is that a famous thing I should have heard of too?"

"It's just a junction of two streets with those names," said Sandrine.

"Barbès was a revolutionary from Guadeloupe," said Hannah. "And Rochechouart was an abbess, the head of a convent."

"How on earth do you know *that*?" I was truly knocked back.

"I'm a historian." She smiled. "And ten years ago I lived here for a year. I was lonely. I had time to look into things." She was less scornful, a bit gentler than Sandrine.

"And did this nun sail out and preach to this revolutionary?"

"Not in person. I think Barbès lived in Paris anyway."

"So," I said, "when you're on the Métro, you don't just think: This is where I get off, nice café, or whatever, and I'll be seeing my boyfriend any moment. You think about revolution and an old woman praying in a convent."

"I guess so. I'm afraid it's too late to change now."

"Isn't it a bit tiring?"

She laughed. "Yes. But it's what gives depth to the day. It's the silver behind the glass. Otherwise, life would be like being permanently on the Internet. Just one-dimensional. Click. Open. Shut. Click."

I didn't have an answer to that. I felt this teacher-type had pretty much understood how my life was. Also, I didn't want to irritate her in case she sent me back to Sarajevo.

"Do you need any more help with your translations?" I said, to remind her of my uses.

"I'll let you know later. Thank you."

I liked the implications of the word "later." Warmth, bed, coffee in the morning. And I didn't have to be at Paname until the afternoon.

Aubervilliers–
Boulevard de la Villette

I T WAS LATE BY THE TIME I'D FINISHED TRYING TO EXPLAIN TO TARIQ
(all because of the name of a stupid subway station) the nature of
France as a revolutionary lay republic that viewed religion as an export
only—preferably to its farthest colonies, like Indochina. He looked interested when I mentioned Algeria, where the *pied noir* schoolteachers
inadvertently gave the local Algerians ideas by talking about the glo-
ries of revolution. It was past midnight by this time, and I hadn't the
heart to send him off into the January night, so I said he could stay in
the storeroom again.

The next day, I began my work in earnest. After breakfast and a
scalding shower, I left my lodgers to sleep on and went down into the
empty Quail Hill street. To avoid two *correspondances* on the Métro and
to stretch my legs, I walked to the Place d'Italie, where the city began to
open up towards its southern boundary and the wide streets let light
into the back of my eyes. On the train, with laptop, notebook and pens
zipped into the shoulder bag against my ribs, I felt that for the first time
in years I was doing what suited me best. At what point in my childhood had I known for sure that this detective work was what I'd been
put on earth to do? I had, after all, had other abilities. I could play the
piano to a half-decent level and had—once, anyway—played on the college tennis team. But in the end all those things had given way to the

joy of setting out alone on a cold morning, awash with coffee, on a mission to redeem the lives of dead strangers.

Looking back to my teenage years made me think about Warren. He was a funny brother for me to have—confident where I was nervous, fair where I was dark; sometimes I found it hard to believe we were related. Warren was also, I think you'd have to say, good-looking—and no one had ever called me that. We were close as children but grew apart in our teens. I read hundreds of books from the library, haphazardly, and I guess this was when my vocabulary became a little ornate. I admired Southern writers like Faulkner and Eudora Welty and I had a long affair with English novelists, so much so that my teacher told me I'd started to write essays "with an English accent." At college, I was up on American feminists—we all were—but for politics I really preferred the French, from de Tocqueville (partly because he seemed to be the only Frenchman in history who'd liked America) right through to Foucault. Jasmine Mendel and I had a special weakness for Julien Benda, who was a famous radical in the twenties.

While I was reading, Warren did vacation work in a canning factory and became interested in the business. I told him I could think of nothing worse than standing on a production line.

"Listen, kid," he said, "I'm not standing on a line. When I'm done with business school I'm going into management; then maybe one day I'll have my own company."

The way he put it sounded reasonable and I wasn't sure enough of my ground to express how the idea appalled me. My father was proud of me for being what he called "philosophical"; no one at work, he said, had ever explained things to him in the same way.

"But she's so *wordy*," I overheard my mother say to him one time. "I can't see how any man's going to put up with that."

"Maybe it's not all about men," my father said. "That's what she'd say anyway. Being a feminist and all." Dad really was a very decent man.

The working title of my postgraduate thesis had been "Work, Family and Gender: French Women in Occupied Paris, 1940–44." My job in Paris now, as I had told Julian, was to develop it into a chapter for a book that my department head was editing. Five years earlier, Professor Putnam had herself published a biography of Jean-Pierre Timbaud, the secretary of the steelworkers' union who, along with twenty-six other hostages, had been shot by the Nazis in retaliation for the murder of a German officer in Nantes in 1941. Putnam wrote with a popular swing that made some people suspicious, but her book had found readers outside the world of university subscription and its short fame attracted more funding to the department (the money, in fact, that had made her relaxed about taking me on).

When I first read the Timbaud book, I'd been shocked at what little support the Resistance had had in France. "Killing Germans was unpopular with most French people," Putnam explained to us, "even among those who resented them. They usually shot about twenty-five innocent French people in reprisals for every German officer killed."

I then read all Putnam's papers on the period. They sure didn't support the story of *La France résistante*. It was murky. When the Statutory Work Order was introduced in 1942, young Frenchmen of a certain age had three choices: to go and toil in German factories for the Nazi war effort; to join the Resistance; or to disappear. For women the alternatives were less clear-cut. Men could be heroes; women had to survive, make deals, raise children. Only a few girls could take risks carrying messages by bicycle in the countryside; life wasn't like that for the women of Paris.

It was well known that for decades nothing had been published in France itself—no firsthand narratives and no analysis by French historians of the four years most people thought best forgotten. I remembered my amazement on turning to the back of the standard work on the period to look for the bibliography. There was none. At the time the book came out—in 1972, thirty years after the events it described—the author, a thirty-nine-year-old associate professor at Columbia, explained the absence by saying no work had been published in France for him to acknowledge, not a single book; he recommended a couple of novels for "atmosphere" and that was it. His own information had come from documents in German archives.

By the time of my own first visit to Paris in 1996, things were beginning to change. In the year before, President Chirac had admitted—half a century after the events—that the French government had been complicit in German anti-Jewish measures; but it was the conviction in 1998 of Maurice Papon, the prefect of Bordeaux, for crimes against humanity that proved the French state had not only authorized the deportation to Auschwitz of nearly 80,000 Jews but had at times competed with the

Occupier in a desire to purge more efficiently, as, for instance, when it volunteered French children and adults from the Free Zone to fulfill the Nazi train "quotas." It was Papon's conviction that had persuaded French historians to overcome their fear of bumping into "Papa" in some town-hall document and begin their own investigations at last.

Many of the books that started to appear had a political agenda of their own and most were written by and about men. For my own researches, I needed raw material—the gush of unfiltered experience. My college had provided me with passes to the library at the Sorbonne and preregistered me with smaller organizations that specialized in the Occupation, Jewish history and women's lives. I'd decided to begin at the Centre Jean Molland Mémorial Franco-Allemand in the Ninth arrondissement, a new venture under a German director, situated a few streets south of the Place Pigalle, near the museum of the painter Gustave Moreau.

Twenty minutes after leaving the flat, I climbed the steps at Métro Saint-Georges and looked around in the bright morning air. It was a small, unexpected square with a statue to a well-known courtesan. Paris knew how to respect its fallen women; those down the hill, the plaque said, had been called *lorettes* after their local church, Notre Dame de Lorette.

The Centre Jean Molland was on a courtyard that opened from the street by way of a small lodge. Inside was the Parisian atmosphere I remembered—old stone walls with modern glass doors and fierce central heating; as I handed over my photograph and waited for my pass to be laminated, I began to feel at home.

My ambition was to be led by the recordings or the documents I studied to make discoveries of my own, to find still-living witnesses of the period. If a young woman had been twenty-two in 1942, for instance, she would now be eighty-six. So it was still possible. I wanted to find someone who hadn't simply been alive but whose experiences might illuminate the whole period.

On the second floor, in a warm audio room that smelled of new wood and paint, I sat down in a booth and called up the index of contributors. It gave brief details of each speaker, but it was not cross-indexed, so I couldn't enter "food coupons," "Germans" or "childcare" in the search box. It was clearly going to be a long trawl, one that would depend on perseverance and a little luck. After a half hour of looking through the catalog, I made a choice.

LEMAIRE, Juliette, born 1920.
File 1. LYAT/WBTJM/KR/1943/8754/235A
Recorded: *9 June 1998.*

The Centre's summary read: "Detail of life of young woman, working class. Relations with German soldiers. Live-and-let-live attitude of neighbors. Black-market restaurants. Involvement in Purge of 1944."

I turned over my cell phone, put on the headphones and pressed the on-screen PLAY command.

Young Juliette Lemaire was a Parisienne who had lived in rue de Tanger and taken the Métro each day from the local station, Aubervilliers–Boulevard de la Villette, to her work in a clothes shop on the rue de Rivoli. I paused the recording and found the rue de Tanger on my *Paris Pratique* pocket map, but the Métro station had for some reason disappeared. It looked a bleak-enough area at the northern end of the Canal Saint-Martin, near the Place Stalingrad. Juliette spoke French clearly, with only a slight Parisian accent, and seemed to have prepared, or at least thought carefully about, what she was going to say.

I was at work one day when two German officers came in from under the arcade. It was raining. They said good morning politely and began to look round. My friend Sophie was working with me that day. There were at least six of us at any one time. You must understand, it was rather a big shop and quite fashionable.

I was afraid of these men with their polished boots and gray uniforms, but Sophie wasn't like that. "They're just lonely men," she used to say. "They have sisters like us at home." Monsieur Flandin, the owner, told us we should always be polite. There were no rules about what you could do. The only thing was not to make a fuss or an incident.

The younger officer had a smooth, fat face and he wanted me to show him some dresses. I didn't like him; he was like a pig with pink eyelashes. His skin was shiny. But with his uniform and his position he thought he was something.

The older officer was tall and dark with sad eyes. Despite myself, I found him interesting. He had more braid on his uniform than the other one and looked as though he was in Paris because perhaps he was too old to be fighting the Russians. He came over to the rack of dresses where I was talking to his colleague. He bowed his head slightly to me, and maybe I imagined this but I think he even touched his heels together. He introduced himself by rank and surname, Major Richter. He said he was looking for some gloves to take back to his wife when he was next on leave. In Rothenburg, I think he said.

"Mademoiselle," he said to me, "would you mind trying on the gloves, so I can see what they look like? You have elegant hands, like my wife's."

Sophie was already at the glove counter. For maybe twenty minutes, she pulled out drawer after drawer of gloves—kid, pigskin, fur, calfskin—and I had to try on each pair, then hold my hand up for him to inspect. Sophie was the supplier and I was the model for these two German men. I was not a shy girl, but I found myself blushing as the older officer looked down at my hands. He was very grave; he didn't smile. It was as though he was weighing up an important military decision, or a work of art. His face was thin and dark but newly shaved.

Eventually, he decided on a beautiful chocolate kid pair with fur lining and fur wrists and raised seams. He wanted to test the softness of the leather but waited till I'd put them down on the countertop. He held them briefly against his cheek, as though the skin on his fingers was too coarse to tell. They were expensive, but he had cash in his pocketbook.

As I was wrapping the gloves in tissue paper by the till, he said, "Forgive me, Mademoiselle, but might it be possible for me to invite you to dinner one evening? There are some beautiful restaurants near the Opéra and I could arrange for my car to take you home afterwards."

I was shocked and I blurted out something about my parents and not being allowed out in the evening. "I quite understand," he said. "Please forgive me. Thank you for your help. And your hands. Goodbye."

I pressed the PAUSE button and looked at the catalog entry again. I saw that Juliette had died nearly five years earlier, in March 2001, aged eighty-one. It was a shame. She sounded like such a nice woman.

The accommodation reached between German soldiers and Parisian women was complicated. In the early days of the Occupation, many of the Germans were embarrassed to be in Paris at all. Although the officers had had to swear a personal oath of loyalty to Hitler, their true allegiance was to the Prussian army of their grandfathers. At the end of 1941, Otto von Stülpnagel, the German military commander in France, had become so reluctant to take the required reprisals against French resisters that he asked Hitler to be relieved of his command. Critics said that his return to Berlin and subsequent nervous breakdown had opened Paris up to the power of the SS, who moved in as a result and had no qualms about reprisals or anti-Jewish measures.

Otto von Stülpnagel was replaced by his cousin, Carl-Heinrich, who hated Hitler so much that he joined a German underground plot to kill him. His relationship with the SS chief in Paris, Carl Oberg, was tense; and for Parisian girls like Juliette Lemaire, with limited means and opportunities, life became even more morally uncertain.

The next section of Juliette's testimony was harder to understand. Perhaps she hadn't sat close enough to the microphone or maybe her voice had grown tired. Most of it concerned her life at home with her parents and the prospects for a working-class girl. She mentioned friends from school days, including one called Georgette Chevalier, who was keen on cycling, and one called Yvonne Bonnet, who was more interested, so far as I could make out, in boys.

One thing we had in common was that we had so much energy. But the war had come at the wrong time of our lives. We should have been working all day and then going dancing on Saturday nights and out on bicycle rides on Sundays. But Paris was half empty and it was quiet. A lot of the young men who might have been asking us out were away in prisoner-of-war camps, and then there was the curfew. So you made your choices, and I think Yvonne thought that in this world gone mad she'd try anything—and that might mean going out with German soldiers if they asked her. She used to tease me for being too proper. She'd say things like, "You're never going to find a husband in your parents' apartment."

Georgette Chevalier used her energies in a quite different way. She was very athletic and very determined. Given half a chance she'd be off bicycling or swimming. One summer she took me climbing in the Vosges Mountains and we became friends over campfires in the evenings. I was worried that she'd joined some organization that would get her into trouble. And so it turned out.

Soon after this, the audio file became too difficult for me to follow, but with a password given to me when I registered, I was able to download a copy onto my laptop to study at home.

By the time I'd finished work for the day, I needed time to decompress, to leave Juliette behind and reconnect with the present-day world. I walked uphill, then turned into the rue Victor Massé. It was a narrow street with ordinary Haussmann buildings, black-painted iron posts to prevent cars parking on the sidewalk and a couple of cheap but respectable hotels. In its unostentatious and slightly cramped way, it was typical of this part of the Ninth—a sort of sub-arrondissement that seemed unaffected by the movements of migration, money or fashion. It had probably never been "hot" or "coming" or "BCBG" or any of the other irritating words I'd seen in magazines. It seemed largely, perversely, French, and old-fashioned. I wondered, as I came to the corner of the rue des Martyrs, why, if all was relatively unchanged, it was so difficult for me to picture the women of the Occupation period—Juliette Lemaire, for instance—walking down this street.

Perhaps something in my imagination was at fault. I had sometimes thought so before, when I wondered if I'd ever quite shed the child's way of seeing "history" as a sort of pageant—something that took place in a different world. At college, we'd been asked to understand that history was neither "past" nor "other" but an extension of the present to which all people, whether they know it or not, are attached. Professor Putnam had recommended that her freshman students attend a lecture in quantum physics to get a first idea of the flexible nature of time. She pointed us to seminars in neuroscience where they discussed the brain's creation of the "self" as an illusion—what they called a "convenient fiction." This, she explained, would not only do away with the "great men" idea of history but would help us see that all private humanity was ultimately, over time and in ways it was our work to explore, entangled in public events. Then in the senior year, she had told us to read *Four Quartets* by T. S. Eliot. She urged us to stick a motto on the noticeboard in all our study rooms: "History is now and New England." Eliot's line (without the "New") was in the final quartet, "Little Gidding," but the idea worked just as well, Putnam said, in the setting of the third, "The Dry Salvages," a rocky outcrop just down the American coast from where we were at that moment sitting in her seminar.

I was excited by all this. I believed in the impact of previous existences on every day I was alive; in more excited moments I came to think that the membrane of death was semi-permeable. This belief was what gave a sense of purpose to my work. It was only on rare occasions that I felt I wasn't up to the task, and then I worried that I'd let down the people whose lives had mattered so much.

The rue des Martyrs sloped downhill between wine merchants and bakers, *traiteurs* from Greece and Spain next to fishmongers and cheese shops supplied only by France. Thinking I'd do a short loop to stretch my legs before picking up the Métro, I took a left into another unremarkable street. A short way down was a secondhand bookshop, with bins of mounted prints on the sidewalk and a window display of old volumes with gilt covers. I went inside and found a woman with gray hair in a chignon sitting at a desk. We smiled simultaneously, each familiar, I suppose, with the other's type. "May I?"

"Please feel free to look around, Madame."

The shop had a back room, down a step, where I found myself alone among the wooden shelves. It was a room I'd been in many times before, in small places run for love not profit—independent shops in Ipswich, Massachusetts, or Burlington, Vermont. I flicked through a book of old photographs from Paris: street corners, bars, gas lamps; solitary dog-walkers at first light; people strolling past the awnings of sidewalk cafés; night owls on their way home. The subjects were familiar to the point of staleness, but the images were well composed and nicely printed in black and white. They covered the years from 1934, the year of right-wing riots and street-fighting in Paris, through the Occupation and into the fifties. One picture held my attention: a woman of about twenty-five, her skin slightly olive, like a Lartigue model, with very dark, almond-shaped eyes and a look that was both demure and defiant. Photographed in 1942, she wore a tailored jacket and a white fur around her neck; the clothes were chic though not necessarily expensive. With her slim fingers and light makeup, she was beautiful in a way that women might appreciate more than men. She looked Parisian in style, though not necessarily French by birth. She was the sort of woman you'd at once want to know better; even if she turned out to be in some way an impostor, she'd entertain you along the way.

For a long time, I stared at the face and felt its living gaze. People say that photographs "capture" a moment, but nothing was imprisoned here, or stopped. This woman was no more "frozen in time" than I would be if I flipped the viewfinder on my cell phone and snapped myself: A shutter's momentary opening was not an interruption of passing time; it was just a contribution to the flow.

I bought the book, exchanging pleasantries with the woman at the desk. It was dark when I went down the hill, pausing at a supermarket to buy dinner. I took an elevator with a cracked-glass door to the first floor, where the fresh food was displayed, filled my basket, paid, and went down to the station at Notre Dame de Lorette.

● ● ●

In the Métro on the way home, I saw a man who, from the back, reminded me of Julian Finch. When he turned around, I saw he had a coarser, less humorous face. Julian was a puzzle to me. His manner was gentle, but some of what he said was sharp as well as funny. Did he use his soft bass voice as a disguise for saying slightly cruel things? And why had he pegged me as a "Joni Mitchell type?" Was he suggesting I was emotionally self-indulgent, some sort of crybaby? Or just politely mentioning the only other Canadian singer he'd heard of? The one thing about Julian you could say for sure, I thought, as I turned into rue Michal, was that he was hard to read. I remembered a party I'd been to in Sylvie's apartment in rue des Marronniers ten years before. Some students were asking him quite normal questions, but all he wanted to talk about was his wife's taste in painting and how she'd found a masterpiece for nothing in a Marais gallery.

The front door of my apartment was not double-locked, and I found, as I let myself in, that I was pleased by this evidence that Sandrine and Tariq would be there.

"I'm feeling better," Sandrine told me as we ate dinner.

Her face no longer had blotches of color; with her hair and clothes washed, she looked much healthier.

"I'm glad. What are your plans?"

Before she could answer, Tariq said, "Is it all right if I smoke a cigarette on the balcony? I'll shut the door behind me."

When he came back inside, I was showing Sandrine the book of photographs.

". . . and these people here, I suppose they're about to go on vacation for the first time ever. Thanks to Léon Blum's government."

"They look excited."

"This is my favorite picture, this is why I bought the book."

Tariq looked over our shoulders. "She's wonderful," he said.

"I feel she's my friend already," said Sandrine.

"Exactly," I said.

I began to turn the page.

"Stop," said Tariq. "I want to look at her."

All three of us looked at the young woman's face, the dark, dark eyes staring back at us.

"There's something about her," said Tariq. "It's like she's familiar."

Anxious that Tariq's feeling for the woman might be less pure than Sandrine's or mine, I closed the book.

"When Sandrine leaves, can I stay on in the little room?" said Tariq. "I can afford to pay for my food and give you some money towards the heating and things. I can do the shopping if you tell me what to buy."

"I'm not looking for a lodger."

"I could help you with any translating you need. I'd be no trouble."

"I'll think about it."

It wasn't that I distrusted the boy or thought he'd misbehave; it was more that I didn't want my routine disturbed by his comings and goings, his worn-out sneakers and crumpled T-shirts. That was not the life of pure thought I'd had in mind.

I found myself too tired to do any more translation of de Musset.

After reading a couple of pages of a 1947 novel called *Les Forêts de la Nuit*, one of those recommended as giving some "atmosphere" of the times, I fell asleep and dreamed of the woman in the photograph. Hiding behind a buttress on the riverbank, not far from Notre Dame, she grasped me by the wrist and told me that her name was Clémence.

SEVEN

Bir-Hakeim

WHEN I'D BEEN AWAY ABOUT TWO WEEKS, I THOUGHT I'D BETTER LET people at home know I was still alive. I sent an e-mail to my father in which I made out I'd got a job in "catering" and a long-term place to stay "in the Seventeenth." It seemed far enough away from the Thirteenth, where I was actually still camping—one day at a time—in Hannah's storeroom, and as an area it was drab enough to reassure him. He didn't reply.

I didn't know what to say to Laila. I took a selfie on the Métro and just wrote, "Guess where I am xx." I didn't want to try too hard, but I hoped she might be worried. I turned my phone off after sending it, so I wouldn't be tempted to check every thirty seconds if she'd e-mailed back.

Hasim seemed to think I was doing an okay job at Paname and Jamal didn't stick my head in the fryer when I told him the Nuclear-flavor chicken maybe wasn't hot enough. In fact, Jamal had turned out to be a solid sort of guy. I told him I'd failed to score at Stalingrad and he said, "Leave it to me." Next day he passed me a little polythene bag. It wasn't like the nice *kif* at home, I guessed it was grown indoors. But he only asked ten euros and it was certainly strong. I just wanted to chill, but I ended up in a white sweat with my heart pounding, worrying that the whole sack of chicken bits was reassembling itself into one big unhappy rooster. Luckily it didn't last long.

A week later, one afternoon when there were no customers, we had a smoke together in the kitchen—just a little bit, in case there was a sudden public clamor for the Anthrax special.

"Have you always lived in Saint-Denis?" I asked him.

"No." He sucked in heavily. "My parents were from Algeria. I was brought up in a camp."

"What?"

It was a bit of a long story and I may have not got all the details down exactly, but the gist of it was this. During the Algerian War, Jamal's parents had been living in a rural village in Algeria with their two small girls (Jamal was not born yet). The Algerians were fighting the French for independence and it became very nasty, with torture and "ethnic cleansing." The Algerian death squads in the region where Jamal's family lived were killing not just the French settlers, the *pieds noirs*, but also their fellow countrymen—Algerians they thought weren't keen enough on the independence cause. Some villagers thought they'd be safer from the massacres if they stuck with the French colonials, so they signed up as a sort of militia to protect the settlers. These fighters were known as "Harkis." But when the Algerians won the war and the French were thrown out, the Harkis were unpopular. To put it mildly. Mobs hunted them down. They made them dig their own graves, then shot them— but not before they'd castrated them, tortured them and made them swallow their French service medals.

Jamal told me all this, sitting on the table, rubbing his hand over the gray stubble on his chin as he inhaled another big one. He didn't seem angry, but maybe he was too stoned.

Tens of thousands of these Harkis were killed in Algeria and the French refused their pleas for help because they didn't want to spoil the terms of the peace with the Algerians. A few thousand Harkis were allowed into France, but they were kept in camps and not allowed to get a job.

"My parents lived in the woods near Lille," Jamal said. "I was born in that camp. My father eventually managed to escape and got us out to join him. But there was never an amnesty."

"So you're illegal?"

"It's more that I don't exist."

"What about Hasim?" I said.

"His father fought against the French," said Jamal.

"So that made it okay?"

"I guess so. His family was allowed to come. In the sixties, I think."

Frozen fireballs. Back in rue Michal, everything was fine, except that Sandrine had disappeared. I got back one day to find she'd taken all her bits and pieces, stuck them in her backpack and vanished. "T, I've gone to England," said a note on the bed. "I asked Hannah again if you can stay. Don't smoke and do make the bed and she might give you a trial run. A few more days at least. Until the next time. Sandrine x PS hope some girl will let you do it with her soon." She'd left a letter to Hannah in a sealed envelope by the router on the hall table.

Hannah had a dinner date that night with someone called Julian Finch and I left early for work the next morning, so I didn't see her to talk about staying on in the flat. It was a pretty slow day in the medina. Underneath it, just behind it, you could see the old town of Saint-Denis, which was as French as they come with its holy Christian cathedral (Jamal said they used to bury the kings of France there), its old clock towers and its pale stone and black slate roofs with the rain running off. But they were like a stage set left over from a previous production. All the action now was between sad-looking Arabs and Africans, older versions of me in a way, with their pale halal meat and rows of odd vegetables and naked chickens with scraggy necks drooping off the stall and bright trinkets and garish clothes and knock-off designer perfumes and striped plastic shopping bags, illegals and refugees haggling in odd Arab dialects right there in the rainy square next to the tombs of the Catholic kings.

"We're not doing enough business, are we?" I said to Hasim at lunchtime. "We should do home delivery. We can advertise on the Internet. Or put some leaflets through people's doors. Clichy-sous-Bois. There's millions in the estates there."

"You don't want to go into those places," he said. "It's dangerous."

"I'll go if you pay me."

"There's criminals there. And people who started the riots last year. Bad people."

"We can get a delivery bike. A moped."

Hasim looked tired. "Not now."

When I finished at three, I wandered over to Basilique de Saint-Denis station and took the Métro, like I did every day. I usually stood, or sometimes sat on a fold-down *strapontin*, but for some reason I was on one of the permanent seats that are arranged like a café table, with two facing two.

I turned to look into the window and noticed my eyes had big black circles under them. I looked like a panda. And it was not just the color, there were rings and flat pouches full of . . . What? Fluid? "Experience?" There were two deep lines between my eyes. I had a beard, which on the corners of my chin had gray patches.

Looking in the mirror was one of my favorite ways of passing the time and I enjoyed imagining the life that lay ahead of a young man who any reasonable observer would have had to admit was quite unusually beautiful. But not this time. This was not the guy who'd looked back at me in the bathroom at home and told me to leave. This was someone older, someone bent by the glass to the rough age of sixty. And I mean "rough."

Turning my head back into the carriage, I saw a woman I knew standing by the doors, holding the upright support. She caught my eye. I wasn't sure if it was me or the older man in the convex window that she was acknowledging, but I felt such a voltage of recognition that I couldn't move.

Every day thousands of women go into this underground world and lose themselves. I'd watched them. They're without gravity, briefly, being anyone. Then they go up and reconnect with their lives and who they are, or who they think they have to be. But for a few minutes every day they're almost anyone. And of all this throng of nameless girls and women that I'd gazed at day after day on the hopeless Line 13, only this one spoke to my loneliness.

Then, in a moment it became clear. I remembered how I knew her. She was the woman in Hannah's book of photographs.

Her head was turned away as she looked towards the other side of the carriage, and I was able to stare at her dress, which was made from some black material that held the line of her thigh as she strained upwards to read something. Then as she rocked with the sway of the train, I could see the outline of a button or strap beneath the fabric at the top of the leg. The neck of the dress was high and loose. Her coat was open and I could see a row of beads and a fur scarf or wrap. Looking away, trying to read the station names, she couldn't have known I was staring. I could picture every detail of her skin—her breasts, her belly, the pull of the muscle in her upper arm where she held the rail. And that face, those eyes. No one could have failed to be intrigued by what they held.

Without catching my eye again, she crushed her shoulder bag to her ribs and got off the train. I waited for a few seconds, then jumped off as the doors were closing. We were at Place de Clichy, and she headed for the *correspondance*. At Charles de Gaulle–Étoile, she changed again, walking fast through the tiled tunnels, and I was only just able to get into the same carriage. I've watched enough cop films but never concentrated on the technique. I wished I'd had a newspaper or even a book to hold up in front of me.

After Passy, we were up in the open air, on a bridge across the river. It was still light with a fading winter sun—on our left was the Eiffel Tower, to the right was what looked like a coal barge lying low in the water. At the next stop, Bir-Hakeim, the woman got off. Same as at Stalingrad, you had to go down from the raised outdoor platform to reach the street. I followed about ten meters behind and noticed that she tossed away her ticket at the top of the steps. It didn't flutter, but fell straight and when I got alongside I saw she'd folded it lengthwise, then across, to make a "V."

Down on the street, she turned without hesitation and began to walk south, beside the elevated track. She walked quite fast (it was cold) with only a slight swing of the hips at the top of her long legs. I now felt easier about following her, as I could do the movie trick of looking into a shop window if she checked her stride. Not that there was much to see on the Boulevard de Grenelle. We went past the red awning of a big café called Gitane, then she went left into a narrow, cobbled street. There was a closed Indian restaurant, and a battered street door painted maroon. She entered the code on a keypad and used both hands to push open the heavy door. I must have been following too closely, because as the door was grinding shut, she glanced back onto the street and her eyes met mine. She didn't smile, but neither did she look away. The door kept slowly closing, and all the time she stood there in the black dress and the high fur collar and her legs like a dancer's with the feet angled like a clock showing five to one.

• • •

For about an hour afterwards, I think I must have just wandered about. Winter afternoons in Paris, I was discovering, have a special feeling. The air is damp and works its way into you. Everything seems out of reach—though this may be something to do with having so little money. Although I could afford a Coke or an espresso in the Café Gitane I hadn't got enough cash to order the *plat du jour* with extra *frites* and linger in the fug.

It also may be connected to the way the buildings look the same. I expect there's a reason for this and Hannah would have told me what it was, along with the dates of the architect. But what it means to most people—the ones like me, who don't know all the history of everything— is that whether you're in the wealthiest bit of the Sixteenth or the scuzziest part of the Nineteenth the chances are the buildings will have black slate roofs and pale stone fronts, balconies on the second and fifth floors, heavy street doors with number codes and so on. They're never tall, they're never short or squat, they seem to have been planned to fit the street. It's *so* not like the medina at home, where they were thrown up any old how, or even like the Ville Nouvelle where you have the feel- ing the French wanted to build as fast as possible.

But in Paris on a winter afternoon, when the sun's gone down . . . Clerks and shop girls and doctors and schoolkids and poor old people who can't afford the rent all go into the same building, where the same modern lift's been driven up through the old stairwell, there's the same parquet in each apartment and pretty much the same smell of cooking in the hallway. When you're sleeping on the floor of Baco's back room on Sarajevo's twenty-first, you'd give anything to be enter- ing one of these heated *immeubles*. Boy, had I wanted to be part of that way of living, to have my anonymous room in an anonymous apart- ment in a building just like all the others in the Nth arrondissement. At the same time, there's something odd about a city where two-thirds of the buildings are the same. You'd think all the inhabitants would at least be looking for a change, for some action outside. The one thing those buildings of Paris suggested to me, I thought as I rambled on up the river that cold afternoon, was the ability to keep secrets. That's what they looked designed for.

Maybe I wasn't thinking too clearly, as I walked between the elevated railway and the black river on my left. Maybe I was in some sort of shock from seeing the woman in the photograph made flesh in the Métro carriage. It had made me forget the surprise of seeing myself so much older reflected in the window. Normally that would have made me stop and think for a minute or two at least. Anyway, what brought me back to myself was a monument set on the quay.

Suddenly I was face-to-face with a life-size group of figures made of bronze. They seemed to represent a family in despair. It was dark and I couldn't see too well, but it looked like two parents holding a baby, two grandparents with another kid, a girl with a doll and then another woman, perhaps a grown-up sister, lying down, resting her head on a suitcase. They had a refugee look, all of them. I shone the torch from my phone on it. The metal had gone green, and the result was a bit tacky, like they'd economized on the materials. Underneath was an inscription: THE REPUBLIC OF FRANCE IN HOMAGE TO THE VICTIMS OF RACIST AND ANTI-SEMITIC PERSECUTION AND CRIMES AGAINST HUMANITY COMMITTED UNDER THE AUTHORITY OF THE SO-CALLED "GOVERNMENT OF THE FRENCH STATE" 1940–44. LET US NEVER FORGET.

The "D" had fallen off the DES in front of CRIMES. It was a bit puzzling. The inscription seemed to be making a big statement but in a small way, like admitting to something without really owning up to it.

. . .

It was hard to know what Hannah thought of me. I think she despised me for being a teenage male, but was a bit ashamed of that because I was an African—hardly a small minority in Paris, but a minority all the same (I'd given her the *pied noir*/Algerian/Berber/Bedouin story when Sandrine was still there). She probably wanted to prove that she didn't have an instinctive prejudice against people like me, but she couldn't keep a look of horror from her eyes when she saw my shoes in the hallway or even worse in the living room. Yet I occasionally had the feeling she enjoyed some present-day company in her peculiar life, which seemed otherwise to be all about the past and dead people.

As Sandrine had predicted, she eventually said I could have a trial as her lodger. The rules about the bathroom and so on were pretty strict and it was clear that if I put a foot wrong I'd be back on the twenty-first floor of Sarajevo before you could say "Tang Frères."

But I was so relieved that I decided to make a real effort.

"Is this Julian Finch your boyfriend then?" I asked when we next had dinner together.

"What? Certainly not. He's someone I knew ten years ago."

"So he's a sort of historical figure too."

She laughed, something I hadn't often seen her do before.

What I was really wondering was whether she had sex with this Julian guy, or at all, or whether she was too old, or maybe waiting for a man who'd marry her. I had the idea from movies and TV that American girls were not like Laila or Wasia and Kashira and my other friends at home, that if they liked you they'd do it without a second thought. My favorite bit of an old U.S. comedy show was when a New York girl listed the names, one after the other for a long time, of all the boys her room-mate, who protested that she was a virgin, had "put out for" on a first date.

But I couldn't square that with how serious Hannah seemed to be. She was small, slim, with exactly two gray hairs in the dark brown-black. She seldom wore makeup and was usually dressed in jeans, unless she was going out to meet this Julian, when she made a bit of an effort, putting on lipstick and a skirt. She was no looker, no Laila, that's for sure, but when she was anxious she had a cute way of pushing her hand up through her hair at the front.

It was a bit awkward when she returned to the subject of my unintended joke.

"Sometimes I think I do have better friendships with dead strangers." She'd opened a bottle of wine earlier and was now pouring a second glass. "Sometimes I feel closer to the subjects of my research than I do to actual people I know at college or in my hometown. Does that seem strange to you?"

Know who she reminded me of? Miss Aziz. When she was trying to make us "think for ourselves" towards the end of class. She used to lure us into discussions by saying more and more crazy things till someone just *had* to join in.

Hannah held the wine bottle towards me. I don't like wine, but it seemed unfriendly to say so, and I let her pour some into my empty water glass.

"What do you think, Tariq?"

Was she drunk? Not on two glasses, surely? I'd had so little wine in my life I'd no idea what it took. Maybe two was enough.

"What do I think about what?"

"Does it seem strange to care more about dead strangers than people you know who're alive today?"

"I don't know."

"Go on! You must have an opinion. Think about it!"

What I thought was: I have a bedroom in a warm apartment with my own radiator. I do buy some groceries and I do try not to leave my stuff around, but that's about all I contribute. And if by way of rent the landlady needs some conversation . . .

Really, I wanted to tell Hannah about seeing the woman from her photograph book, and how I'd followed her. But I thought she'd laugh—tell me I was imagining things. Or maybe boot me out for being some sort of stalker.

"Go on, Tariq! Throw me a bone here!"

I coughed. "All right. I'll tell you something. The other day, I was going up the steps to the Métro at Stalingrad and this girl, this woman, was coming down the other way. I felt we'd met before. Maybe in some other life. No, that's not right. I felt she was my other half, the person I was meant to spend my life with. No that's not right, either . . . I can't explain."

"Go on." She was smiling, but not in a mocking way.

"She seemed to speak to me—not as the guy I am, who makes a mess of things and works in a shit fried-chicken place. I felt she was meant for me as the man I could become, as the man I deep down already *am*— an older, better man beneath all the clumsy, unimportant stuff of being young and useless and being me."

Hannah said, "I think I've had moments a little like that. And what did you do?"

This was a surprising response. I'd expected her to laugh. "I went for a walk to clear my head."

"I can't remember where Stalingrad is."

"Boulevard de la Villette, La Chapelle, round there. Not a very nice area. Top end of the canal. I went down rue de Tanger, I remember, and rue du Maroc. The names reminded me of home. I saw a shop that sells rat traps."

"Tanger," said Hannah. "That rings a bell. I think I came across it in my research the other day."

She reached over to a large notebook on the table. "Yes. Here we are. Juliette Lemaire. One of the spoken testimonies I listened to. She sounded like such a nice woman. She lived in rue de Tanger with her parents."

"Poor Juliette. Maybe it was better then."

"Well, they were quite short of money. But I think it was respectable. And here . . . She took the Métro every day from Aubervilliers–Boulevard de la Villette." She looked up from the book. "I checked and it doesn't exist any longer."

"Let's look online. If the Wi-Fi's working."

I used my phone and eventually we got there.

"There were originally two stations," I summarized from the first hit. "Rue Aubervilliers and Boulevard de la Villette. They joined up in 1942. But in 1946, 'to honor the Russian victory at the Battle of Stalingrad, a section of the boulevard was renamed Place Stalingrad.' And that's when the station changed its name too."

"So it's the same place."

"Yes."

There was a silence. Hannah seemed to be lost in thought.

Thinking I was still meant to be making conversation, I said, "Were the French on the same side as the Russians in that war?"

"Some were, yes. But most were on the other side."

"That sounds complicated."

"It was. Later on, more people changed sides."

But she seemed distant now, as though she wasn't concentrating on my adventure anymore but had lost herself in the loops of the past.

"She was nice, you say, your Juliette?"

Hannah looked back at me. "Lovely, I think. Though I have only her voice to go on."

"Do you think she was beautiful?" I was thinking of my Stalingrad girl.

"Maybe. But what's that got to do with it?"

"But do you?"

"Well . . . She certainly had admirers. And something in her voice. Modest but a little bit confident."

• • •

Eventually I heard back from Laila, saying "You lucky boy! We have exams soon. Miss A. has vanished. Off sick, they say, but maybe she's gone back to the Home Planet! Najat has got a boyfriend, would you believe? He's TWELVE!! Billy says he'll beat him up if he comes anywhere near the house. Saw your stepmother in the medina yesterday, but she hurried on before I could talk to her. Hope you are having a great time. Send me more pics. xx L."

I read it several times in case I'd somehow overlooked the words "I miss you terribly" or, "Here's a link to some pictures of my *qooq*." But the words stayed the same. All I could take out of it was whatever was intended by the "xx." More than x, obviously, but presumably not as much as xxx. After a few days, certain I wasn't going to get anything more out of the message, I deleted it.

Twice when I'd been on the early shift at Paname, I went down to Bir-Hakeim afterwards, at exactly the same time as on the first day, and stood opposite the maroon door. I never saw her. Of course I didn't know if she'd actually been working up there near Stalingrad or whether it had been on a trip to see a friend or buy rat poison.

So then I thought I'd try to catch her first thing in the morning. And one day when I was on the late shift at Paname, I got up very early and went down to Bir-Hakeim. I picked up an old newspaper on the train and was stationed opposite the maroon door by half past six.

Having nothing else to do, I read the paper. It all seemed to be about politics and trade and war. As an economics student, even a lapsed one, I ought really to have been interested, but to tell the truth it left me cold. It was maybe the first time I'd read a newspaper properly and I didn't think I'd be doing it again in a hurry.

The door did open from time to time, and out came old men or children or people in jeans and trainers with earbuds. People came to the door—builders, deliveries . . . After a time I thought that perhaps this wasn't where she lived anyway. Maybe she'd been making a one-off visit to a friend who'd given her the code to buzz herself in.

Then at a quarter past seven the maroon door opened inwards and a familiar figure stepped out. She was wearing the same coat, which fell to just below the knees, and a funny hat. Pillbox . . . Is that the word? It looked like something old-fashioned, quite smart but not twenty-first-century, more like the period of the war when she'd been photographed.

To my surprise, she didn't turn left and head up towards Bir-Hakeim. She turned right and walked quickly down some small streets, with me following, till we came into the big open area at the bottom of the Champ de Mars, with the Eiffel Tower away to our left. I noticed what looked like bullet holes in the stone walls of the École Militaire as we walked past. She didn't take the Métro there either but turned up left, then right into rue de Grenelle and finally down a narrow side street. I was twenty meters behind her when she stopped and went into a shop. I waited a minute, then walked past. It was a sewing-and-mending shop—in the window were the words *"Retouches. Transformations. Tous vêtements"*—very small, and I could see her at the back, behind sewing machines and a rail of hanging clothes, talking to someone and hanging up her coat. So this must be where she worked. I noted the name of the street, rue de l'Exposition, as I headed home.

Colonel Fabien

Allowing Tariq to stay on in the apartment for a trial period was not such a tough decision in the end. He was often at work in Saint-Denis till late, so some days I never saw him. I remembered myself in Paris at almost the same age and felt a flutter of anxiety on his behalf. I also thought a lodger, however callow, would be some company: There was a difference between the solitude I liked for work and its aching sister, loneliness.

For reasons of self-preservation, I'd tried not just to forget Aleksandr but to kill him as a living memory in my mind—awake or dreaming. The strange thing was that on the days I did allow myself to picture what he might be doing, it was always loneliness that I imagined. His wife couldn't offer him what I had. It's not that I was conceited about my looks (far from it) or my conversation or my sexual prowess or wit or value as a companion or anything at all. Except one thing. A perfect intimacy, you might call it. I knew that what we'd found couldn't be improved on. And I knew he knew it too. So why had he cut me loose and chosen to spend his life in what could only be a form of torment, day by day, dwindling, shrinking into half a man without me?

As for my own loneliness, it was something that I'd learned to live with, like insomnia or strep throat; it was, in the phrase I remembered hearing as a child, the cross I had to bear. But it needed watching and the occasional new remedy—so the alarm that sounded when Tariq's trial week came to an end was familiar to me. One week's lodging led to another, by which time he was more housebroken, and then to a third, fourth and fifth. He never guessed what proxy emotional function he was performing—but then he had a Paris room for free, so why would he care?

• • •

It had been Jasmine Mendel's idea that I apply for a position as a post-doc at my old college. When I returned from my two years in Africa, I had no idea what to do next. The experience had been exhilarating but had left me feeling flat. For all the funds we'd raised, the information films we'd made and shown, the clinics we'd set up and the friends we'd made, I knew I couldn't spend my life in this work. Other people could do it as well or better than I could.

Jasmine had a spare room in her Harlem apartment, so I went to stay with her while I worked out what to do next. We sat up into the night talking. We agreed that it was not possible for the wealthiest countries to fund free education for every poor child in the world, but there was something they could do. Just as rich individuals in any country should pay more in taxes, so the leaders of democracies with universal school-ing owed it to poorer countries to share their good fortune. This was not so much in drilling wells or wiping out malaria, it now seemed to me; it was more important that the leaders of developed countries should bring the benefits of *knowing* things, of understanding history, to their dealings with nations where most people had never had the chance to learn anything at all. That, we decided, was the very least of their duty: It was their baseline moral obligation.

While I was in New York, doing voluntary work and waitressing in a bar, the United States, backed by Great Britain, invaded Iraq. Jasmine and I were shocked by the president's ignorance and disappointed that British Mr. Blair seemed to have no better understanding of the Middle East. We bemoaned the failure of Anglo-U.S. privilege, calling it, after a book by our college favorite, Julien Benda, the "treason of the clerks." Their education at Yale and Oxford had obliged these two men to know, to understand and to act accordingly, instead of which they'd sold their birthright in the name of a short-term political gain that had proved—predictably—to be a delusion.

So I wrote to my old head of department at college, Barbara Putnam, and applied for a position. If I couldn't change the politics of my country, I figured I could at least try to understand the lives of those who had gone before. To my delight, she accepted. She said she'd been on the panel when I defended my dissertation and remembered my "earnest clarity." A little condescending, I guess, but it got the job done.

• • •

On my next visit to the Centre Jean Molland, I made a new selection. The summary read: "Begins with an anecdote from childhood. Witness later has involvement with French and German security and at second-hand with foreign agents in Paris."

This kind of direct connection was unusual. The other reason for choosing this woman was that there was no death date on her file, so that, although the recording had been made exactly eight years earlier, there was a chance she was still alive.

MASSON, Mathilde, born 1918.
File 1. LAAT/WTTJM/YS/1942/1074/416A
Recorded: *27 February 1998.*

My name is Mathilde Masson. I was born in Paris in 1918. Papa had lost his leg in the war. He'd got through Verdun but then he was in the wrong place when a shell landed. He was in hospital at the Front, then they sent him back to Paris after the war ended. But he hadn't seen my mother for nearly two years before I was born.

I didn't know about this as a child and I don't know to this day who my real father was. My sister Louise said she knew there was something wrong the moment Papa came home. He refused to pick me up or play with me. He didn't look at me or speak to me till I was six.

His left leg was cut off above the knee. They let him have his job back, but standing up all day hurt the stump of his leg where it rubbed. He worked in the slaughterhouse at Vaugirard. From the age of seven it was my job to massage the stump in the evening. I used to rub it with oil or put powder on where the blisters had burst.

There were three sisters, Louise, Élodie and me. When I was

about twelve, Papa told us we were going away for a few days. We were amazed. Holidays didn't exist in those days. We were a poor family and we lived in Belleville, a poor part of Paris. By then Louise had started a job, so she didn't come. It turned out the trip was organized by a veterans' association. This must have been 1930, a time when most men under forty were veterans. My father was given four days off work.

We borrowed a suitcase from Monsieur Barrault, who lived on the top floor. That was for us girls—Élodie, who was sixteen, and me. My father had a bag of his own. Élodie and I wore our best clothes and had one change each. We went on the Métro to the Gare Saint-Lazare and took the train for the coast. It took hours and hours. We stopped at a station in a forest in Normandy and bought some bread and a cheese from a man on the platform. I remember thinking how quiet it was out in the country. You could hear the birds singing; that's something we never heard in Paris, if you don't count the odd seagull.

When we got to the station there was a horse and cart to take the suitcases, but we had to walk. Papa was allowed to sit up by the driver and there was room for one more. He chose Élodie.

Maman and I walked for half an hour to reach the boarding-house. Our room was at the top, with two beds and a wardrobe. There was a bathroom at the end of the landing and we could see the sea from the window. We were told that dinner was at seven but we could use the big sitting room downstairs at any time. Ellie and I sat down and pretended to read the magazines.

We looked up when we heard someone come in. It was a man, but he didn't look like a man. He had a suit with a collar and tie, but his face was all wrong. He had one ear and some hair, but no nose and just a few teeth stuck into the middle of a hole. He said something we couldn't understand.

Papa came in with Maman. Papa was on his crutches with his wooden leg banging on the floor. He said good evening to the man with no face. The room began to fill up. There were men with no legs and one with an empty sleeve pinned up smartly. There was a man pushed in on a chair with wheels. But mostly it was their faces. Some had no eyes or lips. Others had faces that had been torn up so much that the bits were in the wrong place.

Just before seven, the woman in charge came into the room. She was about thirty-five, but she wore a widow's black clothes. "We're honored to have the heroes of France as our guests," she said. We went through when the bell rang and found our table in the dining room. The waitresses were young women in blue overalls, not like the waiters I'd seen in Paris. They brought some soup out from the kitchen and put it down on the tables. You could hear the sound of the spoon on the china and a lot of slurping noises. Élodie kicked me under the table, but I didn't catch her eye. My father said something like, "You'd think they'd show more respect." Élodie and I both had the giggles, so I looked round the room to try to stop it.

Most of the grown-ups were married, like grown-ups everywhere, but I didn't think I'd ever find a man to marry me. I was illegitimate, I was poor and I wasn't pretty. Not even one of the men with missing faces would want to spend his life with me. I was only twelve, so perhaps it was odd to be thinking like this, but Louise and Élodie felt it too. That's what we talked about. We even talked about Jean, the boy who brought up the water from the yard at home.

The next morning, Maman took Élodie and me down to the beach. We were sitting under an umbrella when the man with no face stopped and raised his hat. His name was Jérôme. I don't know if that was his first name or his second. He was trying to make conversation, asking us where we lived and so on. Maman didn't know whether to look at him or not. If you stared, you could see that one of his eyes, the right one, was almost normal. It was a nice eye. The other one was mostly covered by skin.

We understood that he was asking our names. By now Maman was flustered. It wasn't just the way he looked, but he was paying attention to us when my father wasn't there. And there was something that made me think he might not be poor like us, and that was awkward too.

Élodie whispered to Maman that he was asking if he could take her for a walk along the beach.

Well, she was sixteen and she looked more. None of us could say how old Monsieur Jérôme was, but most of the soldiers there were only in their thirties. He held out both hands to Élodie and she let him pull her up off the sand.

My mother smiled and waved her hand. She just wanted to see the back of him, I think.

Élodie looked back and made a funny face. She was slim but she'd always had thick calves. After a bit, I saw him hold out his elbow for her to take, and she slipped her arm under his. I felt jealous of Ellie. It showed you could change your life. Someone else, a stranger, could come along and just walk you away.

That night at the boardinghouse the dinner was fish, which we never had at home. Maman asked if we should have some wine and in the end Papa agreed. I didn't like wine. My other sister, Louise, had given me a taste when the *patron* of our local bar gave her a glass one day. Louise was always being given things for free. When the girl came at the end of dinner to mark off our wine bottle, she found Papa had drunk it all.

In bed, I whispered to Ellie, asking about Monsieur Jérôme. She said she couldn't understand what he said, but maybe it would get easier. The sun was bright again the next day when all of us went down to the beach. My father had borrowed a woolen bathing costume, which came down to the knee on one side and covered his stump on the other, with a bit of costume flapping loose. He said I could help him into the water.

I rolled down my stockings and left them with Maman and Ellie. I was wearing my dress because I had no costume. It was difficult for Papa to walk on the sand because of his crutches. We reached the smooth bit where the tide had been, but this was worse for him because the end of his crutches dug in even more. He kept swearing as he hopped along. He got down to the water, leaning on my shoulder. He had quite a slight build, not heavy, but I was small too. It was the first time I'd felt seawater, and I was afraid. It was cold and there were bits of weed swirling round in it. We managed to get a bit deeper in, then my father's foot landed on a stone and he swore and nearly fell over.

He said, "We've got to get out deeper; I've got to get my stump in. That's what the surgeon told me. Salt water." I liked the feeling of the sand on my feet, but my dress was soaking by now and I didn't want to be swept out to sea.

Papa's thigh was hard against mine and the fingers of his hand were very strong from his work as they squeezed my upper arm. Now it was up to my waist, so I knew his stump must be in the salt water.

"Turn me round," he said, and we managed to get ourselves back facing the beach. Maman and Élodie were waving at us from beneath the umbrella. I felt Papa's other arm go up as he waved back.

I could feel his body shaking against mine and I thought he must be crying. The seagulls were squawking above us and I was afraid. "Look at me waving," he said. "The stupid whore. Look! Yes, it's me. Here I am waving back, you whore."

He wasn't crying, he was laughing. A wave knocked me forward and I lost my footing. I grabbed my father as I fell and he toppled over with me. I swallowed salt water and came up spluttering. My father was thrashing and shouting, but he couldn't stand up.

Back on my feet, I needed a moment to breathe before I began to haul Papa up. Eventually he managed to pull himself into a standing position.

The next day Élodie helped him, and he stood in the sea for half an hour and he didn't fall over. Ellie was annoyed when Monsieur Jérôme came by and she was still in the water.

My mother just sat on the sand, looking out to sea. She came from the Auvergne; she was one of seven children. At the age of fifteen she was sent to Paris by her father to try to find work. She was living in a maid's room at the top of a big building near the Gare de l'Est when she met my father. He said she was almost starving. She was working as a cleaner in a cheap hotel. She looked on Christ as her savior in the next world and on Papa as her savior in this one. He had taken her out of the tiny maid's room and married her. I remember that second day sitting beside her on the sand, watching Papa lean on Ellie in the sea and wave to us. Maman's face lit up when she saw it and she waved back. I hoped Papa wasn't calling her a whore.

That evening I could see that Papa had been drinking. His face was red and he seemed sad. Ellie and I had both put on our best dresses and brushed our hair for dinner. It was the last night of the holiday. The main course was pork. Papa didn't seem to like it and began complaining that it was too tough to chew. He called over one of the girls in their overalls and told her to bring wine. He'd already finished one bottle.

After dessert, the Widow came into the room and tapped the side of a wineglass with a knife. She was wearing a smart black dress. She made another speech about what a privilege it was to have the heroes of France in her hotel. And Papa stood up and said, "Why don't you give them something they can eat, then?"

Then he stood up, holding a piece of the pork with its bone, and said, "How do you expect a man with no mouth to chew through this?"

Then he gave this demonstration of what a bullet does and how it spins when it hits a bone and can tear your face off as it's trying to find a way out. And if it's a machine gun there's another bullet following.

And the Widow was saying she was only doing her best and she'd lost her own husband and it was a special week.

Then Papa said something like, "It's special so that no one has to look at us for the rest of the year. So you can get us all out of the way in one go."

The Widow was upset, and a man who was not so badly wounded came over to our table and put his hand on my father's arm. Papa pushed him away. He said when he'd been lying among the dead men at Fort Vaux in Verdun he'd dreamed he'd survive long enough to have dinner with men who weren't mutilated. And with beautiful women.

Then he sat down.

Mathilde Masson's French had a strong Parisian flavor and she spoke more quickly than Juliette Lemaire. Every few minutes, I had to stop and replay the recording; even then I wasn't certain I had understood every word. Juliette seemed to have rehearsed what she was going to say, but Mathilde's story had a headlong quality, as though she didn't much care what people made of it.

The Centre Jean Molland summary showed there were six Mathilde Masson files, of which I'd heard the first. I thought of skipping ahead but decided that if the Occupation story was as good as the summary suggested, I needed to understand the background.

I pressed PLAY on the second file.

It was difficult for Papa. It tired him out to stand all day at work in the slaughterhouse and it irritated his stump. When he came home after a long journey on the Métro, he used to take off his wooden leg and sit at the table in his shirt while my mother made dinner. We always had meat because he could get it for almost nothing at work. He used to bring back cheap cuts for other people in our building.

The widow Madame Gauthier could only afford baked endive with a sprinkling of cheese unless he gave her a piece of tripe or something. She lived in hope, the old girl. At ten to six, when the shop was closing for the day, she used to shuffle out and pick a few things off the display, and the shop owner would let her have them cheap if he was going to throw them away. When she came back into the building she'd slow down outside our door on the first floor, make sure we'd heard her. She coughed loudly or called upstairs to her cat. The cat never came; it was just her way of letting us know she was there.

"Give her something, for God's sake," my father used to say when he heard Madame Gauthier outside. Then Maman used to tell one of us to carry up a piece of meat wrapped in newspaper, the nastiest offcut she could find.

Louise said our mother couldn't stand Madame Gauthier because of something she'd said when Maman was pregnant with me. When the bump began to show, she passed Maman on the stairs one day and said, "I see you're keeping in practice, Madame Masson."

Our place was cramped, but there was food and there was a bedroom for Papa and Maman, though the rest of us had to share. There was a living room that looked over the street and a small kitchen at the back that looked over the courtyard with the water fountain. The backs of the next-door buildings all looked down over it. You could see through the windows of the apartments and hear people shouting. If someone left a window open you could sometimes hear a wireless.

I used to sit by the window while my mother was making dinner. I watched Jean, the water boy, filling up his buckets for us. If it was dry he'd have to go to the Wallace Fountain at the end of the street. Louise used to joke that he was in love with me and always trying to catch my eye, but I don't think it was true. I watched the old man opposite getting ready for bed and the young woman who worked as a secretary who used to smoke cigarettes and knock her ash out of the window. You weren't meant to throw things down, but there were broken bottles and boxes and cigarette ends at the bottom that no one ever cleared up. When I saw these people in the street they didn't know I knew all about them.

It was my elder sister, Louise, who looked after me when I was young and Maman was out at work. Everyone said Louise was stupid, and it's true she was no good with spelling or numbers. Papa told her she'd end up working in a shop, like Maman, maybe on the haberdashery counter at the Samaritaine if she was lucky. They all thought Louise was backward, even Maman, who was just a country girl herself.

But I didn't care what they thought. I worshipped Louise. She had a black hat and a fox fur she'd got at the Clignancourt market. She was good at sewing and she made herself dresses from bits of material she picked up God knows where. She knew her way round. She knew how to find a whole Camembert and a piece of steak for next to nothing. At the bar on the corner of our street we'd sometimes get given hot chocolate by the *patron*. And then there were the pictures. I always wanted to go and see a film at the Louxor, which was a sort of Egyptian building near Barbès, but it would have meant taking the Métro, which cost money. Louise found a side door into a picture house in Ménilmontant, near where we lived. It opened into a back corridor and after the film had been running for a few minutes, you could sneak into the auditorium.

Louise did get a job, but it wasn't in a shop. She became a waitress in a café-restaurant in the rue des Francs-Bourgeois, which was in a very run-down part of town, on the old marshes going down towards the rue de Rivoli. There'd been a lot of TB there and some of the houses had been pulled down. Louise couldn't spell, but she could take the orders in her own way to tell the chef.

Sometimes after school I walked up to see her. It took me a long time, but I never minded going through the streets on my own and nobody bothered me.

One afternoon in December, I arrived when it was dark and cold. Louise had been there since the early morning and her shift was finished. "Come on," she said. "Let's go and have fun." She put on her hat and coat and we ran off down the street over the wet cobbles. It was a maze round there, very narrow streets and old houses with bits falling off. Louise led me into a red awning that said CAFÉ VICTOR HUGO. It was very old-fashioned and it had lights in colored-glass shades.

The owner had a big white beard and sad eyes. His chin seemed to rest on his beard as if he were wearing a scarf. He asked if we wanted hot chocolate and Louise said, "This is my little sister Mathilde." "Delighted, Mademoiselle," he said and I wasn't sure if he was teasing me. I said to him, "Are you Monsieur Hugo?" He smiled through his beard and said, "Of course I am." Then Louise said, "And some cakes, please." And Victor Hugo said, "Are you sure? They're full price today."

He gave Louise a look and she said, "That's all right."

The chocolate was boiling hot. Then Victor Hugo brought a plate with two slices of cake and some buns. I said to Louise, "What did he mean, they're full price today?"

And Louise laughed and said, "Sometimes he gives me them half price. And sometimes he gives me dinner for nothing." So I said, "Why?" And Louise said, "I do things for him." "What things?" I said. "You know. Things. When his wife's not here."

That was when I discovered how Louise could always get steak and Camembert. It started with little favors, I think. Later on she made a living from it. I suppose I looked shocked when she told me that first day. But she was so bright and gay about it. She laughed and said, "But you like the cakes, don't you, Minouche?"

I was anxious about Mathilde. Belleville, I knew, had always been a poor part of the city. Once, like Montmartre, it had been a village outside the old boundaries with vineyards on its slopes, but after the Franco-Prussian War it had been drawn into the new, enlarged Paris. While some slum buildings had been cleared, it remained border country and had been one of the first districts to take in immigrants, the Armenians and the Greeks arriving while Mathilde was still a child. Meanwhile, in the Masson household, blond Élodie had the looks, the admirers and the indulgence of her father, Louise was lively and able to look after herself, but Mathilde seemed to have nothing.

The third file of Mathilde's testimony took me through her school days and some early menial jobs working as a cleaner and in a bottling factory. There was not much about dresses or treats or visits to the movies anymore. She talked of work and money and the long hours and of her father's failing health. Élodie married a plumber and moved out of Paris to an apartment in the suburbs. Louise continued her fast life between Belleville and the Marais, still a blighted neighborhood.

In the fourth file, things changed with the arrival of the Germans. At first, it seemed to unify the Masson family, giving them a focus for their discontents. Then divisions began to open up. The father was unyielding in his hatred, but Mathilde and Élodie went with the popular view that if even France had been defeated, then surely no one could resist: German victory in Europe was inevitable and therefore best not delayed.

The big development came in 1942, when Mathilde, at the age of twenty-four, found her first boyfriend. He was a young man who worked in a shipping company with offices near the Opéra. Mathilde's voice became quite different when she spoke about him. She slowed down so much that I could understand all she said without using the PAUSE and REWIND.

Of course Armand was more educated than me. At first I was afraid to say too much, because he listened so carefully. He always assumed that other people were as clever as he was and what they were saying was important. And he'd sit there nodding his head gently up and down behind his glasses.

This made me nervous. We went for a walk in the park at Belleville and I hardly opened my mouth. Slowly I got used to him. I never dared take him home in case Papa was in one of his rages. I wanted him to meet Louise, but I was worried that he'd disapprove. Armand had this way of seeing through people.

After a while, I got to trust him. I told him a few little things about my life so far, being the youngest and all that, and he didn't laugh at me. He said he admired me for getting on with my life. I didn't know what he meant. What else was I supposed to do? He told me he thought I was beautiful, which was a lie, but I didn't mind him saying it.

Armand was very against the government and the Germans. He

said Marshal Pétain was an old fool and that the prime minister, Monsieur Laval, was evil. I said the marshal had saved France twice and was a hero. And we had a free zone with no Germans in it, not like other countries they'd invaded. Surely that was the marshal's doing? But Armand wouldn't be shifted.

He said, "Don't let's argue. Just promise me you'll never talk to a German," and I said, "I promise."

One day Armand gave me a beautiful scarf. It looked expensive and it was wrapped up in tissue paper by the shop. You have to understand I'd never had anything new before. Everything I'd ever worn was handed down from my sisters or bought secondhand.

Towards the end of the month, when he'd been paid, he used to take me out in the evening. There wasn't a lot you could do, because the food was rationed. I'd tell my parents I was seeing a girlfriend from work, then I'd go and meet him in Pigalle, where we listened to a singer in a bar. Armand sat there in his work suit and tie. He couldn't dance—he was a hopeless dancer—but I didn't mind. I used to like watching him, sitting there in his glasses, nodding in time to the music.

What I felt about Armand was the same thing I felt about that scarf. They were mine and no one else's. I can't explain how fierce I felt about him. Because I'd never had anything of my own before.

The next year, which must have been 1943, we decided that when the war was over we'd get married. Armand said things were starting to go against the Germans, especially now the Americans had joined in. I was confused, because most people I knew thought the Germans were sure to win.

It was about this time that Armand sometimes started to cancel our dates in the evenings, because he had other meetings. He didn't tell me what they were. I asked him if they were something to do with the Resistance and he looked shocked and put his finger on my lips. But I had my suspicions.

There were a lot of posters up at that time. They showed the American Uncle Sam and the English leader in Jewish skullcaps, making the war drag on for their own purposes. The posters were put up by the government, which wanted the Germans to win as soon as possible, so we could all eat again. Every time I went to get my papers renewed in the big building opposite the Opéra, there'd be a new poster. Some of them told us to trust the Germans, with pictures of happy children being carried by a blond soldier. On the Métro, the first carriage was reserved for the Germans and the last carriage was for the Jewish people with the yellow star stitched onto their coats.

My friends used to laugh at them—we called them the "Sunflowers"—but Armand told me not to. He told me Colonel Fabien and other men who'd shot dead German soldiers were heroes. And I said they weren't heroes to the families of the hundreds of innocent French people the Germans killed in revenge. Armand said there was a better way of getting at the Germans now. He showed me how to fold my Métro ticket twice longways, then once across at an angle. It made a "V"-for-victory sign. When we got off the train, we dropped them on the platform. In places like Belleville or Couronnes, where the Communist Party was strong, you'd see hundreds of "V"s on the ground. The Germans never knew who'd done it and it undermined them. It began to drive them mad.

École Militaire

APPARENTLY THE WOMAN IN THE PHOTOGRAPHY BOOK TOLD HANNAH in a dream that her name was Clémence. When Hannah told me this, I didn't jump right in and say, "Well, I know where she works *and* where she lives!" After all, Hannah was shocked when I told her about the other girl, the one I'd seen at Stalingrad. Just the coincidence of the Métro stations sent her off into her little world of ancient history. So I wasn't going to tell her about the sewing shop in the rue de l'Exposition. I just said, "Clémence? Nice name."

Up in Saint-Denis, old Jamal had done me proud. He kept the weed coming and I was able to go out on my break and have a puff most days. It didn't interfere with the foot-and-beak-sorting or the surface-wiping. Most of the time I was plotting how to get down and see if I could talk to Clémence, as I now thought of her. The more time passed, the more I became convinced that she held a key. To *what* exactly, I couldn't say, but I had this feeling she could help me find out more about my mother.

All I knew about her, Hanan, beyond the bare facts of her French *pied noir* father and Algerian mother, was that she was a bit older than my father and that she'd been in her midthirties when I was born. At some point I'd picked up the idea that something bad had happened in Paris when she was young, some trauma, but I had no idea what. You'd guess there might have been bullying or rough treatment because she was half Algerian, but that's only a guess and it might have been something else altogether. In a very remote part of my memory there was an idea that *her* mother, my grandmother, had met with an accident and it was this—a parent's death—that was my mother's trauma.

The trouble with my hunch that Clémence might help was that whenever I got down to the rue de l'Exposition the shop was closed. I'd been in Paris long enough to know that most things were shut on Monday. Then there was the Christian weekend. For instance, the family bistro nearest Hannah's flat in Butte-aux-Cailles opened in office hours on Tuesday to Friday (even though there weren't any office workers to eat there because there weren't any offices). On Saturday and Sunday when the families were at home, it was closed. It was also shut all day on Monday.

One morning, I got to the sewing-and-mending shop at about ten o'clock. A man was coming out and locking the door behind him. I asked if the shop was open.

"No," he said, sounding puzzled. "It's Thursday."

"I know. But . . ."

He looked at me oddly, as if I should have known that Thursday was impossible. None of this put me off, it just me made me keener to see her.

* * *

At Hannah's flat in rue Michal, things seemed to be quite settled. Her timetable was regular—leaving at about nine and returning late afternoon from her studies—so I could plan my visits to the bathroom for when she was out. I took my shaving things and toothpaste back to my room after use and made sure I didn't leave my stuff in the sitting room. In fact, I only shaved every second day, to get rid of a black smear on my upper lip, which was one reason I was surprised to see my reflection with a beard in the Métro carriage window.

In the bathroom, I spent a fair amount of time staring at myself in the mirror. I tried to surprise my face, to catch it unawares, so I could see what I looked like to other people. Once or twice I got close to that complete separation from the image that I'd had at home, when the Tariq in the mirror spoke to me. In those eyes I could still read a glorious future—if only other people could see it, too, I thought—and understand how deep and soulful and downright *valuable* this guy was. Someone to be treasured in his brief and brilliant time on earth. I roughed up my hair or flattened it with water. I tried a trace of mascara that Hannah had left out on the edge of the basin.

A couple of times I looked through the cabinet to see if it would tell me anything about her. It was too much to expect morning-after pills and sex toys. I knew that. What I didn't expect to find was five different kinds of lip moisturizer. What is this thing with women's lips? Laila was always at it too. I've had chapped lips only once in my entire life.

Sometimes when I was walking through Saint-Denis to work at PFP or back from Tolbiac to the flat, or when I was going to a movie at the underground multiplex at Châtelet–Les Halles, I'd wonder if the way I looked at all the girls I saw was really normal. At least once a day I'd see a girl or woman, someone between the ages of about seventeen and forty, who I felt this awful longing for. Not as bad as the Stalingrad girl with the short dress over gray tights and the leather bag, who I ought to have married by now if the world had any sense. And not quite the same sense of—I don't know what you call it, destiny, perhaps, as I'd felt when I saw Clémence. But it was upsetting, because if I caught their eye I was pretty sure they felt it too. I wanted to lean forward in the train (it was usually in the Métro) and say, Natalie, Suzanne, Brigitte, let's get off here, buy dinner and take it back to your apartment. Let's stop pretending. You know I'm right. We haven't got a whole lifetime to throw away. I'll get some wine.

What was this machinery of the world, this great clanking, invisible, interlocking thing, whose only job was to screw it up for me, make sure I never even got to talk to her?

And then there were all the others—the ones I thought about in a more down-to-earth way. A middle-aged Parisian businesswoman tapping at her cell phone, a plump schoolgirl with pink hair and slashed jeans, a Muslim mother in her headscarf picking over the vegetables at the market in Saint-Denis . . . What probably made it worse was the fact that at home I'd hardly ever seen a woman naked. There were pictures in the soft-porn magazines which with some difficulty you could get hold of at home. The odd glimpse in an American movie. I imagine there was porn on the Internet in Morocco, but without a laptop there was no way of seeing it. I couldn't afford a laptop and neither could anyone else I knew, except Laila. There was a computer room at college but all the machines had a filter. And there were Internet "cafés," dark little rooms in the medina where you could go and look at a screen with headphones on. A boy in my year said he had seen films of housewives in full *niqab* hard at it, but it was far too risky in a booth where anyone could walk in, and he was a bit of a bullshitter.

Presumably it was my age. I guessed that by the time I was forty or something I wouldn't be obsessed like this at all. And yet . . . suppose that once I'd had a few girlfriends, drunk deep from that well, it might turn out that I wasn't squashing the desire but only feeding it. Then I'd become like one of those smug men of fifty with gray hair and a belly who have a mistress and a wife and are open to other offers. Then, far from fading away, the urge would have taken over my life. I'd be a monster.

Trouble is, I'd never actually been alive before, so how was I to know what I'd feel at forty or fifty? This was, so far as I knew, my first attempt at living on this planet and I was making the whole thing up as I went along.

. . .

The next time I went to the rue de l'Exposition, one afternoon after I'd done the early shift at PFP, I saw Clémence sitting in the window. She was wearing a blue dress and was working a machine with her feet while at the same time squaring up pieces of material under the needle with her hands. I know nothing about sewing, but it looked to me as though she was not just mending a dress but actually making it. Sometimes she stopped and looked down to a table by her elbow, as if to some instructions.

What was I supposed to do? Go in and say, I've seen you in a book, but somehow you haven't aged in sixty-odd years? And in a dream you told my landlady your name. Now I wonder if you'd like to talk to me about my mother, who lived in Paris as a child and as a young woman—though I don't know where.

It wasn't that I was shy. At home, a lot of life takes place on the street and all children speak to strangers. We're brought up like that. And look at the way I'd found myself work in Saint-Denis—I just talked to lots of people I didn't know until one of them offered me a job. I'd never quite understood shyness anyway. What was the worst thing that could happen? Some stranger you'd never see again might tell you to fuck off? Was that so bad? But I wasn't sure how to approach Clémence. And maybe the reason was that I didn't really want to talk to her anyway, I wanted more to *look* at her.

So I went up to the rue Saint-Dominique and eventually found a *maison de la presse* where I bought the largest newspaper they had. It was called *Le Figaro*. Then I went back to the sewing shop and perched myself on the windowsill of a building opposite and began to watch over the top of the open paper.

Her knees went up and down and the dark eyes moved, but her head stayed quite still. She seemed so absorbed by her work that there was no chance she'd look up and see me. Everything about her seemed delicate, the slim fingers, the pointed kneecaps, even the thighs, of which I could see a little when the blue skirt rode up. Her nose was quite sharp and her mouth was pursed in concentration. But although she was delicate, she wasn't fragile. She seemed to know exactly what she was doing. I loved her.

The rhythm of her work began to suggest a tune to me. As I watched the gentle rise of her thighs beneath the blue dress and the exact movements of her hands, I started to sing to myself, very quietly. The words I put to the tune weren't up to much, the first words that came into my head, but the song seemed sad, like the folk songs I vaguely remembered from my earliest childhood. Who can have sung them to me, where did I hear them? Perhaps from my mother, before she disappeared, and maybe she'd first heard them here in Paris in a concert hall or in a bar or maybe just in the street by someone homesick for the countryside.

For an hour or more I sat and watched her work. An older woman with glasses came from the back of the shop and put a cup on the small table next to the sewing pattern, but even then Clémence hardly hesitated and her eyes never left the piece of cloth under her hands. When it was dark, she finally stopped, as though the electric light of the lamp beside her was not enough. She stood up and raised her arms above her head and stretched. She went to the back of the shop and for a moment I lost sight of her, but I felt sure she must have finished for the day. Sure enough, in a few minutes she emerged, wearing the same knee-length coat and small hat on the side of her head. I was looking down hard at the trade figures or political argument or whatever was in the long columns of *Le Figaro*. There was no need to glance up because I knew which way she'd be going.

I gave her about thirty meters, then set off. We were soon on the open area of the Place Joffre, in front of the bullet-marked École Militaire, and I had to hurry not to lose her in the backstreets that led to her porte cochere with the flaking paint.

When she got there, I hung back to give her time to enter the code, go inside and let the door close behind her.

Intending to go up to Bir-Hakeim, I strolled past a minute later. But as I glanced across the road, I saw that she was standing in the entrance, holding the street door open with her left hand. I caught her eye and stopped.

Her eyes met mine, as they had on the Métro. She lifted her right hand and beckoned to me to cross the road and come inside.

• • •

Behind the street door was another world. I was used to this from the doors in the medina, or the gate at Laila's wall that opened up their park-like garden.

Clémence said nothing as she walked ahead of me over a cobbled courtyard, in the far corner of which was an open door onto a stone staircase. There was no lift. I followed her up two flights, where she unlocked a double door from the landing.

We went into a hallway with a wooden floor, then a sitting room, where she pointed me to a chair. She didn't come in, but I heard the sound of a kettle and china next door. The sitting room had a window over the courtyard and a sewing machine on a table. The furniture was old and there was no television or music player or Wi-Fi router or anything electronic.

After a minute or so, Clémence came back and put down two china cups of clear tea and a bowl of sugar on a tray. She turned on two table lamps, but they didn't give much light. She'd taken off her coat and little hat, I noticed, as she sat down opposite me in her blue dress and her pointed knees in their honey-colored nylon covering. She took a cigarette from a small box on the table, lit it and blew out some smoke. She was sitting forward with her elbows on her thighs.

At last she spoke. Putting her head on one side, she said, "What do you want?"

I was shocked.

She spoke in French, and what she'd said was, *"Qu'est-ce que tu veux?"*—not the *vous* that you'd expect on first meeting, but the familiar *tu*. So she was either being rude or she was treating me as an infant.

Yet her tone of voice suggested neither of these things. It suggested kindness. She wasn't asking what I wanted in the way shop assistants say, "Can I help you?" It was more like an offer: "Tell me what you want and I'll give it to you." Perhaps it was more even than that, something like a philosophical question as though the words "from life" or "from me" were understood.

It sounds impossible now I look at it that one question could say so much. But at that moment in her tone I swear I heard a kind of fondness.

My short life to this point had not included anyone speaking to me in this way. It had so far been about trying, and hoping and being frustrated and thinking that frustration, really, was the nature of being alive—attempting to have happiness and finding that there was some glitch in the basic rules of existence that made it impossible.

I picked up the teacup. The drink was very hot, and sweet, made with a bunch of mint, leaves and stalks, like we have it at home.

We heard the clock ticking. I thought about how to reply, of what to say, of all the things I might try to ask of her.

In the end, because it was the only thing that seemed possible, I told the truth. I said, "I want to watch you."

But that's not really what I said, because obviously I spoke in French too. What I said was: *"Je veux te regarder."*

And the *te* was like jumping from a cliff. The sound of it hung there.

She didn't blink, just said *"Comme tu veux."* As you wish.

Then she leaned forward and held out the cigarette box to me. I took one of the unfiltered cigarettes and lit it with a table lighter. It was not like being at Hannah's.

Some time passed then. I couldn't say how much, perhaps an hour, perhaps much less. She talked. I didn't ask her questions, but her low voice filled the room. It was all stories from the past, but they didn't sound like history, like Hannah telling me things. Her father, a town called Annaba, her mother, her sister, back in Paris, a strict school in rue de Vaugirard . . . I didn't really listen, I just looked at her, both exotic and familiar. Her dark hair shining a little when it caught the light from one of the low lamps. The big dark eyes which were like a deer's. I don't mean she looked like an animal, I mean there was something dutiful and patient in them.

At some point during this hour I was able to listen and concentrate on what she said: ". . . in the apartment where we're sitting now. It's all so long ago. A policeman—a man my friend knew because he'd seen him often in the street, usually on Avenue Bosquet—came and knocked on the door at two in the morning. The policeman asked to see his papers and told him to get dressed. He walked with him, down this little street here, onto the boulevard and then only a short way from here to an arena, a well-known place where they had sporting events under a glass dome painted blue. He did what he was told because he had nothing to fear. He wondered what sporting event could be taking place in the middle of the night.

"It was the strangest event that Paris had ever staged. The seats of the auditorium were all taken. There were families with grandparents, families with small children, married couples and people all alone, like my friend. Some lay down, some spilled over from the seats onto the sports area. But there was no entertainment. For five days there were no bicycle races on the wooden track, no football, no clowns or jugglers, no boxing. Nor was there any explanation of what they were doing there. Paris policemen barred the doors. There was no water and nothing to eat. The thousands of people in the velodrome, the old and the young, the rich and the poor, had one thing in common. On their coats they had a yellow star.

"When the police began to move them on the fifth day, a few were already dead from lack of water. The officers herded them all into the same green-and-white buses that might on any other day have taken them to work. They took them to a camp in the north of the city, a place called Drancy. The bakers, the dressmakers, financiers, old people, good-for-nothings, lawyers, road menders, the young brides, the office clerks and the children. And from there they put them on trains that took them to the east, to Poland, where they could more easily be killed."

Ternes

TWO MONTHS INTO MY WORK, I FELT I WAS MAKING PROGRESS. THE problem was that keeping the personal and professional apart was proving more difficult than I'd expected. So much of what I saw and thought—on the street, at home in the flat, working in the archive—seemed colored by some sort of memory-filter made up of the person I myself had been ten years before.

I suppose that at that age—twenty-one—I was a rather solemn girl. My parents were true Americans, descended from German and Irish migrants, the Kohlers and the Slatterys, generations back. They lived in Massachusetts, where they had the advantage of being white and employed; my father worked for a company that imported Japanese porcelain, my mother in healthcare administration. Even as a kid I noticed that not everyone had a timber-framed house with a porch and a small spare bedroom in back; by the time I went to high school, I was aware that having incomes from two parents was also an advantage. In class I met children from the projects near the steel mills. Most of them had only one parent and hardly any seemed interested in learning; to hear them talk, you'd think their life was already pushing them towards gangs and crime.

Our high school was no great shakes, but—so long as you had some backup or encouragement at home—it gave its students a chance at least of getting the grades they needed for college, and the more I read about the world, the more it seemed clear to me that even this education put me in a minority. What chance would I have had if I'd been brought up in a refugee camp or a village in Africa with no school?

At college, I joined marches against violence against women and organized book sales for African famines. Jasmine (affectionately, I liked to think) called me "God's little soldier." By the time I arrived in Paris in the fall of 1995, I still hadn't sorted out what I really thought—or, rather, I knew what I believed but not how to shape a life to reflect those beliefs. Perhaps I had been more confused than I knew—dangerously so maybe, I now thought: a mixture of unresolved contradictions.

"I know what you mean," said Julian Finch when I cautiously referred one day to the way my past seemed to hang over me. "There's no city in the world where you're so aware of your younger self."

We were in a restaurant on the Avenue des Ternes, a room with crimson banquettes and platters of shellfish, where he'd invited me for lunch. It was a sunny day in March and the sidewalk trees were coming into leaf.

"You did seem desperate that summer, I remember," he was saying. "I didn't know you well and it wasn't my place to ask, but I knew you'd had trouble with your Russian poet."

"Playwright."

"He had a poetic air. I felt responsible. You were young. I'd introduced you to him at that library event."

"No, I'd already introduced myself."

"But it was difficult. You were such a mixture. So grown-up in some ways, so confident and firm in your feminism, but somehow vulnerable. Or so it seemed to me."

"You didn't say so at the time."

"Of course not. You have to respect someone else's beliefs. Partly because you want to, and partly because you don't want to put your foot in it. And then there's the distance you have to keep with the student-teacher thing."

I began to laugh. "You really mustn't blame yourself for my Russian."

"But he made you unhappy."

"Not at first. I became unhappy when he went back to St. Petersburg."

Julian nodded. "And was he your first?"

"First what?"

"First real . . . First proper . . ."

"No. The only one. 'First' implies there were others."

I hadn't slept with a man for nearly ten years; the fact was, I hadn't even kissed one—though I didn't say so to Julian.

"I see." He picked up the menu. "Now. Food. In a place like this, we should order the old-fashioned things. That's what they care about. *Pot au feu. Tarte tatin.* Please don't say you're going to have the sea bass."

"Why not?"

"Sylvie ordered it in every restaurant we ever went to. Sometimes it took her twenty minutes staring at the menu before she knew that what she wanted was the sea bass."

While we ate (not sea bass, unfortunately), I told Julian about the Mathilde Masson files and how I was worried about Mathilde's "future." "She wants to be tough. She has this in-your-face accent and attitude. But I fear the worst."

"And you think she might still be alive?"

"There's no death date on the file. Though the Jean Molland's not always up-to-date with its housekeeping."

"Would you like me to find out?"

"Can you?"

"Maybe. I know Leo Busch, the director of the Centre."

"The German?"

"Yes. And I've met his French counterpart too. A nice woman. Florence Something. I could ask them, if you like. It might be confidential, but I can always ask."

"I'd appreciate that."

I'd drunk half the bottle of wine and had no plan to work in the afternoon; out on the avenue, I could see the spring light already starting to fade. I was more than happy to listen as Julian told me a little about his life without Sylvie. ("Being single has some advantages, though to be honest, not as many as I'd imagined. I do miss her.") I just hoped that he wasn't expecting me to reciprocate. There was nothing I wanted to tell him about the intimacy of my connection with Aleksandr and the sharing with him of both my noblest and most shameful private thoughts. What on earth had led me on? Was it a greed for sensation, a hunger to be known better, to become so close to someone else that I would melt into his flesh and disappear? All of this and more, I thought, the "more" being in part a sense that such passion ("love," if that was the word for it) was approved by others—held up as a goal that everyone should aspire to. I had been deceived. Knowing him so intimately hadn't taken me to a higher plane of being, still less brought me peace of mind. Instead, it had created a second person inside me, a sort of Dido full of operatic yearning, who, when Aleksandr left me to go back to St. Petersburg, cried out to heaven at my abandonment. In the years that followed, it didn't matter how many days of quiet work or evenings of friendship I enjoyed. Nothing could calm the pain of the inner bitch sister, permanently in heat, hysterically aggrieved.

Or so it had seemed in my more balanced moments—when I could use humor to gain some distance from this demented person. At other times, I was caught without a defense. It wasn't only at night, when I had surrendered to sleep, but by day, on a street corner, that I might be taken unawares by a sense of loss that obliterated all reason. Once when I was walking in the park at home, I called his name out loud among the trees, then sat down on the grass and wailed. I worried at that moment that I was losing my mind.

"By the way," I said, "I have a new boyfriend now. A young Moroccan who lives with me."

"You dark horse."

"It's a little like having an exotic pet."

"Sounds messy."

"I'm training him. We take it one week at a time. And he knows I'll kick him out if he gets out of line."

"Young men make insatiable lovers."

"He doesn't think of me that way."

"He's how old again?"

"Nineteen, twenty, somewhere round there."

"He thinks of you that way. Believe me. Unless he's gay."

"No, he's not. But, boy, is he ignorant. He knows nothing. It shocked me at first. Now I find it kind of intriguing."

"Are you making yourself responsible for his education?"

"Not in any regular way." I looked down at my coffee. "It's strange. We've become kind of friends. I'm like his mom and his older sister as well as his landlady. And he does interest me. I think that knowing nothing makes him in a way more open to experience."

"That doesn't sound possible."

"I know. But he has no clutter in his head. When he sees something, he doesn't try to figure out what it means, using kinds of precedent or comparison. He just thinks, What's this? Will I enjoy it?"

"But you don't really think of your own education as 'clutter.'"

"I sometimes think I've read too much. I see too many trees up close. Sometimes I'm maybe missing the shape of the woods."

Then we talked for a while about British support for the French resistance, much of which was focused on Paris through a secret network of agents under the code name "Prosper." Julian was enthusiastic about their story, but I was beginning to feel tired.

After lunch, Julian went up Avenue Mac-Mahon to take the Métro home, but I kept walking towards the Place des Ternes. It was by no means a charming part of town, but even this street had its half-closed dramas. In one of Barbara Putnam's papers I'd read how, in 1942, at the Brasserie La Lorraine on the Place des Ternes itself, some of the agents in the Prosper network used to gather and drink on the terrace. They belonged to the Special Operations Executive, a spying-and-sabotage organization that was built up throughout Nazi-occupied Europe. Meeting in public was in breach of their orders and in defiance of every norm of safety and common sense; they even sometimes spoke in English. Their excuse was that they were lonely—nothing more. And by 1943, the Prosper network had been betrayed by its French air-transport officer, who had told the Germans where every secret flight would land and who'd be on it; all that was left to the careless English visitors with their drinks on the terrace was the knock on the door, a rendezvous with German counterintelligence at 84 Avenue Foch and the cattle truck to a concentration camp out east, where they would be killed.

As I came alongside, I wondered which table on the terrace of the Brasserie La Lorraine had been chosen by the lonely agents of Prosper and if any of the waiters there today, in the same black waistcoats and bow ties as their predecessors, fumbling for coins in the folds of the same white aprons, would have any idea that such events had taken place. How many years did it take to forget? How small was the failing of a school or teacher that its pupils might somehow never learn? The human drive to ignorance, as Professor Putnam had once told her seminar group, is a force as powerful as its opposite—as strong as curiosity itself. For many centuries in almost every country of the world, she told us, the ambition of the village elders was that the next generation should know not less than they themselves; they hadn't hoped for progress or enlightenment, just that there should be no net loss of knowledge. It had seemed a modest aim when she first explained. Now I was not so sure.

● ● ●

While the days were filled with the words of recorded women, I found much of my spare time taken up by thoughts of a girl in a photograph. In a fanciful way I'd never have admitted to my professional colleagues, I became sure that Clémence had had something to do with the Resistance. I pictured her not as a country girl who'd persuaded her father to shelter an Allied airman for a couple of days or who'd agreed to run a message on her bicycle to the next village. It was more than that. She'd lived in Paris, where she'd been photographed, and her eyes had the look of someone whose knowledge of secrets had lasted a long time. Her coloring suggested that she might have come from the south, near Spain, from Pau or Tarbes, but Paris had obviously been her sphere of operation. Perhaps she was not even French but had been dropped by SOE parachute. All that mattered for these agents was their ability to pass for French when speaking; nothing else counted, not even their suitability for undercover work.

Studying the photograph in my book, I thought Clémence looked a little like a true-life figure of the Resistance: Andrée Borrel, a young Frenchwoman who on her first SOE assignment found herself sharing several weeks of dangerous activity with Francis Suttill, the English leader of the Prosper circuit. Afterwards, exhausted by all they had gone through together, Suttill sent a message to London to express his gratitude for this exceptional woman. "She is the best of us all . . . Thank you very much for having sent her to me."

There was no life of Andrée Borrel, though she appeared as a minor character in the biographies of others. It was difficult to find out much about her. The British secret services had been reluctant to give information, refusing even to release the letters she had written to her sister from prison outside Paris, while the French didn't include her in their pantheon of Resistance heroines, because she'd worked for a British organization.

⋅ ⋅ ⋅

At the Jean Molland the next day, I decided to finish the Mathilde Masson story, which, distracted by other witnesses, I had temporarily put to one side. At the start of the next file, Mathilde's voice still had the slower rhythm that had made her easier to understand when she first talked about Armand.

It was in the autumn of that year, 1943, that things started to go wrong. Armand canceled our evening out two weeks running. The first time he was polite and said he'd been kept late at work. The second time he said he'd had to stay at home and look after his mother.

The third time Armand canceled, I went to see Louise, and when she'd finished work we went to the Victor Hugo for a drink. It was crowded in there and Louise seemed to know quite a lot of the customers. I didn't see the proprietor, but a couple of men were joking and calling out to Louise across the room. She seemed to enjoy it and shouted back something rude.

I said I was worried about Armand, and Louise said she'd heard he'd fallen in with some bad people. That was the thing about Louise—she seemed to know everything that was going on. It was not like Armand to let me down, I said, because he'd always made such a fuss of me. Louise squeezed my hand and told me not to worry.

Over the next few weeks I became certain that Armand was working for the Resistance, though I didn't really know what that meant. There were a lot of people in Paris now who were not so sure the Germans were going to win after all. They talked about a battle at Stalingrad, where the Germans had lost a million men. And then, what with the Americans joining in and everything, it was looking different. Quite a few of the girls I knew who'd been flirting with the German soldiers outside bars and cafés now walked past them with their noses in the air.

So I thought I should find out what Armand was up to. When we next met, I decided to ask him straight out. It was on a Sunday and we'd gone for a walk in the Tuileries, which was a change from the Buttes-Chaumont. A lot of the earth had been dug up and planted with vegetables. We sat on a bench and Armand opened a little tin box. He said he'd managed to get hold of some nice cheese through a friend who knew people in Normandy. Before I could ask him, he said, "Mathilde, I've got something to tell you, but you must promise to keep it secret." Then he told me he was part of a group who were helping send messages to London. All over France, he said, there were people being armed for the battles against the Germans that would be coming soon. Apparently Armand could remember all these code names and addresses and map references without writing them down, which would have been dangerous. It made me feel proud of him that he was so clever, though I suppose no one was going to ask him to use a gun with his short sight.

Then he said, "What we do now will make a difference for the rest of our lives. When we're old we have to know that we were on the right side."

I remember looking along the gravel paths of the Tuileries when he'd stopped speaking and wondering what all the people there were hiding in their hearts. The ladies with the prams and the old men and the youngsters without a care, what they really thought. I saw a bride in her wedding dress posing for a photograph with her husband behind some trees.

Armand was very worked up. I didn't know anything about the politics, but I could see how much it meant to him. I didn't want to end up on the wrong side when we were old, so I said, "Is there anything I can do?" And he said, "Nothing yet."

That must have been in October. I remember it was still sunny in the Tuileries. Then a bit later Louise told me she'd heard something else about Armand. He'd been spending a lot of time with his new friends. And someone at the Victor Hugo had told Louise that they'd seen him with a woman. They weren't doing anything wrong. They were sitting in a café, close together. But his hand had been on her thigh. They were whispering. And Louise said, "Well, were they talking about parachutes and guns or were they whispering other things?"

She didn't say this to make me jealous, though she must have known it would. She knew how I felt about Armand. I asked her how her friend knew all about him and she said, "Everyone spies on everyone these days. Haven't you noticed?"

I think for the first time in my life I was really angry with Louise. I suppose it ought to have been Armand I was angry with, but it wasn't. I turned on her and said, "I wouldn't trust any of the men you spend time with."

We'd never talked about that before. There were tears in her eyes. She said, "Don't be like that, Mathilde. I'm just trying to warn you."

But I was angry and I said, "I'm not having some bitch open her legs for him."

Louise looked shocked and I began to laugh at her. I was so upset. "You of all people. To be shocked," I said. "You and your special favors in the upstairs room."

Then Louise wiped her eyes and looked at me and said, "You know why I do it?"

I said, "Is it money?"

And she said, "No. I do it because I want to. I do it because it stops me feeling lonely."

I paused the recording and sat back in the chair.

In my mind I could picture the Belleville apartment where Mathilde had grown up and where, presumably, she and Louise still lived at this point in their lives—unless one of Louise's gentlemen friends had found her a room. I could picture the lazy stockpot and the smell of meat cooking (even if Papa had retired by now, he'd still have friends in the slaughterhouse). Now, in 1943, there'd be damp clothes hung up about the place to dry, near the stove or the open kitchen window where as a child Mathilde had looked over the lives of the neighbors. And Papa resting his stump on a chair, glass in hand. Was old Madame Gauthier still stopping outside to call upstairs to her cat? Presumably she'd died a pauper's death by now.

I imagined the bare boards of the landing and the grudged wattage of the hanging bulb. Living on top of other people in this way, sharing a bed with her sister for much of her life, how had Louise managed to feel so lonely that she had to sleep with men for money?

The closeness of other people who were fond of her hadn't been enough. She had needed more. She'd wanted to be known, known intimately, as herself, for herself—even for a short time, even if it meant being known by a stranger.

Sèvres-Babylone

A T FIRST I THOUGHT CLÉMENCE HAD INVENTED THE WHOLE THING. But then I looked it up online and I discovered that the roundup at the Vélodrome d'Hiver, the big cycle track near the Quai de Grenelle, was a famous incident when the Germans were in control of Paris during the Second World War. The bronze memorial I'd seen on the quay that cold afternoon was a tribute, a bit late in the day (fifty-three years, I reckoned), to the 13,000 people who'd been held there before being packed off to an unfinished housing project in the northern suburbs at a place called Drancy and from there in trains to be murdered by the Nazis in Poland. The glass roof of the velodrome had previously been painted blue to put off British bombers, and before the roundup began the windows of the lavatories were screwed shut by the Paris police to prevent escape. The French plan, Operation Spring Breeze, was to arrest a total of 28,000 people to meet the needs of a German "quota." It wasn't "spring," though, it was July, there was no breeze and it was like a greenhouse in the velodrome, with no sanitation. There was dysentery. And of the 13,000 only 400 came back from the death camp.

Up at Paname Fried Poulet, I asked Hasim and Jamal if they knew anything about it. They didn't. But Hasim told me about the thousands in Algiers who'd "disappeared" in the course of the war against France— not just people who'd died in the fighting, but political prisoners who'd been made to vanish by the French authorities. I suppose you only know about the bad things that have happened to your own people. He mentioned massacres.

It must have been a couple of days after this, while we were working in the kitchen, that Jamal asked me if I'd ever read the Koran. This was awkward. I was wary of him after what he'd told me about his childhood in the camp, but I liked him and had never thought to ask if he was religious.

"Not since I was a kid," I said. "I used to go to the mosque a bit. There were classes. But my mother was Christian, I think, so . . ."

He went to the spice cupboard and handed me a dog-eared book. "You can have this copy. It's in French."

"Have you read it, Jamal?"

"Me? No. I'm not a believer. I don't need religion to know what I think. I don't need a god to hate this country, I just need to remember what they did to us."

"So if it's just the same old war between our people and the French, why do the jihadis always talk about religion? Why do they need religion as well?"

I never did hear Jamal's answer to this question because at that moment Hasim came into the kitchen, and for the first time since I'd known him he was smiling. Someone he knew in Algeria, a cousin with money, was thinking about opening up a restaurant in Paris—not in the *banlieue*, but somewhere in the middle of the city. His idea was to bring fast food to the smart areas, where he could charge more for it. Although it was really not for me to say, I was just the kitchen slave, I didn't think ladies shopping for handbags in the rue du Faubourg Saint-Honoré would want to eat burgers and kebabs.

"That's not true," said Hasim. "There's a McDonald's in the Champs-Élysées."

He had a point. As a matter of fact, there was also a Subway with a back entrance onto the respectable street where Clémence lived.

Jamal coughed and wiped his lips. "Listen, boss, those chains have American millions behind them."

Hasim was not deterred. "I like the sound of this Marais place," he said. "It's fashionable. Lots of tourists. They could start a shop there. Take a short lease and see how it goes."

"It's full of Jews, the Marais," said Jamal. "Jews and falafel."

I opened up the latest sack of frozen chicken bits from Transylvania and began to thaw them in the oven while Hasim and Jamal carried on arguing. After a few minutes they began to swear at each other—your mother this, your sister the other. Jamal was against the whole thing on any grounds—religious, financial, anything he could shout about—though it was really none of his business.

And then I had a brainwave. It seemed to me the reason both these tough men were frightened was that neither of them had ever been into the middle of Paris. They'd lived their whole life in the medina that was Saint-Denis—at night in a *cité* tower, dodging past the robbers and the drug gangs, and by day in the sweatshop of PFP. They were afraid that if they took the Métro and hopped off at Filles du Calvaire they'd be arrested for looking suspicious. Whereas, despite what I'd said to Sandrine about people's prejudices, I didn't care. Perhaps because I was young, or just visiting, or both.

"Would you like me to look around for you?" I said. "My favorite restaurant's not far from the Marais. I could walk over and maybe ask a few people who have small shops how much they pay for rent and that kind of thing."

This made both men forget for a moment whether Hasim's mother had been a one-eyed whore and turn on me. In the same way I'm not shy of strangers, I don't take abuse too personally. Maybe I'd got used to it from my father when I was a kid. In any case, by the time it had all died down I'd pretty much got the go-ahead.

• • •

Meanwhile, back in Butte-aux-Cailles, things seemed to be going fine as far as Hannah was concerned. She still hadn't asked for any rent, but I left money on the kitchen table alongside the occasional bunch of bananas or a big pot of the yogurt I knew she liked. I was earning about fifty euros a day at PFP and only needed ten or so for food, so I usually left twenty for Hannah. Nothing was said between us, but it seemed to work okay.

She also asked me if I'd translate something for her. It was an audio file she'd downloaded onto her laptop, so I had to wait till she'd finished using it and gone to bed one night. There was no password or anything on her machine and I resisted a temptation to open her browsing history. What would a middle-aged American search for anyway? Bottom-less Coke and fries? No, she didn't like that stuff. Hot Tanjawi guys with huge . . . No, certainly not that. Historicalbackwaters.com. Possibly. Lipmoisturizersupermart.com. Yes, that would account for most of it, I thought. But I honestly didn't go there. I hovered, but I didn't.

The audio file was a recording of an old woman with a trembly voice. Her name was Juliette Lemaire, and I remembered she was the one who lived where Stalingrad now was. The sound quality was shit. It took me till about three in the morning to transcribe the whole thing, but this is what old Juliette said.

A few months later the German officer, Major Richter, came back into the shop, this time on his own. He was very polite towards Sophie and me and he bought a fine woolen jacket for his wife. The Germans were always buying things, not just from shops like us but even from the flea market at Clignancourt. We still had things they couldn't get at home, which was funny when you think about it. I found out later it was all to do with the German economy and inflation. Their shops had been bare for years.

As he was leaving, he asked if I'd think again about having din-ner with him. He told me the name of a smart restaurant near the Opéra which of course I couldn't dream of going to. For some reason I said I'd think about it.

He said, "When will you decide, Mademoiselle?" And I said I'd tell him if he came back at the end of the week. He said he had to go to some training school, to lecture there, but would look in again the fol-lowing week.

There were no rules about this kind of thing. I knew girls who'd let the German soldiers buy them drinks all night in the cafés round Pigalle and sleep with them if they felt there was something in it for them. And there were smart ladies who sat on the terrace of the Coli-sée on the Champs-Élysées and allowed the German officers to buy them cocktails and dinners and maybe *didn't* go to bed with them. I don't know. But Sophie and I used to think they all had their price.

I wasn't going to sleep with Klaus Richter. He was married, he was German, he was twice my age. I was a young girl with no money and I'd never slept with anyone, because my parents were quite religious and wanted me to marry someone who'd look after me and that wouldn't happen if I'd slept with men before marriage. So that wasn't the problem. But there was something about Klaus Richter that I really did like. He was kind and he had such a sad face. But then again I didn't want to lead him on, I didn't want him to expect anything.

We had a long talk about it at home. Everyone had to make their own choices, and of course most of these decisions weren't about sleeping with the soldiers; they were just about saying good morning or stepping aside on the sidewalk or whether you made a point of not reading newspapers you knew were run by the Germans. But everything was run by them, really, so everyone went along to some extent. You couldn't be a hermit.

My mother was worried about me going out with any men at all. She cared a lot about modesty. She worried about me as an only child. My father asked about what other girls of my age did. My friend Yvonne Bonnet had been out with at least three German soldiers and she was quite proud of it. They'd given her presents—ribbons and combs and some bunches of flowers, nothing very much, but she liked to show them off. I was pretty sure she'd slept with them too, but I didn't say that to my parents.

Anyway, my father was a bit more easygoing than my mother. He said everyone was making up the rules as they went along, so there were no rules. Like most people then, he thought the war would soon be over. The Germans were sure to win and it was up to us to make sure we were their second-in-command in Europe afterwards. He'd had no problems with any of the Germans he'd had dealings with and he saw nothing wrong in planning ahead. He was impressed that Klaus Richter was an officer, and a major at that.

In the end he said, "We've brought you up to behave properly. Now you're twenty-two years old and we trust you. Of course your German is a proper officer, not like those men the Bonnet girl brings home. I think you should go and have a big dinner with champagne and then come home and tell us all about it. And if you can bring back a little something in your handbag, so much the better." That was Papa all over.

My mother tried one last time to stop me and talked about the Church, but I told her not to worry and I said I'd only go if he promised to have me home by ten. I was longing to be independent. I liked going to work on the Métro every day. I enjoyed wearing nice clothes and I spent time in the morning thinking about what I was going to wear. Most of my things were secondhand, but I'd saved up for a charcoal woolen skirt from our shop, because we got a good discount. It was a question of putting the right things together, fabrics and colors, and I liked it if I got the occasional admiring glance from a young man. It didn't mean anything and I wasn't a flirt. It was just that I was young and I was glad to be living in Paris, even at such a strange time. I wanted to stretch my legs, to stretch my wings.

When she talked about her clothes and going to work on the Métro, I envisaged her again as the girl I'd seen coming down the steps at Stalingrad. Not as that girl's grandmother or mother—but as one and the same person.

After I'd finished the job, I moved the new file to the center of the laptop screen. I called it "Shop Girl." I had no idea why any of it was important, let alone a contribution to "history." But my heart was full of longing for her and I felt relieved that she hadn't slept with this Nazi.

• • •

The next day I was on the late shift, so at about midday I took the Métro to Chemin Vert and cut down to the Place des Vosges. Then I walked right across the Marais, along the rue des Francs-Bourgeois. It wasn't my kind of place. It had dusty white stone buildings, expensive clothes shops and tourists. It was old, like the casbah, but not as much fun, less lively, and it was full of men holding hands—*maricones,* as my father would have called them. I went down a smaller street and I asked in a couple of falafel bars and an American diner what their rents and taxes were. The people behind the counters, one of whom was a Jew with side whiskers and a black hat, looked a bit surprised, but they gave me a rough idea or said to call back when the boss was in. By now I was feeling hungry (the fruit and bran on offer at breakfast at Hannah's didn't last the morning) and I thought that before I did my research into property rents I'd go to the favorite restaurant I'd mentioned. It was called Flunch, and it was just next to the Beaubourg building with its grim-colored plumbing.

And Flunch was a really good place. You went down some stairs into this white-tiled underground area where you could help yourself to pretty much anything. There was a grill bar and a hot-meal counter, a big range of desserts and liter cups of Fanta and Coke on draft. But the best thing was that once you'd got through the till there was a whole lot more free. So long as you'd got a main-course plate you could add spaghetti, *frites,* courgettes, rice, broccoli, meat sauce, as high as you could pile it, and the whole thing cost about what I could earn in one hour and a half at PFP.

As I was waiting at the grill bar I noticed an old man with a big white beard who was talking to himself. He was carrying an ancient leather bag in one hand and he was finding it hard to balance his tray in the other. I was carefully pushing my burger to one side of the plate to make maximum room at the free counter when I got stuck behind him. He was trying to explain to the cashier that he wasn't ready for his dessert or cheese yet (he seemed to be planning a five-course meal) and he wanted to eat his egg mayonnaise first before he put his main course on the tray.

"Do you want coffee?" she said.

"Coffee? I haven't had my soup yet," the old guy said.

The cashier only seemed to speak the lines she'd been programmed to say—do you want coffee with that, have you got a voucher—so I thought I should try to help. Eventually we managed to get the old man's piled-up tray past the till. I hadn't the heart to tell him about the free food on the other side.

He stood there looking about him with a lost expression. "I can't see a waiter to tell us where to sit," he said.

"You just sit anywhere." I took us to a vacant place.

One of the things that was great about Flunch was that it was so clean. There weren't any silly women feeding dogs at table, something that had really freaked me out at first in Paris. Also, there were plenty of people like me there, pale-skinned people from the north of Africa, as well as black-skinned men from what looked like Senegal or the Ivory Coast.

"My name is Victor Hugo," said the old guy, wiping some mayonnaise from his beard. "I appreciate your help, young man. I haven't been here before. I tried to reserve a table, but they told me it was impossible. And what's your name, may I ask?"

"Tariq Zafar."

He shook my hand. "What a fine name. Are you a Mohammedan?"

"My parents . . . In a way."

"I think there are many of your co-religionists in this restaurant. And many others who work in the neighborhood as masons and builders. I like to be among such people when I eat. People who put down cobbles in the street."

Although he seemed a bit soft in the head, he was very interested in everything going on around him. He was struck by the advertisements for Flunch itself, which said things like, *"Votre anniversaire? Il faut fluncher!"* in bright colors. He made himself chuckle a fair bit by chanting, *"Je fluncherai, tu fluncheras, il aurait dû fluncher, elles flunchèrent"* and so on.

The clothes worn by the women also seemed to fascinate him and he asked me to explain what lay behind their choice of jeans or dress or miniskirt. I told him I wasn't qualified to say, though on the Métro I'd often wondered the same thing myself. Take my Stalingrad girl, for instance—Juliette, as I now called her. When she washed and dried her hair in the morning, put on some mascara, then decided on that combination of short skirt with boots and loose coat or jacket and strode along the platform at Rambuteau or sat on the seat with the skirt riding up her thigh as she checked her phone, the clean hair falling over her cheek, did she know what an awful effect she had on the boy opposite? Had that been her thought process when she got dressed that morning? To make me and others like me suicidal with frustration, to spread despair through the city?

From this, we moved on to the question of women in general.

"In your religion a man is permitted many wives, I believe," said Victor Hugo. "I have always thought that a most sensible arrangement. And you are allowed by your holy scripture to sleep with your friends' servants, too."

I had a mental picture of Laila's housekeeper, Farida, when Victor Hugo said, "But not with your own servants, I understand."

"Certainly not," I said, picturing my parents' bad-tempered cleaner.

He was struggling with his wine bottle, so I unscrewed it for him with a snap. His eyes widened, but he said nothing.

"We have a lot to learn from other faiths," he went on, as he sipped the wine. "We are a lay republic, as you know, Monsieur Zafar. But people are still intimidated by the teaching of the Catholic Church. I find such things absurd and hypocritical. I believe in God, but not in the Church. God sent great men—writers and musicians and scholars—to be his prophets on this earth, men such as Molière and Racine, who are touched by the divine, but he did not send the parish priest. My wife and my mistress are on the best of terms. Indeed, they are going to the Comédie Française together this evening while I complete some urgent work at home. I adore them both and there is enough of me to go round."

He put down his knife and fork, drained his wineglass and said, "I think I'm ready for the coffee now. Will you join me?"

In the next half hour I learned more about the country I was living in than in all the years of my life up till then. It all made sense the way old Victor Hugo told it. From the Frankish kings and the divine anointing that made them the chosen ones, through the Revolution that had established the Rights of Man for all the world and then the desperate times when only a few good men could keep the flame of freedom alive—like the one (I didn't catch his name) who had escaped from the Siege of Paris in a hot-air balloon, carrying the spirit of France with him, a little flame that must never go out . . . And the French Revolution, he said, was "the greatest step forward taken by the human race since the advent of Christ." And it was the duty of France to bear this burden for all the world.

By the time we'd finished the coffee and agreed what an excellent restaurant it was, I found that I'd also said I'd spend the afternoon with him. More than that, I was to be his colleague or assistant in whatever "work" it was he did.

"My business is underground, Monsieur Zafar. On the metropolitan network. I hope that suits you."

"I love the Métro."

"Then we shall amuse ourselves."

We walked to Hôtel de Ville station before going below ground. Having jumped the barrier in the usual way, I had to wait while Victor

Hugo looked for his pass in the pockets of his big coat. I guessed it was some old citizen's travel permit. He looked ill at ease in the rubber-wheeled wagon with its farting pneumatic doors. He seemed to flinch at the automated announcement that told us which station was coming up next. The male announcer's voice said the name twice. At first he had a questioning note, "Châtelet?" as we began to slow down, and then, as we came into the station, he seemed to grow more confident as he said, "Châtelet," in a told-you-so way.

At Concorde we got off and followed the *correspondance* to the green line, going south. I had a quick suck on a spliff while I waited for the old man at the end of a tunnel.

"This is more like it," said Victor Hugo. "My favorite line, the famous Line Twelve. Mairie d'Issy to Porte de la Chapelle. This is the real Paris, Monsieur Zafar."

Victor Hugo put his hand into his bag and pulled out a large piece of black cloth, about two meters long. With his back to the door into the next carriage, he wrapped the cloth round the two metal uprights that standing passengers hold on to. He fastened it with a stretchy luggage clip sewn into the seam so it made a tall narrow screen. Victor Hugo was now hidden behind it, bar the toe caps of his boots. As we left Assemblée Nationale, he took out some ragged puppets from his doctor's bag and began the show, sticking the puppets over the top of the black cloth.

It started as a cops-and-robbers thing. One mangy puppet was chased by another, who wore a police hat. Victor Hugo did the voices with the cop squeaky and the robber a bit deeper and somehow sounding the nobler of the two. It was better than the beggars' speeches you usually got on the Métro, when a young man told you the story of his life, "I'm looking for work. Yes, I *know* you've heard it all before, but I only need a one-euro coin from each of you."

The people in the carriage stared at their cell phones or their books while Victor Hugo did his performance. Many of them had headphones and gave us only a glance.

After a bit of dialogue, the robber puppet gave the cop a blow on the head. Then the robber took off his mask and became an ordinary citizen. He'd gone straight, that was the idea. Then there was a female with hair made of mop ends and rouge on her cheeks, who I took to be a hooker, and her baby, whose cries Victor Hugo imitated in an old man's falsetto. People began to move down the carriage to get away from us.

Round about Sèvres-Babylone, a new male puppet appeared. It had a plastic wineglass attached to its hand and took over the baby. I thought this new one might be an innkeeper, but at this point Victor Hugo produced a hat from his doctor's bag and sent me down the carriage to collect any offerings.

I don't want to be unkind to the old man. He hadn't got much to work with and he gave it all he'd got . . . but the show was really shit. I managed to collect two euros and forty cents.

We were now passing through Volontaires and there weren't many people left on the train.

"It's time to put away our people, Monsieur Zafar," said Victor Hugo. "We can resume the story tomorrow."

"Isn't it over yet?" I said.

"No, no. The entire story takes three days from Mairie d'Issy to Porte de la Chapelle and back again." He was dropping the grimy puppets back into his bag. "You can join me tomorrow if you like. It's good to have a helper. I start at nine-thirty, when the morning rush has died down, otherwise there are people standing here, in our performance area."

The train was pulling into Vaugirard station. "I remember watching the horses being led into the slaughterhouse," said Victor Hugo. "Just above where we're sitting now. It was a fine sight. But the other butchers didn't like it. They said the dead horses made too much smell and it put people off their work. I loved a horse steak myself. Now it's a park."

He seemed to think it was a tremendous joke and chuckled away into his white, scarf-like beard, a little tear of mirth rolling down his beaten-up boxer's cheek into the mustache. "A park!" We got off at the end of the line. I made for the northbound platform to go back into town while Victor Hugo headed for the exit.

"I shall be at the table by the door at Le Comptoir d'Issy, just up here, from nine in the morning," he said. "I shall expect to see you. Until tomorrow, Monsieur Zafar."

It seemed to take ages for a train to come and I was starting to feel a bit spaced out. This may have been from Jamal's weed, which was unpredictable, I'd found. There was also something about being with Victor Hugo that had unsettled me.

When you're young, when you're a child, you're quite used to not understanding things. Gravity, how to read music, how planes stay up, computer code . . . Everyone's been a child, everyone starts out ignorant. But you don't fret about any of this because there are things that seem more important, like how am I going to pass this exam and why can't I sit up late and drink beer. You'll get round to knowing the hard stuff one day. And yes, my life was none the worse for the fact that I wouldn't be able to rewire a house. There were people to do that for you. Outside the gates of the medina you could see them lined up in the morning. A painter with his pots, an electrician with his rolls of wire and the plumber with his taps and rubber piping all attached to his rickety bicycle. They sat cross-legged on the curb outside the café drinking mint tea, hoping for work. And I knew that my father, Mr. Wise Guy himself, would go to his grave with no idea of even how a simple transistor radio worked.

My problem in Paris that day with Victor Hugo was that it struck me I was going to be twenty any moment, and some of the knowledge gaps could no longer be forgiven. It was starting to be a cop-out to say, I live my own life and I mind my own business.

And that was why as I sat in the empty station at the end of the line, I became aware that knowing so little was starting to make me feel sick.

Eventually the train rattled in and I sat down alone in a dusty carriage. There was nothing much to look at. Above some seats near the door was a notice that said these places were reserved, then gave a list of who was entitled to them—in order. First were the war-wounded, the *mutilés de guerre*. Then *aveugles civils* (people blinded by heredity or illness, not by enemy fire, presumably), then pregnant women and those accompanied by children of less than five years old. I wondered why Parisians needed to be reminded of simple manners and why this was the first time I'd noticed the announcement. Then I wondered what conflict the men might have been wounded in. Had France been in a war recently? I felt another spasm of my new discomfort—the shame of not knowing.

The carriage door was pulled open at the next station by a man of about forty with a briefcase. Normally you lifted a latch and the doors powered apart automatically with a hydraulic belch. (Or did I mean "pneumatic" belch? God, I didn't know *anything*.) The door latch on this bit of rolling stock had no spring, it was like the closing of an old iron gate, and the man had pulled the doors apart with his own hands. Someone farther down the carriage was smoking, knocking his ash onto the slatted wooden floor. When I got out at Sèvres-Babylone to change lines, I had to walk along beside the train. Most of the carriages were green, but towards the front there was a red one: First Class. Its windows were cloudy, but it seemed to have only men inside, a huddle of overcoats.

Then, instead of taking the *correspondance* and heading east, I decided to go up and get some air to clear my head. At the end of the platform was a door with the notice *"Au delà de cette limite votre billet n'est plus valide,"* beyond this point your ticket is no longer valid. As I climbed the steps on the other side of the barrier I saw a drift of abandoned tickets, many of them folded into the familiar "V" shape.

I was glad to be up on the street, even if it was only Raspail, the bully of the Left Bank boulevards. For a moment I stopped to get my bearings. I looked up and found myself opposite a large hotel called the Lutetia.

Suddenly I had to lean against the wall to keep from falling. I was bent by a spasm of homesickness—for the sound of the muezzin's tinny loudspeaker call, for the whitewash of our house and the sparrows in the light well.

Poissonnière

THERE WAS A PHONE MESSAGE FROM JULIAN WHEN I GOT HOME ONE day. "I've been in touch with Leo Busch at the Centre Jean Molland and he was very helpful. I ended up going there myself and made a few photocopies. They took photographs of most of the people who gave spoken testimony. There's one of Juliette Lemaire as an old woman, must have been taken when she made the recording, but she also gave them a picture of herself during the war. I saw a snap of Mathilde Masson too. Leo says he thinks she's still alive. Mathilde, that is. He wouldn't give me her address, but he said if you could assure him of your good faith or something, he'd contact her on your behalf. I told him you were the very definition of good faith, but he needs to hear it from you in person. Plus some ID or letter from your professor, I think. E-mail would do. I can drop the photographs round if you'd like to have dinner one evening. Let me know."

It was typical of Julian to try to squeeze a date out of it, I thought. But when, after an early evening bath, I got dressed in a black woolen skirt and a dark-green sweater I'd bought that day, I found I was almost looking forward to it. Julian had chosen a hipster place in rue Saulnier; he told me it was "important" to go there because they distilled their own gin. After some thought I also put on some tourmaline earrings and a touch of lipstick.

The restaurant turned out to be almost next door to the Folies

Bergère. "So. Frilly underwear and moonshine liquor," I said as Julian brushed his cheek against mine. "Your dream destination, Julian."

"Have a drink. They recommend you have their gin with soda, not tonic. But try not to enjoy it too much."

"I'll try. And that's enough about my puritanical leanings."

"But I've only just . . . All right. I like that sweater, by the way. Is it new?"

"Thank you. Please make the gin a big one."

Rue Saulnier was a dingy street, but in the light of April we were able to sit outside, beneath a blue awning.

"Are you still in the sound archive?" said Julian.

"Yes. I've heard about twenty women now. It's a good collection, but I got a little sidetracked and I started to read about the Resistance. I'm not sure how relevant it was to the life of the average woman in Paris."

"Very little, I'd guess," said Julian. "I think after the Liberation, de Gaulle gave medals to everyone who'd said *bonjour* to an Allied soldier, and it came to about three percent of the population. Which by coincidence was the same number who volunteered for the other side—for Vichy organizations like the Milice. And I guess that was representative of the whole country. At the start it was mostly pro-German, but by the end it was divided down the middle."

"It's not really the active numbers that interest me," I said. "It's more the question of attitude. Everyone must have had a view. They all cared about their own lives, their own country."

"Most people's view was that they wanted the war to be over, I think," said Julian. "That's what my first-ever landlady told me. And they passively supported whatever means would bring that end about most quickly. First the Germans and Vichy. Then, when that wasn't working out, the Allies and the Resistance. Like François Mitterrand. Change horses, back the winner noisily and cover up your false start. Then deny you changed and keep on denying it until the clamor dies down."

"That sounds cynical."

"Some people were. Not all by any means. The most cynical thing was to present your cynicism as inevitable. Even in some odd way as principled. *C'est normal.* That took some nerve, I guess."

"I'm sure it was harder for women," I said. "With so many men away in prisoner-of-war camps or going to work in German factories. And women in all the worst jobs, making less money and having to feed a family."

"Yes, I think they had a harder life for sure."

"You agree with me, then?"

"I do."

"Is this a first?"

"It could be. It's also why I'm looking forward to reading what you come up with. Don't make it all footnotes and sources, though."

"There are certain protocols."

"I know, I know. It's getting cold. Shall we go inside to eat?"

The menu was minimal. Cauliflower, sweetbreads, salmon and pork were on offer, but only in a single word, with no suggestion of how they might be prepared.

"Does it make you long for Mom's turkey and ice cream?"

"Mom's meatloaf maybe. I'll go with the salmon."

Julian chatted with the waitress in his annoyingly good French and chose the wine she recommended.

"You're such a flirt," I said, as the young woman disappeared.

"I was just being polite. And she was nice, wasn't she? I think the day of the surly Paris waiter is over." He poured some water. "You know when we had lunch last time and we talked a bit about that SOE group, Prosper? I've read a bit more about them."

"Really?"

"Not just out of politeness. I was intrigued."

"It *is* interesting. I've become fascinated by the courier, Andrée Borrel."

"She was quite a character, wasn't she? Very active. Bicycles, mountain walking. Her sister called her a *garçon manqué*. I think she was sleeping with the wireless operator."

"Is that important?"

"Maybe it was to her. You never knew if it was going to be your last day before the Gestapo knocked at the door and took you off to Avenue Foch."

"I thought the Gestapo were in the Hôtel Lutetia."

"Strictly speaking that was the Abwehr, the counterintelligence service. Avenue Foch was home to the Sicherheitsdienst, who were part of the SS, while the Gestapo—"

"Poor Andrée."

"Yes. She had maybe eighteen different security organizations, French and German, to deal with. I think he was quite dashing, the radio guy, by the way. Don't look so doubtful."

"That wasn't what was significant about Andrée."

"I know. She was a brave and idealistic woman who died an appalling death. I do understand that. I wish there were a biography of her."

There was something earnest, almost pleading, in the way Julian looked at me that I hadn't seen before. At the end of dinner, he discovered that he'd left the photographs of Mathilde and Juliette at his flat.

"Come back and have a brandy. It's only two minutes' walk."

"Is it? To Strasbourg–Saint-Denis?"

"You must have gone past it."

"No. I took the Métro to Poissonnière because it's on the line from Tolbiac."

"Blimey, that's a long way round."

I began to laugh. "Where do you find these words?"

"'A long way round?' That's—"

"No. 'Blimey.'"

"It's part of being English. Along with a high tolerance of uncarbonated beer. And outdoor theater."

Julian opened a door off the cobbled street next to an Alsatian brasserie. His apartment was two floors up; the hall gave onto a large, parquet-floored living room with a piano and hundreds of books on shelves and tables or piled up on the floor. The furniture was old and covered in woolen rugs and throws; the ocher-tinted light came from lamps with red and orange shades. There was a framed nineteenth-century print of an effete-looking man I took to be Alfred de Musset. The room was scruffy, but the effect was quite pleasant, I had to admit; there were not as many socks and tennis shoes lying about as I'd somehow expected.

"Did you tidy up specially?" I asked when I got back from the bathroom (unmodernized, but surprisingly clean).

"No. I wasn't expecting anyone."

"You didn't forget the photographs—"

"On purpose? No. Genuine half-wittedness. Try this." He handed me a glass of brandy with water. "It's *fine à l'eau*. Hemingway was always banging on about it. Have you ever been to the Closerie des Lilas?"

"Ten years ago I used to walk by sometimes and peer inside and imagine him there. But I couldn't afford to go in."

"It's not too bad if you go to the bar bit, not the restaurant. When I was in disgrace with Sylvie, I used to spend whole afternoons there with the *plat du jour* and a glass of Côtes du Rhône. I'd read a book and spin it out for hours. I'll take you there one day. Here. Have a look at these pictures. This is Juliette Lemaire as an old woman."

He handed me a photocopied image of a white-haired woman in a cardigan with a printed silk scarf tied at the neck. She was smiling, weakly, but with goodwill in her eyes.

"She looks nice."

"And here she is in 1942."

"Oh my God." For a moment I think I stopped breathing. "This must be her friend Sophie with her. This is the rue de Rivoli, isn't it?"

"I think so. That colonnade. The Nazi flag. And the shop looks like it."

"My God, she's so . . ."

The young Juliette was coltish, her tailored dress cut short to show off her legs in their silk stockings. Her hair was not curled with a parting, like Sophie's, but left long and free, almost to the shoulders. She had dark lipstick. A leather bag hung on a long strap from her shoulder. Her eyes were engaged with the camera, smiling at whoever might see her in the years after the shutter closed; she was a girl with nothing to fear.

I surreptitiously wiped away a tear from the corner of my eye. Julian took back the piece of paper and handed me another one.

"And this is Mathilde. It's dated 1998, which I guess is when she did her recording."

Mathilde Masson, the child of Belleville, had a broad face and small, pugnacious eyes. At the age of eighty, her hair was still dark, probably dyed. It was wiry, held in check by grips and slides. She had lipstick and some black coloring round the eyes. The gaze was neither kind nor cowed.

I exhaled as I handed back the piece of paper.

"You can keep them," said Julian.

"Thank you. I like your apartment."

"It's on an eight-year lease. But there's only three years left."

"Was that part of the divorce?"

"It was complicated." He sat down on a velvet-covered couch, facing me. "Sylvie had much more money than I did and it didn't seem right to sell her flat in the rue des Marronniers. So I just got this lease."

"So she got to keep the family home and you have the garret with the smell of sauerkraut."

"Have you noticed? I think I'm used to it now. They're very nice people. I often go down and eat at the bar there."

"It doesn't seem quite fair."

"You think I should have asked for 'alimony' and all that? I didn't feel entitled to what Sylvie had inherited from her family. And I like this flat."

I sipped the *fine à l'eau*, which was both fiery and weak. "What was the final straw between you? But don't tell me if you think it's . . . inappropriate."

Julian laughed. "What a choice of word."

"Was it one of those pretty Dutch students?"

"God no. In eight years of marriage I had only one lapse. At a conference in Berlin. One night. Even then I didn't sleep with her. Just . . . messed about a bit. Apart from that . . . Nothing. Not even flirtations."

"So what was it?"

"Well . . . I suppose I may as well tell you. If we're going to be friends?"

"I hope so."

"Sylvie had been sleeping with one of her colleagues for five years. As well as with a gallery owner in the Marais, and—"

"The one where she picked up the masterpiece for nothing?"

"Indeed. And with her childhood boyfriend. And with the lifeguard at the Keller public swimming pool just over the Pont de Grenelle."

"My God, Julian."

"Yes, I was pretty shocked too. She had what you might call a need. I mean, these were the ones she told me about. It's rather like a criminal who knows he's going to jail asking for other crimes to be 'taken into consideration.' She wanted to get these names out there so there'd be no further proceedings. But I'm pretty sure there were others."

"That must have been hard."

"For a time. I was in shock. My life didn't seem to make sense. But in the end I came to admire her, really. She did what she had to do. She wasn't designed for marriage. Not to me, anyway."

"And are you . . . You know, do you speak to each other?"

"There's no need. We have no children. But I see her occasionally and I find myself being polite. Friendly, I suppose you'd call it."

"And Sylvie?"

"She looks a little . . . underfed. Chic, but hungry. But she also looks happier than before. She smiles more and smokes less. So that's something."

We carried on talking till nearly one o'clock, when we went down onto the rue du Faubourg Saint-Denis. Julian pulled over a cab and briefly hugged me before opening the car door. The embrace was so brief that for a moment I wondered if I'd upset him.

• • •

The next day at the Centre Jean Molland, I called up the last of Mathilde Masson's audio files. I'd brought Julian's photocopied piece of paper with me and gazed at the old woman's face as I listened.

I was tormented by what Louise said about Armand and the girl. I decided I had to have it out with him. So the next Sunday when we were having our walk in the Buttes-Chaumont I said, "A little bird told me you were seeing a lot of a girl who works in the Resistance."

He looked put out. "Who told you?" he said. "I'm not supposed to be seen with anyone. Who told you?"

And I said, "I'm not giving names. But she said you seemed very close." And Armand said, "Of course we're close. We trust each other with our lives." And I said, "No. I mean, close like we are. You and me."

Then he started patting me on the hand and telling me I was talking nonsense. He said he was sorry for the times he hadn't been free to take me out, but it was all very important and soon the Americans would come to France and then the Resistance would help and then we'd get married. He promised me there was nothing between him and any other girl.

I wasn't taken in. "So there is a girl in your group," I said. "What's her name?" He said he didn't know her real name but she was known as "Simone." I asked what she looked like, and he wasn't sure whether he should tell me. Then I got angry and I said, "You're my fiancé. You have to tell me. What's the matter? Don't you trust me?" And he said she was unusually tall and often wore a beret to cover her hair, which was blond. But maybe it was dyed and it might be a different color by now.

So I said, "Is she French? Or is she a foreign spy?" And Armand said she was French, she came from a village near Nantes. She'd worked as a pharmacist's assistant. He said she was very committed to the struggle and that she'd done some sabotage in the Loire region.

We were walking over a bridge by the waterfall next to a funny little building with stone pillars. I'll never forget it. I could feel my life ending. I didn't trust him. Armand. The only man who'd ever shown me any kindness. The man I loved. I couldn't trust him anymore.

And I panicked. I wanted to get away from him. I started to run. Armand was calling out to me and started to run after me, but I screamed at him to leave me alone. I ran to a Métro station and caught the first train I could. I didn't know where I was going.

When I next had time off work, I went to the Café Victor Hugo, where Armand had been seen with the girl. I went inside and saw that the *patron* was working behind the bar. I showed him a photograph of Armand that I carried in my bag and asked if he'd seen him. He said, "You're Louise's sister, aren't you? I remember when she first brought you in, when you were little."

Then he looked at the picture and said, "Yes, I think he's been here." And I said, "Was he with a tall woman? Maybe she was wearing a beret. Probably with blond hair."

Monsieur Hugo laughed and said, "What do you mean 'probably?'" And I said, "I think she changes the color quite often." He was wiping down the top of the bar. "Yes, I remember her. They were whispering together. Lovers' talk, I suppose. I remember thinking he was much shorter than she was—that's why I remember them." Then he laughed into his big white beard and said, "Tell Louise I've got some apple tarts coming in tomorrow."

Well, I couldn't keep going back on the off chance that the girl would be there. I had a job in a factory in rue d'Angoulême on the other side of the Boulevard de Belleville, and I only had Sunday off work. But my day finished before Armand's and I knew where his office was, near the Opéra, so I could follow him and see if he met her again. I suppose it sounds mad now, but I can't explain how much

I hated this Simone bitch. I didn't care what her beliefs were or how brave she was or anything like that. I couldn't bear the thought of her opening her legs to him. I'd done it, sex, with Armand. I know we weren't married and everything, but we'd been careful and it meant a lot to us. And I thought of this girl, and to her my little Armand was probably just a toy. She did it to amuse herself. And would she have taken care of him anyway, made sure his glasses didn't get broken, made his coffee the way he liked it?

One night after work I sat in the window of a café in the rue Cambon, which was a very expensive street that I couldn't afford—it was full of smart clothes shops. That slut Chanel had her shop there. She was sleeping with German officers in the Ritz all through the war, Louise told me, and getting her pick of paintings and furniture from Jewish flats she'd informed about. I had to be careful to drink only one small coffee; I didn't even ask for a glass of water, and the waiter kept looking at my shabby coat. But I had a view of the front door of Armand's office, and the light in the café was dim so I knew he wouldn't see me. He was supposed to finish at five-thirty but he often stayed late. Eventually he came out and began to walk quickly up the boulevard. It was a time of year I like, and the trees should have been in blossom, but they'd all been cut down for firewood and the buildings alongside were stained black by the cheap fuel. It's funny how you remember these things. Then he went up rue de Sèze to Madeleine, where he went down into the Métro.

It was good to get down there. By this time walking on the street for more than five minutes was suspicious. On the Métro the police could check your papers easily, so that's how you traveled if you had nothing to hide.

Armand was buried in the evening paper and he wasn't looking around at all. It was as though he wanted not to meet anyone's eye, and that made it easier for me. We went about ten stations up the line, past Pigalle, though I don't remember where he got off, maybe Jules Joffrin.

He still didn't look around; he scuttled off and I had to hurry to keep up. I knew he wouldn't look back, because that would have been suspicious. A German soldier got out of the front carriage, the red one. There were other Germans inside and Armand must have seen them.

Up on the street, he kept moving fast with his head down, not looking back.

We were in Montmartre, a part of the city I didn't know at all, but I guessed he was going to meet Simone and the other people in their group. It was an odd-looking place he stopped at. It didn't look like the normal apartment buildings in Paris, if you know what I mean. It looked a different-color stone; it looked foreign, Russian or something. This was in rue Damrémont, I think. The front door opened very quickly—I think he used a latchkey—then he was gone.

There wasn't a café in the right place this time, so I just had to walk up and down on the sidewalk opposite. It was dark by now and, as I said, I didn't know the area, and in those days a girl couldn't be alone at night without people getting the wrong idea. Then there was the question of the curfew, and you couldn't be out at all after that.

So I walked up and down the street for ages, pretending to look into shop windows. A couple of men made remarks, but nothing much. As it got close to the curfew I knew I'd either have to go home or find somewhere to stay. I didn't have the money for a room, but I went into the nearest café-bar and asked to speak to the owner. I gave him a hard-luck story about how my husband had taken all my money and I couldn't get home. I said I'd sweep and clean and wash all the dishes if he let me sleep in a back room or even on the floor. He went and spoke to his wife and she gave me a cloth and a mop and told me to get working. I said I'd start after curfew. If Armand hadn't come out by then, he'd have to spend the night. I knew he wouldn't risk being seen.

I watched the door of the building but no one came out. I just hoped he hadn't gone out through a back entrance. Then I went back to the café and began to work. I swept the floor clean of all the ash and broken glass. It was made of red tiles, I can still remember it. Then I scrubbed it on my hands and knees, and with each movement of the hard brush I imagined the floor was *her* face and I was tearing off the skin.

What right had this woman to steal Armand? I didn't go around Paris sleeping with different men, taking other women's husbands. I wanted just one man. And I was the only one who understood him and knew how to look after him. I hadn't asked much from life; he was all I'd ever had.

The owner's wife said I could stop cleaning, because they were going to bed. She showed me a small sitting room in the back and said I could sleep on the couch. She was all right. She was a bit suspicious, but she could see I'd done a good job. She brought me a carafe of water and a glass and there was some bread and a small piece of ham left over at the bar, which she said I could have. There was no butter; there never was.

Although the couch was quite comfortable I didn't sleep at all, because I was frightened of sleeping past five in the morning, when the curfew ended. I got up and went back to the bar and polished some more glasses and wiped all the sticky stuff off the bottles and put them back neatly, then tidied the shelves. I watched the clock above the bar.

It was still dark when I went down the back corridor and opened the door at the end. It wasn't very nice, two footprints and a hole and a tiny sink and it hadn't been cleaned for a long time, but I washed as well as I could in cold water and tried to comb my hair. At about two minutes past five I let myself out of the bar and onto the street.

For about an hour I hung around opposite the building Armand had gone in, and this time the door did open. Two people came out. They were Armand and a tall woman and they began to walk quickly down the street, arm in arm.

They went down into the Métro and I followed them, but they weren't interested in anyone else, so it was easy. They got out at Saint-Georges and walked for about ten minutes till they came to rue Milton, on the other side of the rue des Martyrs. Outside a small apartment building, they stopped and he kissed her on the lips. She clung on to him for a bit, then opened the front door with a key and went inside. A minute later I saw a second-floor light come on.

Armand turned and walked down the hill. I slumped to the ground, with my back to a wall. I stayed sitting for a long time. Eventually I managed to stand up and dust myself down. I'd been sitting against the wall of an elementary school. I looked across the street to take a note of the number above her door.

The next day I went to the prefect of police in Belleville and reported an enemy of the French state living on the second floor, at number 12, rue Milton, Ninth arrondissement.

Censier-Daubenton

Hasim had second thoughts about a new restaurant in the Marais when I told him how much it was likely to cost in rent and taxes.

"I think it's just that area," I said. "There's plenty of cheaper parts of town, I'm sure. Near where I live in the Thirteenth, for a start. Or somewhere out by the Périphérique."

"You can't charge enough in those places. It needs to be somewhere that people pay a lot. Saint-Germain-des-Prés. They charge tourists eight euros for coffee there."

Business plans were not my strong point, so I left him to it. I was beginning to be sick of PFP. Although the money wasn't bad, the shifts were long, Hasim was depressed and the work was revolting. The many hours there also prevented me from searching for whatever it was I'd come to Paris to discover.

There was no doubt that I'd been quite lucky to find both a job and a place to live. Maybe it was because I didn't try too hard. This was a part of my character that annoyed my father. "You just drift along expecting things to fall into your lap. You've got to engage with life," he told me. For some reason, things tended not to have a big impact on me. I wasn't scared to ask the shopkeepers of the Marais about their overheads and I'd volunteered to deliver fried-chicken pieces to the frightening *cités* of the *banlieue*, because I trusted to my own luck. If some badass gang leader threatened me, I'd just run. I was quick enough on my feet. Maybe this was something to do with being nineteen, though I was beginning to wonder if I ought occasionally to worry a little more. Not as much as Hannah, who seemed on the edge of a nervous breakdown from listening to a sound recording, but just a bit. The only thing that made me feel really uneasy was how little I'd been able to imagine my mother and her life in Paris. Had she lived among the North Africans in Saint-Denis or in some other ghetto? I didn't think so. Her father was a Frenchman, and I pictured them in one of those typical *immeubles,* a little shabby, on the fifth floor with a balcony.

I wished now that when I'd left Clémence's apartment that afternoon I'd made some arrangement to see her again. At the time I wasn't thinking straight at all. I'd stumbled out onto the street with my head whirling. It was partly the nature of what she'd told me. To think that those events had taken place just across the road from where we sat in her old-fashioned *salon* drinking mint tea. That the people who herded them in and locked them up, then put them on buses, were not Germans with guns and dogs but the gendarmes they saw every day on the street. I decided that I needed to find out more. Feeling a little self-conscious, as though my father were watching and applauding, I embarked for the first time on some "research." Only on the Internet, admittedly—but I read that later in the war the velodrome had seen recruitment rallies for young men who wanted to work for something called the Milice, which as far as I could make out was a force of uniformed thugs put together by the French government to do the Germans' dirty work. So . . . No more family picnics at the velodrome watching the cyclists whiz round the banked wooden track. It was no wonder that a few years later they pulled the whole place down. You wouldn't want those memories to spoil a big sporting event. Frozen fireballs.

But more than what Clémence had told me, it was the *way* she spoke that had shaken me. The strange familiarity that was almost tenderness. And I couldn't put it all down to Jamal's weed, because I hadn't smoked for a few days. (We were waiting for a new consignment from Jamal's man. He lived out in some high-rise in Sarcelles where Jamal wasn't keen to pay a call.)

Meanwhile, it was getting close to my birthday and I thought I should mark the day. It wasn't that I was proud of having clocked up another year of not having slept with a woman. (Twenty I was now. It was getting to be ridiculous.) No. It was more that I thought I should ask Hannah out to say thank you for having let me stay in her storeroom all this time. And it was a chance to go somewhere a bit less greasy than PFP and to give Hannah a break from the permanently closed restaurants of Butte-aux-Cailles and wherever it was she went during the day to listen to her old ladies.

In my wanderings I'd gone just off the Boulevard Haussmann one day, into the rue Vivienne. It was too expensive for me, but right in the middle I'd spotted a wine bar whose blue awning said VINS, TAPAS, ESPACE D'ART. I didn't drink wine and I knew nothing about art, but I liked tapas. We had them at home sometimes (there were a few Spanish places in the Ville Nouvelle that Laila and I had been to after lectures) and the good thing about tapas was that they were cheap—olives, hard cheese on a stick, fried squid rings and little gray anchovies. Even the omelet with potato bits that Laila loved was not expensive. Hannah was sure to be on some sort of diet, too, so if I had a smoke first, then drank Coke it really wouldn't cost much. I could ask Jamal and Hasim and maybe tell my landlady she could bring a date to make up the numbers.

The next time we were both at home, I suggested it. "You can ask your boyfriend," I said.

"I don't have a boyfriend," said Hannah.

"What about that man you're always having dinner with, Julian?"

"He's not my boyfriend. He's a Brit. He's just an old acquaintance. But you should ask people. It's your party."

"I don't know anyone in Paris." Baco? Not a party type. Clémence? The masseuse from . . .

"What about your friend Sandrine?" said Hannah. "Remember her?"

"I don't know how to find her," I said. "It's weird, she was part of my life, night and day, for a really important week or so and then . . . Nothing."

"Life's like that, I'm afraid. Some chance meetings shape your whole existence. Others have no meaning at all."

"She didn't even leave an e-mail."

"There'll be more encounters like that," said Hannah. "Random. If you don't like it, you can always believe in an afterlife, or an endless number of lives, in which case these people will turn out to have a role. Their purpose will become clear. Or you can just let them go. Say thank you to your god or your destiny for having met them. Then . . . Gone."

Not sure where she was going with this conversation, I said, "Anyway, I'm asking the people from work, Hasim and Jamal."

"Will they come?"

"Probably not." It was starting to look like the smallest party in town. "But you can ask anyone, Hannah. Think. Who in the world would you most like to see?"

"I guess it would be Jasmine Mendel. She's my best friend. I was at college with her. I think I told you."

"Send her an e-mail."

"I don't think she'd fly over from New York for tapas."

"I'd buy dessert as well."

• • •

A great deal of my day in Paris, I think it's fair to say, was spent just wandering round. That's why I felt sorry for the young men from the high-rises who dared go only as far as the Gare du Nord and strike a few poses before scuttling home. But there was nothing to be frightened of in Paris. You could go anywhere you liked—all the smartest bits, the most Catholic or old French, places called Faubourg or Royal, it didn't matter. You couldn't afford to *buy* anything, but you could still walk along and gaze through the shop windows and read the menus of restaurants that charged 125 euros for dinner. This freedom was one of the things I liked most, and because I'd never been to a big city before it took me by surprise. In the movies I'd seen, New York was full of gangsters, alien invaders or explosions. There probably *were* films of people going shopping and meeting friends in a bar, but I'd never seen one of those. And my idea of Los Angeles was of a place of guard dogs where the lawns had a notice saying ARMED RESPONSE and you had to be worth a million dollars to get a cab into Beverly Hills. Either that or a drug district where you got murdered. So to be able to wander free down some streets that even I'd heard of, like the Champs-Élysées, was a thrill. And I discovered cinemas that didn't show just superheroes or cartoons, but films with men and women doing ordinary stuff. Some of these were boring, I admit, and some of them were filthy in a surprising way—you'd suddenly get a close-up of a druggy man's *zib* or a woman cutting a bit off her *qooq* (these Catholic directors like to shock you, I think). I wouldn't say I enjoyed any of the films that much, but I'd never seen anything like them at home and I felt glad they were there—for me and a few others in the afternoon.

Trying to get up the courage to tell Hasim I wasn't going to work at PFP anymore was difficult. For some reason I thought they'd want to keep me on and they'd make a fuss and maybe threaten to report me to the police for having no papers. But if I failed to turn up to work one day, that might make them feel more like getting rid of me. So early one morning, when I should have been on the Métro to Saint-Denis, I zipped over on Line 6, Direction Charles de Gaulle–Étoile, and switched onto Line 12 down to Mairie d'Issy.

It took me a moment once I was up in the open air to get my bearings. I'd expected an end-of-the-line *banlieue*, a ghetto of one nationality, maybe Colombians, Poles—Pygmies for all I knew, with every shop offering weird meat and money orders home. In fact, it was at a junction of five streets, open and bright, where most of the people could have passed for French. I spotted Le Comptoir d'Issy, a slightly upmarket place, and when I pushed open the door, I saw the figure of Victor Hugo sitting by the door, next to the coat stand, with his old doctor's bag in his lap.

"Monsieur Zafar, good morning. Allow me to buy you some coffee before we set off. I thought you'd be back. Curious to know how the story goes on, are you?"

"Yes," I lied. "Thank you."

"I have a fancy for Line Seven today. The travelers of Line Twelve are starting to know my tale too well. We shall have to change at Madeleine. Are you familiar with it? The church?"

"No."

"Never mind. We change again at Pyramides and then we can take our time as we travel to Porte de la Villette. I am considerably further on in the story than when we last met. I shall endeavor to fill you in while the train is stationary."

"Don't worry, I'm sure I can pick it up as we go along."

There was the usual going through the pockets of his overcoat as Victor Hugo searched for his Métro pass while I waited on the other side of the barrier (I'd recently taken to buying tickets from my wages), but we got there in the end and were able to set up shop in a clean carriage leaving Pyramides.

It turns out I'd missed too much of the story to be able to make much sense of it. The character with the wineglass, the innkeeper, as I thought of him, seemed to have turned out a thoroughly bad man. The policeman was back on the scene, still pursuing the criminal-turned-hero.

At Opéra, old Victor began to tell me another tale. At first, I wasn't sure if it was part of the puppet story or not.

"The Opéra, Monsieur Zafar. It was the building in Paris that Adolf Hitler most coveted. He spent only one day in Paris after the Germans had occupied it. A simple tourist's *Rundfahrt,* as he himself might have said. But it was the Opéra he instructed his architects in Berlin to imitate.

"Of course, this was before the ceiling had been redecorated by a Russian Jew. The Opéra itself was considered the high point of the redesign of Paris by the vandal Baron Haussmann, who tore down the old streets and replaced them with vistas that all looked the same. The Opéra itself smacked of the Teutonic, so it was not surprising that it was the place Herr Hitler most admired."

There was quite a bit more of this while the train was held. Eventually, he got back to his story about the ceiling. "So, forty years ago, they decided to smarten up the Opéra inside. They commissioned an elderly Russian painter called Chagall. For months he lay on his back on top of a scaffold, for all the world like Michelangelo in the Sistine Chapel, painting away. And for months he went to the same café for lunch in his paint-spattered overalls. One day, the *patron* finally said, 'I see you are a decorator, Monsieur.' And Chagall nodded. The *patron* said, 'And what is your specialty? Outdoors? Masonry? Walls?' And Monsieur Chagall thought for a long time, then said, 'Ceilings.'"

Victor Hugo was still chuckling away into his beard at the Gare de L'Est and seemed to have lost interest in his own tale. He was talking a lot about the sewers of Paris, which he called the "intestines of the Leviathan" and a new group of threadbare puppets he'd pulled out of his bag called "Les ABC." Every time he used the word "ABC" he gave me a dig in the ribs, to signal some sort of joke, and eventually I understood that it sounded the same as the word *"abaissé,"* meaning "debased," I suppose, or "low grade." Well, they'd certainly come out of the bottom of the bag.

We got off at the end of the line, which was my old friend La Courneuve–8 Mai 1945. Victor Hugo, I'd gathered by now, didn't recognize the stops where a line had been extended, so for him Line 7 stopped at Porte de la Villette. Anyway, we switched platforms and took the southbound train and he more or less got his performance back on track, with gunshots and fighting in the street, though this was hard to conjure up with no props for barricades.

For some reason the travelers on Line 7 south were in a generous mood and I collected enough money after Censier-Daubenton to pay for lunch at a Chinese restaurant near Les Olympiades—one that old Baco had once recommended. Victor Hugo said he'd never eaten food from China before. He seemed surprised that China *had* food. A waiter banged down a teapot and some small cups, then brought a pile of baskets with bits of steamed things inside. Some smelled of fish. One that was easy to recognize was a dish of chicken feet (rejects from PFP, perhaps). There was a bowl of rice and soy sauce in another pot. I tried to show Victor Hugo how to use his chopsticks, but he kept firing the food over the paper cloth. He did get a grayish bag of something up to his lips, but it burst and spread its gloop into his beard.

"We must not despair, Monsieur Zafar," he said. "I shall approach like Napoleon at Austerlitz. I shall feign weakness to draw the enemy on, then take their center by surprise. What is this sauce? A beef stock?"

"Soy," I said.

"I beg your pardon?"

"Soya beans. Fermented, I suppose."

"How ingenious!" he said. "And I can see that these are the feet of barnyard fowls."

"Yes, I wouldn't have those."

But he'd balanced one on his chopsticks and was nibbling at the end where the nail was.

"And does the Chinaman take wine with his lunch?"

I picked up the laminated menu. It looked like a no. "Would you like some Coca-Cola?"

"No, thank you."

Some parts of the lunch were not too bad and it went better for

Victor Hugo when he gave up the chopsticks and used the serving spoon instead. "Most ingenious," he kept saying as he took the lid off another small basket and sniffed its contents, but I didn't think he'd become a regular at the Dragon Vert.

The sun was shining when we parted as the best of friends near the wavy-roofed pagodas of the Olympiades. I didn't make a date to meet again, but I may have left the impression that I'd get down to Le Comptoir d'Issy one day soon.

What I was really wondering as the old man disappeared with his props was whether I'd be able to find Beijing Beauté Massage and reach the end without being interrupted by a howling baby. But that moment I noticed that my phone, which hadn't been working underground, was vibrating in my pocket. I turned down the call, but listened to the message, which was Hasim telling me that if I didn't get myself up to Saint-Denis he would perform a certain act on my mother. My grasp of his brand of Algerian Arabic wasn't great, but I'm pretty sure what he threatened was illegal.

• • •

It was a warm day late in May and there was blossom on the trees, so I decided to walk for a bit. From the Place d'Italie I took Avenue des Gobelins going north, towards the center of the city. You wouldn't want to go south, obviously, or you'd get back to Maison Blanche and Maurice the lorry driver, with his giveaway pedo shirt-and-tie. How many miles had he put on the clock of his Iveco since I'd been in Paris? Back and forth with only French pop music for company—plus any young people he might have picked up at the roadside.

And weird Sandrine. Not that I really understood any of the people I'd met in France. Not just Sandrine, but Hannah, Victor Hugo, Jamal, Clémence . . . The only halfway-ordinary guy I'd met was Hasim. It wasn't that he and I were similar. I hadn't screwed up my life by starting a terrible restaurant in a sad suburb attached to a city I didn't dare go into. I wasn't all hung up on religion and race and history and marriage and whatever else was making him look so down in the mouth. I liked the country I came from. I missed it. And as for Paris, I liked that too and I had no fear of walking down its Frenchest streets. But what I mean is, the way that Hasim's mind worked was clear to me. Life had pissed him out of a camel's cock, as he might have put it, but he had to make a living and a life in a two-room flat on the eighteenth floor in the frozen fireball of Medina-sur-Seine.

It was odd. He and Jamal both spoke French as their first language, but they hated the country and the old-style French people they called *fils de Clovis* (meaning, as Victor had explained, that they were descended from the first divinely anointed king of France, white man Clovis). They also hated the Jews, which was the main reason Jamal disliked the idea of the Marais. It was not that they'd actually met any Jews, because there were none in Saint-Denis or in any other part of the *banlieue*. I'd once asked Jamal why this was and he just grunted. "They can't live here. It would end badly. They know that."

At the top of Avenue des Gobelins, as part of my decision to know and understand more, I made an effort to take in my surroundings. I could see a tall, domed building on what looked like a hill—and a hill, or a *butte* as the locals call it, is a rare thing in Paris, so I thought I'd make for it. I took a few random turns and the streets became narrower and one or two had cobbles, I was proud of noticing. At one point, on rue du Cardinal Lemoine, the road fell quite steeply towards the Seine. I could see over to the other side of the river, past where my favorite Flunch must be, near the Beaubourg thing, then on past the Opéra, up, up, as the ground rose towards Pigalle, over Montmartre and right up to the tower blocks of Saint-Denis and Sarcelles, which loomed over the city in the mist. I thought of all the boys my age with no work or college, in drug gangs, wearing English-football shirts, looking down on the closed city they were barred from, as if waiting for their time to come.

The building with the dome looked like a Christian church and it was called the Panthéon, but it turned out to be kind of empty. The leaflet said that famous people's ashes were inside, but I could only see a few marble statues and a pendulum swinging on a long wire that hung down from the ceiling. I was about to leave when I saw people going down some stairs into what was called a *crypte*.

This turned out to be a warren of cold underground chambers where the lights shone on various tombs. Most rooms had a chain across the doorway, so it was hard to make out the names carved in the stone inside and there were only a few placards to tell you who was who—the majority being soldiers or important politicians. Trying hard to concentrate, I did notice a few street names (Jaurès, Gambetta), but what brought me up short was a chamber with three white tombs in it, one of which had the name of Victor Hugo. There was nothing to say who he was, though the dates beneath his name were 1802–1885 and I made a mental note to tell my new friend that some statesman or inventor shared his name.

After the Panthéon I walked on until I came into a park next to rue de Vaugirard with gravel paths among the trees. It had children playing in sandpits and lots of bored-looking young mothers, sitting on the benches, rocking a pram to and fro as they chatted to a fellow childminder or checked a phone in the palm of the other hand. There were couples mooching along between the lawns and flower beds beneath the scabby trees. Everything seemed to move at half pace and the afternoon hung heavy. It made me feel unhappy and alone, so I got out of it as fast as I could.

After walking for maybe fifteen minutes down the rue de Babylone, I veered towards École Militaire and before long I found that I was in the rue de l'Exposition. This wasn't planned in any way, I barely knew where I was, but my feet were drawn to this narrow street. I bought a *Figaro* from the usual place and perched on the wall. The shop was open, but the sewing machine in the window was not in use. I saw the woman with glasses who had brought Clémence her tea at the counter with the clothes rail behind.

It was about half past four, so there was at least an hour before the shop might close. The man I'd spoken to before came out with a bunch of keys and looked both ways up and down the street as though someone he was expecting was now running late. He looked at his watch and set off towards rue Saint-Dominique. I waited for an hour, but no one went in and no one came out.

Eventually, I crossed the street and pushed open the door. Although I didn't feel shy, I felt I should try to be polite. The woman behind the counter at the back of the shop was wearing an apron. She took off her glasses and settled her hair, which was a dark-orange color.

"I was wondering if you could help me, Madame. I'm looking for the lady who works here."

"Who?"

"The one who sits at the machine in the window and makes dresses."

"I don't know what you mean. There's me and Monsieur Fournier. No one else works here."

"But I've seen her and I had tea at her apartment." I wanted to say what Clémence looked like, but I thought it might be a mistake to describe her to an orange-haired old crone who was denying her existence.

"I'm sorry. Perhaps you've mistaken the shop."

"Her name is Clémence. Does that name mean anything?"

"I'm afraid not. I need to close up now, Monsieur. Goodbye."

It was starting to grow dark and I had been out almost all day. At my age your legs don't ache, you don't clutch your back and groan like Jamal after a long day at the fryer, but just at that moment I did feel an odd fatigue. It was all I could do to move my feet down the street or calculate which was my nearest Métro station. École Militaire, probably. But Bir-Hakeim would take me direct to Place d'Italie on Line 6. And so on my way there I inevitably went down a small street—rue Humblot, I noticed it was called—with a maroon-colored street door whose paint was flaking.

I looked up at the building and wondered if one of the lights was hers. But then I remembered that her apartment was on the far side of the courtyard with no window onto the street. I looked at the keypad let into the stone beside the locked doors. How many four-figure combinations can be made by the digits 0 through 9? I expect there's a formula to work it out.

The chances of my finding the right four by chance were next to none. And to my exhausted mind, those odds precisely represented my chances of ever opening a door onto a happiness that life had so far at every turn kept closed to me—the girl coming down the steps at Stalingrad, all that and more.

In anger more than sadness, I pressed four numbers at random.

A woman's voice came through the metal grid. "Hello."

"Hello," I managed to say back.

"Who is it?"

"It's Tariq."

Then there was a pause. I thought I could hear someone crying.

I said, "Can I come in?"

"Not today."

"Can I come another time?"

There was a further silence. "Hello?" I said.

"On Tuesday."

"At what time?"

"At this time. At six."

Belleville

I WAS APPALLED BY THE DEVELOPMENT IN MATHILDE'S STORY AND surprised there was no mention of it in the summary of the audio file, no health warning from the Centre's archivist. If I'd come across the incident in the first week—when my identification with Mathilde was so great—I might have excused her cruelty. But it was too late now. My reading into the lives of female agents and *résistantes,* many of whom ended up in camps where they were tortured or killed, had hardened my attitude.

The following day, I had an e-mail from Leo Busch, the Centre's director, telling me that the documentation I'd submitted was in order. He'd been in touch with Mathilde Masson, who told him she'd be happy to receive a visit from an American researcher. Busch warned me that the old woman was not in the best of health and that her willingness to be visited might have less to do with an interest in history than a need for company. They'd spoken on the phone and Busch had found Mathilde difficult to understand; *quand même,* nevertheless, he wished me the best of luck with my researches.

In reply to another e-mail, Busch gave me the address of the building where Mathilde had grown up; so the next day I took the Métro and emerged from Belleville station onto the boulevard that ran along the old city boundary. I began to walk up the hill, where a funicular had once connected the heights of Belleville to the Place de la République

down in Paris proper. As I climbed between the Chinese restaurants
and cheap supermarkets, past graffiti-covered alley walls, I tried to picture the hill in Mathilde's time—traffic-free except for horse carts, with
native Parisians and a handful of Armenian immigrants, their shoeless
children playing at the roadside while the parents were at work in
nearby factories. It was hard to imagine things I'd seen only in films
about the early life of Edith Piaf.

When a loop brought me down to the address Busch had given off
the rue des Couronnes, it became easier. Although the building was
much less slum-like than I'd imagined, quite elegant in a modest way, I
knew enough of my subject's life to be able to picture her stern face as
she pushed open the street door at the end of a day's work and went
upstairs, dodging Madame Gauthier and her cat, breathing in the smell
of whatever meat her father had picked up from the slaughterhouse.

I stood for a long time opposite Mathilde's home. Oddly enough, I
had no desire to go inside, to pry further, but I did wonder about the
sisters. Did they in the end think themselves lucky to have an apartment
at all, to have two parents when so many children had lost a father on
the Western Front? Did they hate being poor? Did they dream of "love"
and "escape?" Until Armand had come along, the only male, besides the
father, who seemed to figure in their lives was Jean, the young man from
the Alps whose job it was to carry up water from the fountain in the
courtyard to the eighteen apartments inside. Boys from the Alps were
the strongest, Mathilde said, accustomed at home to carrying milk
churns hung from yokes across their shoulders; and sturdy Jean had
been the subject of remarks between the girls. In the end, only Élodie
had made it to the suburbs. Louise had taken her self-prescribed cure
for loneliness, while Mathilde had found a chance of something better
stolen from her; the girls had been like insects beneath a stone, protected
by ignorance from understanding their position. As I put these thoughts
into words, I knew I'd put quote marks around "love." I wasn't sure
whether this was proper—a good professional habit to stop me under-
valuing the role of work in women's lives—or whether it showed a
growing conviction that love wasn't real enough to base a life on.

For a little longer, I gazed at the old building, the brick and stone
washed in sunlight that seemed indifferent to the past. I heard a seagull
overhead, then went down the slope of rue des Couronnes, across the

boulevard and into rue Jean-Pierre Timbaud opposite. I hoped this might have been the journey to work taken every day by Mathilde—though in 1942 her walk to the factory wouldn't have taken her past rows of burka shops. Outside the cafés, the men from the Maghreb smoked and argued, drinking tea and Fanta; and for all the female clothes on sale, there were no women visible. So unexpected was the lurch into a different culture that it took a moment or two before I fully registered the name of the street: Timbaud, like the trade unionist shot for his Resistance activity, the subject of my own professor's book. In Paris, where almost every street name was a nod to history, this could hardly be coincidence. Later I'd check that, before it was renamed, this had been the rue d'Angoulême, the site of Mathilde's factory. As the narrow descent opened up into a square, or triangle at least, I saw an old metallurgical works, now converted into an industrial museum or maybe loft spaces. Among the memorial plaques to workers' international struggles was one to the memory of Jean-Pierre Timbaud. With its Café des Ingénieurs, or Engineers' Café, the area had a post-industrial feel, and I became certain that this was where Mathilde had worked six days a week before her afternoon walk in the Buttes-Chaumont on the seventh. How much on a cold winter Monday must she have looked forward to the factory's whistle on the far-off Saturday. How fiercely had she urged her life away.

Then I walked on through a part of town I'd never visited. I had a feeling I was near Père Lachaise cemetery and thought I might wander like a tourist down the chestnut avenues, among the tombs, but I took a wrong turn and found myself on Boulevard Voltaire, one of those wide Paris roads whose raison d'être is to connect more interesting places. Among the travel agents and the peeling plane trees, the *immobiliers* and photocopy shops, there was still, even here, the occasional porte cochere that might have led onto a courtyard with a history to conceal. I remembered how when I'd first come to Paris it exasperated me to think that I'd never have the time to push open every door and see what lay behind. What then had I hoped to find, I asked myself as the traffic barreled along beside me. A door, a key—one life that by its individuality would open up a world.

By now I was outside a shop called Wash-Wash—a launderette, I guessed, for visiting Americans. "*Sans rendezvous!*" it told the passerby: no appointment necessary. But it turned out, when I looked more closely, to be a place for cleaning motorbikes. And what was the turnover in *that*? How many messenger boys or gray ponytails or Vespa-riding clerks made a note in the diary to head down to Wash-Wash on Boulevard Voltaire on a Sunday morning? It would have been a good place for Armand to meet Simone and other members of his circuit, somewhere quite forgettable. Or for me to meet Tariq. "Is that *sans rendezvous?*" he'd ask with that wide-eyed look of his. "No, Tariq, very much *avec.*"

Tariq was in my thoughts because of Leo Busch's warning that Mathilde was hard to understand. Given my problems with spoken French, I thought I was sure to struggle. I could have asked Julian to go with me, but although his French was better than mine he was not a native speaker; his understanding didn't seem as instinctive as Tariq's. I was in any case reluctant to let Julian see me at work. Over the years I'd developed one or two ways of winning the confidence of people, and I didn't want him to tease me about them afterwards.

With Tariq, it was different. He wouldn't notice anything. He wouldn't know which number world war it was, why the Germans were in Paris or why most French people tolerated them, having changed their tune from 1940's *sales Boches*, "filthy Germans," to 1942's *sales anglais*, "filthy English." He'd probably be looking at the screen of his cell phone while Mathilde talked, but it would be a comfort to have him there.

• • •

The appointment was made by Leo Busch for the following Thursday afternoon. Mathilde lived near the Place des Fêtes, on Line 7 *bis,* a loop attached to the regular Line 7; she'd be expecting "a colleague" and me at four o'clock.

When the day came, a breezy morning in May, one of those days when the world seems bright again, I wasn't feeling at my best. Aleksandr, for a long time dormant in some zombie hinterland, had burst into my dreams the night before and left me shaken, as he could, for many hours (it was sometimes days) to come.

I couldn't allow him to derail my work, so I had to confront, for a moment at least, the power he still wielded: I had to face him down. But at once my mind began to wander . . . Suppose there were six billion people in the world, three billion of each sex. Of these, perhaps one billion were over fifty and one billion under twenty-two. So I had one billion potential mates! Allowing for the fact that many of them wouldn't like me at all, and being as choosy as a reasonably sane and halfway friendly person might be, could you narrow it down to, say, one in a hundred of that group? Picky or whatever. But even that still left (I checked the math on a piece of paper) one hundred million attractive men I could have had an okay life with. (My guess, only a guess, was that few women in fact narrowed it down that far; many were content with number 567,297,441.) But anyone in your top fifty million was going to lead to something dangerous. Then suppose by the most unlikely chance you came across a man in your top million or thousand or hundred. What then was the capacity for pain? And what, dear God, if he was in your earthly, conceivable top ten? I hardly dared to picture Number One himself. At that moment he was probably chopping trees in a Venezuelan jungle in a loincloth and a sweaty headband, unaware of his appalling power.

When I'd finished this calculation, I felt better. I even smiled. But then I saw the strangeness of my logic. I hadn't for a moment thought the narrowing odds would bring me happiness as I came closer to the other half of me. No. I'd assumed that the person I most loved would most utterly destroy me. And what, as my therapist might have asked in her hot Boston consulting room, does that say about you, Hannah?

At one o'clock I went out to a local café and had the dish of the day— "*Le dos de cabillaud, Madame? Bien sûr*"—and, for the first time on my own, a lunchtime glass of wine. The cod was good, but the wine made me feel hazy, so I had an espresso and went back to the apartment to find Tariq. It had been easy to enlist his help and he took obvious pleasure in planning the Métro trip.

"I've never been on the Seven *bis*," he said excitedly, and while the train rattled along I saw his brown eyes staring first at himself in the reflection opposite, where his face was elongated by the glass, then at the advertisements in the stations where we stopped. I suppose it was just a boy thing, a male thing, but I envied his self-absorption. He was either admiring himself or thinking of his next pleasure. In my own head I barely seemed capable of seeing anything for what it was any longer. Everything seemed connected to, or shaped by, something else— to an incident long ago, to wider meaning or significance: to history and loss.

I could feel a headache starting up in the usual place behind my temples and I was afraid that the meeting with Mathilde mattered too much to me. I'd already done enough work to provide a draft chapter for Barbara Putnam's book, so it was not anxiety about the professional outcome of the interview that was troubling me. What was making my head hurt was the fact that I felt answerable to these women. It was up to me to discover and put right whatever might have happened to betrayed Simone; only I could forgive Mathilde for what she'd done, because only I understood the extenuating facts of her life. And then there were the others I'd come across, like the admired Andrée Borrel; or those I'd perhaps imagined, like Clémence; and it was for the stressed machinery in my brain to redeem their deaths and give them a better chance in some hypothetical second life.

The Place des Fêtes, Party Square, almost at the end of the line, was anything but festive. Tower blocks with orange and tan paintwork were ranged around the sloping square—a pedestrianized area with a dirty glass pyramid, a handful of tubed saplings and a shuttered carousel.

"My God," I said, struck by a spasm of guilt. "We must buy some flowers for Mathilde. I'd quite forgotten."

"There's a Monoprix over there," said Tariq.

"No, I think we can do better," I said. I wanted time to gather myself. On one side of the square was an alleyway with a bazaar that sold household goods; next to it was a florist with potted plants and some old tulips. At the back of the shop I unearthed something fresher, a bouquet tied with straw.

"Are you all right?" said Tariq, as I fumbled with the coins.

"Yes, I'm fine. I'm just going to get some water to drink. Can you hold on to these?"

Tariq's cell phone guided us to Mathilde's block and we went through the street doors. Inside, it was like a run-down hospital, the walls gunmetal gray in whorled, unfinished plaster.

"I'm surprised there's no security code," I said as we walked past rows of mailboxes to the lifts.

"It won't start till later," said Tariq. "It was seven at the Olympiades." How come this kid knew more than I did? Street wisdom—something else for me to learn.

The elevator was larger than in most Paris buildings, part of the design, not squeezed up later through a stairwell. The doors shuddered open on the twelfth floor, where a diagram showed the way to apartment 1206. The ceiling was low above our heads, and the windowless way was lit by sodium wall lights.

"Here," said Tariq, pointing to a number on the wall, beside a gray door.

I lifted my hand, then hesitated.

"What?" said Tariq, looking up from his phone.

I knocked. Almost at once I heard shuffling footsteps, then the sound of locks and chains, none of which sounded heavy enough to be effective. As the flimsy door was pulled open, I searched for the living face of my witness. When I saw it at last, it was at a lower level than mine, the figure of Mathilde Masson reaching only to my shoulder. I had a vision of her as a child, standing in her wet dress in the sea, with her father clinging on.

"Come in, come in."

We did as we were told and found ourselves in a room with some old brown furniture, among which were a couple of plastic garden chairs.

"I brought these for you," I said, holding out the bouquet.

Mathilde took it with a sound that might have been surprise or gratitude and put it on a hatch that opened onto a small kitchen. There was a blue budgerigar in a cage by the window that overlooked the square far below. The room was warm and airless.

Without waiting to be asked any questions, Mathilde began to speak. Her voice was thinner and harder than on the audio files and she spoke more quickly. I felt thrown. I had a list of questions, beginning with inquiries into Mathilde's health and how she came to be living in the Place des Fêtes, which was not so very far from the Belleville of her childhood and . . . But the old woman hadn't even asked me to sit down before she began to talk. I was still fumbling in my bag for notebook and pen.

Mathilde sat in an armchair that seemed to have come from the time of the Occupation itself, though it had a remote control beside it and was lined up on a small television. Since I hadn't been offered a seat, I perched on the edge of a garden chair and nodded to Tariq to do the same. I was so fascinated by the old woman's physical presence that I found it hard to concentrate on what she was saying.

Interrupting her story, Mathilde turned to face me. "Are you American?"

"Yes."

"What are you doing in Paris?"

"I'm sorry, I thought Professor Busch had explained. I'm writing a chapter for a history book about women in the—"

"What's it got to do with America?"

"Nothing specifically. It's history. It's a record; it's of interest to all people who—"

"And who's he?"

"He's my colleague, Tariq. I thought Professor—"

"Is he an Arab?"

"His home's in North Africa, I believe."

Mathilde's face grew hard. She had smeared lipstick on her mouth and black color round her eyes, so that with her dyed hair she looked like something from a Weimar nightclub.

The set expression resolved itself at last. "I like Arabs," said Mathilde. "Monsieur Rashid brings up my shopping."

I didn't dare look towards Tariq.

"There's people from all over the world round here," she said. "There's even French people I remember from where I grew up. The Arabs are fine. It's the Jews I can't bear."

"Madame," I said quickly, "could I please ask you one or two questions about the Occupation? And perhaps if you could speak quite slowly and remember that I don't speak French that well."

"I thought all Americans were fat," said Mathilde.

"No. Anyway, could I ask you a few questions? You remember you did some recordings for the Centre Jean Molland. Perhaps we could start with those."

"I saw a notice in the paper. I thought I could help. I had things to tell them. People told such lies afterwards."

"I've listened to the recordings. They're very interesting. What was your parents' attitude towards the Germans?"

Mathilde considered for a moment, and I felt pleased to have her attention. I'd been embarrassed by what she said about the Jews—not on my own account, because I could handle historical context, but, weirdly enough, on Tariq's. I didn't want him to have a bad impression of "us"—Mathilde and me.

"My father hated the Germans," said Mathilde. "But my mother quite liked them. She liked their green uniforms and their funny shaved necks. She was a stupid woman. We didn't see that much of them where we lived. They liked the cafés on the Champs-Élysées. And the Bois de Boulogne. They liked boating on the lake. But why would they come up the rue des Couronnes? There weren't even any good brothels."

Once she'd started, Mathilde was able to keep going. Much of it was familiar, but I didn't want to risk missing some jewel, so I scribbled as fast as I could in my notebook.

". . . ration coupons, but there was nothing to buy with the coupons, so what's the point of a ticket that says you can have half a loaf of bread if there isn't any bread in the bakery?"

"And why did you stay in Paris when so many people left?"

"Are you crazy? We didn't have friends in Burgundy. We didn't have a country manor house! We were peasants. Paris peasants. I'd only ever been out of Paris once in my life, to go to the seaside when we were young. It was a veterans' association who paid for us to go to—"

"You talked about it on the recordings." I didn't want Mathilde to waste energy on things I already knew. "And would you say that life was harder for women than for men in those four years?"

"Of course not. The men were either in prisoner-of-war camps or they had to go and work in Germany. We just carried on in the factories like before the Germans came. I still got paid."

"So what was your feeling about the Germans? You personally?"

"I didn't mind them. I felt sorry for some of the young ones. They didn't know how to behave, they looked embarrassed. Later in the war it was different. They were older. They'd come back from Russia. They were broken. Like ghosts. No, they were all right, the Germans. It was the English we didn't like. Because they kept the war dragging on. And the Jews."

"Yes, but what about—"

"And the Russians. The Bolsheviks. We didn't want them to win the war. Of course."

"And the Americans?" I suddenly couldn't help asking.

"We didn't know anything about the Americans," said Mathilde. "Until they came parading down our streets when it was all over."

"All right. Now if I may, I wanted to ask you about your fiancé, Armand, and his work with the Resistance."

"Did I tell them about that? On the recording machine?"

"Yes, you did. You said quite a lot about Armand and how you planned to get married. Then you told how someone had told your sister, Louise, that he had been seen with another woman who—"

"That bitch. That filthy whore."

Well, I'd registered Mathilde's coarse language on the audio files, but it was somehow a surprise to hear it on the twelfth floor, in person, with the bird looking over from its cage. As Mathilde continued talking, I remembered how she'd said that she and Armand had been lovers—"I'd done it, sex, with Armand"—and as I tried to focus on what she was saying, I looked at her legs in their dark wrinkled nylons and blue rubber clogs and imagined her parting them for Armand in . . . maybe his parents' flat when they were out, a room near the Victor Hugo found by Louise or among some bushes in the Buttes-Chaumont . . . Then I looked at the old woman's hands with their ropy veins and imagined them caressing her lover, little bespectacled Armand. I felt ashamed of these thoughts, for a moment, but then put my shame down to bad practice. It was really quite all right to picture these things. History was not a pageant; it was real and now.

Mathilde waved her speckled hands in the air and spit gathered in the corners of her mouth. I risked a glance across at Tariq, but he was looking down at the screen of his cell phone, presumably killing goons on it.

"Could I, please, Madame, ask you to talk a little bit more slowly? Thank you. And do you know what happened to Simone after you reported her to the prefect of police?"

"She was arrested, I should think. People were arrested all the time."

"And then what happened to her?"

"I don't know. I expect she had a trial and went to prison."

"In France? Or did she go to a concentration camp? In Germany? Or Poland?"

"How should I know? They wouldn't have told me, would they?"

"What about Armand? Did he know what happened to Simone? Did he know it was you who followed him and reported her?"

"I sent him a note to warn him she was in trouble and that he'd better be careful. I didn't see him again."

"Never?"

"I saw him once in the street. Twenty years later. He was gray and bald and he had a child with him. A girl of about ten."

"Did you speak to him?"

"No. He saw me and tried to cross the road, but I moved on quickly. I got on a bus. I didn't want to talk to him."

"And you never married."

"No."

"And what about Louise and Élodie?"

"Ellie went to live in the suburbs. She had four children, but I hardly saw them. Louise went to live in Marseille with a man she met through her work."

"Did she write to you?"

"Lulu?" Mathilde smiled for the first time. "No, she couldn't write. But I went down to see her once. Her husband fixed it."

"And . . . Was she all right?"

"They moved out of the town into a village. They adopted a little boy from Spain. They all came to Paris once. She was . . . just the same. She never changed. We went out to a dance hall, the four of us. In Montmartre. She made me dance with her husband while she danced with the Spanish boy. She said, 'Come on, Minouche. You can borrow my husband, but make sure you give him back.' Then she whispered in my ear, 'He took me a lot of finding,' and we both started laughing."

Sensing that Mathilde was starting to flag, I looked down at my long list of questions. "How do you think the women of Paris managed during those four years? What was the main way in which their experience was different from men's?"

Something about the way it came out made it sound like a test paper. I found myself blushing. "Give examples," I might as well have added.

Mathilde snorted. "It wasn't very different for people like us. When you're poor you just do what you have to do."

"But from the history of the—"

"You only think about the factory. Work. And when you might get time off. But mostly we were thinking about food."

For a few more minutes Mathilde continued with her rattling reminiscences. She reminded me of the actress Arletty. Professor Putnam had once played us a recording of her to give an idea of a certain type of Parisienne, of the accent and the attitude known as *parigot*. Mathilde, like Arletty, wasn't interested in shades of righteousness. How difficult it was when contemporary witnesses seemed unaware of the meaning of what they'd lived through—though to me that difficulty was also the most interesting part of it: the way that personal experience shrugged off the judgment of others.

Mathilde's voice was weakening and she was growing restless in the armchair. I wondered if she needed the bathroom—not that she'd have been shy to say so.

When, reluctantly, I stood up to leave and started to express my thanks, Mathilde said, "They gave me a hundred thousand francs for denouncing that slut."

"Really?"

"I didn't ask for it. They just handed me a piece of paper to sign and then gave me an envelope at the police station."

"What did you do with the money?"

"I bought a hat for Louise. I gave some to my mother for food. The rest I gave to the veterans' association that had paid for us to go away to the seaside. When I was a child."

"That was nice of you," I said, happy we were parting on a note of decency. But Mathilde only grunted.

After the handshakes and goodbyes, I waited with Tariq at the elevator. When I tried to get into it I found my left leg wouldn't shift.

"I can't move!"

"What?"

Slowly my foot came up from the carpet tiles. In the time we'd stood waiting for the elevator to come to the twelfth floor, my shoe had become stuck tight by a piece of chewing gum.

From the lobby we walked out into the spring evening.

"What a foulmouthed old girl," said Tariq.

"I couldn't understand everything she said."

"Neither could I," said Tariq, as we headed for the Métro. "But don't worry. I've got it all here."

"What?"

"I recorded it on my phone."

Place des Fêtes

I WAS SO EXCITED ABOUT SEEING CLÉMENCE AGAIN THAT I COULDN'T sleep, I couldn't do anything really. I did manage to speak to Hasim and tell him I wasn't coming back. He shouted at me for a bit but then calmed down.

"So what are you going to live on?" he said.

"I've saved some money. And I think I'm going home soon."

"All right, boy. If you come back, you know where to find us. Jamal says hello."

"Say hello back."

Hasim wasn't such a bad guy. He had this fear of authority, which I'd assumed was because his business was somehow shady, didn't pay tax or something, but in fact I think he was just a law-abiding person who was always hoping for a break. Meanwhile, I'd built up a reserve supply of Jamal's weed. It was powerful if erratic stuff and I usually needed only a little bit to be hammered for about three hours. I was wondering how I was going to pass the time till my Tuesday meeting with Clémence when Hannah asked me if I'd help her with some old woman she was going to see. Mathilde, her name was.

She lived in a cool part of town. We went on the 7 *bis*, which I'd always wanted to have a ride on. It wasn't as clean as some of the lines, to be honest. The trains had orange seats and there was no announcer to tell you which station you were coming into, you had to work that out for yourself. At the Place des Fêtes even the benches on the platforms were orange—what you could see of them beneath the sleeping tramps or *clochards*. (Victor Hugo had told me that they'd got that name because they used to go into the old food market at Les Halles when the bell or *cloche* was sounding at the end of the day and they'd get given food that was otherwise going to be chucked out. I was starting to learn stuff in Paris, I really was. I could tell my father—if he ever asked.)

Anyway, up in the open air, there were big tower blocks and some shops with good cheap stuff in them and a huge Monoprix and a burger place. Almost the only thing missing was a Flunch. The lift in the building went really fast and the flat when we got there had a brilliant view.

Hannah seemed to be in a bit of a state. I saw her taking some pills out of her bag and swilling them down in a flower shop with water from a bottle of Vittel. I didn't ask what the matter was. I'd once asked my stepmother if she was feeling okay when I saw her take a tablet and got a twenty-minute lecture about minding my own business.

It was painful to watch. Hannah was like an interviewer on television, but the old woman wasn't playing. She just talked. I noticed Hannah struggling to keep up so I switched on the RECORD feature on my phone. Hannah kept trying to bring her back to the point, but it didn't work. She was begging for some sort of big judgment on the past, but Mathilde didn't see beyond what she'd done day by day. I don't think the old woman was trying to be difficult, it was more that she just didn't understand. I guess she'd never been to school. Or if she had, it was so long ago that she'd forgotten the whole business.

The other thing about old Mathilde was that she had a really disgusting vocabulary. Maybe when you get to be very old you don't care anymore, or perhaps she'd gone a bit crazy, like old people do. I was quite glad that most of it seemed to be flying over Hannah's head. Anyway, I thought her life up there looked pretty good with this Monsieur Rashid bringing up her groceries and the caged bird and the television opposite her chair. If that's old age, it doesn't seem so bad.

The next day, back in rue Michal, Hannah asked if she could listen to the recording. We sat together at the table in the sitting room. Every now and then I'd stop the playback and rewind. Sometimes this was to reassure Hannah that we'd got it right, sometimes it was because I hadn't heard it the first time and needed to listen again.

We came to the bit about the boyfriend, Armand, and this woman he was in some sort of Resistance group with. Simone her name was. I tried to translate for Hannah. "'It drove me mad to think of that bitch sucking his cock. He had a lovely cock, it was very hard and it had a special taste. It was mine to suck and I used to stroke his balls and make him cry with pleasure when I bent over and let him lick—'"

"God, Tariq, stop it for a moment. Did she really say that?"

"Yes."

Hannah was red with embarrassment.

I said, "I think she was jealous."

She began to laugh. "I think you could say that."

"I don't know if 'cock' is really the right word," I said. "At home we call it a *zib*. But I've heard 'cock' in American films and I think—"

"Yes, you're probably right. Is there much more of this?"

"Quite a lot more."

Maybe the phone would reach the end of its recording capacity soon. That was my best hope.

I pressed PLAY again. Mathilde's voice said, "At night I used to lie there thinking of her putrid . . ."

I stopped it again and said, "I'm not sure about that word."

"What was it? I didn't catch it."

"*Chatte.*"

"Oh dear. Maybe we can use a word in your language for that too."

"All right. *Qooq* should do."

I began to translate again. ". . . 'her putrid, hairy *qooq*. And him . . . fucking,' I think we'd have to say, 'her disgusting *chatte*.' Or *qooq*. And . . ." I stopped. "I'm afraid it starts to get a bit rough here."

"Give me an idea."

"I don't think you'll want to use it in your book."

"Probably not. But I don't want to be squeamish."

I was beginning to sweat a bit. "It's about Simone's breasts and her . . . her back parts. You know, there's a lot of pig stuff and *merde* and, er . . . stuff I don't even understand myself. To be honest."

But I wasn't being honest. I understood it; I just didn't want to translate. Old Mathilde really wasn't keen on Simone. A bit of me admired her passion, but, really, some of the things she said.

Finally, Hannah stood up from the table. "All right. I think we've got the point. Can we go to the last bit now? When she was talking about how she reported Simone to the police? There was something there. About how she went back a second time?"

I was dreading this bit even more than the sex parts or when she'd referred to Armand as *un vrai petit con*. (I tried to explain that *con* here maybe just meant really 'stupid' rather than being another version of *qooq* or *chatte*.) I had the impression that Hannah felt protective of Mathilde, that she really liked her for some reason. Not because she was a nice person but because she was her special find. Or maybe just because she was a woman and she thought women always had a bad time.

I found the section and pressed PLAY. "'They didn't give me enough money, the police. They were supposed to give me more than that. Marshal Pétain had asked everyone, every schoolchild in the country, to inform. I didn't even know you got money for reporting an enemy of the state, but when I told people back at the factory they said the police had shortchanged me.'"

"Wasn't there something else?" said Hannah.

"Yes, there was."

I found it in the end.

Her voice was tired by this time and it sounded scratchy, but the words she said still came out quite clearly from my cell phone.

Mathilde said: "'Next time I denounced someone I made sure I got the full amount.'"

Hannah asked me to stop the recording there. Then she went into her bedroom and shut the door.

● ● ●

When I arrived at the entrance to Clémence's building, my problem was that I didn't know the code and there was no chance that four random numbers would work again. I went across the cobbles and looked up at the façade, hoping for a sign or a light, but of course the apartment was on the courtyard so I don't really know what I was expecting to see. I had some of Jamal's best in my pocket, and not for the first time I wished I'd brought my *sebsi*, the little pipe I used at home. Instead, I rolled it all into a paper, lit up and smoked it quickly. There was no one else in the cobbled street to catch the smell.

It was six o'clock, the appointed time, and I was in the right place.

But what on earth was I doing? Going to see a woman who looked like someone I'd seen in an old photograph book. Was that a good way to spend a Tuesday evening in early summer? There was more to it, though. Something I had to understand. There was also the sense that she lived in a world that was denied to me and to which she alone had a key.

As I ground out the stub-end of my smoke, I looked at myself in a shop window for a few moments, turning from side to side. My face grew older as I watched. The man in the glass shook his head as if to say, "I don't believe you, boy. Are you really going to do this?"

Then I turned back because I heard the street door grinding on its hinge, and there was Clémence standing on the threshold. I watched as Tariq crossed the road and as she kissed him lightly on the cheek.

When I'd had this sense of watching myself before—talking to my father at home or to the man beneath the railway arches at Stalingrad—it had lasted a few minutes as a complete switch or transfer. This time, it was intermittent. For the next hour I was in and out of myself.

Upstairs in her apartment, she sat me down in the same armchair. I took a cigarette from the offered box and she leaned over me with the table lighter, then went to the kitchen and came back with mint tea, hot and sweet, just like the time before.

"I have to go out in an hour," she said as she sat down. "I have people to meet."

"You sound anxious," said Tariq. He used the *tu* form: *"Tu as l'air un peu inquiet."*

"It is a little fraught, I suppose. It always is. And you?" *Et toi?*

"It's nice to be here again."

"What do you want? Really?"

"Just to be here. To watch you. And to listen. If you'd like to tell me things."

She smiled and pulled away a shred of tobacco from her lower lip. "Of course."

I said, "I went to that place you told me about. Drancy. Where they kept the people before putting them on the trains." (I hadn't been there or anywhere near it. I'd only looked at it on Hannah's laptop. But I wanted her to think well of me.)

"That was good of you. What did you make of it?"

Tariq fumbled for words. "I think if I'd owned the place opposite, the Hôtel Vouvray, I would have let people stay for free. And maybe I'd have lent them binoculars so they could see their children or their parents in the yard when they did the roll call. Wave to them. Get a message to them."

Clémence smiled again. "Maybe."

"Tell me more about yourself," said Tariq.

The room was full of smoke and the lights were very low. Clémence leaned forward to the table and took a cigarette, then she sat back in her chair, kicked off her shoes and put her feet on the table.

I had severe couch-lock. I'd blasted in a bit more *kif* than I'd meant to out on the pavement there, and I knew I couldn't move a muscle for a while. So I just sat, looking at Clémence's long legs, the pale color of her calves and the darkness higher up, and the sweep of her hand as she gestured. And hearing her voice was as good as listening to the sweetest music from home I could imagine, played through the best hi-fi in Paris.

When you're as stoned as this you don't take in precisely what's said—it's more of an impression. What I remember is patchy, but it was something like this.

". . . as a little girl at school in rue de Vaugirard. The teacher was a nun, an old woman in a gray habit with a headdress and glasses. There were so many girls in class and in the afternoons they'd take us sometimes to the Jardin du Luxembourg. It took ages to get there; Vaugirard is such a long street. We were Catholic girls and we knew all the saints and kept the feast days. Life was very ordered, and at home my father was kind and my mother was strict and that was the way it was. Of course I would have liked a brother or sister, but a sad look in my mother's eyes when I raised the subject made it clear that that would never happen. Somehow we had a sense that this life was almost perfect as it was. We wanted it to stay the same forever. The cakes with sugar on top from the baker at the end of the street on Friday afternoons. Mass on Sundays in the big church so I could wear my new hat. And lunch afterwards with neighbors and the doors open onto the terrace. Even my mother was laughing. But I was afraid. I was scared of other countries. Wars. I was afraid that the life we'd made might not survive.

We couldn't take intrusion from other people. Other ways of thinking, other peoples, other gods."

It wasn't clear to me exactly where young Clémence had lived, which arrondissement, because, as she said, the rue de Vaugirard goes on forever. You couldn't say exactly when either, except it seemed to be a long time ago. Something about the way she spoke made me think of black-and-white films. Maybe it was a particular movie I'd seen one lazy afternoon recently—one in which a class of schoolboys is being taken off to exercise by the PE teacher, walking briskly along the rue de Vaugirard, and two by two they disappear down side streets, into shops, till there's no one left following the teacher as he marches on.

At some point I think that Clémence was singing, a sort of folk song or lullaby. The language was a version of French, but not the one I'd learned as a child and not the one I'd been speaking all day. It was a mixture of what seemed like peasant French with bits of Spanish, Italian and Arabic. That's what it sounded like to me, anyway. It was perfect *kif* music, nonsensical and haunting. I watched as she wiped away a tear.

As the effects of the drug began to wear off, I became aware that she was talking about a different country now. The dream of a Catholic city in black and white had given way to somewhere in Africa. I couldn't say which country, though it was somewhere on the north coast, by the sea.

". . . the white buildings of the bay. The arches of the viaducts built up into the old town on the hill. The stepped alleys of the casbah and the palm groves of the boulevards along the sea . . . And friendships in the villages they'd built up over generations, the families who'd come once from Angers or Toulon with the local farmers and the clerks, the Arabs and their quiet women. In the schools near the port, the children of the settlers studied with the local boys and girls, learning the history of a country that they'd never visit, revolution, rights of man and rule of law, the rise of science and the writers who had entertained the world— *Le Misanthrope, Les Misérables, La Comédie Humaine* . . . And then the world wars and the intrusion of another world, of another Europe . . . Then civil wars, the killing of the children and the women and the massacres of entire villages . . . And all that was left was the belief in a god who wasn't there. That was all they could think of to hold themselves together. And now we have the war that never ends. But for a while—before I lived—there was a time when the springs in the hills ran through the wells of the casbah, through the bars and terraces of the big hotels below and out into the bay where the boats came in, unloaded, set sail again, all day until the sun went down."

Looking back, I've had to join up some of the bits and pieces here, but the images are clear in my mind. And then Clémence was singing again, in the same mixed language as before, a story of a shepherd on a hill and a child who never came home.

When she'd finished, she stood up and looked at her watch. "I must go and change," she said. "There's not much time."

"All right."

"I'm me."

"What?"

I was puzzled. What she'd said, in French, was *"Suis moi."* As far as my slow brain could tell, that meant "I'm me." She'd just dropped the *je* at the start, as people do.

But who *is* that? I wanted to ask.

She shook her head as she went to the door. *"Non. Suis-moi."* She beckoned.

Then I understood. *"Follow me." Suis-moi.* Of course. Even Hannah would have got it.

Tariq put out his cigarette and went down the hallway after Clémence, into a dimly lit room with a brass bed under a lace coverlet. There was a threadbare rug on the parquet.

She pointed him to a chair, then went through a door and closed it behind her. He heard the sound of a shower running.

He looked round the room. Above the stone fireplace was a painting of a saint. On the mantelpiece were two candles and some old porcelain. Over the bed itself was a crucifix. Light came from a bulb under a ceramic shade hung on a flex from the ceiling and from a dim lamp by the bed. There was an old wireless on a side table and the curtains were drawn.

The door from the bathroom opened and Clémence appeared in a dressing gown. She sat down at a table in front of a mirror and caught Tariq's eye in the reflection.

"Can I stay?" he said. "That's all I want to do."

"Of course," she said.

He gazed over as she rubbed some cream into her face and neck, then drew mascara along her lashes. She combed her hair, then rolled a dark lipstick over her mouth, leaning into the reflection of the mirror on the table.

Tariq looked as though he hoped the performance would carry on. But after she'd dabbed some powder on her face, she stood up and turned towards him. She took off the dressing gown and threw it on the bed. She had nothing on beneath it. From the top drawer of a chest she took some stockings and, sitting on the side of the bed, rolled them up her legs, then fastened them to a sort of belt she'd taken from a lower drawer. Tariq looked at how her breasts fell forward as she reached behind her thigh to the back fastening.

When she was satisfied with the arrangement, she looked towards Tariq and found him still staring.

He looked down at his feet.

"Come here," she said.

I stood up from the chair and went over to the edge of the bed. Then I knelt down and put my arms round her bare waist, let my hands slide down, under the straps, held her tight and rested my cheek against the hair between her legs.

For a minute I stayed still, while she stroked my head and spoke softly. I couldn't make out the words, but I found them calming. She said nothing distinct, kept murmuring, stroking my hair. She began to sing again.

SIXTEEN

Louvre-Rivoli

JULIETTE LEMAIRE HAD BEEN TO DINNER WITH KLAUS RICHTER NOT
once but twice, I discovered. There was nothing underhanded or
false about Juliette, but there was something close to naïveté that made
me feel anxious as I listened to her story in the sound booth.

Maxim's restaurant, where German soldiers (or French citizens
without scruples) could eat anything they wanted for cash, had been the
venue on the first occasion. Juliette had been too nervous to eat but had
listened in fascination as Richter talked about his childhood in a village
on the river Tauber near Rothenburg. He told her how he hated it when
the Nazis lit on his home as a model of "Germanness," then expelled the
Jewish townspeople. "That was not the country I'd grown up in, which
was one of music and art and high Christianity," he told Juliette, as she
smuggled a petit four into her handbag. He spoke of Riemenschneider's
wood carvings and the wine so lovely it was unknown outside Franco-
nia because "we drank it all ourselves!" He described how he fell in love
with the daughter of a concert pianist in Rothenburg.

Delivered home to the rue de Tanger by ten o'clock as promised,
Juliette sat up with her parents describing the splendor of the room—
the gilt-framed mirrors and plush seats—and the food she'd barely
touched, including a Bresse chicken with foie gras beneath the skin. Her
father had urged her to make a better meal of it if she was asked out
again.

The second dinner, a few weeks later, was in a restaurant near the Opéra, a place with shellfish on ice in the windows. Juliette hadn't liked it as much as Maxim's, because through the window she could see the Kommandatur, where she and her friends were forever waiting to have their papers stamped. This time she had managed to eat a little: grilled sole and then some Brie. The butter in a small silver dish was the thing she'd loved, more than the wine or the fish or the cheese.

Juliette's voice was that of an old woman, but it carried still a sense of youthful doubt, of not knowing whether what she'd done was permitted, overlooked or asking for trouble.

The second time, I'd taken a lot of care with the way I looked. My mother said I should put my hair up, but that wasn't my style and I wore it loose. She said my dress was too short, but I said it wasn't, and anyway I wore a light coat open over the top and new gray stockings I'd got from the shop. I didn't have an evening bag, so I took my usual one on the long strap, which I wore diagonally across my front. Papa said I looked like a bandit, but I said it was to keep it safe on the Métro. I always wore it like that. I didn't mind, because I felt free and light on my feet.

Klaus looked very proper in his uniform, clean-shaven, with the gray beginning in the hair above his ears. He was polite to the waiters and friendly to some people he knew at another table. He had clean fingernails and hands that stayed steady when he lit a cigar afterwards. Then, with the coffee, he began to talk more about his wife. He told me they had two boys, but they were too young to be soldiers, thank God. Then he pushed a small package across the table and said it was for me. In it was a pearl necklace with a gold clasp. I'd seen similar things in shop windows in the rue du Faubourg Saint-Honoré, but no pearls as pure as this. I thought I could get away with it, for a moment. A single row at the collar under a blouse . . . No one would know it was expensive.

But I pushed it back and thanked him. Then I said we shouldn't meet again. And he told me . . . things I can hardly bring myself to repeat even now. He said he was in love with me. It sounds ridiculous—a high-up officer and a girl from a shop, and this was only the fourth time we'd met, but maybe he was. He said he'd first seen me coming up the steps at the Louvre Métro station on the rue de Rivoli and followed at a distance to find out where I worked. It had taken him a week to pluck up the courage to come into the shop with his fat friend. This made me like him more. We both began to laugh, but my mind was made up. I was frightened by the feelings he was stirring up in me. I had an urge to kiss him and I was scared of where it might lead.

He apologized for going too fast. He said, "It's the war, Juliette. We're living at twice the normal speed." He spoke good French with hardly an accent. He said he wouldn't mention love again if I would just let him see me. Perhaps one Sunday we could go on the lake in the Bois de Boulogne. He said he could arrange for some fresh produce to be delivered to my parents—he mentioned eggs and ham. Outside on the street, he gripped my hands. He pleaded with me, but I was crying by now. Why? Was I frightened of what people might say or think of me? No, I didn't care about those people scuttling off down into the Métro, each with their own little secrets. I didn't care what they thought. I was just scared of the feeling inside me.

We stood there for a moment. Then he took a deep breath and walked over to his car. He gave instructions to the driver and opened the door for me. I let him hug me before I climbed in. I didn't look back, because my face was ugly from crying. All the streets were empty, so it took no time to get home, because all the streets were empty.

I paused the recording, put down the headphones and looked back over my notes. In my months in Paris, I'd listened to many witnesses, panning for gold, and it had taken me a while to come back to Juliette Lemaire. Although I'd warmed at once to the sound of her contralto voice, I'd also felt there was something flighty about her—this shop girl, this *midinette*—and thought I was more likely to find hard truths from women like Mathilde Masson, the daughter of Belleville and Verdun.

I saw now that I'd underestimated Juliette. She'd left school at fourteen but later begun to read books to educate herself; after the war, she'd found a place at some sort of night school. Her aim had been to learn dressmaking, to have her own clothes shop one day, but she'd been sidetracked by the idea of becoming a schoolteacher—an ambition she made good at the age of thirty, by which time she was living in the south of Paris, deliberately far from where she'd started out.

Over the years, I'd gained a sense of when I was in the presence of true witness. A lack of emotion was a good sign, as was an ability to live with contradictions—a willingness just to report experience and leave the judgment to others. And Juliette Lemaire was perhaps after all the one I'd been looking for—well balanced, unafraid and present in the capital at all important times.

I restarted the recording in the summer of 1944, the days of the Liberation. Juliette hadn't joined in the euphoria that most people felt. She'd seen fighting at the École Militaire, as Free French units fired on Vichy recruits inside, leaving the walls marked by bullet holes. There were certainly plenty of people in Paris who, although they'd done nothing to express it, had opposed the Occupation and envied their country cousins—people who'd been able to make real gestures of support in haylofts, bicycles, messages and so on. For the frustrated *résistants* in Paris, long-held resentments became violence in the streets. But most of the people Juliette knew were not like that: They'd supported Marshal Pétain until a few weeks earlier. She found it hard to understand how so many of them went to cheer General de Gaulle on his march down the Champs-Élysées; none of the general's new admirers had protested at the death sentence pronounced on him as a traitor in his absence in 1940, and none had answered his call to go to England and join him. Yvonne Bonnet, the friend of so many German soldiers, waved her flag in a frenzy, but Georgette Chevalier, the only person Juliette knew who'd taken any action to support the Resistance, was still held in a concentration camp. And the defeat of the German army in Normandy had been achieved by the Americans, Canadians and British, with only one division, the radio said, of Free French soldiers. Juliette didn't know how many men that was, but not many.

There was now official talk of America and Britain as "our friends, the Allies," but for four years she'd walked to work past propaganda posters portraying these two countries as enemies—as Jews and Bolsheviks. It was not that she'd ever really believed that Mr. Churchill was a moneylender, a Shylock in a London bowler hat, but the change of heart was too quick to be convincing. Meanwhile, on the streets many people joined the manhunt, for fear they might otherwise themselves become the quarry; some of the most ardent avengers were those with the most to conceal.

Juliette spoke of how the courts heard the cases of those who had collaborated with the now-defeated Occupier. But, she said, everyone had collaborated. "Collaboration," after all, had been the official national policy, announced by Marshal Pétain, who had used the word proudly to describe the nature of the partnership he'd agreed upon with the Führer. How could it now be treason?

There were to be no trials in the old courts, because they had all worked under Vichy and were by definition therefore tainted. But it would take too long to wait for "clean" courts to be set up by the new government, so some of the first hearings were with soldiers sitting as judges. These military sessions at first had powers only to detain people to await trial by a proper civil court in due course, but those in charge were frightened of the anger of the mob that might be provoked by any delay. So, with some misgivings, they also gave the military tribunals the powers of judgment and sentencing.

To tell the truth, I found out most of this much later on. At the time it was chaos. Newspapers were limited to a single page and no one really knew what was going on, just that there was this sense of urgency. What I remember most about August and September was not the joy of liberation but the rush—the tearing hurry to avoid a civil war. It was more important to maintain order than to have justice. The people first in line were politicians like Pétain and Laval, then regional prefects who'd been too close to the Germans, then journalists and writers who'd been open in their support. Then of course there was the Milice. At Annecy they arrested a hundred members of the Milice who'd been active in rounding up Jews on behalf of the French government, in torturing and killing people suspected of being in the Resistance. The trial lasted only a day, and seventy-five Milice men were shot by a firing squad the next morning. But I had cousins in the southwest, where the Milice had done exactly the same things. When de Gaulle's men arrived in their town, the Milice men also presumed they'd be put on trial and sentenced to death. But all that happened is that they were given new uniforms. They were told they were now to form a military reserve for the new republic. The same men. This happened throughout the country. Later they became the basis of the riot police, the CRS.

The new government was trying to run ahead of the mob. The situation was desperate and General de Gaulle understood that. But it meant there was no real justice. Firing squad or a new uniform—you didn't know which to expect.

One morning in September, perhaps three weeks after the Liberation, I was walking to the Métro to go to work, when I was stopped in the street by three men. They each had different armbands. One had a hammer and sickle, one a big "V" and one a cross of Lorraine. They asked me my name and said I was under arrest. I said under whose authority and they said the FFI. Since the FFI, the French Forces of the Interior, were the people officially in charge of the transition, I went with them to the police station, where I was put in a back room with eight other women. I think we all knew what was coming.

Later that day, my name was called and I was taken in a van to a large building near Porte de la Chapelle. I don't know what it was usually, but there was a room with three men in military uniform. Two men stood up and read out statements. I was too frightened to take in all of what they said. One statement was from the manager of Maxim's restaurant, who had himself been arrested. Another was from a female neighbor or "friend." I was asked if I'd slept with a German soldier and I said no. I said I'd twice had dinner with an officer, but that was all. There had been no law against it so far as I knew. German soldiers and Parisian women mixed freely in public. I said that in my work I often came into contact with soldiers at the shop.

It was over quickly. They had more important people to deal with and I was told I was free to go: I was not a "horizontal collaborator." The senior soldier in charge was quite polite; he wasn't angry, like so many people at that time. But outside the building there was a crowd being held back by two police officers behind a barrier, and they were spitting and shouting. They were too many for the police to control. They broke through and I was grabbed and dragged down to the street to a barbershop. They put me in a chair and held my arms and legs while the barber shaved my head. Then they pushed me out onto the street again, where I ran for my life. In the crowd of people shouting, I saw the face of Yvonne Bonnet.

Somehow—for all the pushing and spitting—I still had my hand-bag with me, still wearing it like a bandit. And when I'd run as far as I could, I stopped by a draper's shop near Château d'Eau and bought a meter and a half of blue cloth, which I wound round my head like a turban. I was too ashamed to go home at once, so I hid among some trees in a park and waited till it was dark before I went back to my parents.

Many other women had a far worse time of it. They were sent to the Vélodrome d'Hiver or to Drancy to wait for the proper courts to be set up. At Drancy, they were beaten by the same guards who had beaten the Jews.

About a year later, after the concentration camps had been liber-ated, I saw Georgette Chevalier. By now she knew of all the medals that had been handed out to people who'd joined the Resistance only a few weeks before the Liberation. She wasn't bitter, though. And she refused to give the name of the person who'd informed on her. I told her what had happened to me and she said, "To think when we sat next to each other at school. That it would come to this." Then she put her arms round me just as she had when we'd huddled by the camp-fire in the Vosges Mountains, and I began to sob. I was ashamed that I'd not been more like her.

She said, "It's all right. We know what we did. I can sleep at night. So can you. But this will never, ever go away. Not until every last per-son who lived through it is dead."

And she was right. I still don't know when that will be. Even a child who was ten in 1944 will have some memory. So maybe when even the last of them has gone—in the year 2034, perhaps.

And as for me, I suppose I'm an old woman now, even if I don't feel old. I have no shame. I feel only sorrow that my one life turned out like this. My youth came at the wrong time. I moved out of Paris in the end. I married a decent man, we had two children and we lived in a village in the Loire, where I taught at the elementary school. In all the years I lived there, in all the parents' meetings and evenings with friends of our age, no one asked what I'd done in Paris during the Occupation. It was a closed subject. We lived a sort of half-life all those years, the sixties and seventies and so on, quite comfortable in its way in our new house with enough to eat and summer holidays, and with friends nearby. But so much was never said.

So I'm glad to have put down these memories at last and I hope that young people who listen to them will understand a little of what happened. What will they do with the knowledge? Can understanding the past help you to live better? That's not for me to say, but I feel pleased to have come to the Centre Jean Molland these last few days and I am grateful to the people here for having invited me.

By the way, my hair never grew back to what it had been before. It went gray when I was still young and I always had it cut before it reached my shoulders. I was never again that girl tripping down the steps from the raised platform of the Métro with my coat flying open and the whole world in front of me.

For three days after listening to this, I shut myself in my bedroom in the flat in Butte-aux-Cailles. I left a note for Tariq, asking him not to disturb me. I heard his footsteps come and go, his coughing in the morning from the coarse weed he smoked. But he'd become a more considerate lodger, closing the door quietly, no longer lighting cigarettes in the living room. I liked his euro offerings by the fruit bowl too; they made me feel kindly towards him.

In my room, I went over the downloaded Juliette file as well as my comments on the last recording at the Jean Molland and my interview at Mathilde's apartment. Then I looked over the notes I'd made on further oral witnesses and on documents from other libraries I'd visited.

With my rereading of the standard books, I was ready to start writing. I'd include some new statistics I'd discovered from documents at a Jewish library in the rue de Turenne as well as extensive quotation from the eyewitnesses. I'd gotten hold of some new data on pregnancy rates during the Occupation and some figures on women's pay; taken all together, it was enough to be a contribution.

The problem I wrestled with in my room was that the academic form seemed a bad fit for the task; there was so much I'd have to leave out. The testament of Mathilde and Juliette had been difficult to bear, to take on board, but it was harder still to think that my chapter might not do justice to their experiences.

Emerging from my reverie, I found two missed calls and a text message from Julian. And when we met two days later in his flat above the Alsatian brasserie, I outlined the problem to him.

"Perhaps you should think of writing a book of your own," he said.

"Yes, but what?" I pushed my hand up through my hair. "God, I can't do a sort of Heroines of the Resistance thing with pictures of pretty girls."

"Well. Let's think. Have a cup of tea. That's what we do in England when we have to work something out." He lifted the pot. "Just because such books have been a bit cheap before doesn't mean to say you couldn't write a serious one. Something that gave a real feeling of the nature of the experience. Maybe six essays. Or eight, or ten. Pick your most exciting or illustrative cases. See what they say about the nature of patriotism or nationalism or whatever we call it. Because it's certainly interesting that British women died for France. And also because British and French patriotism are completely different emotions. Ours is a bit shamefaced and populist; theirs is the province of the intellectual. So your women's stories would be gripping in themselves but also a way of getting at something abstract and almost academic. Then it would be a proper book you could be proud of."

"No one's going to commission me to write that. I'm unknown."

"That means you'd be cheap. They wouldn't have to pay you much. Write a clear, solid outline. That's what I did with de Musset. I tried to make it sound irresistible, a low-risk thing for them. As though they couldn't lose."

"And—"

"I'll put you in touch with my editor."

"That's very kind, Julian, but really . . ."

"Really what?"

I was thinking, "really," that no one had talked to me with such sympathy since Aleksandr, ten years earlier. It was as though Julian had given a lot of thought to it.

"I remember Aleksandr urging me to write a book," I said.

"Your Russian poet?"

"Playwright."

"I know. Tell me about him. You never really have."

"I think I might need another cup of tea first."

"When it gets to six o'clock we can have something stronger."

"Why not before?"

"The pubs don't open till six."

I felt I was beginning to understand Julian's idea of humor.

"Okay," I said, "I'll come clean on tea alone."

Botzaris

For a few days after what had happened between Clémence and me, I felt strange. Sensations I had no name for seemed to take me over. The good thing was that in most ways I felt calm—part of the world in a way that I had never done before. I felt connected to . . . to what? My home, my family, my past . . . Something to do with who I was, deep down, where I'd come from. Berber, Bedouin, Muslim, French, African . . . I was all these things, but I no longer felt limited by them. I sensed that I was part of something larger, more invigorating.

Two days afterwards, I had an SMS from Jamal, asking if I'd go and meet him at a café in Sevran, a notoriously hard-line Muslim suburb some way out on the RER.

"Is Hasim still angry with me for quitting?" I texted back.

"Nothing to do with H."

Something to do with drugs then, presumably—something not even Jamal wanted to spell out.

On the way to my rendezvous, I found that something seemed different, and it took me twenty minutes on the dirty RER train to see what it was. I wasn't looking at the women in the carriage in the same way as usual. I still noticed that some were more attractive than others, but I didn't picture in detail what each one might be like beneath her clothes. I was able to think about other things. Perhaps the change would only be temporary, but I had to admit that while it lasted it was something of a relief.

From what I'd read in advance online in an English popular newspaper, I expected Sevran to be full of men in Taliban headgear and women in burkas. But it turned out to be an ordinary suburban town, still French, with just a few more immigrants than average. I met Jamal in a run-down café with a green sign showing a racehorse and the letters PMU. It was famous, according to the newspaper, for not serving women. The proprietor put down his cigarette and welcomed us. Jamal ordered coffee, I asked for Coke. The place was poor, but it wasn't threatening. The bar guy was really nice and there were three girls at a table by the door. So much for the newspaper.

"Why are we meeting here?" I said.

"It's my day off work and I'm visiting a friend," said Jamal. "Listen, boy, you know you said you're going home soon."

"Yes. I've saved enough money for an airline ticket. But I haven't decided on a date yet."

His face broke into a smile. "Will you do something for me? Deliver an envelope to someone in Tangier."

"What's in it?"

"Money."

"What do I do with it?"

"You hand it over. And that's it."

"Is it legal?"

"To give money to someone? Of course it's legal."

"It's not some terrorist thing, is it?"

"No. I told you. I'm not religious. And I'm a man of peace. I think those terror people are crazy."

"So who's the money for?"

"People like me. To help them with their lives."

"And where's it from?"

"A charity in Saint-Denis."

"All right." I was thinking about the flight. I'd only been on a plane once before, when I was about three and my mother took me to Paris. So I'd been told.

"Have you read the book I gave you yet?" said Jamal.

"The Koran? No. And you just said you're not religious."

"I'm not. But the charity has religious backing." He smiled again. "And for your own sake. Your education, boy. You ought to know what we don't believe in."

"I'll have a look. I'm not a big reader."

Jamal looked at me over his coffee. "I don't know exactly who'll come to meet you in Tangier. It'll be no one I know."

"You don't know anyone outside Paris, Jamal."

"Sure. But suppose this guy's a believer. That's another reason it might be better if you had an idea of what he believes in. It would be polite."

"Okay. I'll try."

It was not just that Jamal had never been outside Paris, he'd hardly ever been out of Saint-Denis. But there was concern in his eyes as he looked at me. And maybe a little embarrassment as well—from shame at the narrow life that was all that history had allowed him. I felt like an actor in an old-fashioned play: a young messenger being dispatched by a homely uncle worried for his safe journey.

His gaze held mine. As I think I've said before, Jamal was a decent guy. I put my hand on his shoulder.

"I'm having a party on Friday. For my birthday. Do you want to come?"

"Where is it?"

As soon as I told him, I knew there was no chance. He was never going to come into the Second arrondissement.

"I may be busy. I'll have to see."

Busy . . . Of course. The social life of Medina-sur-Seine, the cocktail parties, the receptions . . . "Okay," I said. "See how you go."

. . .

When I let myself into Hannah's flat, there was a woman there I didn't know.

She stood up with a smile and said in English, "Hi, I'm Jasmine Mendel. I bet you've heard a lot about me."

She thrust out her hand and I shook it.

"I've come for your birthday party."

"You what?"

"Hannah told me about it. And I wasn't going to miss it for the world."

She had brown hair and a big smile. She gave off energy like the powerful compressor that thuds away by the permanent roadworks at the medina gate. I liked her straightaway, but I was worried she was teasing me.

"It's all right, man. To level with you, I had some time off work. And, like all Americans, I adore Paris. So when Hannah e-mailed me, I made a reservation that afternoon."

"So, it's not just my party that—"

"No, don't worry. But there is a party, right?"

There was. We met at the tapas place in the rue Vivienne, like I'd planned. Inside, the walls were bare stone, so it was like being in a cave. There was Hannah and Jasmine and Julian Finch, the guy Hannah was always having dinner with, and me. Jamal and Hasim didn't show, but Hannah had also asked two people from the library where she went to listen to her old ladies—a Frenchwoman called Florence and a German called Leo. So there were six of us, which was not much of a party, but it was better than nothing and the food was really great and they all said how good the wine was too, though I was drinking beer.

Jasmine was curious about everyone and kept asking questions about how we all knew each other. She seemed especially interested in Julian, the Englishman, and when we sat down at a table with candles on it, she put herself next to him.

Although he must have been over forty, this Julian was friendly to me, not treating me like some sort of strange pet that Hannah had picked up. He asked me about life at home and my college and he seemed to know a lot about Morocco. He said he'd been to Fez and Marrakesh but not Tangier.

I noticed Hannah looking anxiously from time to time at Jasmine and Julian, but I didn't know why.

It was interesting to see older people getting drunk. They were all so used to wine that they probably didn't notice how their behavior changed. After another bottle or two, we had dessert, then Florence, the Frenchwoman, and Leo, the German, both said they had to go. They'd drunk the least. I was meant to be paying because it was my party, but Hannah said she'd invited Florence and Leo, so they were her guests, and Julian said he'd like to pay for me, as his birthday present, so I ended up paying almost nothing, not even for the taxi, which Jasmine, who'd drunk the most, paid for when it dropped the four of us back in Butte-aux-Cailles, showering euros on the pavement.

Hannah said that as it was my birthday I could smoke in the apartment, so I had a little of Jamal's best to get my levels up to theirs. Jasmine insisted on a giant toke as well.

Somehow we got onto people's problems with understanding French. Julian said he had trouble when he first arrived if he was invited to somewhere *sans vin*.

"I expected a dry evening," he said. "So I stopped at a bar on the way. Turned out it was the number of the house, *cent vingt*. A hundred and twenty."

"I had a moment the other day," said Hannah, "when I heard someone say, *'Mais après tout nous sommes tous daddons.'* I looked up *daddon* in the dictionary, but there was nothing there. Finally I worked out she meant we were all descended from Adam. *Nous sommes tous d'Adam.*"

"Speak for yourself," said Jasmine. "I'm a *daddon* till the day I die."

"After we had the *onglet* and the *anglais*," said Julian, "I invented a story for Hannah. The *quand* one. Do you remember?"

"Not word for word," said Hannah.

"It was something like . . . *Quel cant qu'on raconte quand que le Comte est con qui recompte ses comptes. Quant à la conte du concombre, par conséquence, quand il danse le can-can dans le camp à Caen . . .*"

"However you look at it, everything comes out *con*," I said. "Story of my—"

"Tariq!"

I think it was Jasmine who called out my name, pretending to be shocked, but it could have been Hannah. It certainly wasn't Julian, who carried on chatting to me while both women went to the bathroom. He was quite handsome in a middle-aged way, like one of those film actors who play the dad of the troubled teenager. Or maybe the slightly inspiring high-school teacher. He had a really nice jacket too.

But the thing you noticed above and beyond all else about Julian, the thing that was so obvious that it was almost embarrassing—so obvious that even I was aware of it—was that he was completely obsessed by Hannah.

In the tapas bar he'd kept glancing past Jasmine and Leo to check on her. Now when she came back into the sitting room with a bottle of wine and wrestled with a corkscrew, the look on his face was like nothing I'd ever seen. It was as though he'd never really looked at a girl before and was struggling to get to grips with a miracle of nature.

Perhaps I'd changed. The weed, what had happened with Clémence . . . I don't know. But to see someone look at someone else like that . . . It was touching, to be honest. And Hannah did look nice that evening. She was no beauty, as I've said, but the light caught her hair, the black and brown together, as she worked away at the cork.

You could see that Julian wanted to help, but something made him hesitate. Not wanting to patronize her? Enjoying the flush on her skin? I don't know, but I decided to try some wine from a bottle that was already open and see if I could get to like it. It tasted fine.

"And I so love your British accent," Jasmine was saying.

"Thanks, but I'm afraid there's no such thing," said Julian. "There's Scottish, English, Welsh and Northern Irish accents. Hundreds of each. But no such thing as a British accent."

"Don't be so snippy, Julian," said Hannah, still wrestling with the bottle.

"I didn't mean to be. The French have never understood either. They always say English to mean British. Even their politicians. But the idea that a nation is composed of four parts is really not that complicated. It does make you wonder about the French claim to being such a reasonable and intellectual people if they can't even grasp that. I don't say Burgundians to mean French."

"How's the research going, honey?" said Jasmine.

". . . particularly hard on all the Scots and Welsh and Ulstermen who lie buried beneath French soil after their attempts to keep Alsace-Lorraine for France to be known as 'English.' It's a bit—"

"It's a bit . . . overwhelming," said Hannah with a gasp as she eventually pulled the cork out. "I've got more material than I can use and some of it doesn't seem to fit the academic pattern. Some of the oral witness, the audio files, have been . . . surprising."

"Are they reliable?" said Jasmine, who was sitting close to Julian again.

"I think so. Tariq's helped me a bit. With translation and so on."

Maybe it was the wine, or the weed, or both, but I found myself saying, "What makes you think these women in the recording booth were telling the truth? They were all pretty old and they might have been forgetful. But also, has it ever occurred to you that they went in there and just made the whole thing up?"

Hannah pushed her hand back through the front of her hair. "There are ways of checking. And if I can't verify anything, I'll put it at arm's length. Or drop it."

"That's what I'd do if I were them," I said. "Just go in and make up a good story."

The conversation began to really spin along then, with everyone talking over each other.

For the first time in my life, I felt I was getting the hang of wine. Maybe we had the wrong stuff at home, because this French wine gave you a real blast. There were no palpitations or white sweats, you just felt really fond of everyone.

Take Jasmine, for instance, who'd come all the way across the Atlantic to see her friend. That was so nice of her that I wanted to cuddle up and put my face between her breasts in the clean white shirt she'd put on for the party. And Hannah, still shooting anxious glances that I couldn't read at her two friends but looking so vulnerable. I'd never thought of my landlady that way before, but I wanted to put my arms round her—not to bury my face in her sweater, à la Jasmine, not at all, just to somehow look after her a bit. And there was Julian, this English guy, and the hilarious efforts he was making not to gawp at Hannah.

I had some more wine.

"Warren sends his love," said Jasmine. "He was in New York last week. You know he's moving to Heinz? He's doing real well."

"Who's Warren?" I said.

"My brother," said Hannah. "He's kind of a big shot in canned goods. If you see what I mean."

"I tried to get him to come," said Jasmine, "but he was going to Pittsburgh. And then I said what about your parents, why don't they come to Europe, come and see you, and he said they don't have passports. Is that true?"

"I guess so," said Hannah.

"And are you having a good time in Paris, Tariq?" said Jasmine.

"Wonderful," I said, which was at that moment true.

"What do you like most? The Eiffel Tower? The Latin Quarter?"

"No, I like the Métro best."

Everyone began laughing, so I laughed too as I poured myself some wine. "I like the stations. Their crazy names. I love the funny smell, like gas and burnt rope. I like the girls I see in the carriages. And the people I come across there. One day I met this guy who does a puppet show every day on Line Twelve. He's called Victor Hugo."

"I bet he is," said Jasmine.

"Sometimes he'll go on another line, though, for a change. And we've been to this place called Flunch, where you can eat as much as you like."

"What's your favorite station name?" said Julian.

"So many to choose from," I said. I was really flying now. "I like the long weird ones like Réaumur-Sébastopol. But I like short ones too. Botzaris. Hannah teased me that I didn't know any of these guys they were named after. Or the famous dates in history."

"Yeah, it was all Botzaris to you, wasn't it?" said Hannah.

"Yes, but some of them are just streets or places, aren't they? Bastille? Invalides. Charles de . . ."

They were all laughing even more by now and I suddenly wasn't feeling quite as good as a minute ago, so I made an excuse and went to the bathroom, where I fished out my cell phone and did some searching. Had I made a stupid mistake? Bastille, for instance. Don't tell me there was a painter called Auguste Bastille. No. All clear, it was just a prison, just a place. What other ones had I mentioned? Marie-Louise Invalides, a famous dancer? No. Fine. Charles de Gaulle–Étoile. It was Étoile because of the star shape of the roads radiating from the Arc de Triomphe. Obviously. And Charles de Gaulle?

The Wi-Fi labored for a moment, then . . . Whoa. I mean . . . *Fuck*.

I was really feeling sick now. My brain had turned to alcohol. I bent over the toilet. Frozen fireballs. Charles de fucking Gaulle.

• • •

Two days later, when I'd recovered, I went down to Mairie d'Issy early in the morning and teamed up again with Victor Hugo. I felt in need of some of his old-timer's wisdom, whether it was reliable or not. He seemed happy to see me, but it didn't work out like one of our usual mornings.

Victor was in a thoughtful mood and said he lacked the energy to do his puppet show. So we got off together at Assemblée Nationale (someone had blacked out the name on the platform and written "Palais Bourbon" in its place) and walked along the riverbank. This was an area I hadn't visited before. There were tourists with cameras and baseball caps, driven along by their guides, clutching water bottles, photographing themselves against the backdrop of the Seine.

As we walked, Victor Hugo talked to me about the Bible and told me the stories of Moses and Samson and Gideon and Joshua and Jonah and David and Bathsheba and Solomon and Saul and Elijah. I must say that even to someone who'd seen a lot of action movies, these episodes of battle and sex and disembodied voices were pretty gripping.

"But enough, Monsieur Zafar. What am I thinking, telling all this Jewish folklore to a Mussulman? Forgive me. I was intoxicated by the power of narrative and found myself unable to stop." He coughed. "Not for the first time, I must confess."

We had arrived at a bridge that led to an island with a cathedral. Notre Dame, I presumed. Victor Hugo gazed over.

"Of course my own country once hoped to be a Mussulman power." The phrase he used in French was *une puissance mussulmane.*

"Really?"

"The idea was to enlighten the Arab world, to bring it science, law, the rights of man, then form an alliance with them against our common enemy."

"Who's that?"

"The Americans."

"But that didn't happen."

"No."

"What stopped it?"

"World wars. Other European countries. The Germans and the English."

"Was that all?"

"No. As a result of the wars, the countries of the Maghreb, the men of Algeria, Morocco, Tunisia—people who had once loved us, or at least lived alongside us—came to distrust France as much as they despised the other Europeans. So they decided to remove us. And because they were so poor, so beaten and so spread out, the only flag under which they could come together was the flag of their vanished god. They brought a god into politics! And that was the end for France. After that, there was only massacre, torture and despair. The end of our oriental dream."

He was starting to lose me here, but he sounded mournful. He took me by the elbow. "See here," he said. "This bridge. The Pont Saint-Michel. Look."

I looked. I saw tourists.

"An awful place for your people," said Victor, still holding my arm. "The last chance of friendship between our countries ended forever on this spot. It was from this bridge that the police threw the bodies of the Mohammedans into the Seine. To conceal how they had beaten and killed them."

"When was this?" I said.

"Let me see . . . Forty or fifty years ago. Quite recently."

I calculated, splitting the difference. Forty-five years ago would make it 1961, when my mother was a child in Paris. Perhaps her father had been one of those involved. But no, he was French or at the least French Algerian—*pied noir*, black foot maybe, but white skin. But his wife, my Algerian grandmother . . . Suppose that was the trauma of my mother's childhood. Her own mother (Algerian Granny) killed, then thrown by riot police into the river.

"It was an infamous day," said Victor Hugo, releasing my arm and looking into the brown water of the Seine. "Hundreds of people were murdered by the police because of the way they looked. The police had been given a free hand by the man in charge, whose name was Papon. He said they could do whatever they liked and he would cover for them. During the war, twenty years before, this Monsieur Papon had been concerned with rounding up the Israelites in a bicycling arena farther down the river to our left—whence they were dispatched to a place in Upper Silesia known for its manufacture of chemicals and there exterminated by gas poisoning. He was not a good citizen of the republic, Monsieur Papon. He had not drunk deep from Pascal or Voltaire, from Racine or Montaigne or even from my own more modest work. He had turned his back on the clear stream of enlightenment and drunk from the puddles of the midden. Like a beast."

I was now thinking too much about my grandmother to concentrate on the history lesson. I wondered if there might be a way of finding out if she had been one of the victims of this man Papon's massacre. Or perhaps my French grandfather. Had he been tanned enough by the Algerian sun to pass for brown in the eyes of a crazed riot policeman?

"For weeks afterwards," Victor Hugo was saying, "the bodies of Algerians and Moroccans were washed up on the banks of the river, like the jetsam from an oriental merchantman that had been scuttled in the night."

Was there perhaps an official casualty list, I wondered? And what name would I search for, what in fact *was* the family name of my grandparents? Although I knew my father's parents, I'd never met my mother's—French Grandpa and Algerian Granny. They'd never been mentioned at home, so there was no need to add a surname to distinguish them from the Zafar grandparents.

"For many years," Victor Hugo was saying, "we were fascinated by what we called the Orient, though North Africa is not really very far to the east. But at the end of the nineteenth century, Paris was in love with the Tuareg and the Berber, with their kilims and their arches and their metalwork. We had grand exhibitions on the Champ de Mars with pavilions of the Orient. Our poets smoked hashish and our artists painted odalisques. It was a fashion, it was a game we played with the people of the Maghreb as our toys. Until we lost interest. And for that, and for the massacres, your people have never forgiven us."

A few minutes later, Victor said he had to be on his way. He had a rendezvous with someone—his wife, I guessed, or perhaps his mistress. He didn't say, but he looked pleased at the prospect.

"I do hope we'll meet again, Monsieur Zafar," he said, holding out his hand. "I have enjoyed our promenades."

"Yes, I hope so, Monsieur Hugo."

After I'd watched the old boy shuffle off towards the Boulevard Saint-Michel, I went down some steps to the edge of the river itself. I sat on the embankment, my legs hanging loose, and gazed into the water. I wished I'd been like Hannah Kohler, who knew everything about her family and the history of the countries from which they'd long ago emigrated to America. She understood herself, her ancestors and her obligations to them. Her earnest work, it struck me, was a thank-you letter to the generations who had enabled her to know her place.

For people like me—or Hasim and especially Jamal—there was no such luck. I would never meet my grandmother or her French-born husband, though I had a feeling I would have liked them both. He was an adventurer in Algerian exile and must have been a free spirit to have married a local girl. And she too must have been bold—to have left home and gone to live in Paris, this wonderful, difficult place.

It was not their ghostly absence that I felt, as I sat by the river, staring into the silent water. What haunted me was the sense that their secrets had left a permanent void in my life.

EIGHTEEN

Barbès-Rochechouart

I T WAS GOOD TO SEE JASMINE AGAIN AND TO SPEND TIME WITH HER after Tariq's birthday. I was especially grateful for her company after my earlier promise to Julian to "come clean on tea alone" had led me into difficulty.

I had begun by sharing with Julian a description of my first visit to Aleksandr's apartment. He lived off the rue de la Goutte d'Or—near the department store with windows full of wedding gowns and its name, TATI, written up in the colorways of the striped laundry bag that was everywhere at the time. It was like being in Kampala (as I imagined it, anyway, not yet having visited) as I came down the steps from the Métro and turned off the boulevard, past the hawkers selling faux–designer suitcases, into a narrow street of butchers' shops. Pigs' trotters, split longways, were lined up in neat rows; in one place, above raw joints of chicken, a sheep's head was oozing on a spit. The smell of meat was so overpowering that it was a relief to come to a fruit counter, where the bananas were laid out by color, from bright green through yellow to black, catering to tribal custom. Beyond the food shops there was a djel-laba store and a kiosk that sent money orders home. On almost every face I saw a longing for Africa.

After the next corner, a street door opened on a different world. I crossed a courtyard and walked up a wide stone staircase to the first floor, where I knocked. Once inside, I was out of Africa, back in France, back with my Russian, and from this point on, as I talked to Julian, I began to edit my account of what had happened.

The truth was that from the start there was a scary kind of candor. I thought it was a sign of Aleksandr's passion for me that he should be so honest; he seemed to have no time for caution. His directness was born of experience, I guessed, and when we spoke French (which was most of the time, my French being better than his English), I was able to respond without feeling as vulnerable as I might have felt in my own language. I told him everything—what I dreamed and longed for, even how to touch me. I was young and I was small, and he was a man of forty-five, solid and heavy on my frame. Sex was the gateway to intimacy, and sex intensified that closeness all the time, but the intimacy itself had something else—a joyous feeling of having squared a circle, of having somehow cheated death.

I understood that with my boyfriends at college, I'd been only going through the motions. In Aleksandr I had found what the poets wrote about, and it was different in kind. Body and soul, no holding back, and the more I offered, the more I believed in what I found. It was as though he'd revealed to me that being his lover was my purpose in being alive, and always had been. It was not so much that I'd previously imagined I had a different function; it was more that I hadn't known till then that I had a raison d'être at all.

In the version of all this I offered Julian, I tried to play down the sex and dwell on the elevated conversations in which we'd discussed . . . The problem was that I could barely remember what on earth we had discussed. Surely when I had come back to bed in a T-shirt, carrying tea or wine, we must have touched on Pushkin and Tolstoy and the failures of Communism; we must at least have talked about his childhood and how his grandparents had weathered the Revolution. Or something. Yes, there was the time that he'd said I should write a book, though I couldn't say what sort of book he'd had in mind. A play, was it? I could recall in some detail his admiring commentary on Paris when we were out on the streets and in the bars, his admiration for the men of the Enlightenment and for France's continuing battle to be both revolutionary and democratic. But what I remembered best of what Aleksandr had whispered to me in the rue de la Goutte d'Or was more personal and much less elevated.

"Interesting area," said Julian, when I finally paused for breath. "Zola country."

I guessed he was trying to change the subject in order to spare my embarrassment, so I doubled my efforts to make what had happened ten years ago sound more like a meeting of minds. The truth didn't sound grand enough.

"He was a wonderful companion in the city where I'd been so lonely. But it wasn't just the relief of having company, you understand. It was much more than that. We were identical in the way we . . ."

". . . in his novel *L'Assommoir*," said Julian, just carrying on. "It's been translated as 'The Boozer' or 'The Knockout Shop.' Lots of people think it's his very best, though in my view it's not as good as *Germinal* . . ."

". . . though I did know, of course, that he was married," I said, "but they were separated. And anyway we had so much in common that . . ."

". . . and Gervaise the poor laundress lies dead for days at the bottom of her sordid building in the rue de la Goutte d'Or before anyone finds her . . ."

I wasn't going to give in to Julian's delicate attempts to spare me. "Though I'm not defined by one affair that ended badly," I was saying firmly. "I'm not a victim. All love affairs end badly, unless they just fizzle out, which is itself a bad ending anyway."

". . . and Gervaise is living in a cardboard box beneath the stairs. The place was built around a courtyard. Perhaps the very same one that your Russian lived in."

I looked down. I had nothing left to say on this subject and I knew if I kept talking I would start to cry.

It was only when Aleksandr left me one day, without warning, to go back to St. Petersburg that I began to see that his candor and his urgency were not the mark of his commitment but a sign that he was short of time; he'd never looked into changing the return date on his ticket. It turned out he was "separated" from his wife only in the sense of living in a different country. The intimacy of his pillow talk, which I'd taken as a measure of how deeply he was wrapped up in me, was his way of not engaging in anything more serious—on topics where, I later suspected, he was frightened of being bored by my opinions.

Of course, I didn't tell Julian how many weeks I'd sobbed and torn at the bedclothes, loathing my gullibility as much as I had hated Aleksandr. I didn't say how many years the feeling tortured me. Even to myself I could never admit how much—for all I felt humiliated and abused—I had continued loving him. I couldn't admit it because I couldn't tolerate the idea that I was that deeply flawed.

All I could do was wonder what had happened in my life up to that point to make me so vulnerable. I looked back at my childhood, searching for a clue, but in the middling household with the confident brother and the slightly baffled parents ("But she's so *wordy* . . ."), in the functional high school where I had friends enough, and in the town with steel mills replaced by IT start-ups, there seemed nothing unusual—no trauma, no denied reason for being so defenseless. So maybe it was just the way I was.

For ten years I'd tried not to revisit, let alone revive, the earlier person I had been, that Dido full of angry yearning. It might have been my real or truest self, but I preferred another version—one that worked, had colleagues and friends and went about her business eagerly. And as I gave Julian an idea of the years that followed, he grew less embarrassed. He seemed happy to ask about my time in Africa and my return to college as a postdoc, intrigued by my failed dates with other men, amused by the sound of the all-powerful Professor Putnam.

By the time I'd finished the account of what Julian had called "your Russian poet" and its aftermath, I felt tired, though no longer ill at ease. We sat in silence for a time, each picturing, I suppose, the fragments of the fallout—the bits and pieces of what I'd once been. I knew my story sounded in some way unconvincing, because I'd failed to convey the depth of the emotion. I didn't have the words. But the odd thing was that I no longer minded. I was under no obligation to convince anyone, even Julian; my task was to survive: to heal, somehow, and move onward.

"It's nearly eight o'clock," said Julian at last.

"Does that mean the pubs are open now?"

"It certainly does. And the restaurants. And for once you're going to let me pay. You won't be abandoning a principle or betraying your sisters. It's what friends do sometimes. Give each other presents."

I stood up. I felt relieved. I felt more than that, in fact. I felt reborn.

• • •

We went to a noisy café-restaurant in a backstreet near Oberkampf. Outside, beneath an awning, people sat smoking efficiently, like dogs in a laboratory. Indoors, the ceiling was decorated with scenes from a circus, and I thought it best not to say that I'd always been afraid of clowns.

Julian was thrilled to be allowed to pay at last, to be the host, and spent a long time consulting with the waitress about the wine.

"The trouble with organic is that it often tastes of beetroot," he said when she'd gone. "Or worse. I was trying to find if they had something that tastes like wine."

In the course of dinner, I found myself being gently probed about Aleksandr. Julian kept his language simple. "It must have knocked you back a bit" was one of his British openings; but I found it much easier to respond to this kind of thing than to the pseudo-scientific terms of Dr. Pavin, the Beacon Hill therapist.

"Well," I said, "it sure put me off men."

"But you're naturally affectionate. And optimistic. So you must have felt an urge to . . . to try again at some point."

"I did feel that, yes. But I was able to control the urge. I couldn't risk a repeat."

"So you consciously shut down the better part of yourself."

"I made some hard choices. But I wouldn't say it was the 'better' part. It was a different part, that's all. Perhaps the 'better' bit was the intellectual part, the worker."

"Don't you think that the urge to affection, towards trust and the giving of yourself—for all the risk involved—is a noble urge? To love. It's life-giving, life-affirming, whatever you want to call it. And in that sense 'better' than self-protection, however logical that may be?"

"No, I think it's just a different way of living. Love is danger. I made a choice, no more than that."

The food had arrived, and with it some red wine that tasted, to Julian's relief, of wine. I found myself thinking about the men who'd asked me out over the years and how I'd developed strategies to stop them. It was difficult at the time to be honest. I'd told Jasmine that I had difficulties with the act of sex, though in fact I'd enjoyed it with Aleksandr to an extent that seemed almost indecent. To some of the men I hinted that my interests lay more with my own sex; to others, I mentioned entanglements, obligations . . . With one, I simply broke down and cried, sobbing till (I saw through parted fingers) he left.

After a few minutes, seeing me lost in thought, Julian said, "How much longer are you going to stay in Paris?"

I looked up. "My grant runs till the end of June, but I have a little cash saved up. The apartment lease lasts until September. Then I have one more year in the department. Putnam said I might do some teaching back home next year."

"Might you extend your time here?"

"I doubt it. I'll finish writing the chapter, but I don't think they'll want me to stay."

"It's certainly an interesting area, the Occupation. I've done a bit more research of my own."

"Hey, you stick to your Romantic poets with the long hair. This history stuff is mine."

"I was thinking of offering a guided tour. It would make me some pocket money. *Les Années Noires*. Four Years We Must Forget. Or, rather, not. It takes you round some nice parts of Paris. The Opéra, the Kommandatur in the building opposite, which is now Berlitz and Air Maroc. Then onto the Métro and over the river to Bir-Hakeim and the site of the Vélodrome d'Hiver and the grudging little monument to all those packed off to Auschwitz."

"Yes, but you're going to need some human touches, I think."

"I can take them to Avenue de Suffren, near the Eiffel Tower, where the Tambour sisters lived. Germaine and Madeleine. Incredibly brave women. But some fool resister had left a briefcase on a train with documents full of names and addresses. Number 38 Avenue de Suffren was a death trap. The Gestapo had watched it for years. Then we'd swing down to Sèvres-Babylone, to the Hôtel Lutetia, where the Abwehr set up shop, then up to Avenue Foch, where SS Security chose to put their headquarters because it was Marshal Foch who'd taken the German surrender in 1918."

"That's quite a grudge."

"When I walk past number 84 Avenue Foch and look up to the little maids' rooms on the top floor, where the SD used to torture their prisoners, I sometimes think I can hear the ghost of a woman crying."

I said nothing.

"You look sad," said Julian. "Don't you like the food?"

"What? No. I like it. What is it?"

"Duck something." He looked at the small menu. "Pithiviers. Whatever that is. Tart. Pie. It's not bad, is it?"

"It's great. No, it's just that I was thinking. We talk so much about the importance of remembering. Of redeeming the lives of people who have gone before. Of educating children so they don't make the same mistakes. What if that's all just pious nonsense?"

"What do you mean?"

"Well. What, really, is the difference between the commemoration of an atrocity and the perpetuation of a grievance?"

Julian breathed in. "I think we know."

"Don't just dismiss the question."

"I'm not. Only a few years ago the Serbs were massacring Bosnian Muslims to get their own back for the way the Serbs were beaten by the Ottoman Turks at the Battle of Kosovo in 1380-something! The whole Serbian identity is built on the myth of Kosovo Polje. Wouldn't it be better if they'd just forgotten? Six hundred years is a bloody long time to brood."

"Sure is." I was beginning to feel a little worn down, but Julian carried on.

"What happened to the ANZAC forces at Gallipoli in 1915 was the making of Australia. The anniversary became their national day. But it also preserved a feeling of anger against their British commanders. It made resentment a key part of who they are. Though Britain lost twice as many men as Australia and New Zealand."

I looked down at the table, fearing I was about to lose the ground I'd gained earlier that evening. "That was great," I said, standing up suddenly. "I'm sorry, but I think I should be getting back now."

Julian put his hand on my wrist. "I'm sorry. Was I . . . I didn't mean to go on."

"Not at all. I'm just tired."

"Do you feel all right?"

"Yes. Just tired. I got a lot . . . off my chest . . . Earlier on."

"I'll find a taxi."

. . .

Tariq had been all but invisible since the evening of his birthday party. The next day he'd offered his room to Jasmine, who'd previously been sharing my bed. I said yes and thanked him for his offer. Tariq took himself off at once, saying he'd be back when Jasmine returned to New York at the end of the week.

In the drunken haze of the birthday evening, I hadn't thought much about his embarrassment over General de Gaulle. The conversation moved on in his absence and it was a while before he returned, pale-faced, from the bathroom. Who was I to judge him anyhow? Back in my freshman year I'd had plenty of de Gaulle moments of my own, and they'd just spurred me on. It was less a "love of learning" than a desire not to be shown up that had made me sit an extra hour in the library and grind things into my memory.

Reluctance to laugh at Tariq's ignorance was part of a deeper shift I felt starting to take place. I couldn't put it into words yet, but there was some sort of tectonic rumbling . . . I sighed. There was no time now to think about some reshaping of my life's foundations. I had work to do. It was a question of laying out papers on the table in the living room, making plans, cutting, pasting, and starting again, as I began to shape my chapter.

There was the sound of a key in the door and Tariq came in, carrying a small backpack.

"Are you okay?" I said. "Where have you been?"

"I went to see an old friend. A Chinese woman on the twenty-first floor of the Olympiades. Has Jasmine gone?"

"She left this morning."

"I liked her."

"I could see that." I found myself smiling as I settled back to work.

When Tariq had had a shower, he came back and sat down in the sitting room with a can of Coke. I looked up reluctantly from my table, over the top of my glasses, but he didn't budge.

"Good party, wasn't it?" he said.

I took off my glasses. "Yes. It was a good evening."

"I liked your friends."

"Thank you."

"So that's the guy you're always having dinner with."

"Julian? Not 'always.' Sometimes."

"But he's not your boyfriend, right?"

"No. I told you."

"He takes you out?"

"He always tries to pay, if that's what you mean by 'taking out.'"

"And what do you talk about when you're on a not-date with him?"

"Why do you ask?"

"I just wondered. I saw him . . . looking at you."

"We talk a lot about my work."

"Is that all?"

"The other day I did tell him about . . . more personal things. We talk about the past, mostly. He's done some work in my area, as a matter of fact. He's made some suggestions."

"Like an extra researcher?"

"In a way."

"And does he try it on with you?"

"God, no." I laughed. "It's not like that between us. He's a Brit who talks about the pubs being open and having another cup of tea."

Tariq squeezed the empty Coke can with an irritating noise. "Do you think he's maybe . . . laughing at himself? Living up to some idea you have of him?"

"A little bit, I guess. But he's still not . . . It's more complicated. Believe me. Now I need to do some more work, so if you could . . ."

"Is it?" said Tariq, standing up.

"Is it what?"

"Complicated?"

I put on my glasses again and opened the Masson file.

● ● ●

That evening I had an e-mail from Julian with a poem attached. It was called "The End and the Beginning," and it was by a Polish writer called Wisława Szymborska. "This is what I was trying to say the other day," Julian had written. "But obviously she puts it better." The poem was about how, after every war and every atrocity, the mundane act of clearing up has to begin. Bridges need to be rebuilt, bodies are buried, life continues. After a few years, some people can still recall the reasons for the disaster, some are starting to be bored by the subject. It ended:

Those who knew
what was going on here
must make way for
those who know little.
And less than little.
And finally as little as nothing.

In the grass that has overgrown
causes and effects,
someone must be stretched out
blade of grass in his mouth
gazing at the clouds.

It was good, I thought, and seemed somehow universal. But it was not the last word. It made me more determined still to visit Natzweiler, the concentration camp in the Vosges Mountains—a trip I'd been postponing for a while. It was a camp for men, but I knew that Andrée Borrel had been murdered there, along with three other women of SOE who had parachuted into France. It was the only Nazi concentration camp on French soil and interesting for that reason; I also wanted to pay my respects to Andrée, a woman after all described as "the best of us all"—a phrase that had haunted me since I first read it. An Internet search showed it was reachable from Strasbourg, though there seemed to be no railway station nearby and no buses. I'd have to rent a car.

As I was tidying away my papers for the night, I came across the photocopy of "La Nuit de Décembre" by Alfred de Musset, which I'd never finished translating. I quickly read myself back to the point where I'd stopped: the poet followed everywhere by someone who looked exactly like him, not so much a double as an alter ego . . . How this figure had watched him as a child, a student, a lover and so on, sometimes benign, sometimes frightening—an apparition at his father's deathbed and a companion on his travels through Europe.

The next part of the poem was more confessional. It concerned the memory of a love that had been lost. The poet was alone on his bed, imagining the warm absence of his lover. He gathered up some physical mementos, strands of hair, some letters—the *"débris d'amour."* He looked at the relics, the eternal vows of a single day, "tears wept by eyes which tomorrow will no longer recognize them."

Without the presence of the double, the poem became suddenly fierce. I stopped reading and put it to one side. There was only a page or so left and I thought I might try to finish my translation on the train to Strasbourg.

In the early evening of the next day, feeling a little housebound (what my old Lyonnaise landlady liked to call *"casanière"*), I decided to go for a walk in the city. I thought I remembered Julian telling me that de Musset had once seen his alter ego coming towards him in the Tuileries Gardens. Or was it the Jardin du Luxembourg? There was another famous poem, by Verlaine, called "Colloque Sentimental," about the ghosts of two lovers in a *"vieux parc solitaire et glacé,"* an old park, lonely and frozen. Perhaps I'd been thinking of that. I quickly looked the poem up and found that it was only a few lines long. The two ghosts walk towards each other, asking if their love had ever truly existed. "Do you still see my soul in your dreams?" The last line was: "The night alone heard their words." This poem also seemed too powerful for comfort, and I pushed down the lid of my laptop on the open file.

At any rate, I'd go to the Tuileries, because I'd never been there before. It was not part of the Left Bank I'd gone looking for as a student, nor of the place of slums and factories that I'd recently been frequenting. It belonged to a part of the city where space had been no object to the monarchs and emperors who'd laid out the vistas. Emerging at Louvre-Rivoli, going up the steps, I pictured Major Klaus Richter doing the same thing: getting out of the first-class German carriage at the front of the train, spotting the leggy Juliette with her handbag worn bandit-style on its long strap and the carefree swing of her hips as she climbed the steps and set off down the rue de Rivoli. Beneath the arches of the street, down the long colonnade, I could all but see the hanging Nazi flags that brushed her shoulders.

Inside the gardens there were busts and statues celebrating the Romans who'd invaded Gaul—an influence so important to France but quite unknown in my own country, or in Tariq's for that matter. None of the inscribed names meant anything to me and I doubted whether they were familiar to the others who passed the stone beards without a second glance.

I walked down an avenue of horse-chestnut trees, the dust gray-white on the hard ground. On my left was a silver-birch plantation and a notice that told me it had once been the site of a *manège*, or riding school. It was twilight, but the gardens were still full. From being the private pleasure ground of kings, the Tuileries had become, in the French way, a garden for the People. I sat on a bench and thought of those who'd trodden these paths. The enchanting Gilberte Swann as a child chasing a metal hoop, adored from afar by the young Marcel of Proust's novel . . . Mathilde Masson and her keen Armand, who'd sat together over their rationed picnic, perhaps on this same bench, as he told her he was part of a Resistance group.

A slight, dark-haired woman of about my own age, dressed in a similar sundress with bare legs, walked across my eyeline towards the children's play area, where she leaned over and lifted a small child up into her arms.

I had come to the Tuileries for gentle exercise and peace but found my mind raging with thoughts that wouldn't quite connect. In a narrow avenue, behind a screen of pleached hornbeams, a young married couple posed for wedding pictures, the photographer hurrying them to catch the last of the light. I stood up and breathed in hard. It was time to go.

The park was beginning to empty as I walked towards the eastern end, where it joined the courtyards of the Louvre. Here the graveled paths gave way to a green lawn, on which were hedges of box and yew. As I walked between them in the first moments of night, I heard rustlings from inside the foliage, then saw male arms and legs sticking out. Everywhere I looked the bushes were alive. A few feet in front of me, two men crawled out, then stood, adjusting their clothes.

Behind the lawn was the museum, a nation's cultural identity in colossal stone; beside it was the glass pyramid, a *grand projet* grasp at immortality by a president whose name I couldn't bring to mind. On the grass there were scores of abandoned fast-food cartons and bags, half-liter polystyrene cups with lids pierced by plastic straws, among which the satisfied couples were beginning to pick their way towards the rue de Rivoli.

Filles du Calvaire

I NEVER QUITE KNEW IF VICTOR HUGO WAS TELLING THE TRUTH, SO BACK at the flat I did an Internet search into the Paris events of 1961. There was plenty there. Things in the Algerian War were out of hand, with massacre and torture on both sides. Some wild Algerians had brought their struggle to the streets of Paris and had killed about a dozen cops in the course of the year. So the government called in Papon, who'd been a district torturer in Algeria, rounder-up of Jews at the Vélodrome d'Hiver in 1942 and later on was convicted of crimes against humanity. Just the man. He introduced an eight-thirty p.m. curfew on all 150,000 Algerians in and around Paris and sent in police squads to Algerian districts to rough up anyone of "North African appearance." He told his men to be "subversive" and that he would cover for them. A demonstration against the curfew was planned, but police blocked every station and road into the city center. Despite this, about 30,000 Algerians were able to gather and protest. The police, many of them old Vichy militiamen who'd escaped trial in 1944, grabbed as many as they could and bused them off to detention centers, where they shot some, tortured some and knocked out others with truncheons or pickax handles. Then, from bridges all through the city, including one at police headquarters near Notre Dame, where Papon was watching, they tied their hands and threw them into the river.

Most of what I read stressed how hard it was to know the exact numbers, since it had all been denied at the time and the police archives were still closed. There'd been a few campaigns and books by journalists in recent years, but the biggest source of information on the numbers seemed to be "citation needed."

Although I could now more or less understand all this (something I couldn't have done in January, when I first arrived), I knew there was no chance of finding out the truth. I had no real basis for thinking that either of my grandparents had been involved. I had nothing more than an unreasonable suspicion—or maybe just the hope of bringing their story to an end in my mind.

I decided to concentrate on a matter that was easier to deal with. I chose a day for my flight home and looked for the best deal. For all that I had learned in Paris, the thought of home was exciting. I had already begun thinking of the covered market and the spice shops in the medina just behind, where the red powder was troweled out of sacks and put on scales with brass weights. I had missed the cakes in the café at the Rif Cinema and I particularly missed the fried-squid shack on the steep hill up to the casbah. I was starting to think about our house as well, not so much the people as the view from the roof terrace over the sea between the shirts flapping on the line.

Don't get me wrong. I wasn't feeling sad or beaten. Paris might have exhausted me, but it hadn't got the upper hand. No. My meetings with Clémence had changed my life for the better. I'd also learned so much from Victor Hugo. He'd told me about what he called the destiny of France. According to him, it was the historic duty of his country to be a light and an example, the guardian of freedom for the world. In his version of events it was the French, not the Jews, who were God's chosen people. He believed in a god, he said, but not in the clergy. "Whoever teaches about the invisible world is a priest," he told me. "All thinkers are priests."

It's only fair to admit that I'd also benefited from the example of my stern landlady. I was more impressed by seeing someone who actually lived in a serious way than by my father telling me to work hard while pouring whiskey down the throats of his would-be business partners. In all the long months I'd spent in the city of Paris I'd discovered through the people I'd met—through Clémence, Hannah and Victor, through Hasim and Jamal, through Juliette at Stalingrad and even a little through Baco and Sandrine and the cleaner in Beijing Beauté Massage—how many different ways there were of being alive.

And to be quite honest, there was also an e-mail I'd had from Laila. It was much longer than her usual I'm-having-too-much-fun-to-bother-writing type of message. It began, "Hi, Tariq. How are you? You've been away for ages! When are you coming back? I MISS you."

I spent about five minutes enjoying that before I went on reading. "I ran into your father in the medina yesterday and he seemed very anxious about you. He asked if I would come and have tea with him and your stepmother and talk about you and what the matter was. He said you haven't rung or answered his e-mails. Anyway, I went round to your house yesterday evening.

"They're worried. They want to know what you're doing. I said so far as I knew you were looking for where your mother used to live. I know that wasn't your real motive, you were just fed up with life here. But it was the best I could think of. Your father has spoken to the people in the college office and they say that if you sit your exam in August and you get a good grade you won't have to drop a year. Please do that, Tariq, because I really don't want you to be in the year below me! Think of my reputation with Wasia and girls like that. It wouldn't be that much work and I could help you with the revision.

"What's new here? Najat has 'broken up' with her twelve-year-old boyfriend and spends the evening in her room listening to gloomy music! Billy is getting good at tennis and beat me yesterday. Miss Aziz has been seeing something of a mysterious man who picks her up outside college in his Mercedes. He has aviator shades and a cream linen suit. I don't think he's from the Home Planet, but maybe Riyadh. Or Qatar. Ugh! But we can trust Miss A. to play it cool, can't we? She's not going to spend the night with him in a hotel on the bay. Please!

"I've thought about you a lot, Tariq. It bothers me that you're in Paris with all those Christian women. City of Light and you a young man of good family. Frozen fireballs, count me OUT! I want you to come back. I think we're a pair, you and me. We understand things.

"Tangier needs us, frankly. There's a lot of rough boys from Tétouan hanging round the Ville Nouvelle lately, and some of those building projects, out towards the airport, they're getting a bad reputation. This is so, SO real. So come back with your Paris accent and all the euros you'll have saved up—you have made some money, haven't you? And then come and see me for dinner and we'll get Farida to make the lemonade you like and have a big barbecue in the garden and light some candles and play cards all night and have fun. Beer too. Don't dare not to answer me. I miss you. Love, Laila xxx"

• • •

It was all I could do not to dance along the rue de Tolbiac, past the Lycée Claude Monet. (I know. Don't tell me. Revolutionary leader? Chemist?)

At that moment I had a text message and was disappointed it was not a follow-up from Laila. "Tariq, it's Julian Finch. We met at your birthday. Hannah gave me your number. Could I buy you a beer this evening? Something I wanted to ask you. J."

Free beer? *Allez.* We met at a bar near Filles du Calvaire. It was a run-down sort of place with a sticky floor and an old mirror advertising a liqueur called Fap' Anis, *"celui des connaisseurs."* Perhaps the whole thing reminded Julian of an English "pub."

He asked me about myself and what I'd been up to in Paris. I was able to make him laugh when I described the chicken bits and how we cooked them at PFP. I told him about Hasim and Jamal. He said he'd definitely try a Nuclear special next time he was up that way.

"Do be careful, though," he said. "This money you're passing over back in Tangier. Don't get involved in anything, will you?"

"Jamal's a nice guy," I said.

"Yes, but he might not have nice friends."

"He had a bad start in life. He was brought up in a kind of concentration camp. Near Lille. Because his dad had fought alongside the French in Algeria."

"We've tried to forget all that," said Julian.

"Why?"

"Most of the Harkis were left behind in Algeria. They begged to be rescued, but de Gaulle told them they were the victims of history. The Algerian loyalist women paid to whip them. I've read they even cut bits off them while they were still alive and fed them to dogs. The few that made it over here were kept in camps, like your friend."

"It's not surprising Jamal seems so against France," I said, trying to sound wise, though really I was just feeling pleased that I now knew who de Gaulle was.

"The Harkis and their children had a special case. But the other Algerians, the majority, just hate the French because of the way they behaved over there."

I mentioned the police massacre of 1961 and asked if there was any chance that there would ever be a list of victims' names.

Julian shook his head. "I don't know much about it. But the files are usually closed for fifty years in these sorts of cases. And they'll never publish the names."

"Why not?"

"Well, for one thing I don't suppose they have them. Do you think the corpses were identified? After they'd fished them out of the river I should think they simply burned them. And did the dead people have papers on them anyway?"

"I don't know." I was trying not to picture it all too closely.

"And there's another reason," said Julian. "The urge to forget. The desire not to know. Have you ever noticed that if you confront a French person with something difficult, they don't dispute it? They just look at you and wait till you've stopped saying what they don't like."

"There was a guy in a bar. I mentioned about Zidane being sent off in the World Cup Final the other day. He didn't say anything. He just stared at me."

Julian went over the sticky floor to get more beer.

"It wasn't just the Harkis," he said, as he sat down again. "Thousands of *pieds noirs* came back to France and they were hung out to dry. Teachers, clerks, engineers, people who'd faithfully served their country in difficult conditions. They had no welcome back and no financial help. They were told they were on the wrong side of the settlement. No one wanted to know them. The wrong side of history."

He drank some beer, then smiled.

"Still. I didn't come to talk about the darker parts of French colonialism," he said. "And I don't believe they're any worse than some murky bits of British history. I wanted to ask you a favor, Tariq. As you know, Hannah and I are good friends."

"Yes, you—"

"I'm worried about her. She seems so fragile at the moment. It's as though all this work has got on top of her."

I nodded, though I wasn't sure what he meant.

"Would you mind keeping an eye on her for me? I have to go to London for a while. In fact, I may stay there for good."

"You're not coming back to Paris?"

"I need time to finish my book. I did so much reading up on the Occupation and so on that I missed a deadline for my own work. My publishers have given me two weeks' grace."

"So it's a book thing. A deadline."

"Mostly. But other things haven't quite worked out for me here. I can't go on pushing at a closed door. I have to respect . . . the will of others. The integrity. I admire it."

Julian looked very sad. "Can you do that for me?" he said. "I'll give you a phone number. Call me if you think there's a problem."

"What kind of problem?" I said.

He breathed in. "I think that in some odd way the strain of work and the nature of the things she's been dealing with—women fighting lonely battles and so on . . . I think it's opened some old wounds of hers. It's as though her work and her private feelings have overlapped in a way she finds difficult to manage. I'm afraid she's close to breaking point."

"Does she ever have boyfriends?" I said.

"She did once. Years ago. A Russian."

"Really? How on earth . . . A Russian? I mean, what was he like?"

"A bad man." Julian finished his beer. "Perhaps that's unfair. I only met him twice. But I didn't like him. He seemed cruel."

To ease an awkward moment, we concentrated on practical details—when he was leaving (the next day), when I might be leaving (soon), and how to be in touch (for some reason he was ditching his French cell phone in Paris, so gave me his sister's landline number in England). We talked about what he might do in London—work, teach, write—where he'd live, what would happen to his flat in Paris.

"So you'll be here for maybe two more weeks?" he said, as we stood up to leave.

"About that," I said.

"That's better than nothing. It'll be reassuring for me to know you've got an eye on her. Hannah likes you, by the way."

By now we were standing outside on the street.

"Would you say goodbye to her for me?" said Julian. "Tell her I was called away. A bit unexpectedly. Say de Musset needed me."

"Won't you see her to say goodbye?"

"No, I think it's best not."

"Okay. I'll tell her. De Musset."

"Do you want a taxi?" Julian said.

"No, I'll take the Métro, thanks."

We shook hands. As he was walking away, he turned round and called out, "Give her my love."

. . .

I watched as the car disappeared, feeling a bit lost myself. I had the scent of home in my nostrils, it was true, and I'd almost run out of money, so I wouldn't be able to stay much longer. But before I left for good, there were a couple of things I needed to do. For a start, I wanted to see Clémence one more time.

When I'd left her apartment there'd been no talk of meeting again. Rather the opposite. She gave me to understand that what had taken place between us was something that by definition can only happen once, like an introduction, or a death. Nor had we discussed such simple things as whether she actually lived in the flat or merely had use of it from time to time. I had no phone number for her and I doubted that she had a cell phone anyhow. But the nature of what had passed between us made me feel indebted to her. My lie about having been to Drancy to see it for myself was beginning to trouble me.

So after I'd watched Julian disappear, I decided I should put it right. I went to Châtelet–Les Halles to take the RER Line B. I disliked the RER almost as much as I loved the Métro. The underground building site that passed for a terminal, the announcements in English and the disappointing station names . . . They had nothing like Mairie des Lilas.

When I eventually got to this historic place called Drancy, it was . . . It was disappointing. It was just a big, three-sided, low-rise housing block. It was pretty run-down, but I'd seen worse. In front, on the open side, there were a few meters of rail and one of the cattle wagons they'd used to deport the Jews. There was an ugly curved memorial stone on which children were climbing. There was a plaque on the ground in a gray brick surround saying Esplanade Charles de Gaulle (the guy seemed to be everywhere now). On it were some words I couldn't make out and a date: 18 June 1990. Souviens-toi, it said. "Remember." But they themselves had forgotten for almost fifty years. Can an apology that late really be effective?

Anyway. I asked myself what would Clémence want to me to do— or feel? To concentrate. That's what she'd have wanted. Yes. To imagine. So I pretended to be Hannah, going round with my teacher glasses on, knowing everything. I walked down the long colonnade with its thin metal pillars and apricot-colored doors. There was a notice in one ground-floor window: *"Protection Maternelle et Infantile."* A bit late now. At the foot of one staircase was a memorial to a poet called Max Jacob, who'd died on the spot before they could put him on a train to the east.

The grass in the big area in the middle needed mowing and was full of dandelions. Three African men sat on metal benches in the sun, listening to the children's voices, drinking Coca-Cola from the can, smoking cigarettes.

I couldn't get any sense of "history" at all. There was just the idle present. A radio playing by an open window. Some birds singing. The men with nothing to do.

Did it matter if once, more than sixty years ago, some terrible things had been done here? I would bet any money that none of the people living here now, mostly immigrants by the look of it, knew or cared about it. They had their own difficulties.

These thoughts didn't seem good enough. So I decided I should try one more time. Not to make an effort would be like making those people die twice over.

Sitting on a metal bench, I shut my eyes. I pictured what Clémence had told me. It was nighttime in my imagination and an old green Paris bus was arriving, packed with tired, bewildered people. The local gendarmes were pulling them off the bus. The open end of the three-sided rectangle was blocked off by wooden fences, with barbed wire and sentry posts. The gendarmes pushed them through the gates, where German soldiers got them into lines with the end of their guns. Rows of them, just where I was sitting on the bench. Maybe it was raining. They were given numbered staircases to go to and were kicked along by boots and rifle butts. Children were torn from their mothers. Perhaps each staircase had its chief, not a soldier but one of those interned, a Jew. Someone in the darkness who took them to a straw mattress on the floor. To sleep. Before they took a train to somewhere they were too tired to imagine.

My eyes were squeezed shut with effort and I heard the sound of children's footsteps going up the stairs. I was with them, just for a moment, right behind them, as they climbed, watching the calf muscles of their bare legs. And I hoped that maybe it would have meant something to them to know that many years later, someone, even just a nobody from Africa like me, would come to listen to their voices. I tried to believe it might have been a comfort for them to think—in the last hours of their lives—that in an act of remembering they were, for a moment at least, something more than footsteps in a concrete stairwell.

● ● ●

After this excursion, I didn't feel up to much, so for a few days I stayed in the flat. In the end, I got the necessary energy to go up to Saint-Denis and make a call on Paname Fried Poulet.

Hasim was away, but I let myself in by the kitchen door and found Jamal up to his elbows in flour and spices.

"Thought you weren't coming, you little cocksucker."

"I had other things to do."

"Got your plane ticket?"

"Yes. I leave on Wednesday."

Jamal pulled his hands out of the mixing bowl and ran them under a tap, then he turned to me. "You do hate this country, don't you?"

"France?"

"Yes, boy. France. They tortured us and killed us. And your country the same."

"No. They gave us independence."

"They let you go because they couldn't fight two wars at once and Morocco was less useful to them. And what they did to my father and mother. That camp. He escaped by stealing a passport one night. He got a job as a laborer, building tower blocks for new immigrants outside Lyon."

I remembered Maurice the pedo lorry driver: "Too many Algerians in Lyon, that's the trouble. Always have been."

"My mother died in that camp," said Jamal. "My father and my sisters and me, we then lived in a shantytown." *Bidonville* was the word Jamal used—a town made of empty cans.

"I know it was bad for you, Jamal. But . . . none of these things happened to me."

"But you still hate France, don't you?"

"No, I don't. I like France. Of course I know there were bad things done. But it's the same with any European country, isn't it? England's just as bad." I thought of Miss Aziz's puzzled history lesson. "Or Germany. They were far worse. And I like it here in Paris. I've learned so much."

Jamal banged a tray of chicken pieces into the oven. "All right, kid," he said. "I suppose you've met a girl. A woman."

"Maybe."

"Don't let them ruin your life. Women."

"Why would I do that?"

Jamal went to one of the store cupboards and took out an old chicken sack. He pulled out a thick envelope, which he handed to me. "This is the money. There's a phone number inside."

As I was leaving, he gave me a small plastic bag of *kif.* "And this is for you. Use it before you go to the airport, then throw it away if you haven't finished."

We shook hands. Jamal smiled at me. "*Na'al abouk la France*," he said. Fuck France.

I smiled back. "Thanks for the weed, Jamal."

For the last time, I crossed the medina that is the Saint-Denis market square—the black slate roofs and the halal meat, the buried Christian kings of France and the exiles of the Maghreb, the black burkas and the limp *tricolore* on the town hall. Frozen fucking fireballs.

• • •

I was leaving just in time from a cash point of view, as I'd spent what was left of my savings on a silver bracelet for Laila that I'd seen in a shop in the Marais. I was down to my last forty euros, and even with cunning use of the Flunch fill-your-plate scheme and Hannah's fruit bowl I was always feeling hungry.

But I still had eight Métro tickets left, and using one of them I took myself to Bir-Hakeim. Down the steps and onto the Quai de Grenelle, past the Franprix with the elevated track on my right, past La Gitane with its red awnings and blackboard outside (dish of the day, as ever, was *entrecôte* or *dos de cabillaud*) and on down to rue Humblot . . . Apart from the cobbles and the Royal Rajasthan Indian restaurant (on which the metal shutters were drawn down to the pavement), it was a very unremarkable street. From the maroon street door a woman in a hat was emerging and I ran towards her, calling out, "Clémence! Wait!"

She turned to look at me and I saw in a moment that it was someone else. The old-fashioned clothes were similar, she was the same age and height, but it was another woman's face. She smiled at me as she put her key into her bag and began to walk. Even her smile had something of Clémence in it—a look that said, "It's all right, I know you and I understand."

Waiting till she'd reached the end of the street, I set out to follow her. Almost at once we were in a square, the Place Dupleix, which was loud with the noise of children playing in the dust. They pushed and screamed, with a sound like seagulls. Behind them was a church with a pointed spire. Clémence, or her sister, walked on quickly, looking at her watch, past a glass-roofed bandstand inside the park.

We left the square and passed between some modern buildings and a low-rise block of flats. At the junction with a busy road, she waited to cross by a café and I hung back. Then we were off again, and at the next crossroads, she turned left into the broad, tree-lined Avenue de Suffren. After a while, she seemed to slow down, checking the numbers on the buildings.

The atmosphere had changed from the calm of rue Humblot. We were now near enough to the Eiffel Tower for the pavements to be full of tourists, mostly Japanese, or Chinese (I'm not good at knowing the difference). There was a shop with its name, Parapharmacie, in green lettering and a row of hire bicycles in their docks.

The buildings behind were tall and grand, old Paris. As Clémence hesitated, I crossed the road and stood behind a tree. She went to the intercom at the entrance to number 38, a double chestnut door. I saw her heave her shoulders up, as though bracing herself, or breathing hard. She clutched her bag in both hands, then nudged the door with her hip. It opened inward. She looked round one more time, almost as though she was searching for me, glanced up to the sky, then stepped inside and disappeared.

Jacques Bonsergent

I TOOK STOCK OF MY WORK AND OF HOW MUCH LONGER I NEEDED TO spend in Paris. Although I'd finished my investigations, one thing still worried me: the story of Mathilde's family going to the seaside in Normandy. I wondered why Mathilde had included it in her memories of the Occupation when it had taken place so many years before. Presumably the archivists also thought it was relevant—or they'd have cut it.

Old Masson, the slaughterhouse man, the butcher of Belleville: Perhaps he was significant in a way I hadn't understood. He was certainly from a memorable generation of men. According to the standard figures, the French casualties of the First World War numbered 1,358,000 dead and 4,266,000 wounded, of whom 1,500,000, including Mathilde's father, were permanently maimed or disabled.

These seats are reserved. 1. First. Before all others. *Aux mutilés de guerre.* One and a half million of you.

Among more than *five and a half million* casualties. Perhaps this was the significance of the seaside boardinghouse. And this figure was what lay behind everything that had happened during the Occupation years: the official policy of Collaboration so proudly announced by the marshal (the same man who twenty years earlier had been the hero at Verdun); the self-seeking of some citizens, the indifference of others; the racial hatred and propaganda and the deportations to the death camps;

the acts of heroism. Everything. Because the idea of another five million was not bearable. It was not thinkable.

It was clear to me now that old Masson had been a tough, tough man. His journey to work would have tested even a youngster with both legs. From Couronnes to Convention, which was the station nearest to the old slaughterhouses, I counted twenty-three stops. There was only one change of line, at Pigalle, but with no escalators that would have been hard work for a man on crutches. And with one and a half million *mutilés* at large, of whom perhaps a third or more would be seeking work in Paris, he wouldn't even have been guaranteed a reserved seat on the train. No wonder he drank so much.

The next day, I decided to retrace Masson's daily steps. Line 2 took me overground past Stalingrad and Barbès, the Tati store and the little Africa of painful memory. At Sèvres-Babylone, beneath the Hôtel Lutetia, my eye was caught by a performance at the far end of the carriage. An old man with a thick white beard plied a pair of grubby-looking puppets above a black curtain he had rigged between the chrome uprights. Passengers seated nearby were studying their phones or shoes. The puppeteer was undeterred, apparently trusting in his story, which seemed to be both adventure and morality play. Among the puppets whose names I caught were Marius and Cosette.

At Convention, I had a fifteen-minute walk to the site of the old slaughterhouses, now the Parc Georges-Brassens. Might old Masson's trade union—or at least his able-bodied colleagues—have provided him with a ride by bus, or even by horse and cart?

The entrance to the park itself was marked by two bronze bulls, face-to-face on rectangular pillars; inside, there were flower beds planted red and orange, a stone-edged pond and gravel paths under plane trees. It was an "amenity," I thought, for the people in the blocks of flats that rose from the slope behind it; but however much it was now appreciated by women pushing children in their strollers, it was hard to picture the sheds where the animals had been rounded up each day, the hoses washing down the floors, the foaming red drains, the butchers' vans loading the carcasses for the restaurant kitchens in Clichy or Saint-Germain.

On a long loop, uphill and around, among the municipal planting, I was hoping for some sense of the past, of the place where Mathilde's father had worked; but in the empty benches, the blanched concrete of the apartment blocks behind and the occasional smack of a runner's foot in the dust, there was only the thin texture of the day.

I was making for the main gates when I stopped. In my nostrils was the strong smell of horse. I turned and sniffed, then followed the aroma towards the edge of the park. I expected to see a riding stables somewhere along the way, tucked in behind some trees. I listened for the sound of clopping metal shoes. But although I passed an area with colored swings and slides and a *crèche maternelle* built in the same nursery-school style, there was no sign of anything to do with horses.

Eventually, beside the street, I came to the former stables, where in old Masson's day the creatures had been brought to wait for the final stage in the journey from pasture to table. I remembered reading how local people had complained about the smell of horse at Vaugirard, much worse apparently than that of dead cows or pigs or chickens.

Yet no horse had been brought here for almost fifty years. Beneath a pitched glass roof, the handsome iron-framed building, open on all sides, was now a market for secondhand books. There were some collector's items, but most were uniform editions of the works of Rousseau or Voltaire, rescued from old houses and for sale by the meter as interesting wallpaper. In a second stable were illustrated comic books, some still current and some that time had frowned on, like the colonialist elephant, Babar, or Bécassine, the dumb Breton girl. Whatever their warmth or weakness, the books were discussed by dealers and the buyers only as curios; it was not part of the transaction that anyone would read them.

. . .

As I walked home later from the Métro, I hoped that Tariq would be in. He'd have no answers, no explanation to the riddle of the horses, but he was someone to talk to. And I still believed his ignorance of the past made him in some way more receptive. It was only a day or so before his birthday party that I'd told him so. "I like your stories of the girls you see on the Métro. The encounters you're always having. I think maybe it's because you have so little baggage. You're not always making connections, saying, 'Things must be this way because of what happened during the Commune,' or whatever. You just ricochet through life like a pinball in a machine. You see things for what they are today. It's a gift."

"Really?" he'd replied. "I assumed it was the drugs."

But Tariq wasn't there, and it had never been part of our arrangement that he'd leave a note. So for some hours I did what I always did, deciding what most needed my attention—reading, writing, tidying, e-mailing, planning ahead.

None of it distracted me. I could concentrate neither on the meager information I'd found concerning the Natzweiler camp nor the salad of lettuce, lentils and roasted walnuts I made for dinner. I could think only of horses.

I had sensed the presence of animals that weren't there. Smelling was not quite as bad as seeing or hearing, which would have been delusional—or psychotic. But even so . . . Could there be such a thing as temporal synesthesia—a condition in which you confused not two senses, like sight and smell, but in which different eras became merged? Could it be that my brain, made hyperactive by the shortcomings of the present, had actually experienced, through smell, the richer past?

And if so, I thought, pushing my hand up through the front of my hair, did that mean that I was going insane?

Moving the half-eaten dinner to one side, I began to type into the search field of my browser. *"Chevaux." "Parc Georges-Brassens." "Manège." "Equitation."* For some minutes it coughed up only things I knew. I noticed that my hand was shaking as I typed "Parc Georges-Brassens pony rides." Low down on the first page I saw the word *"poneys."* The French spelling. I clicked the link and found a blogger who confided that the Parc Georges-Brassens was his "third favorite" public space in Paris. This faint praise was followed by the disclosure that small children could be offered pony rides on certain days of the week. The last time had been three days earlier. It was a pungent animal to be detectable after almost seventy-two hours, but there was an old photograph of three children in hard hats on three small ponies and in the absence of any better explanation it would have to do.

I'd printed out my rail ticket to Strasbourg and now filled in some details of my driver's license online to save time at the car-rental desk.

I made sure I had the right clothes to wear—a linen dress, light cardigan for the evening, comfortable shoes for walking—and two books to read on the train. Then I took a shower and washed my hair.

A cup of chamomile tea, I thought, would ready me for an early night, but I found my hand still shaking when I poured the boiling water. I wished Tariq would come back. I wished Jasmine had still been there. Perhaps I could call her in New York—the timing would be fine.

But it was neither of these people that I most wanted to talk to; nor was it my parents or my brother or my professor or any other of my friends and colleagues at home or in Paris. I saw suddenly—with a clarity that almost blinded me—that the person I most wanted to see, and the only person I would ever need to see again, was Julian Finch.

"Le numéro que vous avez demandé n'est plus attribue," said the recorded message on his phone. The number you have dialed is no longer recognized. Please hang up and try again.

There was the sound of a key in the door.

"Tariq. Hi. Where have you been?"

"Oh, you know." He smiled hazily. "Hanging out."

"Have you been smoking?"

"Jamal gave me a whole lot and I need to get through it before I take the plane. But don't worry, I won't smoke here."

"Doesn't look like you need to."

Personally, I was high on certainty. Julian would be able to explain and support: today and in the future, as far into it as I could see.

"Listen, Tariq, I'm going out for a bit."

"Where to?"

Normally, I would have told him to mind his own business, but the release of energy that came from admitting something so long denied had made me light-headed. "I'm going over to Julian's apartment. I couldn't get hold of him on his cell phone so I'm going over there."

"Really? Why are you doing that?"

"What do you mean?"

"Didn't he text you or anything?"

"What are you talking about?"

"He's gone back to London. He told me to tell you that he said good-bye. Something about de Musset."

"He *what*?"

"He said, 'Say de Musset needed me.' He left his French cell phone behind."

"When did you see him?"

"About five days ago. We met for a drink. I meant to mention it, but I've hardly seen you, and—"

"You met for a drink?"

"What's so odd about that?"

"But Julian's my . . . *my* friend."

"Yes, but he asked me if I'd keep an eye on you."

"He asked you to *what*?"

"Nothing. He's staying with his sister, he said. Do you know her?"

"No, of course I don't know his English sister."

"He left a number for emergencies. A landline."

"Where is it?"

"I think it's in my other jacket."

"Well, go on."

While Tariq went to his room, I tried to understand the change that had taken place in my life.

Tariq came back into the sitting room, looking uneasy.

"Have you got it?"

"I think I must have left my jacket in a bar last night."

"For fuck's sake, Tariq."

"I'm sorry." He turned to go, then stopped. "He said to give you his love."

• • •

Two days later, Tariq left for Morocco.

And the following day was the one I'd booked for my visit to Natzweiler. To be sure to arrive within the opening hours of the concentration camp, I had to leave Paris early in the morning.

Bastille, République . . . The famous names went by on the Métro; then Jacques Bonsergent, which was, depending on what you knew, either the place where you acknowledged a young wartime resister executed by the Germans or an area with a coming club scene. A few months ago, I would have admired one way of living and despised the other. Now I was not so sure. I'd looked up the names of the puppets, Marius and Cosette, and found that they were characters in *Les Misérables*, a novel I'd never read on account of a vague prejudice against musical theater. So there it was: I hadn't read the most famous novel of the nineteenth century. Nor had I known till Julian told me that the rue de la Goutte d'Or was the setting of another nineteenth-century novel almost as famous as Hugo's. I hadn't even checked whether Georges Brassens was a painter or a singer. You couldn't know everything, I thought, as my train arrived at the Gare de l'Est, and that being the case, there were after all no polarities of enlightenment and darkness; there were only degrees of ignorance.

Just inside the station was a Marks & Spencer deli, where I bought a ham and mustard mayonnaise sandwich to eat on the train. The shop name made me remember what I'd once been told by my brother: that these sandwiches were made for the retailer by the American Heinz corporation in a factory in an English town called Luton, known for its population of Muslim immigrants. A small number of families made up the workforce, Warren said, looking after one another, bringing in their cousins to cover holiday breaks. But were they happy, I wondered as I paid for the sandwich, to be handling ham? The Indian Mutiny had been started by Muslim colonial soldiers unhappy that the bullets—or possibly the rifles—they were handling had been greased with pork fat. Or was it Hindu soldiers and cow fat? And if so, then . . .

Stop it, I thought. The urge to connect everything is going to drive me crazy; I must try to focus on the present.

On the concourse of the Gare de l'Est, I looked for the platform number of the Strasbourg train and found my seat with ten minutes to spare. I settled by the window, sandwich and Evian in hand, and opened my book.

It was impossible to concentrate. I looked at the landscape, forcing myself to pay attention, to study it as a naturalist might. Mostly flat, only slight undulations . . . A parallel motorway with boxy little cars of near-identical design . . . Wind turbines, a silver-birch plantation . . . Green wheat fields with lines of chalk showing through the earth . . . Deciduous trees with balled rooks' nests.

Everyone else in the carriage was either asleep or playing with their cell phones. The man next to me had a cowboy jacket that gave off a smell of cheap leather.

The farther east we went, the hillier the ground became. Now there were orchards of pears and apples and inclines that grew steeper, the first foothills of the Vosges.

Andrée Borrel and her three SOE colleagues had been brought here, perhaps on this very line, from a prison near Paris—Fresnes, I was pretty sure, though had there been a diversion through Karlsruhe in Germany? Sometimes in the course of these deportations there were moments of lightness. Freed from their solitary cells, the women were able to play cards, smoke and swap stories. They at once resumed both their service identity and their lives as ordinary people, chatting, laughing in the relief of camaraderie. No one really knew what was happening, not even the Germans who guarded them and sometimes joined them at whist. No one knew what awaited them at Natzweiler. It had a gallows and a gas chamber, but it was not an extermination camp and only a minority died there—those marked "Nacht und Nabel," Night and Fog, distinguished by a yellow badge that meant they were not expected to return and could be worked to death. As for Andrée and her three friends, the processes of Nazi logic were perhaps still unresolved at this point in their journey.

Glancing round the carriage, I strained to hear the four women, talking in low tones, punctuated by inappropriate laughter. Professor Putnam had urged us to believe that death was not a locked door but that earlier lives were permanently present and available. But the extent to which I felt these women near me now was beyond historical empathy and I thought I should try to rein it in.

What was known about Andrée Borrel? Very little—though I had collated all the mentions of her I'd found in published books and in documents from archives I'd visited. Photographs showed a determined face, between stolid and beautiful, depending on the light. She had left school young and worked in a dress shop, then behind the counter at the Pujo *boulangerie* on Avenue Kléber near the Étoile. It was too smart an area for Mathilde or Juliette, but it was not far from German military headquarters and I wondered if Klaus Richter had ever bought a cake or croissant from her. Andrée hated the puppet Vichy government and loathed having Germans in her country. She joined a Resistance network in the south but, when it was uncovered by the Germans, escaped to London, where she was trained by SOE. Photographs showed her in the uniform and cap of the FANY, an army nursing unit that gave military cover to SOE operatives. On being dropped back into France, she found herself at once sharing several weeks of dangerous activity with her English circuit leader, Francis Suttill. It was he who had described her as "the best of us all." She had fallen in love with the circuit's wireless operator, a man called Gilbert Norman. When the Prosper circuit was betrayed and broken, she was sent to a prison outside Paris, where she kept her spirits up by writing letters to her sister on cigarette papers and persuading guards to mail them for her.

Though little celebrated, Andrée was a real, historical figure. Mathilde Masson and Juliette Lemaire were real as well, though known only to a few researchers like me—remembered by their families, perhaps, but not much more. Georgette Chevalier, Juliette's friend, had lived and worked for the Resistance but was mentioned in no books. "Simone" was a code name for someone whose real name Armand had never known—or at least had not disclosed to Mathilde. And Clémence . . . Well, a woman had been photographed and her image had appeared in my dream. She had been alive in Paris at the time, but what she had actually done—and who she really was—could never be known. The historical, the real, the possible . . . I knew I needed to cling on hard to these ghostly distinctions.

At Strasbourg SNCF station, I collected the key from the car-rental desk and went to a multi-story parking lot, on the roof of which I saw my designated white Renault. Once I'd found the road out of town, it was almost a straight line to Struthof, the village in the valley at whose railhead the women would have arrived. It was a beautiful day to drive towards the mountains and, despite the nature of the past I was revisiting, I found my spirits lift.

From Struthof, I began to climb, gently at first, then more steeply as the road followed S-bends up the hillside. When I'd finally learned to drive, at age twenty-five, it had been on automatics, so I found the stick shift a little difficult. I hadn't expected anything quite so mountainous, but then remembered reading that the site of the camp had once been a ski station. Swallowing to clear my ears, I went past a small sign by the road that read Chambre de Gaz; it had the familiar lettering of signs throughout rural France announcing Chambre d'Hôte, the local bed-and-breakfast.

Natzweiler was beautiful. The air was clear among the fir trees and the distant ring of mountains. I could hear thrushes, blackbirds and chaffinches; I remembered a phrase my old landlady had liked—*heureux comme un pinson*, "happy as a finch." I parked the car and went into a modern reception building, where a tour party was gathering around a drinks machine. It was more organized than I'd expected, with a bookshop and an audiovisual room.

The entrance to the old camp itself was a short walk up the slope, and here the sense of a mountain resort began to fade. Above the double gates of timber and wire was a wooden board with the words KONZENTRATIONSLAGER NATZWEILER-STRUTHOF. I showed my ticket and took a site plan from the kiosk at the gate.

The camp was on a steep slope, into which was cut a series of flat terraces. At the top was a group of low-built wooden huts, where the prisoners had been housed, and just beneath them, on the first terrace where everyone could see it, was a gibbet, its noose still in place. Around the wired perimeter were sentry boxes, painted blue-green, and beyond them were trees and mountains under a huge blue sky. Wanting to be alone, I waited for the tour party to go down the terraces.

The arrival of Andrée Borrel and her three friends had been observed from an upper hut by a male English SOE officer, who saw at once that the women were being singled out for special treatment. Andrée had for some reason, presumably as part of a failed disguise, dyed her hair blond and was wearing a shabby fur coat against the cold. She had been a tomboy, mad for cycling and mountain climbing, but by the time of her arrival was weakened by prison and malnutrition. She came from a humble family—*des petits gens*, "little people," as one colleague noted— and had to be taught not to smoke or eat on the street, things that might betray her background as an Avenue Kléber bakery assistant when trying to pass herself off as a habitué of a smart café. But her resourcefulness and enthusiasm set her apart, "the best of us all."

The hike uphill from Struthof would have taxed her even at the height of her fitness, I thought, as I began to walk down the side of the camp towards the prison and the crematorium at the bottom of the hill. Perhaps they'd had to drive the weakened prisoners up. What could Andrée have been expecting—Andrée the indefatigable, the one who volunteered for the worst and most dangerous jobs?

At once, the women were told that they were to be inoculated against typhus, a scourge of such camps, and to begin with they were not suspicious, though they did refuse to take their clothes off without a female doctor present.

I went into the prison where they'd been held, a low green single-story timber construction with a pitched, felt-covered roof. The empty cells opened from a stone floor that ran the length of the building.

There were no other visitors. I stopped in the corridor and listened for female voices. Vera? Here. Andrée, *tu es là?* Sonia? I may have spoken out loud.

Next door, the crematorium building was of the same design but had a tall tin chimney, supported by four metal guys that were pegged into the hillside. Inside, the atmosphere was different. There was a room with drug cabinets and a mortician's white porcelain table, the trappings of Nazi medicine.

All the German guards were used to hanging prisoners as encouragement or example and to cremating the bodies of those who'd been worked to death. But this was not an extermination camp, and they weren't practiced at simple murder. Through an uneasy chain of command there came an order from Berlin that the four women were to be executed—not in the camp's own gas chamber, which was in an outhouse of the local hotel-restaurant down the hill, but by lethal injection. There was some reluctance among the camp medical staff (they were hoping to have a party to celebrate the departure of the senior doctor the following day) and they tried to shift the task onto others. Alcohol was taken while the furnace was stoked and given two hours to reach full heat. All the other prisoners were told to stay in their huts and to draw the curtains, on pain of death.

On a bench in the crematorium building, Andrée Borrel, Diana Rowden, Vera Leigh and Sonia Olschanezky—one French, two English and one Polish woman—were injected with the camp's last supplies of phenol. But although the injections were administered by trained doctors, the procedure was clumsy, the dosage was guessed and the quantity insufficient. The women became comatose, but they did not die at once.

I walked down the corridor into the room where the iron furnace stood, its doors still open and its mouth gaping. Into the flames on metal stretchers they had loaded the bodies of the four drugged and dying prisoners; but when her turn came, Andrée was still conscious and fought back, tearing flesh from the face of her murderer with her fingernails as he pushed her into the flames.

Perhaps this was not the selfsame furnace but merely one like it. You could never know for certain. I put out my hand and touched the metal, hoping it was the same hot rim that Andrée had grasped to save herself—the last thing on earth her fingers had touched.

Then I turned and went outside the building, sat down on the bench and lowered my head into my hands.

. . .

When I had composed myself, I went to the foot of the hill, to a small memorial garden with a white cross of sacrifice and plaques of remembrance let into the wall behind. They represented every country and every group of people who had been imprisoned, persecuted or killed in the camp.

A group of three visitors was emerging, dazed, from the crematorium. As they went past on the bank above me, I heard a female voice say, in French, "I had no idea." *Je n'avais aucune idée.* The woman was in tears.

Then, my own eyes dry, I began to climb up the terraces, back towards the entrance. Standing by the gallows, I looked down one last time and to my amazement saw an eagle flying above the crematorium, over the stiff firs and off into the blue skies of the mountains behind. I had never seen an eagle before.

Back in the parking lot, sitting in the white Renault, I felt a great weariness. I needed to get back to Paris as fast as possible and would take an earlier train from Strasbourg if I could. I left the site, not bothering to look at the commandant's house, ignoring the sign to the gas chamber a short way down the hill.

After a few minutes my strength began to fail me and I knew I'd drive off the road with fatigue if I tried to get back without resting first. Halfway down the mountain, driving slowly, working through the gears, I saw the name of a hotel. I hadn't noticed it on the way up, but it could hardly have come at a better time. I turned off and followed the signs, which led me through iron gates, onto a gravel area in front of a white-painted building with a view over the valley.

A board announced the Hôtel du Parc. I pushed open the double glass doors onto a hall with a parquet floor and a couple of palms growing from painted urns. To the right was a wooden reception desk with a dial telephone; on a board were hanging room keys with tassels. Every hook was taken, as though no bedroom was in use. I tapped the bell on the desk.

While I waited for someone to come, I walked down the hall and, through more double glass doors with half net curtains, looked into a dining room, where a dozen tables were laid. On a couple of them stood bottles of wine that had been part drunk, then recorked. I put my head round the door and caught a smell of floor polish and old flowers, perhaps potpourri or dried chrysanthemums.

"Madame?"

I turned around quickly. A woman in widow's black was standing in the hall. "Did you ring?"

"Yes. I wondered if you had a room."

We went back to the desk. The widow was no more than forty-five, I thought, although her face was expressionless, the color drained from it.

"It's number fourteen, isn't it?" said the widow, handing over the key.

"I haven't . . . I mean, yes, that's fine."

"And you'll be dining with us?"

"Yes . . . yes, I think so."

"Please don't be late, Madame."

"Of course."

The woman was unsurprised by my lack of luggage and seemed to expect me to find the room myself.

I went to the staircase at the end of the hall and climbed the steps on a threadbare runner. At the top, off the landing, was a corridor with rose-print wallpaper. Room 14 was the last on the right and the old key turned satisfactorily in the lock.

On the bed was a green cover, beneath which were blankets and white linen sheets, mended in places but quite clean. There was a bathroom with a shower and bidet and a smell of failed plumbing. Through the window, I could see the ground rising up the mountainside towards the camp.

Thinking I'd sleep, have dinner, then set off again, paying for the room but not staying overnight, I took off my dress and shoes and lay down on the bed, on top of the blankets but with the cover pulled up over my shoulders.

There was the sound of German voices singing in the next room. Andrée Borrel, her eyes wide with fear, knocked on my door and asked if she could hide beneath the bed.

I woke up. I had fallen asleep and begun dreaming so fast . . .

There was another knocking at the door and the manageress, the widow, told me I was late for dinner . . . But, no, that was also a dream. My hair was damp on my forehead when I awoke this time.

Next door, the Germans were not singing anymore but talking loudly.

Julian Finch was sitting on the edge of the bed. "I love you," he said. "I always will."

I was awake, putting on my dress for dinner. It was a relief to be awake and I must stop myself from dropping off again. If I fell asleep, I would be lost forever—I would fall through the floor of time.

More footsteps came to the door. It was Andrée again, in a bakery assistant's overall. "They've taken Julian," she said. *Ils ont pris Julian.*

This time I awoke for sure. Yes, this was reality, this was consciousness. All the other times I had only *dreamed* that I had awoken, but this time . . .

Now Andrée was kneeling by the bed, praying, her big eyes closed. I wanted so much to help her, but the tide of sleep was overpowering and it sucked me down once more.

There was a rapping at the door again, louder. It was the widow. "They are coming for you, Madame."

To be certain that I was finally awake, I must move my body, I must shock myself. Pushing back sleep, I reached inside to summon up movement. None came.

What I did find was the ability to make a noise, to scream. It was the loudest I could manage, perhaps no more than a moan in reality, but enough to force my eyes open.

I pushed myself up off the bed, expecting to discover I was still asleep. But no. It seemed all right. I got to the bathroom, ran cold water and splashed it on my face and neck. I looked at myself in the mirror above the basin.

"It's all right," said the face.

And I heard neither the Parisian accent of Andrée nor the tones of the local widow but my own American voice. "It's okay."

Still not trusting that I was back in reality, I went to the window and looked out. It was beginning to grow dark, as was proper to the hour of the day. I walked briskly around the room, checking I had my bag with its books to read on the train, my half-finished bottle of water, my notebook and cell phone. I slipped on my dress and shoes again, touched different surfaces: porcelain, wool, linen—the iron *espagnolette* at the window. At the feeling of each different material I grew more confident.

Awake, alive, in the present day, in a hotel between Natzweiler and Struthof in the foothills of the indisputable Vosges, Hannah Kohler walked down the corridor to the landing, clattered down the stairs, making as much everyday noise as possible, and went into the hall.

"Dinner is ready, Madame," said the manageress. "I thought you'd like the table by the window tonight."

"No!"

I pushed past her and ran to the front door, where I fumbled in my bag. I found a fifty-euro note and tossed it onto the reception desk. Then I went outside and climbed into the white Renault. I took a breath as I stuck in the key and started the engine.

Denfert-Rochereau

W HEN I SAID GOODBYE TO HANNAH, I FELT SAD. AND THERE WAS A tear in her eye when she hugged me.

"Watching you change and grow has been just great," she said, standing back, holding on to my wrists, sounding more American than usual. "You know that, Tariq?"

"Thanks," I said.

"No, really. I feel you're starting to understand things."

"Charles de Gaulle?"

"More than that. Tell me why you first came to Paris."

"I wanted to escape. I guess I hoped to find something too. I don't know. What do you think?"

"I think that without knowing it you realized it was time to engage with the world. You couldn't live forever on the screen of your cell phone. I know your idea of finding out something more about your mother was kind of vague. But maybe it was the first stirring of some hunger in you. The need to understand."

I was starting to feel embarrassed. "I'll send you some more money one day," I said. "When I make my fortune. I owe you for . . . all this."

She laughed. "Don't bother. Life goes around. Next time we meet, you'll be the one with the spare room and I'll be the penniless guy on the run. I just hope you'll let me in."

"Of course I will. Especially if I'm thirty-one and you're nineteen."

This came out a bit wrong, but she didn't take offense. She just said, "And I hope I'll be as good a roommate as you've been."

"I'm sorry about not passing on Julian's message."

"You'd better get going or you'll miss your flight."

"Okay. What are your plans?"

"I'm going to a concentration camp tomorrow."

"You have all the fun."

I gave her the last of Jamal's weed in its plastic bag. "I couldn't quite get through it all."

"But you gave it your best shot. That's what counts."

She could be quite funny, really. I don't know why she'd kept her humor hidden all this time. I had her e-mail, I could be in touch, but I still felt sad.

Down on rue Michal, I headed for Place d'Italie. I had to get off the Métro at Denfert-Rochereau and I felt some regret as I left that tarry smell, the dazzling adverts and exotic names (I'd look up D-R himself when I had a moment). I wondered if I'd ever come back to Paris again, and if so what type of man I'd be. Where would I fit in among the grown-ups I'd seen rattling through the underground world? Would I be a father? A businessman? Rich or poor? Would I be married? To Laila? To the girl from Stalingrad?

But then I thought: Suppose you never really do grow up—suppose it's all an illusion. It sure wasn't something I could picture ever happening to me.

I trekked over to the RER station, where with my last euros I bought a ticket for the airport, Charles de Gaulle. But of course. Who else would they have named it after? My new best friend.

It was more like a supermarket than how I'd imagined an airport, full of the smell of perfume advertised by pouting women and rows of liquor and watches and headphones and cameras and laptops. If I'd not been such an unbeliever I might have felt quite disapproving. As it was, the sweet smell just made me a little nauseous as I took the shuttle train to another zone.

The flight was called and I made my way to Gate 21. I had a seat over the wing and the plane was only half full. It took hours for every-one to settle down, for all the safety stuff with the old-fashioned life jackets, but then the pilot opened up the engines and I thought I was going to burst through the back of my seat. The nose lifted and . . .

Above the Paris clouds, the sun was shining. A female attendant in a funny hat and scarf and thick orangey-brown tights brought beer and wine for free. I raised my plastic glass to old Jamal and all at PFP. *Merci, mes amis.* Cheers. And to Hannah Kohler . . . May your Ladies of the Occupation bring you joy.

The plane rumbled along, bumping over pockets of air, the wing tip staying level with the clouds on the far horizon. It was difficult to put a name to the feeling as we traveled through the bright sky. Happiness, maybe. Something unfamiliar. I sat back and shut my eyes, tired suddenly, my head full of Victor Hugo and Saint-Denis, white wine and the old-fashioned flat in rue Humblot.

• • •

I woke up as we were making our descent. I only had my backpack, which they'd let me bring on board, so I didn't have to wait for luggage. The taxis weren't parked outside the terminal building but up the slope behind a fence. I opened the envelope of money Jamal had given me. I thought they'd want me to get a cab into town.

The car, like most of them, was an old beige Mercedes. In the months I'd been away, even more breeze-block buildings seemed to have been put up along the highway. Maybe some of them had plumbing, or fire sprinklers, but probably not. We drove in through the smarter suburbs, past the big cemetery and the road to the American School of Tangier and into the Ville Nouvelle. I hadn't warned my father I was coming back, but Victor Hugo had told me the parable of the prodigal son from the Bible and I was hoping that if I surprised him the old man might go and find a fatted calf to kill.

To prepare myself a bit, I got the taxi to drop me at the Café de Paris, at a busy junction near our house. It was a middle-aged place I'd never wanted to visit, but I had money in my envelope and time to spare. I ordered an ice cream, with an avocado and almond juice to drink, and left a large tip when I'd finished. Then I walked down to the Grand Socco, the big square. Here was the covered market I'd missed—the bread hags at the entrance selling their dusty loaves and the cats prowling among the stalls. And just up the hill was the Rif Cinema, where I'd spent so many teenage hours, and its café with the fresh cakes, and opposite that the white gate into the medina with the plumbers and painters squatting on the curb with their pipes and brushes, hoping for work. It all seemed so dirty after Paris (the smart bits of Paris anyway) and the street kids, boys of no more than eight or nine, out of their heads on glue and *kif*. It might be running on a low charge, with most people having no work, but in its own way, I thought, it knew what it was doing.

As I approached our house, I began to walk more quickly. I climbed the outside steps and found our first-floor doorway open, as it always was. The air was fresh and clear inside.

My stepmother came out of the kitchen to see who was there. For a moment she didn't seem to recognize me. Then she began to cry. We hugged awkwardly.

"I'm going to ring your father. He'll be so pleased. He'll want to hear all about it."

Then she was on the landline. "Yes, he looks fine. A bit thin. He smelled of alcohol, I thought."

She came back into the hall. "I rang your father," she said. "He'll be home for dinner."

"That's good," I said. "I'm going to have a shower and lie down for a bit in my room."

"We'll have dinner on the roof. The weather's perfect."

Dinner on the roof? No one did that. "Thank you," I said, and kissed her on the cheek—though not in time to prevent her telling me again that the weather was looking just right.

Everything in my room was as I'd left it. I picked up the economics texts, the notebook, the printout of the essay for Miss Aziz that I'd never finished, last year's birthday card from Laila. There were some clean clothes in the drawers, and after I'd had a shower, I lay down on the bed in fresh boxers and T-shirt, wishing that the *moucharabieh*, the wooden screen that gave onto the landing, had offered a bit more privacy.

It was getting dark when I awoke and I could hear my father's voice from the roof. I pulled on some jeans and went upstairs.

"Tariq. My dear boy."

He opened his arms and I let him hug me. He looked older, his crinkled gray hair just a bit more gray, his new glasses thicker than the ones I remembered.

We sat at the *taifor*, which had whiskey on it, and Coca-Cola and cold beer, which I guessed was for my benefit. For once, my stepmother had taken down the shirts on the clothesline, so we could see across the water almost as far as Europe.

"And did you find any old friends of your mother's in Paris?" My father's voice was kind.

"No . . . No, I didn't. I met some other people. Interesting people."

"What nationality?"

"French, American, English, Algerian. Some mixed."

"I saw your friend Laila the other day. She said you won't have to repeat the year."

"If I pass the exam."

"You'll pass. You're your mother's son, thank goodness, not an old fool like me. Have a drink."

He poured me whiskey with Coke and ice. I'd never known him to be like this before. He must have decided not to be angry.

My stepmother was also having a drink, something she only did about once a year. It was a fiery thing called *mahia*, made from dates, I think, which she drank with *limonada*. So we all sat round the low table and I told them a bit about Paname Fried Poulet, but not too much about Jamal or Hamid and nothing about the money in my backpack.

"I've made a special dinner, something I learned from my grandmother," said my stepmother. "She used to call it the food of princes."

"The woman was a peasant," said my father. "But a good cook," he added quickly when he saw my stepmother's face.

To start, we had an omelet made with different kinds of wild mushrooms. Then my stepmother brought up a lamb tagine—a good one, with the best bits of lamb cooked for ages and slices of apricot and lots of juice to go into the couscous with chickpeas that she served alongside it. It wasn't a fatted calf, but with a second whiskey and Coke and the sun going down over the sea, it was pretty good, and I told her so.

"Thank you, Tariq," she said. "My grandmother called it—"

"The food of princes?" I said. "Cheers."

. . .

The next day I had to fight off the urge to call Laila. I felt it would be better to sort out my other business first, so I rang the college and made an appointment to see Dr. Ahmed, the head of department.

When I got there, I was told by the secretary that Ahmed was not available but that I could have a talk instead with his deputy, Miss Aziz.

"Fine by me," I said. The truth is that, apart from handing in essays, or a quick excuse for not, I'd barely spoken to the woman face-to-face before. Even when I'd been in a ten-student seminar with her, I'd managed to keep my mouth shut. It was strange, then, that I felt I knew her so well.

Miss A. was wearing trousers and a white shirt buttoned to the neck (the black skirt and the strip of escaping white lace had never made a second appearance, alas). She had a surprisingly high voice, girlish, almost piping. She seemed uneasy to be sitting in the head of department's office and dealing with a disciplinary matter. She put on some reading glasses and lowered her chin, as though trying to make her voice sound graver. Before I went to Paris, I would have felt pretty awkward with her, but now I felt sympathetic. She was a girl, a woman, and as such would always have a hold on me, but she also had a job to do, a role to fulfill, and was perhaps (I was only guessing here) as full of private fears and general weirdness as I was. Which is not to say I wasn't aroused when she stood up, went over to a filing cabinet and squatted down to open the lower drawer, making the trousers cling to the outline of her thigh and her round backside. She had bare feet in leather sandals and her toenails were painted red. Her feet were like a little girl's. I shifted a bit on the chair and tried to concentrate. I wondered if she'd seen much more of the shady-sounding man in the aviator sunglasses. I didn't want her to go off with him to Qatar or Riyadh or some burning Gulf shithole, I wanted her to go off with me. Perhaps I could be like the men in the old days and have several wives. I'd have Miss Aziz and Laila, Clémence of course, and maybe Farida from Laila's house. Jasmine Mendel on a Tuesday. And Hannah to keep us all on the straight and narrow. And the girl from Stalingrad, naturally—Juliette Lemaire, if that's who she was.

"And you've missed two full semesters," Miss Aziz was saying, "so you'll need time to revise and catch up. Suppose you sit the exam at the end of the month?"

I remembered an important science test at school, when I'd scored four percent in the practice exam. But the night before the real thing a month later, I opened the course book and read it through. It was a revelation, and I managed to get the required mark with a couple of percent to spare. Two weeks to catch up should be enough. And Laila would help me revise.

"I'm glad you've come back, Tariq," said Miss Aziz. "If you pass, I'll be teaching you again next year. Maybe you can give us a talk about Paris as part of the European history module."

"Thank you, Miss Aziz. I'd like to do that."

I stood up and held out my hand. I think she may have blushed a little as she shook it, but perhaps I imagined that. Her skin was a lovely pale brown, perhaps incapable of changing color any more than her violet-black hair.

Back at home, unable to delay any longer, I called Laila and told her the plan. She sounded pleased to hear from me. We talked for ten minutes or so till I said, "Can I come round and do some revision at your house?"

"I don't think that's a good idea."

"Why?"

"We'd get distracted."

"Go on. Please."

"In fact, I don't think we should meet until you've done the exam."

"What?"

"I don't want you to be in the year below me. I want to sit next to you. Once you've taken it and passed it, you can come to dinner the same day. I'll get Farida to make everything you like."

"Laila, you're being a tease."

"I'm not. I really think it's for the best."

"Have you found another boyfriend?"

"Certainly not! It's only you, Tariq. I promise. I think about you all the time."

"And if I do as you ask, will you make it worth my while?"

There was a pause and I wondered if I'd gone too far.

"I might."

There were no words I could find to answer that.

Before the exam, I needed to deliver the money. I opened the Koran, thinking I could do what I'd done with the science book and at least be able to say something sensible if asked about it by Jamal's friends. My memories of the holy book from when I was young were pretty positive, because the handful of classes I'd gone to at the mosque were designed for children. They made you feel lucky that the Prophet had come and that you were among his followers, and the things you had to do—like being kind to widows and orphans and not drinking alcohol—all sounded fine.

But I hadn't looked at it since I was ten, because my mother had been a Christian (I think) and my father believed in nothing. I'd thought very little about religion myself, though obviously I knew about the new fundamentalists, the jihadis, and what they'd done. Then in Paris I'd got an idea of Christianity from Victor Hugo. He told me that the Jewish religion was based on the best-ever myths and stories and the Christian religion on the most revolutionary teaching, and he gave me some examples of that (love your enemy and so on).

What this Koran offered was simple enough. The truth. The other guys got it wrong, we got it right. Moses and Jesus were good men, but the Prophet was the real thing. And if you don't believe that now it's been explained to you, then you'll burn in hell for all time. I took on board the importance of this warning, but, then, after a hundred pages or so, I began to wonder when the book was going to show its hand. When would it reveal the facts or teachings that made "my" religion the boss over the others? The lack reminded me a bit of the comments I used to get on my mathematics exams: "You need to show your workings." But it began to look as though the special authority was in the assertion alone.

Soon, I switched to economics revision. Laila had mailed me her lecture notes and I had the course books. I found my concentration was better than it had been before I went to Paris. Knowing now a tiny bit about European, or at least French, history, made it more alive. It was no longer all Botzaris to me, and I began to feel confident about the exam.

Next day I went back to the Koran and tried to bring the same enthusiasm, but the repetitions were beginning to get to me. I knew that if I didn't believe in God I would be condemned to the fire for all eternity, because I had been told that on the page before. I made myself persevere—though it was a bit like being locked in a room with my stepmother.

When I felt I'd read enough, I rang the number in Jamal's envelope. I thought the man who answered would be suspicious and would demand false names and heaven knows what, but he sounded all right. We made a rendezvous in an area of new buildings on the way to the airport. He said he'd meet me by the side of the main road.

Near the open vegetable market above the Grand Socco there's usually a line of taxis, and by chance I found the same beat-up Mercedes and friendly driver who'd brought me from the airport. As we sped out of town, I began to think about what this money was for. Jamal was a bitter man, and in his place who wouldn't be—given what had happened to his Harki parents? He was a funny old dog in many ways, Jamal, but he was also a friend and a top supplier of weed at knockdown prices. I imagined the money was going to help people in his extended family, here or in Algeria. In turn these people would be outsiders, like him, men who hated France and what it had done. The money would buy them some comforts and ease their lives. I hadn't thought much further than that. The people I was going to meet were just friends of friends of a friend, a deep-fryer of chicken bits in a nowhere street in Saint-Denis.

When we reached the half-finished buildings by the highway that the man on the phone had described, just before a big hoarding on the left that advertised ferry crossings to Spain, I told the driver to stop. I gave him the fare shown on the meter, plus a big tip.

"If you wait here, I should be back in a few minutes. Then I'll give you more money."

"I can wait." He showed a gold tooth when he smiled.

We were early, so I stood in the open where I could be seen. As so often in my country, I had the feeling I was being watched anyway, so there was no need to do anything. They'd come when they were ready. After four or five minutes, a boy of about thirteen appeared from one of the unfinished apartment blocks and signaled me to follow him. He looked a bit like Laila's brother, Billy, though poorer, in ragged shorts and plastic sandals. We went down a dirt road for about a hundred meters, then into an area of uninhabited building works. I followed him inside what would one day be the reception hall of some flats, then down the service stairs. He knocked at a basement door and we went in.

There were two people inside, an unshaven man with a red baseball cap and a woman in jeans with a white blouse and a black headscarf.

They were both a little older than me—about twenty-five, I thought. For some reason I was thrown by the fact one of them was female—though also a little relieved.

Red Cap, who sounded like the man I'd spoken to on the phone, did the talking at first. He asked me questions about Paris, how long I'd lived there, where I'd stayed, who I knew. I suppose he wanted to make sure I hadn't been followed or that I wasn't some kind of informer. Meanwhile, the woman looked impatient and muttered to Red Cap in a dialect I couldn't follow. I began to feel uneasy. I had an urge to be back in the steamy kitchen at PFP.

But no. It's all right, I told myself. Jamal's a good man. His life has been tough, he has some weird ideas, but he's my friend. He's my homely uncle, my *kif* pal. He wouldn't land me in danger. Have faith.

The woman asked if I'd like to help them by running some messages. To Brussels, maybe.

"No, thank you. I've brought the money. That's what I agreed to do."

"Who gave you the money?"

"A man in Paris." I didn't like to say Jamal's name. "He said he was a friend of some people you know."

Red Cap was impatient. "We don't know this man. He's just a go-between. But you have the money."

"Yes."

Then the woman asked if I'd go along to a meeting in Beni Makada and stay to listen to some speaker there.

"No. I have an exam to do. I'm going to finish my studies. I may get married." I was saying anything now—but I knew Beni Makada was a bad part of town. "Here's the money."

I handed the envelope to Red Cap, anxious that he might ask where the missing notes were. But he didn't check it.

The unplastered room was lit by a bulb that hung from a wire held in a corrugated plastic tube. They hadn't finished installing the electricity and it was dusty in there.

We all looked at each other in silence. I began to edge towards the door. It occurred to me that these two were quite low down in whatever organization they worked for—that they were making things up as they went along. There were no rules in this game, so I needed them to think my agreed role in it was over.

"I guess I'll be on my way." I kept it light.

"Wait," said the woman. "What was the name of the Prophet's mother?"

"What?"

She took my wrist. "The name of the Prophet's mother," she said.

"Er . . ." I cast my mind back to childhood. "Aminah."

"What are the first words of the holy book?"

For this, I had only to think back to the day before and Jamal's battered French edition. "'In the name of Allah, the most gracious, the most merciful . . .' Er . . . 'All praise to Allah, the lord of, of . . .'"

"The universe," she said.

"That'll do," said Red Cap, now standing very close to me. "This meeting never happened."

The woman, equally close on the other side, said, "Never."

I confirmed. "Never."

"*Allahu akbar*," said Red Cap. God is great.

"Sure," I said.

Then I went swiftly outside and followed the boy down the dirt road to where the old Mercedes was waiting.

• • •

I never heard from them again. No incidents since then have made me think the money went to a bad end, and I like to think they used it for welfare—food, medicines, a few luxuries for the hard-pressed. Even plane tickets to go to Europe. Because however much men like Hasim and Jamal despised the place they lived, it gave them more opportunities than where they'd come from. I'd run an errand for a friend—a good friend, as it turned out—and that was all. And after a few days I did what I've always been able to do with troublesome thoughts—put the whole thing out of my mind.

Free now to concentrate on economics, I revised in my bedroom, by day and by night. After lunch, I'd sometimes go for a sleep on the roof terrace, where there was a comfortable sofa in the shade. I often lay there daydreaming about Clémence in her old-fashioned apartment, remembering the things I'd seen and done. I pictured the sewing shop and her sitting in the window, with her knees rising and falling. I remembered the folk song that had suddenly come to me as I watched from across the way. And the street door on the Avenue de Suffren beside which she, or the woman so like her, had hesitated and looked round. I thought a lot about Hannah and hoped that Julian was wrong about her being at her wits' end. I'd sent her an e-mail, but she hadn't answered. And as I was drifting off to sleep I thought most of all about Juliette Lemaire tripping down the steps from the Métro at Stalingrad, her coat flying open over her short dress and leather boots, catching my eye for a second as she passed.

The day came for the exam, and I went into college. Miss Aziz met me at the reception desk. She took me by the elbow and smiled. She was wearing a white linen dress down to her feet, where I could see the red-painted toes peeping out, a loose black hijab, mascara and dark lipstick.

"We're going to the old seminar room because it's nice and cool in there. I'll be invigilating the first paper and Dr. Ahmed will be here for the second paper after lunch. Have you done all the work?"

"Yes, I think I've got a grip on it."

She drew the blinds in the small room to keep out the fierce sun and gave me a glass of cold milk and a banana. I sat at a table facing the wall and when the minute hand on the clock had reached the top of the hour, she opened an envelope and put the question paper down beside me.

As usual in exams, the questions weren't the ones I'd wanted, but I had something to say on most of them. Where I ran out of relevant information, I wrote about other things, thinking they'd like evidence that I'd done some reading and was serious about the subject. Miss Aziz sat behind me in an armchair where I couldn't see her. After two hours, I heard her cough quietly and stand up.

"How was that, Tariq?"

"It was fine, thanks. Not perfect, but okay. How soon will I know the results?"

We were walking down the corridor towards the canteen. "Are you in a hurry?" She sounded amused.

"Yes, a bit. But I don't expect any favors. You know . . . It's all my fault anyway."

"I can look at both papers tonight. Dr. Ahmed's finished next year's syllabus planning, so I should think . . . by Friday?"

"If I left you my cell-phone number, might you be able to . . ."

"We'll see."

The second paper was a bit more statistical, not as interesting but easier to get right. I kept knocking down the obstacles it posed, while Dr. Ahmed himself snored in the chair behind me. It seemed a pity to wake him when the time was up, but I had nothing left to say.

It was two days later that I received an SMS that said: "Dr. Ahmed has not had time yet but won't differ by more than a point or two from my marks. I've read both papers twice and confirm that you have passed with merit. K.A."

I was still wondering what the "K" stood for when I hit the Forward button to Laila.

We agreed to meet on Saturday.

● ● ●

During the two-day wait, I worried that Laila would no longer like me. I was also anxious that she might have changed. She'd always seemed more grown up than me in some way. Although I was the one who'd done the daring thing, disappearing to Paris, perhaps she'd also found a way of moving on. Moving further.

Or what if she was unchanged but somehow didn't feel the same? I reminded myself of all the things I'd loved about her. The quickness of movement, the intense sympathy she could show, the way I was never afraid to admit to fear and weakness in her presence, the way we laughed, how it was us two against the rest.

When I got to the house on Saturday afternoon, she opened the door from the street into their huge garden.

"We're having a tennis game," she said. "Can you play?"

"Of course I can."

"I'll lend you a racket. You can borrow Billy's tennis clothes. Some neighbors are coming."

I needn't have worried. There was so much more to her, so many things I'd forgotten, starting with the way she never bothered to say hello, because there was always something more important to tell me. Oh, Laila.

"I got you a present."

"It's too much," she said, when she'd torn off the tissue paper. "But I love it."

We were walking up a paved path through the grass towards the veranda at the back of the house. Laila kept staring at me, not looking where she was going. I was worried she might trip over.

"Did you miss me?" I said.

"Just a bit."

She stopped, put her arms round my neck and kissed me on the mouth. "You're just the same," she said.

"Is that a good thing?"

"Oh yes. Come inside. I'll show you where you can change your clothes."

There was something different about Laila. I had the idea that she'd made her mind up about something.

These neighbors turned out to be older than us, maybe twenty-four or -five, a brother and sister, and they were good at tennis. My knowledge of the game was based on having watched satellite tournaments on Eurosport 2 in the college common room. I'd played a handful of times on the public court, enough to be able to get the ball over the net. Laila was better than me, but not much, and she missed a lot because she seemed to be looking at me, not the ball. I suggested it might be a more equal game if she played with the other guy against the girl and me. It was pretty hot, and after about an hour Farida came out with a tray.

"This is Laila's favorite drink," she told the guests, her cow's eyelashes fluttering. "I'm the only one who knows how to make it."

Well, I happened to know that Laila's favorite drink was Bacardi with Diet Coke, but I went along with Farida, and to be fair the drink was pretty good. It had lemon and syrup and ginger and soda water and something else you couldn't put your finger on.

"It's called a Scherzo," said Laila. "It's an old Italian recipe. It's named after a bar in Ferrara."

I think she'd just made the whole thing up, but the brother and sister went on about how much they liked it. We were all sitting on a grass bank and I had an idea the brother was a bit too interested in Laila and I wished he wouldn't keep telling her how brilliant she was at tennis. He had very hairy legs sticking out of his white tennis shorts, which he kept crossing and recrossing as though he wanted people to admire them.

To my horror, Laila asked them if they'd like to stay to dinner. I tried to catch her eye, but for the first time she was looking the other way. The sister hemmed and hawed a bit, then made a call on her cell phone and it was agreed that we'd play a bit more, then they'd go home and change and old Farida could prepare some extra chicken to stick on the grill.

When we'd finished tennis and the pair of them had gone away for the time being, Laila took me into the house so I could have a shower and change back into my own clothes.

"Why did you have to ask them to dinner?" I said as I followed her down one of the long, cool passageways.

"I'm just being a good neighbor."

"But he's a jerk. And it was our special—"

"Oh, he's all right, really."

We had reached the staircase. "Can I come into the shower with you?" I said.

"Shh . . . Farida might—"

"Farida's plucking the chicken."

We went upstairs and along to Laila's bathroom. Her father was abroad on business and her mother never came to this part of the house. It was a big place anyway, so it was all quite safe. We went inside the bathroom, which was painted dark green, a lovely color, and had an open shower area. I kissed Laila on the lips and she held me.

"Aren't you going to look in the mirror?" she said.

"What?"

"I've never seen you able to resist."

"No. I . . . I've stopped doing that. After something that happened in Paris. A place called Drancy."

"Drancy?"

"I got outside myself. I entered into other people."

"You entered . . ."

"Stop repeating me." I laughed. "You're like an echo."

She laughed. "Well, if you're not Narcissus anymore, then I suppose I'd better not be Echo."

"Shh. Kiss me again."

"You're all sweaty."

"Of course I am. That's why I'm getting in the shower with you."

Laila went to the door and looked down towards the gallery where the stairs came up. She was laughing in the way I liked, when she couldn't stop. "Just for you," she said, and kissed me again.

And I knew then what the change in Laila was. She saw me now as something I was not. In her eyes I'd become somehow beyond criticism—so I was liberated from the burden of being me. It was a shock. But I was confident, because I knew that in order to become this hero, all I had to do in the thrilling new world into which I'd stumbled was to be myself.

I sat on a wooden chest by the window while she locked the door. She took off her shirt and bra and I watched her breasts fall forward as she released them. The water was pouring down from an overhead sprinkler the size of a dinner plate. She was too shy to look at me. For tennis she'd been wearing loose thin trousers made of cotton, like pajamas, with a drawstring.

She stuck her bare arm under the water to test the temperature. She was wearing the bracelet I'd given her. Then she pulled the string, pushed the trousers to her ankles and stepped out of them. I was looking at the way her hair brushed her shoulders. She had her back to me now and she pulled down the tiny white thing she wore under the trousers. She reached out for the shampoo from a shelf inside the shower and began to wash her hair.

"Come on," she said.

I whipped off Billy's tennis clothes and went in under the warm waterfall with her.

Later, we had the best dinner of my life so far and I didn't care that the brother and sister were there. Farida kept bringing salads and barbecued meat and more drinks onto the veranda, where we lit the candles and the hurricane lamps and played some music through an outdoor speaker.

The exercise from the tennis, combined with the beer, was having an exhilarating effect. But what was making me feel like a god was what had happened in the bathroom after the shower, when our bodies were still hot and dripping.

And I'd like to go into detail about how we managed it and how moved I was when Laila put her hand back between her legs to find me. But when I caught her eye in the darkness at dinner, I felt that there were some things I'd need from now on to hold back; I knew that what had happened would have to remain between us.

Austerlitz (by day)

I N THE APARTMENT IN RUE MICHAL THERE WAS A DIRTY T-SHIRT UNDER Tariq's single bed and the remains of a bag of *kif* on the nightstand, but otherwise no trace of him.

On the table in the hall, the Wi-Fi router flickered, but the front windows onto the street were shut. In the bathroom, the tub was dry and the towels hung folded on the rail. The stove in the kitchen was clean, the crockery put away and the kettle cold.

In the sitting room, a closed laptop on the table was surrounded by notebooks with yellow stickers marking pages; inside, the handwriting showed lines and words highlighted in different colors. A *Paris Pratique* street plan lay on the floor beside the worktable, open at "15ᵉ Est," with Parc Georges-Brassens circled in ballpoint.

On the coffee table in the middle of the room was a photocopy of "La Nuit de Décembre" by Alfred de Musset. Alongside it was an English prose version of its closing stanzas. "On my curtain I saw a shadow pass; it came to sit on my bed . . . Are you an idle dream? Or is this my own image that I am seeing in a mirror?"

A separate piece of paper was headed: "The Vision responds to the Poet." It was followed by some scribbled words. "Not guardian angel . . . not god, not demon . . . But I will be with you always until the end of your days, when I shall sit on your tombstone."

After the final stanza of the poem was a translation of what the Vision said:

Heaven has entrusted me your heart.
When you are in pain,
Come to me without worry.
I will follow always on your path,
Though I can never touch your hand.
My friend, I am Solitude.

Under it was written in French, *"Ami, je suis la solitude."* The line was repeated five times in the same American hand, twice with the word *solitude* crossed out and "loneliness" substituted. Next to it was written "Andrée B." Under that, "Louise Masson."

Beneath the coffee table, lying on its side on the floor, was an empty brandy bottle. A packet of cigarettes had been opened and two of them had been half smoked; an empty sheet of 400-mg ibuprofen lay curled beside the ashtray.

In the main bedroom, the closed curtains moved a little in the breeze from the open window. On the floor was a discarded linen dress, on top of which was a cell phone, switched to silent. From the bed where I lay, half dreaming, half imagining the quiet rooms and the clues and indications that they held, there came, no doubt, the sound of low breathing and, some time in the late afternoon, a reluctant movement as I pushed back the duvet and opened my eyes.

So I climbed from the bed, searching for a clock or watch, and was reassured by the silent screen of the phone. There was time. Towards six o'clock in the evening, the bathtub was almost full. Emerging from the kitchen, cup of tea in hand, I went into the bathroom, brushed my teeth and sank into the hot water. For a long time, I lay still, my head resting on the back of the tub, staring upwards. Then I washed and rinsed my hair and thoroughly soaped and sponged the rest of me. Wrapped in a towel in front of the mirror, I turned on the hair dryer.

Back in the bedroom, almost revived, I began to act more quickly as I decided what to wear. Slacks, jeans and a skirt were thrown on the bed before I chose a black dress. It was more formal than I'd intended, but an amber necklace gave it a lift. In the bathroom again, I put on mascara and a dash of lipstick. I leaned back from the mirror. My thick dark hair never looked chic so had to count as boho. The final look was armored, yet feminine, I hoped: sophisticated enough, but ready for anything. Shame about the face. I stopped at the door, went back and put on more lipstick.

It was a brisk ten minutes to the Place d'Italie and then down into the Métro and up towards Bastille, where I would change. At Austerlitz station the train emerged from underground and pulled up in the open air, where it was still summer daylight. There was a short delay, and then we were on the bridge over the Seine; here even the world-weariest commuters looked up and out of the window. Away to my left I could see the blunt nose of Notre Dame, like an outsized tugboat pushing its way upstream.

I rested my forehead against the glass.

The second train rattled west and I checked the address on my phone. Emerging from the station, glancing at my *Paris Pratique* for help, I went down a passage, an arcade, and out on to a smaller street, where I saw the name of the restaurant. It was almost like old Paris, before the alleyways had been swept away by Haussmann to give the police a field of fire along the new boulevards; you could imagine Thérèse Raquin and her lover living nearby in their sinful apartment.

I checked my watch. Five past eight, five minutes after the appointed time. I would walk once round the block and then . . .

Pushing open the door, I found a tall desk by the entrance and a gray-haired woman who politely welcomed me. "Yes, Madame. Monsieur is already here."

My legs felt uncertain as I crossed the parquet, weaving between the tables on my heels; I was weak and had to concentrate on walking, not nudging the elbow of a diner with my hip, not finding myself fold and give way from the knees. He was sitting with his back to the entrance so I could have the seat on the banquette with a view out over the room.

He had never really missed a beat since the winter day more than six months ago that we'd met again at the Mauri Sept: not one. Julian jumped as I touched his shoulder. He stood up at once and offered his cheek, but I threw my arms round his neck instead.

"Is this all right for you?" he said, indicating the seat opposite.

A waiter brought a menu and two glasses of champagne.

"I don't like champagne," said Julian, "but I thought . . ."

I felt I should say something, but found it impossible to speak. I waved to Julian in an encouraging motion. He began to talk about the menu and the weather.

He looked over his reading glasses as if to ask if I was ready yet, but I made another keep-going movement with my hand. I drank some champagne, which seemed to help.

Eventually, I said, "I'm glad you came back."

"It was easy. But I needed you to ask."

"I know."

"How did you find me?"

"You can't disappear in the twenty-first century. Even when Tariq lost the number it wasn't hard. The e-mail bounced back, but I knew you'd given Jasmine a different one."

"You sly old fox."

"Jasmine and I have no secrets."

"Nor did I want you to."

"But you were pleased I made the effort?"

"God, yes. I just needed it to come from you. You do understand that, don't you?"

"Entirely. I've been . . . I've been so . . . stupid. To see what was . . ."

"It's all right." I noticed that the rims of his eyes had turned fiery red. "Now tell me what's been going on."

"Aah . . ." I managed to smile at last. "How long have we got?"

"Quite a long time, I think."

As the waiter took our order and carried the menus away, I began to tell Julian about my visit to Natzweiler. He asked me questions as I went along, but not in a way that broke the concentration I thought it necessary to give the story. Then I told him about the visit to the old slaughterhouses at Vaugirard.

"How do you explain the horse smell?" I said.

"I don't know. I suppose they may have changed the day of the pony rides so the ponies had been there a few minutes before."

"Probably."

"Or maybe not. Some things have both banal explanations and more interesting ones. To some extent we're free to choose, aren't we?"

"Anyway," I said, after a pause. "What about you? That's what I want to know."

"Nothing to report. I'm just treading water."

"Have you moved back to London?"

"For the time being. But I haven't found a tenant for the Paris flat yet. So I'm staying there for a couple of days."

"But why did you move?"

"I wanted a change. Things seemed stuck."

The waiter was a Parisian, a man of a certain age in a long white apron and a black bow tie. He'd brought a half bottle of white wine with the first course and now uncorked some red.

"I'm sorry I was a few minutes late," I said.

"You can't be precise with the Métro."

"There was a man playing the accordion in my carriage."

"Did he ask for money?"

"No, but I gave him some."

"Do you always give money to buskers?"

"Only to accordionists."

"Why?"

I felt Julian scrutinizing me, not unkindly.

"I don't know." I began to relax for the first time. "I suppose I still cling to some old American idea of Paris. There should be accordions."

He smiled and shook his head.

The waiter brought the main course, which was steak with a copper dish of potatoes and a lamb's lettuce salad. I had let Julian order for us both.

I asked, looking at the plate. "*Onglet?*"

"*Français*, I think."

He poured more red wine. I was starting to feel drunk and half-raised a hand to stop him, but then let it go.

"What are your plans now?" said Julian. "When you finish your chapter—and your apartment comes to an end?"

"I'm not sure. I e-mailed a draft of the chapter and Putnam was very positive about it. The faculty has money at the moment. I think if I came up with a good research topic they'd probably let me stay."

I could hardly believe what I was saying—I was making it up as I went along. And in any case my next career move was not the important topic between us.

Waiting to see how Julian would respond, I leaned back against the dark wood of the banquette and looked round the room. The shaded wall lights showed couples, small groups of friends, a solitary gourmet at a window table. In the loud murmuring of voices and the sound of glass and china, I could sense my anxiety starting to recede. It was going to be all right.

Meanwhile, it was difficult to look at Julian. Having so completely changed my mind about him, I felt shy. I wanted to tell him about what had happened in the Hôtel du Parc. While it remained unexplained it still frightened me, and he might be able to help me understand; but more importantly, I wanted him to be a part of it. I couldn't do it now. But there would be time, surely there would be time.

"Did the publisher like de Musset?"

"They were polite about it, but I think they'll only print a few hundred copies."

"I finished 'La Nuit de Décembre' the other day."

"That took—"

"I'm a slow reader, Julian."

"And you liked it?"

"Yes. I've always found French Romantic poetry a little . . ."

"Lightweight?"

"Yes. But I loved the ending of this. I didn't see it coming."

"It's very sad. 'Ami, je suis la solitude.' But I think he's earned it. The rhythms are so good."

"Yes. What is this autoscopy thing? Was it just a literary device?"

"They don't really know. It's an actual phenomenon, though rare. It's probably a perceptual disturbance in the brain, some sort of time lag. You know, like déjà vu, when things have just gone out of synch for a moment. You can feel it slip out, and you can almost sense it click in again."

"I suppose everyone's caught themselves unawares in a mirror or a shop window," I said. "Or when you're lost in a book and you pull back and suddenly become self-aware because your leg's gone to sleep."

"Yes, you re-envisage yourself. Reimagine. And of course this intermittent self-awareness, that we can switch on and off at will, is a key human faculty." Julian began to laugh. "I remember in a strange hotel room in Rome going to the bathroom in the middle of the night and thinking, there's some bastard in here, and getting ready to fight him. I'd forgotten the wall mirror."

"And was this intruder drunk too?"

"Startled more than drunk, I'd say. Anyway, the research says that in some people it can be a pointer to a more serious illness."

"But not in de Musset."

"Not at all. I think he enjoyed it, then exaggerated it for poetic ends. But as with most things in the brain, they don't actually know."

After we'd had coffee, Julian said, "Would you like to come back to my flat for a *fine à l'eau*? For old times' sake?"

"Yes, I would. I'd like that."

We found a taxi outside, though once we were alone in the back of it, I felt a sense of awkwardness again.

As the car turned onto the Boulevard des Capucines, I said, "If you'd like to, then I think you could put your hand on my knee at this point."

"Are you sure?"

"Shhhh." I silenced him by leaning over and kissing him.

He put his hand on my knee and ran it up over my thigh. "You have lovely skin," he whispered.

I looked across the back seat at him. "Blimey," I said.

Up in the apartment above the Alsatian brasserie, Julian prepared the drinks. When we were about to settle among the piled books in the ocher light of the lamps, he suddenly gripped my wrist and said, "Stop. Before you sit down, can I make you a proposition?"

"What is it?"

"Come with me."

He led me into the hallway. "That's the bedroom off to the right there. Bathroom there. Kitchen at the end. But there's this other room here. I have no use for it, but it's quiet, it overlooks the courtyard. It has the sun in the morning. You could use this table as a desk; you could have a sofa bed. There's even a little shower room through there."

"Are you asking me to move in with you, Julian?"

"Yes, I am. But a woman should have a room of her own as well."

"So long as I don't have to sleep in it."

"My dear Hannah, you can sleep wherever you like."

In the sitting room, we sat down at last on the velvet-covered couch. "One thing I need to tell you," I said.

"What?"

"I really don't like *fine à l'eau*."

"Try it without the *eau*, maybe? I just thought it would satisfy your Hemingway fantasy."

"I gave that one up ten years ago. Along with the Russian poet. Maybe we could have wine instead."

"I have a bottle I've been saving."

Half an hour later, I put my hand on Julian's chest, to keep him at arm's length.

"There's something else I need to tell you," I said.

"Go on."

"I don't trust happy endings."

"Me neither."

"They belong to airport books where a peasant woman is violently abused in the first chapter and six hundred pages later her granddaughter opens a department store on Park Avenue."

"Traditionally a chain, I think," said Julian.

"Anyway, the point is, for the last hundred years or so happy endings have been considered . . ."

"Vulgar?"

"Yes. So I don't want that."

"Well, Hannah, please be reassured that I'm not offering that. For a start, it's not an ending. It's the beginning of a new chapter, or just an interlude perhaps. There's only a short time on the lease here. And secondly, the happiness bit. I can't promise that either. But I think it'll be fun. In fact, I'm sure it will be."

"Why are you sure?"

"Because I love you so much. I love your earnestness, your passion, your endeavor, the way you push back your hair when you're anxious, your clothes, your voice. I love the way you care so very much about the fate of people you never knew. It's inspiring. It's magnificent."

"You're going to make me cry."

"I just can't tell you how much I admire you and what you've done and what you stand for. I admire you so, so much. You have no idea."

"I thought I just made you laugh. And that's why you teased me."

"I'm afraid the teasing was a way of showing my affection."

"And when did you know that you loved me?"

"I think I always did. But to begin with it was perhaps clouded over by desire."

"Don't lose it. The desire."

"No, no. Don't worry. But I think it was when I became resigned to the fact that you'd never think of me that way, that I'd never be more than an extra researcher or a sort of louche uncle. That's when I came to love you not just for your eyes and the color of your hair. You know, with the brown and the black at the same time, but it's not streaked. It's both at once, it's . . ."

"I know. It's a thing. Can't help it."

"Anyway, that's when I saw how much I loved you."

"When you accepted that you'd never have me?"

"Yes. Is that perverse enough?"

"I think so."

"And you?"

"Oh dear," I said. "My story's not so well shaped. I was a dumb idiot and one day I stopped being a dumb idiot. I opened my eyes. I saw for the first time. I saw your kindness, your gentleness. I saw your good-will. And your pale-blue eyes. And I saw what a shallow, self-pitying little bitch I'd been."

"Nonsense. What you were was wounded. It needed time."

"And kindness."

"Thank you."

"And weirdly enough, a word from my lodger. He asked me questions about you and how you'd behaved towards me. I was irritated at the time. But when I thought about it . . ."

"I like that boy," said Julian. "Can I tell you something?"

"Anything you like. Always."

"When you first told me about your Russian, I thought there must be more to it. I thought you were keeping something back. I thought maybe you'd been pregnant, had a child, given it up for adoption or—"

"Like Joni Mitchell."

"I thought there must be some further trauma. That you'd followed him to St. Petersburg and been arrested. Or—"

"I did think of doing that. Shooting his wife on the Nevsky Prospekt with a pearl-handled revolver."

"But I think that's when I knew how much I cared for you. When I saw how hurt you'd been by love alone."

I was crying now, I must admit.

"In a way, there was a murder," I said. "I killed a girl in me. There was a more full-blooded, truthful version of myself that I killed off in the interests of a manageable life."

"But ten years," he said.

"I may have killed the girl in me, but I couldn't kill off the idea of him as well. And I suppose it was because I couldn't bear to lose the hope. I chose the grief instead. To keep the hope alive."

"One love . . ." He breathed out slowly.

"Mathilde," I said.

"Jesus."

I think he was crying too by now.

I said: "It's over."

After a few moments, when we were both calm, Julian took my hand and said, "This happy ending . . ."

"Yes," I said, sitting up straight. "You've been very reassuring. You've told me that it's not an ending and that it may not be happy."

"What I meant was—"

"I think what you're offering is a sort of so-so interlude, with love and a chance of fun. Was that it?"

"More or less. Does that still sound too vulgar?"

"No. I can live with that."

"So you'll move in?"

"Yes. But one other thing. When I've borrowed a toothbrush, climbed into your bed and made love to you in a drunken way, you won't be able to call me Mrs. Jellyby."

"I don't want to. And when will you move your stuff in?"

"Tomorrow, if that doesn't look too pushy."

"No. In fact, tomorrow would be ideal."

"*T'es heureux comme un Pinson?*"

"What?"

* * *

I woke with a headache in Julian's bed a few hours later and went to the kitchen for some water. There was a new Vittel in the fridge. Unable to find a glass in the darkness, I drank direct from the bottle, the cold water pouring down my throat and splashing onto my chest.

Then I went into "my" room and stood naked at the window. It was raining onto the cobbles below. I thought of Jean, the Alpine water boy who'd carried up the pails to Mathilde's apartment at Belleville from the fountain in the courtyard. I heard a hiss of tires from the direction of rue du Faubourg Saint-Denis and imagined Richter's black car as his driver took Juliette home to her parents' after dinner in the Place de l'Opéra.

Somewhere over the mausoleums and the cobbled avenues of Père Lachaise the sun would be starting to come up; in Saint-Denis and Sevran the timer was counting down the minutes till the taped muezzin called . . .

The metal grille at the window of the Café Victor Hugo rattled in a gust of morning breeze, and the Chinese women on the Boulevard de Strasbourg were going off to sleep. In the rue de la Goutte d'Or, the brushes of a road-sweeping lorry chased the butchers' blood down the drains. A janitor rattled his keys as he began his descent from the station at Pigalle along the empty streets to the school in rue Milton. In the back of the large *boulangerie*, formerly the Pujo, on Avenue Kléber, the ovens were giving up their first-baked loaves, while underground in the sidings of Mairie des Lilas, the night-shift workers in their rubber boots were hosing down the Métro carriages for the day ahead.

By midday the tourist buses would be unloading on the Place de la Concorde. This way to the *bateau mouche*, the riverboat. Down to your left is the famous bridge with the padlocks. Please help yourself to a bottle of water at the front of the vehicle. After lunch we're having a ride on the Grande Roue de Paris, the big wheel you see over there. Please make sure you have some sun cream to protect your skin. We meet by the ticket booth at three.

Acknowledgments

With boundless love and thanks to Veronica Faulks.

My thanks also to Rachel Cooke, Roland Philipps, Margot Speed, David Bellos, Heather Milke and Tom Holland; to my literary agents Clare Alexander, Lesley Thorne, Lisa Baker, Joaquim Fernandes and Nicola Chang; to my London publishers Jocasta Hamilton, Rachel Cugnoni, Najma Finlay, Glenn O'Neill, Tom Weldon, Gail Rebuck and David Milner.

A hefty thank you to Steve Rubin, Barbara Jones and Ruby Rose Lee at Henry Holt in New York.

In Paris, *merci* to Tim and Stephanie Johnston; Margaux and Romain Roudeau chez "Juvéniles" in rue de Richelieu; Charles Trueheart and Anne Swardon; Claude Bilgoraj, Daniel Jeffreys, Florence Noiville, Sylvia Whitman and Lauren Elkin.

For help on the ground I am grateful to Christopher Leach in Tangier and in Paris to the inexhaustible Mlle. Jessica "the Terrier" Terrier.

I came across the poems of Wisława Szymborska quoted by David Rieff in his book *In Praise of Forgetting*. I am also indebted to *The French Intifada* by Andrew Hussey, subtitled *The Long War between France and Its Arabs*; *Lonely Courage* by Rick Stroud; *Algeria, France's Undeclared War* by Martin Evans; *Flames in the Field* by Rita Kramer; and *The Novel of the Century* by David Bellos, about the phenomenon of *Les Misérables*.

Paris in the Third Reich by David Pryce-Jones was published in 1981 but, so far as I know, has not been bettered for detail or illustration. The book referred to by Hannah in Chapter Six is the classic *Vichy France: Old Guard and New Order, 1940–1944* by Robert O. Paxton (Alfred A. Knopf, 1972).

S.F., 25 MARCH, 2018

About the Author

SEBASTIAN FAULKS is the author of thirteen previous novels. They include the U.K. number-one bestseller *A Week in December*; *Human Traces*; *On Green Dolphin Street*; *Charlotte Gray*, which was made into a film starring Cate Blanchett; and the classic *Birdsong*, which has sold more than three million copies and has been adapted for the stage and as a television series starring Eddie Redmayne. In 2008, Faulks was invited to write a James Bond novel, *Devil May Care*, to mark the centennial of Ian Fleming. With the approval of the Wodehouse estate, he wrote a new Jeeves and Bertie novel, *Jeeves and the Wedding Bells*. In between books he wrote and presented the four-part television series *Faulks on Fiction* for the BBC. He lives in London with his wife and their three children.